DUBIOUS

THE LOAN SHARK DUET (BOOK 1)

CHARMAINE PAULS

Published by Charmaine Pauls

Montpellier, 34090, France

www.charmainepauls.com

Published in France

Cover design by Kellie Dennis (www.bookcoverbydesign.co.uk)

ISBN: 978-2-9561031-0-3 (eBook)

ISBN: 978-1-5488215-0-0 (Print)

Created with Vellum

1

Valentina

I never take the yellow glow of a light bulb or the blue staccato flicker of the television screen for granted. Looking for signs of life is an ingrained habit for people like me, people who live in fear. Already from the corner, I strain my neck to look at our floor. Then I stop dead. The rectangle of our window stares down at me. Black. Dark.

Oh, my God.

Charlie!

My palms turn clammy. I wipe them on my tunic and sprint up the remaining stairs to the second floor, almost tripping on the last step. A jerk on the handle confirms the door is locked. Thank God. Someone didn't break in, attack Charlie, and leave him for dead. I drop my keys twice before I fit them in the lock. From inside, Puff starts barking.

The damn lock mechanism resists. One of these days, the flimsy nickel is going to break off in the door. I force until the key turns. In my rush to get inside, I stumble over Puff who runs out to greet me. He scurries away with a yelp and his tail between his legs.

The darkness is menacing. Flicking on the lights doesn't expel the emptiness or the sick feeling pushing up in my throat. A hollowness settles in my chest as I take in the bowl of half eaten Rice Krispies and the glass of milk on the table.

"Charlie!"

Even if I know what I'll find, I run to the bathroom.

No one.

"Dammit."

Leaning on the wall, I cover my eyes and allow myself one second to gather strength. Something wet and warm touches my calf. Puff stares at me with his hopeful, sad eyes, his tail wagging in blissful ignorance.

"It's all right, baby." I pet his wiry hair, needing the reassurance of his warm little body more than he needs my caress.

Lightning rips through the sky, the sound lashing out a beat later. I close the curtains. Puff hates thunderstorms. After feeding him, I lock up and knock next door, but, like ours, Jerry's flat is dark.

Damn him. Jerry promised me.

It's a wild guess, but I'm betting on Napoli's being Jerry's favorite hangout. It's the only place he ever goes.

The rickety framework clangs under my trainers as I charge down the two flights of stairs. It's after eight. Having a car thief as a neighbor keeps me protected to an extent, but only from criminals lower in the hierarchy than Jerry. There are the drug dealers, mafia, and gangs to be reckoned with. I remain alert as I go, checking the abandoned houses, parked cars, and alleys. Staying under the streetlights, at least the ones not broken, I walk like my mom taught me--like I'm not a victim.

The brewing storm dissolves, taking with it the rain that would've washed away the neighborhood's stench and soot. It's summer, but the smoke from the cooking fires gives the Johannesburg air a thick, wintry smell as I cross from Berea into Hillbrow. Most buildings in Hillbrow no longer have electricity. When crime took over, people who could afford municipal services moved to the suburbs, turning the city center into a ghost town. Shortly after, the homeless and others with more sinister goals invaded the deserted skyscrapers. The door and windowless buildings look like skulls with empty sockets and gaping mouths. Doors have long since been used for firewood. What is left is the carcass of a city. The vultures have picked the meat off the bones, and now there are only the scavengers who prey on each other, and if I'm lucky tonight, not on me.

The walk to Napoli's takes almost forty-five minutes. I'm scared, and my legs ache from standing in the veterinary clinic all day, but worry over my brother outweighs fear and exhaustion. By the time I get to the club, I'm close to collapsing. It's not the first time Charlie has disappeared. From experience, I know the police won't help. They have their hands full with murder cases and so many missing persons they don't have enough space on milk cartons to post everyone. Anyway, most of them are corrupt. I'll more likely get gang-raped by officials in a police cell than get assistance. I have to find my brother myself.

A group of teenagers in dirty vests sniffing glue at the corner shout insults.

The tallest climbs to his feet, his skin shiny with perspiration and the whites of his eyes like saucers. "Yo, white bitch. What ya doin' on my block?"

"Hey!" A meaty bouncer in a T-shirt with a Napoli's logo shuts them up with a look.

The bouncer doesn't stop me when I push through the entrance, but I feel his eyes burn at the back of my head as I walk down the black-painted corridor into the brightly lit interior. A song from a local rave-rock band blares from oversized speakers. The walls are covered in street art, the day-glo colors popping off the bricks under the fluorescent lights. The club smells of poppers and disco machine smoke. There's every kind of generalization inside, from the dark-suited Portuguese to the gold-chained Nigerians. Half-naked women do the rounds, most of them looking spaced out.

Please let them be here.

I run my gaze over the bar and the roulette tables at the back. On the left, raucous cheering is directed at the flat screen where a horse race is taking place. The spectators go quiet when they notice me. One of the men touches his buckle and widens his stance. A sign says the money lending office is upstairs. There's a queue outside the door. That's where gamblers and people who can't make the rent or pay off the mafia sign away their lives, pledging interest of up to a hundred and fifty percent on loans that will literally cost them an arm and a leg.

The men playing darts turn their heads as I pass. Shit. I'm getting increasingly anxious. As panic is about to seize me, I spot Jerry's orange afro in a circle of heads at one of the card tables. Charlie sits in the chair next to him. Almost crying with relief, I push people with plastic beer cups in their hands out of the way to reach my brother. Charlie's curls fall over his forehead, and his eyes are scrunched up in concentration. He's wearing a Spiderman T-shirt and his flannel pajama bottoms. The attire makes him look vulnerable despite his age and bulky frame. Anyone can see he doesn't belong here. How dare the sick son of a bitch who runs this cesspool allow my brother inside?

"How could you?" I say in Jerry's ear.

He jumps and gives me a startled look. "What are you doing here?"

Charlie is studying the cards in his hand. He hasn't noticed me, yet.

I press a hand to my forehead and count to five. "You said you'd watch him for me."

"I *am* watching him."

"He's not supposed to be here."

"He's a grown man."

"My brother is not accountable for his actions, and you know it."

Charlie looks up. "Va–Val! I'm wi–winning."

For now, my focus remains on Jerry. Alcohol and gambling are not his only addictions. "What did you give him?"

"Relax." He gives me an exasperated shrug. "Orange juice, that's all."

"Come, Charlie."

I take my brother's arm, but the croupier snatches my wrist.

"He's not going anywhere until his debt is paid."

My mouth drops open. How could Jerry let this happen? He knows I barely make ends meet. I jerk my arm from the dealer's grip. "How much?"

"Four hundred."

"Four hundred rand!" That's almost half of my weekly wage.

"Four hundred *thousand*."

The strength leaves my legs. Letting go of Charlie, I brace myself with my palms on the tabletop. We may as well carve dead on our foreheads.

"It's impossible." I can't process that amount. "In one night?"

The croupier regards me strangely. "Charlie's a regular. He's been running a tab, and his time's up."

"Jerry?" I look at him for an explanation, a solution, to tell me it's a joke, anything, but he gnaws on his bottom lip and looks away.

I slam down a fist, rattling the plastic chips. "Look at me!"

The table goes quiet, but not because of my outburst. The men's heads are turned toward the landing on the upper floor. When I follow their gazes, I can't miss the man who stands under the light, his hands gripping the rail. He wears a dark suit, like the Portuguese, but he's anything but a generalization. He's nothing short of a monster.

His body is muscular. Too big. There's not enough space in the room for him. He drowns everything in power and dominance. He's not young, but he isn't old, either. Rather than defining his age, his years give him the distinguished edge of men with experience. Thick, black hair falls messily over his forehead, the wisps brushing his ears. His features are rogue, wild, and uncompromising. The lines running from his nose to his mouth are deeply etched. They're the kind of lines men with hard, rough lives wear. A ghastly network of scars runs from his left eyebrow to his cheek. Under the disfigured patchwork, his complexion is tanned. The ruggedness of his skin gives the impression of being marred by bullets. A short-trimmed beard and moustache cover some of his imperfections, but the damage is too vast to hide. It's a face you don't want to see in the dark and definitely not in your dreams. It's a face that stares straight at me.

Heat of the scary kind crawls over my skin. When I look into his eyes, it's as if a bucket of ice is emptied down my shirt. An unwelcome shiver contracts my skin, and my fear turns from hot to cold. His irises are blue like the far-off glaziers I've only seen in pictures. Everything about him seems foreign. Out of place. Dangerous. He's the kind of bad that's even out of Napoli's league.

"Fucken fuck," Jerry mumbles when he finds his voice. "Gabriel Louw."

I've lived here long enough to recognize the name. His family runs Napoli's. If Hillbrow is the crime capital, Gabriel Louw is the king of the money lords. They call him The Breaker. He's a loan shark, and I've heard stories about him that make my blood freeze with their brutality.

The best time to run is when your opponent is distracted. If we have any chance of getting out of here alive, it's now, while Gabriel holds the attention of the room with unyielding demand. Taking Charlie against his will won't work. He weighs twice as much as me, and when he gets obstinate, he's an unmovable, dead weight.

"Let's get an ice cream," I whisper in his ear, "but you have to come quietly."

Charlie knows about being quiet. We practice it enough times when we hide from the mafia, pretending we're not home.

Charlie gets up like I silently prayed he would and allows me to lead him to the door. I pinch my eyes shut and wait for someone to shout, grab us, shoot, or all three, but when I glance back Gabriel lifts a palm, and the bouncer steps aside for us to exit.

Outside, I suck in a breath of polluted air. Clutching my brother's arm, I walk him back to our side of the tracks, which isn't much better, but it's all we have. He talks, and I let his voice soothe me, trying not to think. When we're home, I'll go over what happened. For now, I'm too preoccupied with lurking dangers.

At Three Sisters, I buy Charlie a cone with vanilla ice cream dunked in caramel, his favorite. It's not until we round the corner of our building that trouble strikes again. Tiny leans in the entrance, smoking a joint. When he sees us, he straightens, takes a last drag, and flicks the butt into the gutter.

"Well, well." He wipes his hands over his dreadlocks and saunters over. "Hello, sunshine. Tiny was looking for you." There's an edge to his voice. "Where were you?"

"Ice crea-cream," Charlie says.

"Is that so?" Tiny stops short of me. He's not Nigerian or Zimbabwean like most of the people on our block, but Zambian. His skinny frame towers over me, his black skin lost in the darkness of the night, except for the whites of his eyes and teeth. "You've got money to spoil your ol' brother here, but not for Tiny's tax?"

He calls himself the Tax Collector. He's not the landlord, but he gathers 'tax' on the rent from everyone who lives in our building. He's a mini-mafia within a bigger mafia, but dealing with him means I don't have to deal with the bigger mafia, and he's the lessor of two evils.

Putting his nose in my hair, he sniffs. "You smell like smoke. Club smoke. Who were you with?"

Tiny pretends he owns me. Mostly, he pretends I like him. In reality, he's a coward, but he still has the power to hurt me. I know this from a split lip and blue eye.

"You're dating now?"

"It's none of your business." Charlie's key is not on the cord around his neck. I'll have to ask Jerry about it later. I fish my key from my bag and hand it to Charlie. "Go up and lock the door."

Charlie takes the key, but doesn't move.

"Go on," I urge. "I'll be right up."

"O–okay." Charlie takes two steps and stops.

I give him an encouraging smile. "Quickly. I don't want you to catch a cold."

Tiny grabs hold of my hair. I close my eyes. *Please, Charlie. Obey.* I don't want him to see this. When I lift my lashes, my brother is climbing the stairs on the side of the building.

"Got the money?" Tiny pulls on my ponytail.

The bond on our flat is fully paid. My parents paid cash for the property years ago before anyone could predict how crime and dilapidation would render their investment worthless.

"We don't pay rent," I bite out. This means nothing to Tiny, but I have to try. God knows why, but I try every time.

"You still owe." He grins, flashing a row of straight teeth. "Tiny can't let you stay without paying tax. What example will that be for the others? Give it up, Valentina."

I freeze. "Don't you dare say my name."

He scoffs. "That's right, because you're my bitch." He yanks on my hair. "Ain't it so, *bitch*?"

"Go to hell."

"Now, now. That's no way to speak to Tiny." He clicks his tongue. "Who's gonna protect you if Tiny ain't around?" He tilts his head. "Won't ask you again. Where's Tiny's money?"

I swallow. "I'll have it by the end of the month."

"You know the rules. The fifteenth is payday."

"Please, Tiny." Tears burn at the back of my eyes. A cold weight presses on my heart.

In the middle of the dirty road, he pushes me down to my knees in the gravel, the stones digging into my skin. His eyes take on a feverish light as he unties the string of his sweatpants and lets them fall to his ankles.

"If you bite again, you'll walk away with more than a shiner. This time, I'll break your arm."

Taking the root of his dick in one hand, he grips my hair in the other and guides my mouth to his cock. Disgust wells in my throat.

He pushes against my lips. "Suck me, white bitch."

I don't do anything of the kind. I tune out of the moment and become an empty shell. It's a routine he knows well. He lets go of his penis to catch my jaw, squeezing painfully on the joints until my mouth opens of its own accord. Then he simply uses me, pumping and shoving until I gag. Tears roll over my cheeks. The saltiness slips into my mouth, mixing with the taste of sweat and filth. Mercifully, like always, Tiny comes fast. Not even a minute later, he ejaculates with a grunt and shoots his load into my mouth. When he pulls out, panting like a pig, I turn my head to the side and spit.

He chuckles. "One of these days, you're gonna swallow."

I wipe my mouth with the back of my hand. "When you're pretty and your parents are rich."

"Come on, baby." He pulls me up by the arm, his dick hanging limp between us. "Give Tiny a kiss. Let Tiny taste himself on that useless mouth of yours, because you sure as fuck don't know how to suck cock."

"Let go." I jerk free and snatch my bag up from where it has fallen on the ground.

His laugh follows me down the road as I run to our flat, hating myself as much as I hate him.

Jerry leans on our door as I come up the stairs. He looks away, avoiding my eyes. He must've left Napoli's shortly after us. That means he slipped past me in the street while Tiny got off in my mouth.

"You're a scumbag." I try to push him aside, but he doesn't budge.

"Val…"

"Did you get a kick out of watching?"

He shoves his hands into his pockets. "I'm sorry."

"For being a peeping Tom or dragging Charlie to Napoli's?"

"I couldn't resist the temptation. A Napoli's VIP pass doesn't happen every day."

"Four hundred thousand rand, Jerry."

"We'll sort it. Don't sweat."

"Right." The only way to *sort it* is to disappear, and we have nowhere to go. "How long has this been going on?"

He scratches his head and has the decency to look guilty. "A few months."

"You dragged Charlie out there at night, without my permission?"

"Come on, Val." Jerry braces his shoulder on the door. "I said I'm sorry."

I knock for Charlie to open. I'm physically and mentally too exhausted to fight now. "Whatever."

I cook and clean for Jerry to keep an eye on Charlie while I work, and although Jerry is a thief, he's not physically mean, at least not to Charlie.

After a while, when Charlie doesn't open, Jerry takes Charlie's key from his pocket and hands it to me. Puff barks as I unlock the door. He waits with a wagging tail.

"Good night, Jerry."

"Can I come in?"

"It's late. I need to study." I use the excuse even if I know there's no way I'll focus on a textbook tonight, but it's the quickest way to get rid of Jerry. Otherwise, he'll stay until four in the morning.

"Oh, come on. Just an hour."

I close and lock the door on his plea, waiting until his shoes shuffle down the landing. I brush my teeth three times before I fix Charlie scrambled eggs and toast for dinner, put him to bed, and settle down on the sleeper couch with Puff.

Sleep doesn't come. I think of Charlie and the handsome fifteen year-old boy he'd been. He was one of those all-rounders who was good at sports and first in his class. He was my big brother. My hero. Two years younger than Charlie, I was in primary school when he went to high school. He fetched me when the bell went at the end of the day, carried my schoolbag, took my hand, and walked me to ballet practice. We didn't tell my parents he made a deal with Miss Paula to work in her garden so I could carry on dancing. If they knew, my father would've demanded he worked for money to buy *necessities*, those necessities being booze and cigarettes. Charlie helped me fit the ballet shoes Miss Paula lent me and waited the hour the dance practice lasted before walking me home to fix me a sandwich. He could've hung out with his friends, but he didn't. He took care of me.

If the accident hadn't happened, if I didn't want a stupid piece of chocolate cake that night, Charlie would've been Charles. My brother would've grown into the man he was born to be. Like every night, I weep into my pillow, shedding bitter tears that won't help one damn bit. Brain damage is irreparable.

Puff cries at the door, letting me know he needs to go. The sun is up, but it's barely five. I wait downstairs on the cracked concrete while he does his business against a dead tree and throw a stick for him to fetch a couple of times. Beside himself with joy, he trips over his paws to lay the broken branch at my feet. Puff is always a happy dog. One morning, yelping coming from a garden trashcan alerted me. I pulled out a starved, dirty, flea-ridden puppy. To this day, Puff is scared of trashcans.

He's not done playing, but I have to call Kris and tell her I won't make it to work today. I hate leaving her in the lurch, but I've got to figure out what to do. Four hundred thousand rand isn't going away. Maybe I can explain about Charlie's condition at Napoli's. Maybe if Jerry backs me up, we stand a chance. Napoli's is part of the big fish. They make mince of petty criminals like Jerry, but he's a regular, no less with a VIP pass. They feed on addicts like him. They need his business.

Back inside, Charlie is up. He offers me a smile that breaks my heart, because it's a smile that hasn't grown beyond fifteen years. Ruffling his hair, I turn to the kitchenette so he won't see the tears in my eyes. I call Kris, but her phone goes straight onto voicemail. Perhaps she's in the shower. I leave a quick message, telling her I won't be in and that I'll call back later to explain.

"Are you not going to wo–work?"

"Not today." I open the cupboards and scan the contents. There isn't much. Charlie eats like a horse.

"What's for brea–breakfast?"

I can't tell him how sorry I am. We can't have mature discussions about guilt and penance. "How about cookies?" The simple treats that make him happy are all I can offer.

"Cho–chocolate?"

There are flour, powdered milk, one egg, and cocoa. I can concoct something. If I could, I'd give him the world.

I heat the two-plate, portable oven, and let him mix the dough. While the cookies bake, I shower and dress before sending Charlie to do his morning grooming. At the same time the timer on my phone pings for the oven, there's a text message from Jerry.

Run.

A tremor rattles my bones. I shiver, even if it's hot inside from the oven. Hurrying to the window, I peer through. A black Mercedes is parked across the road. A woman sits in the front, but with the glare of the sun on the window I can't make out anything other than her black hair. A man in a suit gets out from the driver seat and another from the back. He holds the door. A third man folds his large frame double to exit, adjusting the sleeves of his jacket as he looks up and down the street before turning his head in the direction of our window.

Gabriel Louw.

My breath catches. I jump back before he sees me. Charlie comes out of the bathroom and starts making his bed like I taught him.

"The coo–cookies."

They're burning. I switch off the oven and use a dishcloth to dump the baking tray on a cork plate, trying not to panic.

There's no backdoor or window. The only way out is through the front. We're trapped. I lean on the wall, shaking and feeling sick.

Please, don't let him kill us. Scrap that. Rather let him kill us than torture us.

Everyone from Aucklandpark to Bez Valley knows what The Breaker does to debtors who don't pay. He has a reputation built on a trail of broken bodies and burnt houses. Puff, always sensing anxiety, licks my ankles.

Footsteps fall on the landing. It's too late. Fighting instinct flares in me. My need to protect my brother takes over.

I grab Charlie's hand. "Listen to me." My voice is urgent, but calm. "Can you be brave?"

"Bra–brave."

Puff barks once.

The knock on the door startles me, even if I expected it. I can't move. I should've taken Charlie and run last night. No, they would've found us. Then it would've been worse. You can't outrun The Breaker.

Another knock falls, harder this time. The sound is hollow on the false wood.

"Stand up straight." Don't show your fear, I want to say, but Charlie won't understand.

No third knock comes.

The door breaks inward, pressed wood splintering with a dry, brittle sound. Three men file through the frame to make my worst nightmare come true. They're carrying guns. Dark complexions, Portuguese, except for the one in the middle. He's South African. He moves with a limp, his right leg stiff. Gabriel is even uglier up close. In the daylight, the blue of his eyes look frozen. They hold the warmth of an iceberg as his gaze does a merry-go-round of the room, gauging the situation to the minutest details with a single glance.

He knows we're unprotected. He knows we're frightened, and he likes it. He feeds off it. His chest swells, stretching the jacket over his broad shoulders. He taps the gun against his thigh while his free hand closes and opens around empty air.

Tap, tap. Tap, tap.

Those hands. My God, they're enormous. The skin is dark and rough with strong veins and a light coat of black hair. Those are hands not afraid of getting dirty. They're hands that can wrap around a neck and crush a windpipe with a squeeze.

I swallow and lift my gaze to his face. He's no longer taking stock of the room. He's assessing me. His eyes run over my body as if he's looking for sins in my soul. It feels as if he cuts me open and lets my secrets pour out. He makes me feel exposed. Vulnerable. His presence is so intense, we're communicating with the energy alone that vibrates around us. His stare reaches deep inside of me and filters through my private thoughts to see the truth, that his cruel self-assurance stirs both hate and awe. It's the awe he takes, as if it's his right to explore my intimate feelings, but he does so probingly, tenderly almost, executing the invasive act with respect.

Then he loses interest. As soon as he's sucked me dry, I cease to exist. I'm the carpet he wipes his feet on. His expression turns bored as he fixes his attention on Charlie.

Taking back some power, I say, "What do you want?"

His lips twitch. He knows I'm bluffing. "You know why I'm here."

His voice is deep. The rasp of that dark tone resonates with authority and something more disturbing--sensuality. He speaks evenly, articulating every word. Somehow, the musical quality and controlled volume of his voice make the statement sound ten times more threatening than if he'd shouted it. Under different circumstances I would've been enchanted by the rich timbre. All I feel now is fear, and it's reflected on Charlie's face. I hate that I can't take it away for him.

"I'll only ask you once," Gabriel says, "and I want a simply yes or no answer." *Tap, tap. Tap, tap.* "Do you have my money?"

Spatters of words dribble from Charlie's lips. "I–I do–don't li–like them. Not ni–nice me–men."

The man on the left, the one with the lime green eyes, lifts his gun and aims at Charlie's feet. It happens too fast. Before I can charge, his finger tightens on the trigger. The silencer dampens the shot. I wait for the damage, blood to color the white of Charlie's tennis shoe, but instead there's a wail, and Puff falls over.

Oh, no. Please. No. Dear God. No, no, no.

It has to be a horror movie, but the hole between Puff's eyes is very real. So is the blood running onto the linoleum. The lifeless body on the floor unfurls a rage in me. He was only a defenseless animal. The unfairness, the cruelty, and my own helplessness are fuel on my shocked senses.

In a fit of blind fury, I storm the man with the gun. "You sorry excuse of a man!"

He ducks, easily grabbing both my wrists in one hand. When he aims the gun at my head, Gabriel says, his beautiful voice vibrating like a tight-pulled guitar string, "Let her go."

The man obliges, giving me a shove that makes me stumble. The minute I'm free, I go for Gabriel, punching my fists in his stomach and on his chest. The more he stands there and takes my hammering, my assault having no effect on him, the closer I come to tears.

Gabriel lets me carry on, to make a fool of myself, no doubt, but I can't help it. I go on until my energy is spent, and I have to stop in painful defeat. Going down on my knees, I feel Puff's tiny chest. His heartbeat is gone. I want to hug him to my body, but Charlie is huddled in the corner, ripping at his hair.

Ignoring the men, I straighten and cup Charlie's hands, pulling them away from his head. "Remember what I said about being brave?"

"Bra–brave."

So much hatred for Gabriel and his cronies fills me that my heart is as black as a burnt-out volcano. There's no space for anything good in there. I know I shouldn't give in to the darkness of the sensations coursing through my soul, but it's as if the blackness is an ink stain that bleeds over the edges of a page. I embrace the anger. If I don't, fear will consume me.

Gabriel gives me a strangely compassionate look. "You owe me an answer."

"Look around you." I motion at our flat. "Does it look like we can afford that kind of money? You're a twisted man for giving a mentally disabled person a loan."

His eyes narrow and crinkle in the corners. "You have no idea how twisted I'm willing to get." Gabriel grasps Charlie by the collar of his T-shirt, dragging him closer. "For the record, if you didn't want your brother to make debt, you should've declared him incompetent and revoked his financial signing power."

"Leave him alone!"

I grab Gabriel's arm and hang on it with my full weight, but it makes no difference. I'm dangling on him like a piece of washing on a line. He swats me away, sending me flying to the ground, and presses the barrel of his pistol against my brother's soft temple where a vein pulses with an innocent life not yet lived.

"Va–Val!"

He cocks the safety. "Yes or no?"

"Yes!" Using the wall at my back for support, I scramble to my feet. "I'll pay it."

Charlie cries softly. Gabriel looks at me as if he notices nothing else. His eyes pin me to the spot. Under his gaze, I'm a frog splayed and nailed to a board, and he holds the scalpel in his hand.

He doesn't lower the gun. "Do you know how much?"

"Yes." My voice doesn't waver.

"Say it."

"Four hundred thousand."

"Where's the money?"

The ghost of a smile is back on his face. Behind the scarred mask is a man who knows how to hurt people to get what he wants, but for now he's entertained. The bastard finds the situation amusing.

"I'll pay it off."

He tilts his head. "You'll pay it off." He makes it sound as if I'm mad.

"With interest."

"Miss Haynes, I assume." Despite his declared assumption, he says it like it's a fact. Everything about him shouts confidence and arrogance. "Tell me your name."

"You know my name." Men like him know the names of all the family members before they move in for the kill.

"I want to hear you say it."

I wet my dry lips. "Valentina."

He seems to digest the sound like a person would taste wine on his tongue. "How much do you earn, Valentina?"

I refuse to cower. "Sixty thousand."

He lowers the gun. It's a game to him now. "Per month?"

"Per year."

He laughs softly. "What do you do?"

"I'm an assistant." I don't offer more. It's enough that he already knows my name.

He regards me with his arms hanging loosely at his sides. "Nine years."

It sounds ridiculous, but the quick calculation I do in my head assures me it's not. That's almost five thousand per month, including thirty percent interest on the lump sum. I can't call him unfair. Loan sharks in this neighborhood ask anything between fifty to a hundred and fifty percent interest.

"Nine years if you pay it back with the lowest of interests," he continues, confirming my calculation.

Of course, I'm not planning on staying a vet assistant forever. It's only until I qualify as a vet in four more years. By then, I'll be earning more. "I'll pay it off faster when I get a better job."

He closes the two steps between us with an uneven gait. He's standing so near I can smell the detergent of his shirt and the faint, spicy fragrance of his skin.

"You misunderstood my offer." His eyes drill into mine. "You'll work for *me* for nine years."

My breath catches. "For you?"

He just looks at me.

"Doing what?" I ask on a whisper.

The intensity in those iced, blue depths sharpens. "Any duty I see fit. Think carefully, Valentina. If you accept, it'll be a live-in position."

I know what *any duty* implies. He's no different than Tiny. Loathing fills me.

Gabriel regards me as if he's making a bet with himself. "Either I shoot your brother and you walk away, or he's free, and you work off his debt."

"Give me whatever contract I need to sign, and I'll find my own way to pay you."

He chuckles. "It's my terms or none."

What choice do I have? My knees feel shaky, but it's hardly the time to be weak.

"I'll do it." As I say the words, a ball of ice sinks to my stomach.

For a moment, he looks surprised, but then his expression becomes closed-off. "You have five minutes to pack."

"I have a condition."

The amusement is back on his face. He taps the gun on his thigh and waits.

"I want my brother's safety guaranteed." If I'm not around, Charlie will need protection. I don't want a repeat of what got us into this mess.

"Fair enough. He'll have my protection."

"I need to call someone to fetch him. He can't stay alone."

He takes his phone from his pocket, punches in a code, and pushes it into my hand. "You'll use mine until we've ensured yours isn't compromised."

Turning my back on them, I type my only friend's number. While I'm dialing Kris, the man with the dark eyes searches my purse that hangs over a chair in the kitchen. I watch the men from the corner of my eye, my hand shaking as I wait for Kris to take the call.

"It's Valentina," I say when she answers.

Dogs bark in the background. "I didn't recognize this number. Do you have a new phone? I saw you called earlier, but I haven't listened to your message yet."

"Kris, listen to me. I need you to fetch Charlie. Can he stay with you for a while?"

"What happened?"

"Charlie made debt at Napoli's. I'm with the creditor."

"What?" she shrieks. "You're with a loan shark? Where?"

"My place. Things have changed. I'm going to work off Charlie's debt, but he can't stay alone." My cheeks grow hot as I add, "It's a live-in position."

"What about your job here?"

"I'm sorry. I know how much you need me."

It's always hectic at the clinic, and I feel bad for what I have to do. Kris is one of the best vets I know. She gave me a job when nobody else would, and I hate turning my back on her.

Gabriel checks his watch. "You have three minutes."

"I have to go. Will you call me when you've got Charlie?"

"I'm on my way."

"Thank you, Kris." I glance at Puff's body, forcing down my tears. "You'll have to--"

Gabriel takes the phone from my hand. "Hello, Kris." He keeps his piercing gaze trained on me. "The door to Valentina's flat is broken, but don't worry. I'll have it replaced." He cuts the call. "Two minutes. I suppose you'll pack light."

Stress drives me as I shove the few outfits and toiletries I own in our only travel bag. What will become of Charlie? For now, he's alive. I'm alive. That's what I need to focus on.

Gabriel's cronies help themselves to the cookies cooling on the table. Gabriel says nothing. Only his disturbing stare follows me as I move through the room.

I've barely zipped up my bag before he says, "Let's go."

Adrenalin from the shock makes me strong, strong enough to walk to my brother with confident steps and take his tear-streaked face in my hands.

I go on tiptoes and kiss his forehead. "Remember what I said about being brave. You can do it." I want to say I'll call him, but I don't want to lie. "Wait for Kris. She'll be here soon."

Gabriel takes my bag and steers me to the door, stopping in the frame to say to the man who shot Puff, "Stay with her brother until the woman arrives and bury the dog. Have the door fixed before you go."

The man nods. He's shorter than Gabriel, but not less muscled.

I look over my shoulder and take in everything I can--Charlie's haphazard hair, his soft hazel eyes, and the washed-out Spiderman T-shirt--because I don't know if I'll ever see him again.

2

Gabriel

The petite brunette stiffens when I take her elbow to steer her down the stairs. Her face is ghastly white, and her whole body trembles, but she walks with a straight back. I have dragged men three times her size kicking and screaming to a tamer fate than the one awaiting her. She has guts, but I already knew that from last night.

On the pavement, I take her hand to help her down the curb. Her delicate frame grows even more rigid, but she doesn't resist. Magda turns her head to the car window when we approach. She startles at the sight of the woman I have in the iron grip of my fingers, and then her expression turns stoic. My mother isn't happy. This isn't what she ordered. Tough luck. It's not going to happen the way she wants today, but I've got some explaining to do.

Magda gets out, her eyes shredding me to pieces.

"Put her in the back," I say to Quincy, handing Valentina over like a parcel.

Magda waits until Quincy shuts the door and walks to where we're out of earshot. "She was supposed to be dead."

"I made a deal."

"What deal?"

"Nine years for Charlie's debt."

She blinks. "You're *taking* her?"

I cross my arms. "Yes."

"You want to fuck her."

I don't deny it. There's no point.

"It's not that simple, Gabriel."

I saw her. I wanted her. I took her. Yeah, it's that simple.

"That wasn't the plan," Magda insists.

"The plan changed."

She throws her hands up in the air and starts pacing the sidewalk. "The price was death."

"Charlie has brain damage." That's a tougher price than death. To me, at least. "We shouldn't have granted him a loan."

"Well, we did. Retard or not, showing mercy is showing our enemies we're getting soft."

"Nine years are not exactly mercy." Not with what I'm planning for Valentina.

"She has to die."

"I never go back on my word. People in our business trust us because I keep my word. Rhett and Quincy heard me make the deal."

The charcoal lines around her eyes wrinkle. "What did you promise?"

"A live-in arrangement."

"Arrangement?"

"I said she could work back the debt."

Underneath Magda's controlled exterior she's simmering. A vein pops out on her temple. "Fine. You want to play doll? Have your fun, but we're setting her up to fail. When she does, she's dead and so is her brother."

A sharp pain jolts into my damaged hip. I make a conscious effort to relax my body, muscle by muscle.

"Come on." Magda is already on her way back to the car. "I'll figure it out on the way home."

For the first time, I regret never giving a fuck about professional relationship building. I don't care what people think or about anyone but my daughter, but Magda has always cast the net out wide, catching everyone she can put in her pocket. Her network and influence stretch much further than mine. She carries all the authority in this organization. Sometimes, I have the ugly suspicion the business is the only reason she married my father, so she could take it over. She makes a hell of a tougher loan shark than he ever did, and he was a scary bastard.

I get into the back with Valentina while Magda sits up front with Quincy.

"Drive," she tells my bodyguard.

Quincy and Magda are quiet, I guess because of the girl. An intense awareness of the woman next to me and my power over her spreads through my body, making me hard.

Fuck me. I own her.

She's mine.

The thought gives me a head rush. She's so small she looks like the doll Magda accused me of wanting to play with. Upright, Valentina barely reaches my chest. Her bones are fragile enough to crush under the lightest pressure. If I hug her too tight, her ribs may crack. I can wrap one hand around her slender neck. How hard I choose to close my fingers will be the discerning factor between life and death. Yet, she attacked me when Rhett shot her dog. She gave *me* an order when she told me to let Charlie Haynes go. She's strong and loyal.

I'm both fascinated and jealous of her love for her brother. No one has ever fought for me like that, and I doubt anyone ever will. Throwing *any duty I see fit* into the package was a test. I wanted to see how far she was willing to go for Charlie, not that her decision would've changed anything. I took ownership of her the minute I laid eyes on her. Last night, I already knew I was going to take her. Regardless.

When the club manager at Napoli's called to let me know my mother's target was in, the said target being Charlie, my plan was to go in, take Charlie out, and then his sister, who would've been home alone. Making examples of people who don't pay is standard procedure. Some people don't fear for themselves, but they always fear for their families. By Magda's design, Valentina would've been the sacrifice to serve as a reminder to our debtors as long as they owe, their families aren't safe.

Then I stepped out of the office, and there she was, all tits, ass, and legs. No woman, except for the prostitutes, goes into Napoli's willingly. A nerve pinches between my shoulder blades when I think of what could've happened to her had I not been there. She's either extremely naïve or stupidly brave. After this morning, I suspect the latter.

Come to think of it, I don't get how she survived here this long. According to Jerry, she's been residing in Berea for six years. The shithole she lived in is in drug valley. It's a surprise the drug and sex lords haven't kidnapped and sold her or a street gang hasn't raped and killed her yet. There are infinitely dark things that can happen to an unprotected, beautiful girl in this neighborhood.

I watch her from the corner of my eye. In the twenty minutes we've being driving, she hasn't said a word. Her brown hair is long and wavy, curling down her shoulders. A clean smell clings to her, like fragrance shampoo or body lotion. I like it. Complex perfumes give me a headache. In the white shorts and yellow tank top, her toned legs and rounded breasts are exposed to me. So is the vein that pulses under the golden skin of her neck. Her fear excites me. Her courage intrigues me. Long, dark lashes shutter the expression in her brown eyes from me. She's pretending to look through the window, but I know she's aware of me, and the gun resting in my lap.

The weapon is cool in my hand. I'm long since past the stage where my palms get sweaty before a job. I don't mind the killing. I live in a violent city. Only the toughest survive, and I'm a survivor. I won't hesitate to pull the trigger if anyone threatens or harms my family. Lay a finger on my property, and I'll break it off. I was the kind of kid who took pleasure in breaking other boys' toys. I still break. Mostly bones, these days. When it comes to hearts, I only break what's already broken. That way, I don't have to take responsibility for anyone's feelings. Now I've taken responsibility for a person on a whole different level. At least there's no risk of breaking Valentina's heart. She already hates me, and with what I'm planning for her body, she'll only hate me more, but she'll need me with equal intensity. Of that, I'll make sure.

Her gaze widens fractionally as we pull up to our property. It's a double-story mansion on big grounds surrounded by a six feet-wall fitted with electrified barbed wire and twenty-four hour, armed guards. In this city, only people with money are safe. She keeps her face perfectly blank as we clear the gates. The original Frank Emley design dates from the early 1900s and combines various styles with a strong Victorian influence, iron work, stone walls, and art nouveau stained glass windows. It's smack-bam in the heart of Parktown, in the middle of the homes of the bankers, diamond dealers, politicians, and everyone else who can be bought.

Quincy parks and opens the door for Magda first, then for me. While I'm stretching my stiff leg, he lets Valentina out and hovers with her purse and travel bag in front of the fountain.

"I'll take that." I grab her possessions and grip her arm to lead her up the porch steps. My fingers overlap the small diameter of her upper arm. This is the point where I expect her to kick in her heels and scream, but she remains eerily calm.

Magda overtakes us on the stairs. "One wrong move, one wrong word to anyone, and Charlie is dead. Get that?"

Valentina tilts her head away from my mother, a tremor running through her body.

Marie, our faithful old cook, opens the door. Her face freezes when her eyes land on the young woman.

"Prepare the maid's room," Magda says. "I'll brief you later." She enters ahead of us. "Gabriel, bring the girl to my study."

Before I can argue, Magda is gone. Marie's gaze remains fixed on the woman at my side. May as well get the introduction over with.

"This is Valentina," I say. "She's property."

Marie nods as if I bring *property* home every day, but she understands. She's been around the block. She scurries away without offering me my usual drink.

I steer Valentina to my mother's study and close the door. Whatever Magda is cooking up, I already don't like it. The sight of my mother's personal bodyguard, Scott, standing behind her chair with a pistol clutched in his hand makes me rest my hand on my own weapon tucked into my waistband. The threat is clear. Defy Magda and Valentina will end up like her dog--with a bullet between her soft, mud-brown eyes.

Magda addresses my tiny charge. "I understand you'll be *working* for us." She points at the chair facing her desk. "Sit."

I let Valentina go. She obeys, balancing on the edge of the seat. Mirroring Scott's stance, I remain standing, just in case.

"What are your skills?" Magda asks.

Valentina's lashes flutter as she lifts her eyes to me. They're big for her small face and hauntingly sad, but proud, also.

"Answer when you're being spoken to," Magda says in the headmistress voice she reserved for chastising me as a kid.

"I'm an assistant."

Magda's mouth pulls down. "That's it?"

"I also cook and clean for my neighbor."

Magda taps her fingernails on the desktop. After some time, she says, "You'll work for us as a maid and whatever else Gabriel expects from you." My mother gives me an acidic look, as if the sight of me gives her indigestion. "You'll work Monday to Friday until dinner's been served and the kitchen is clean. On Saturday, you're off from five in the afternoon. You're expected back by eight on Monday morning. If we have events at home, we expect you to work, regardless of afterhours."

The maid idea pisses me off, but the leisure time unleashes a rage in me, not that I have any ground to stand on. It's Magda's business and her debt to collect. I'm only the dealmaker. My new toy better not try to escape. I bet that's what Magda is bargaining on. It'll give her the reason she wants to eliminate Valentina and terminate my *idiotic* deal, as she put it.

"You'll keep the house tidy," Magda continues, "and with tidy I mean spotless. Everything on the inside of the building is your responsibility, except for the cooking. Marie takes care of that. If I need you to cook, I'll tell you. If you poison any one of us, you and your brother will die slow and painful deaths. Understand?"

Her throat moves as she swallows. "Yes."

"Yes, Mrs. Louw or ma'am."

Those dark eyes flash with defiance, but she averts them quickly. "Yes, ma'am."

"If you fail in any of your tasks, the deal's off, and you're dead." A sardonic light sparks in Magda's eyes. "Work well for…" She looks at me and waits.

"Nine years," I fill in.

"Work well for nine years," Magda continues, "and Charlie's debt will be paid off. We won't pay you a salary. The money we would've given you will go toward the settlement of your debt. I don't allow servants to eat from our table, but you may use the kitchen facilities to prepare your meals. Since you won't earn cash, my son will pay you an allowance for food and personal commodities. Any questions?"

"Is there a routine I need to follow? What do I do, exactly?"

Magda gets to her feet. "You'll figure it out. You start immediately."

Valentina follows Magda's lead, getting up from her chair with consternation on her face.

Before she goes, there's one thing she needs to understand. I grab her face in one hand, digging my fingers into her cheeks. "Run from me and you'll wish I shot you today."

Her body is close to mine, and I can smell her scent. I fill the olfactory gap I couldn't place in the car. Raspberry. She looks like a dove with her wings tied, but she doesn't falter under my stare.

"Are we clear?" I ask softly. I never raise my voice. I don't have to.

"Yes."

"Good." I let her go.

Her hand goes to her jaw, touching the imprint of my fingers.

"Marie will show you to your room," Magda says. "You'll find her in the kitchen."

I hand Valentina her travel bag, but hold onto the purse and remain standing since I haven't been dismissed.

The minute Valentina is gone, I say, "She doesn't know the way."

Magda goes to the wet bar and pours a tot of Vodka, which she dilutes with orange juice. "Letting her find her own way is her first test."

"Meaning?"

"The hidden cameras will record any traitorous acts she may conceive in her simpleton mind, and you'll use it to your advantage to break her." Magda takes a sip of her drink and walks back to her desk to pick up the internal phone that connects to the kitchen.

Marie answers on the first ring with a professional, "Mrs. Louw?" that comes over the speaker.

"Order maid uniforms for Valentina and linen for her room."

"Any preference, ma'am?"

"Black."

"The uniform or the linen?"

"The uniform. Make the linen..." she thinks for all of one second, giving me an over-easy smile, "...white." She hangs up and continues, "Black and white. Has a nice ring to it, doesn't it? It'll remind her of what she became--our servant and your plaything."

"She won't run," I say, a challenge in my voice. I just found Valentina. I'm not about to kill her on Sunday.

Magda smirks, swirling her glass. "That's not why I gave her Sundays off."

"Why did you?"

"To give her the illusion of freedom. Of fairness. For now, I'll let her believe she has a chance. People without hope can't be broken." My mother lifts the glass to her lips. "You see? I'm giving us both what we want. You get to break her, and I get to kill her."

Hatred laces Magda's words. The fact that I want this woman enough to defy my mother elicits Magda's scorn. I have no doubt she'll make Valentina pay for causing me to stray from the not so straight and narrow path cut out for me.

At my silence, Magda says, "You understand we can't let her meet her end of the bargain? That'll be weak."

"I promised her nine years."

"I have no intention of letting her live that long." Her smile grows until it invades all of her face. "She's bound to screw up sooner than later."

A sudden insight startles me. Magda is happy with the turn of events. She wants Valentina to suffer, and she's relying on my natural disposition to make it happen.

Valentina

MY THROAT ACHES from pent-up tears as I leave Mrs. Louw's study. If I had any hope that Gabriel's mother would have compassion and help me, it's been eradicated in that room. She's worse than her son, her blackness far colder.

I'm sick to my stomach with worry over Charlie. I need to call Kris and check that he's all right, but Gabriel gave me my clothes and held onto my purse with my phone. I can't allow myself to think about this morning or Puff. Not yet. For now, I need to be strong.

With the imminent danger of death over, reality crashes down on me. Despair seeps into my pores. The calculation is harrowing. I'll be thirty-two before I walk free. *If* I ever walk free. There's no doubt in my mind Gabriel will kill me without blinking an eye. I know men like him. My father was one. The servant role isn't only to pay off a debt. It's a means of degrading me. I have no issue pulling the hair from Gabriel's shower or scrubbing his toilet. What's killing me is sleeping under his roof and eating food he pays for. I'm forced to allow my enemy to take care of me. It feels personal and wrong. The last thing I want from Gabriel is any kind of care. I'll talk to Kris and negotiate to work Sundays. That way I'll still be able to pay for my studies. No matter what, I'm not giving it up. It's my only hope, our ticket out of Berea. I'll just have to put my plans on the backburner for nine years.

After getting lost in corridors and too many rooms with sofas and chairs--How many lounges can one family need?--I finally locate the kitchen at the far east end of the mansion. The size of the house overwhelms me. It's going to be a hell of a job to keep the place spotless.

Marie waits for me in a sterile looking kitchen, a hostile expression on her face. "I better show you around."

Wordlessly, I fall in behind her. We go through the ground level with its reading, sitting, television, entertainment, and dining rooms, and up a flight of stairs. The bedrooms and bathrooms on the first level are luxurious and comfortable. As we move along, my heart sinks lower and lower. It's too much.

"Who's currently cleaning the house?"

Marie looks at me as if I asked her for a gold coin. "A cleaning service. I presume since you're here, they'll be fired."

Poor people. They're going to lose a big contract, but at least they're free.

At a wooden door with an intricate carving, she stops. "This is his bedroom. Next door is Miss Carly's. Mr. Louw's mother is at the opposite end."

She knocks on Miss Carly's door and opens it without waiting for a reply.

A girl of about sixteen lies on her stomach on the bed. The room is one of the prettiest I've seen. It's decorated in blue with whitewashed furniture.

"Carly," Marie says, "this is Valentina. She's the new live-in."

Carly lifts her head to look me up and down before burying her face in her iPad again.

"His daughter," Marie says, closing the door. She lowers her voice. "She sometimes lives with her mom, but she's mostly here."

So, Gabriel and Carly's mom are separated or divorced.

We explore the house until we end up back in the kitchen. Only the kitchen is surgical white. It's not a room the inhabitants of the house *live* in. There's no breakfast nook, books, or flowers, not a trace of warmth. It's a functional room equipped for the staff. This is where Marie pauses the longest to show me the adjoining scullery where they keep the household appliances and a fridge for the staff.

"You can keep your food here," Marie says. "The one in the pantry is only for the family."

Cleaning products are neatly stacked on the shelves on the wall. Everything is tidy and in its place. At least there are a state-of-the-art vacuum cleaner and washing machine to work with.

"Do you know how to operate these?" Marie points at the washing machine and tumble dryer.

I nod, even if I don't. I washed our clothes in the bathtub, but how difficult can it be to figure out a washing machine?

"The washing has to be sun-dried," Marie explains, "unless it rains. Mrs. Louw doesn't believe in wasting electricity."

From the scullery, a door leads to the maid quarters. This is where I'll be sleeping for the next nine years. I put my head around the frame. The room is small, the double bed taking up most of the space, but the cream-colored carpet is clean, and the mattress looks new. The paint is white, and there are no foul smells or damp to darken the walls. A connecting door gives access to a small bathtub with a shower nozzle fitted inside, a basin, and toilet. It's much better than what I'm used to. There are no linen or towels, and I didn't bring any, but I don't ask.

"Well," Marie dusts her hands, "I'll let you get on with it. Your uniforms will arrive later. For now, you'll have to work like this." She gives my legs a disapproving look.

"Can I have my phone?"

"You'll have to ask Mr. Louw about that."

The minute she's gone, I use the bathroom to splash water on my face. The enormity of the situation pushes down on my chest. I can't breathe. Needing air, I open the window, letting the breeze on my wet cheeks cool me. From here, I have a view over an enclosed courtyard. There's a circular clothesline in the center and a wheelbarrow pushed up against the wall. Through the open door giving access to the backyard, the blue water of a pool is visible.

Since I don't know how to go about my new job with the massive size of the house, I decide to dive into the deep end and swim. It's an approach that always works for me. For the next few hours, I work out a plan of action as I go, starting with laundry and dusting, then vacuuming and finally washing the floors and windows. My mind is filled with Charlie and Puff, and even if I can't fight my tears, I can hide them while I bend my head over the mop. As I mourn for Puff, I let my hate for Gabriel and the guy who shot him ripen. The only ray of hope in this nightmare is that today is Wednesday. On Sunday, I'll see Charlie.

In the late afternoon, Gabriel summons me to the reading room. Stepping inside, I'm taken aback by the presence of an elderly man dressed in a Mandela style shirt and chinos.

Gabriel turns to me. "This is Dr. Samuel Engelbrecht. He's going to take a blood sample and examine you."

I look between the men. "What for?"

Gabriel ignores my question. "Are you on birth control?"

The wind is knocked out of me by the implication of the question, even if I expected it as an inevitable part of the deal I'd made. If the doctor recognizes the shock on my face, he doesn't acknowledge it.

"No," I force through dry lips.

The doctor offers me an impersonal smile. "Take off your clothes and lie down on the couch, my dear."

I can't move. I'm stuck to the carpet.

"How long do you need?" Gabriel asks.

"Twenty minutes."

"I'll be back for her."

On his way to the door, he stops in front of me. "If he hurts you, I'll kill him."

Dr. Engelbrecht chuckles over his open doctor's case. "It's not nice to make jokes like that."

"It's no joke."

Gabriel says it with a smile, but his words send a shiver down my spine. He walks from the room, shutting me inside with the doctor.

"Come now," the doctor says, "I don't have all day."

It's embarrassing to undress in front of a stranger who knows my employer is going to fuck me. My whole body blushes as I kick off my trainers, push down my shorts, and peel off my top.

He must see many patients at home, because he's well prepared. A disposable sheet is already spread out on the couch. I keep my eyes fixed on the ceiling as I lay down, trying to go someplace dark in my head.

He fits on a pair of surgical gloves. "Bend your knees."

"What are you going to do?"

"Don't worry, my dear, it's just a pap smear. You're supposed to do it every year. First time?"

I nod. It's not like I have money for doctors' visits.

He chats through the examination to put me at ease, but I'm tense, and when he takes the sample it hurts. He lets me get dressed before he takes my blood. He's just about done when Gabriel steps back into the room.

He walks to the couch where I'm sitting with my arm on the armrest while my blood runs into a vial. "How did it go?"

It's the doctor who answers. "Very well. I'll have the results tomorrow."

I guess Gabriel wants to be sure I'm clean. Can't blame him, seeing where I come from.

"Depending on the hormone level results," Dr. Engelbrecht continues, "I'll drop off an oral contraceptive." He removes the needle and gives me a cotton swab to press on the wound. After packing the samples in his bag, he removes the gloves, shakes Gabriel's hand, and takes his leave.

I stare at Gabriel when we're alone, heat burning under the neckline of my top. "You could've warned me."

"It would've stressed you unnecessarily."

"I'll be the judge of that," I say, jumping to my feet. "I may be working for you, but it's still my body."

"No, beautiful." He gives me a calculated look. "I beg to differ."

I don't have a reply. All I can do is rush past him, escaping the unsettling situation, and for now he lets me.

THE HARD PHYSICAL labor is an outlet for my anger, frustration, and even a bit of my fear. As I don't run into anyone while I'm cleaning, a false sense of calmness settles over me, but I start to stress again when I realize I can only manage the ground level in whatever time of the day is left. At least the house is immaculate. I can start with the first floor tomorrow. I won't manage unless I work on a rotation basis, deep cleaning some rooms only every second or third day.

I don't stop for lunch, and I never had breakfast. By the time I walk into the kitchen at sunset, I'm famished, sweaty, and tired, but everything downstairs is sparkling clean. Marie is stirring a pot on the stove. The delicious fragrance of tomato and beef stew fills my nostrils. My treacherous stomach gives a growl. My body doesn't understand pride or honor. It's ruled by the simple survival needs of hunger and thirst. Taking a glass from the cupboard, I fill it under the tap and drink deeply.

Marie wipes her hands on her apron. "I kept you a sandwich." She motions at a plate under a fly net on the counter with a white envelope next to it. "Mr. Louw left your food allowance. He said you won't leave the property before Saturday, but if you write down what you need, I'll order it for you. We have a delivery service that comes every day."

Of course they do.

Glancing at the wall clock, the housekeeper continues, "I'm off. The dinner is ready. Mrs. Louw is going out, tonight. Set the table for Mr. Louw and Miss Carly in the informal dining room. Make sure the kitchen is clean and the table set for breakfast before you go to bed. Mr. Louw usually sees to his own breakfast as he eats before I get on duty. I'll be in at eight."

A soft meow sounds from the door. I look down into a pair of yellow eyes flecked with green. A gray cat, his tail and paws tipped with white, runs inside and rubs against my leg.

I bend down to pet him. "Hello, you. What's your name?"

"That's Oscar," Marie replies.

From her tone, I gather she doesn't care much for him.

"He's Mr. Louw's late grandmother's cat."

Pleased with the attention, the tabby flops onto his side. He stretches when I scratch his chin.

"Nothing but a nuisance," Marie says with a click of her tongue.

This makes me like her even less. I don't trust people who don't like animals. "He seems quiet enough."

She snorts. "Pisses everywhere. You'll see how much you like him when you have to clean it."

"Has he been neutered?" I lift a back leg for a better look. Yep.

A puff of air escapes her lips. "Like I'd know." Marie takes her jacket and purse from a hook behind the door. "See you tomorrow at eight." She shuts the backdoor behind her with a firm click.

Curious, I tear open the envelope with my name on it and peer inside. I'm surprised to pull out eleven five hundred rand bills, five hundred more than my monthly wage. It's a lot more generous than I expected. I contemplate refusing the money on the principle, but I don't have a choice. Without an income, I can't take care of Charlie and pay for my studies. Or eat. Feeling my hunger with full-blown force, I refill my glass with water.

At the sound of the running tap, Oscar twitches his ears.

"Are you thirsty? Where's your bowl?"

When I move toward the door, he jumps to his feet and scoots past me to the scullery. There, next to the dishwasher, are two porcelain bowls, one filled with water and the other with kibbles. It doesn't take me long to locate the bag of pet food under the sink. It's a cheap brand, one with more fiber than nutritional value. Typically, it's manufactured to fill, but not to nourish. I top off the food, rinse the water bowl before refilling it with fresh water, and make myself at home on the floor next to Oscar where I feed him pieces of the ham and cheese I dig out of the sandwich. Not the healthiest meal for him, either, but at least it's tastier than the cardboard they're feeding him. The food makes Oscar my new best friend. As I set the table and bring the laundry in from outside, he stays by my side, stealing hopeful glances at me that I can only reward with caresses, at least until I have my own groceries.

It's late, but I'm worried I won't have time to catch up with all the outstanding work tomorrow, so I fold the clothes I can and put the shirts and dresses for ironing aside. As I wait for the iron to heat up in the scullery, I hear sounds in the kitchen. Immediately, my stomach tightens. How, I don't know, but I know it's *him*. It's as if the air thickens, making it difficult to breathe. I pinch my eyes shut and hold my breath, hoping he'll leave, but the iron hisses and spits, giving away my hiding place.

At the sound, Gabriel sticks his head around the corner. His eyes fix on me, and then on Oscar by my feet. It's difficult to read him. He's looking at me like he's appraising me or trying to find fault. I hate that he makes me fear. I hate even more that he makes me curious. I try not to stare, but the scars on his face have a magnetic pull on my gaze. What kind of weapon creates such scars? What kind of man survives it? I can't look away from the challenge in his stare.

Finally, the harsh lines of his mouth soften a fraction. "You better serve dinner while it's warm." Abruptly, he turns and leaves.

I let go of the breath I was holding, my chest deflating as his presence fades and the air decompresses again.

Carly sits at the table opposite her father, a smart phone in her hand, when I enter with a tray loaded with dishes. She doesn't look up from texting as I place everything in the center of the table. In contrast, Gabriel's eyes follow me around the room. I become intensely aware of my clothes and the state of my body. My skin is shiny with perspiration. I need a shower. To add to my discomfort, he inhales audibly as I sweep past him.

When the tray is offloaded, he nods at me. "Serve us, then leave."

I lift the lid on the bowl of rice and carry it to Carly. "Rice, miss?" I try to hide my discomfort as I'm forced to grovel and bow to my brother's enemy.

No reply. Her head remains bent over her phone, causing her wheat-colored hair to fall in a veil around her face. I hover until the slam of Gabriel's palm on the table make both Carly and I jump. The cutlery and glasses clatter from the force.

"Put away your phone, Carly. If I see it at the dinner table again, I'll confiscate it."

She glares at him with a cool, blue gaze. "Then I'll have dinner at Mom's."

A muscle twitches under one eye before he narrows both. "You're welcome to, but since *I* pay your allowance, your phone stays here."

She throws the phone down on the table, the mobile hitting the wood with a thud. "Fine."

"Valentina asked you a question."

She looks at me as if I'm the reason for their argument. "What?"

"Rice, miss?" I repeat, keeping my face void of emotion.

"For God's sake." She sighs with an exaggerated eye roll. "Call me Carly. I hate to be called miss."

"Rice, Carly?" I say flatly.

She steals a glance at her father and mumbles, "What the hell ever."

Gabriel's knuckles turn white around the stem of his glass. I can't get out of there fast enough. The atmosphere is so thick with tension I want to choke. I return to my ironing and listen, but there's nothing but the clanging of their cutlery and the clinking of their glasses as the meal progresses in silence.

By the time they're done, so am I. All the shirts are folded to perfection, a hated curse pressed into every, neat line. The dining room is empty when I clear the table. Loud music comes from upstairs. I don't want to contemplate the difficulties of Gabriel's relationship with his daughter. I don't care.

When I get to my room, there are towels and a heap of linen on the bed, together with my purse. In the cupboard, I find three black maid's dresses in my size. There's no key in the lock and no chair or other piece of furniture I can push against the door, not that it will do me any good. I made a deal with a monster, and the only way to survive is to honor it.

The first thing I do, is extract my phone and call Kris.

She answers immediately. "Tell me you're all right."

"I'm fine."

"Where are you?"

"At Gabriel Louw's house."

"Did he…?"

A flush works its way up my neck. He will, but I can't tell Kris. She's got enough on her plate. "No. How's Charlie?"

"He was upset when I fetched him, but he's calm, now. He's watching television."

"Thank you, Kris." I blink away the moisture in my eyes. "I didn't know who else to call."

"You did the right thing to call me. I was worried sick about you."

"I'm sorry."

"I tried your phone several times. Why didn't you answer?"

"I was working."

"Doing what?"

I clear my throat. "Maid."

"Maid or whore?"

"Kris, please."

"Val, you're worth more than that."

"I'm doing what I have to." A sudden wave of tiredness washes over me. "Can you please keep Charlie until the weekend? It's a lot to ask, but I've got no other options. I'll come visit on Saturday, and we can talk."

"Okay." She gives a relieved laugh. "I thought you're a prisoner or something."

"Can I say hello to Charlie?"

"Of course. Hold on."

She calls my brother's name. A second later his sweet voice comes onto the line.

"Va–Val?"

"Hey, how are you doing?"

"Bu–burgers."

"Kris made burgers?"

"Ye–yeah."

"You're going to stay with Kris for a while. I have a new job, and it requires that I stay in."

"Wi–will you vi–visit?"

"Every week."

"Whe–when?"

"Saturday."

"Sa–Saturday."

"Don't worry about a thing. I'm going to take care of you."

"Ta–take care."

"I'll see you on Saturday, okay?"

"Sa–Saturday."

"I love you, and remember to be brave."

"Lo–love you, to–too."

I hang up and stare at the phone for several seconds, battling to process how quickly our lives have changed. It's no use crying over things I can't change. I've gotten through bad situations before. I can get through this.

Exhausted, I make the bed and have a quick shower. I try not to think about the fact that it's *his* water or that I have to sleep in a bed that belongs to him, between his sheets, under his roof. Too weary to dry my hair, I pull on my nightgown and get into bed. My thoughts dwell on Charlie and Puff as my head hits the pillow. I want to say a prayer for them, but I'm so tired I fall asleep halfway into it, only to be jerked awake to a familiar and threatening presence in the room.

3

Gabriel

My new toy wakes with a soundless gasp. Purposefully, I let her fall asleep first. Disorientated, her defenses will be down. It makes it easier to see the truth. For the moment, the only truth is the fear in her eyes.

It's not so easy to see the truth in myself, because I don't know what I feel, except for the physical. Her intoxicating smell dominated my dining room and hardened my cock. I don't know what it is about her that brings out my lust. I only know I want her like I've never wanted a woman.

Straightening from the doorframe, I prowl to the edge of the bed. She watches me with her big, murky eyes, her chest rising and falling to the rhythm of my steps. Gripping the sheet, I pull it down slowly. She clings to the fabric, but after a second she lets go, surrendering to the inevitable.

It's the chase. That's what I want to tell myself. It's not that I need to lie to myself. It's just hard to find the truth in the fucked-up slush I call my heart. Maybe I simply want the things I glimpsed in her, the bravery and the love that made her strong enough to take this--what's happening right now--and nine more years of it for the sake of her brother.

My mind tends to be overactive. It rarely shuts down, not even in sleep, but all of my logical thoughts still as I stare down at her body. She's laid out stiff and straight on the white sheet, her hair fanning over the pillow. I reach for the button of my collar. As it pops through the buttonhole, she gulps. Her fingers dig into the sheet. If her body tenses any more, she's going to snap like a twig.

I'm many things, including a killer. I know I'm a scary son of a bitch. I own mirrors, and I'm not afraid to look in them. I see what she sees in her eyes. They're wide and moist in the light that falls from the scullery. The room isn't cold, but she shivers in her nightgown. Inexplicably, this touches me. The women I usually fuck don't shiver. To soften it for her, I turn the scarred side of my face away when I switch on the light of her room.

With the sheet discarded at her feet, I take the hem of her nightgown and move it up over her body, exposing her thighs, cotton panties, and her full breasts that, like her eyes, are too big for her body. She's perfect. Her calves are toned and her ankles tapered. I can see her pubic bone beneath the humble fabric of her underwear, and even the sight of the simple cotton hardens my cock. Careful to tamper my lust down a notch, I take my time to study the swell of her stomach and the way her breasts slightly flattens to the sides. Her nipples are a dark pink, exactly like I prefer. For the moment, those peaks aren't contracted, but I know how to remedy that, despite her fear. I've had enough partners to accurately read a woman's body and give her what she needs.

To ease the tightness in my chest, I undo two more buttons, letting the cool air wash down my torso. When I climb onto the foot of the bed, the first sound leaves Valentina's lips. It's something between a sob and a gasp. I much rather prefer a moan. I fold my hands around her narrow feet. She jerks as if I shocked her with a stun gun. Slowly, I run my hands up her legs, over her hips, and up her ribs. Goosebumps break out over her skin. Careful not to touch any erogenous zones, I reverse the path, keeping the touch light. My cock twitches in the constraints of my pants, pushing painfully against my zipper, but this isn't about me. It's about setting her at ease and bringing her pleasure. After a long time of stroking her like this, she's still incompliant, but her muscles are less tense. With each caress, I move closer and closer to her breasts, until my fingertips skim inches away from her nipples. Even as they finally contract for me with the tips turning into little pebbles, she fights it, pursing her lips almost as hard as she's squeezing her knees together. She's holding back, watching my every action, trying to contemplate my next move instead of giving over to the feeling.

"Close your eyes, Valentina."

"Are you going to rape me?"

I chuckle. "No."

"Then what are you doing?"

"Getting to know your body."

"You're not going to fuck me?"

"Eventually, yes. When you beg me."

Her eyes glisten like cold tiger eye gemstones. "That will never happen."

"You talk too much. Close your eyes and shut your mouth, or I'll be forced to blindfold and gag you."

My words have the desired effect. She seals her lips and pinches her eyes shut. I retrace my movements, starting a slow rub from her feet to the underside of her arms. After a few minutes of stroking her like this, a flush spreads over her skin, marring her neck and the upper curve of her breasts. The erogenous zones of her body will be filling with blood, making her breasts heavy and her sex swollen, preparing her for penetration. This is the cue I've been waiting for. Drawing circles around her hardening breasts, I close the spiraling trace of my fingers until I'm outlying her areolas. I watch her nipples tighten more, extending into kissable pinnacles I ache to feel on my tongue. Ignoring the hunger that makes my balls draw tight, I roll her nipples between my thumbs and forefingers and am rewarded with a gasp that sounds very different now. There's a crescendo of pleasure and an undertone of shame. The mixture is an intoxicating sound, one I take perverse pleasure in. I want to own her feelings, her whimpers, her pleasure, and her breaths. Like a signal, her hips lift. I know what her body is asking for, and I know she'll fight it. I need total surrender.

Letting go of her pretty tits, I wrap one hand around her neck, applying gentle pressure. The touch is both dominating and protective, and the way she reacts to it will tell me everything I need to know about how to make her happy in bed. To my surprise, her head lifts slightly, pressing her neck harder into my palm. Valentina is a natural submissive. My favorite kind of conquest.

Keeping my hand in place, I reward her with a kiss on each nipple. Her lips part on a soundless moan, and her eyes fly open. She blinks at me in surprise. She either expected me to bite her, or she's battling to process the sensation. Holding her gaze, I flick my tongue over her right breast, sucking the delicious nipple deep into my mouth. Her back arches off the bed, and a soft cry falls from her lips. At the sound of it, she goes completely still. Instead of fighting her arousal, she lies back like a corpse, her eyes fixed somewhere on the ceiling. Her muscles unclench, going slack under my hands. This won't do. I won't let her hide from me in her mind.

"Look at me."

The command is at direct odds with my earlier one, but I'm learning to read and understand her reactions. Of course, she ignores me, wandering around in the void she has created in her head.

"If you don't look at me right now, we're going to start over. This time, we'll practice in front of the mirror."

Slowly, she turns her gaze back in my direction until she's watching me from under her lashes.

"Good girl. Keep on watching me and tell me what you feel. If you stop talking, we start from scratch."

"What?"

She furrows her eyebrows, but I don't give her time for another question. I resume the task of licking her nipple like it's my favorite candy. When a suppressed moan slips from her lips, I lift my head to give her a hard look.

"Valentina, I won't tell you again. How does it feel?"

She licks her lips, watching me as I lave her breast with my tongue.

"It feels ... hot." She flushes bright red. "Wet. I mean..."

"Good?"

She bites her bottom lip.

"Carry on." I move to her other breast.

"Uh... Soft. Ah! Hard."

She cries out as I nip her with my teeth. "Tell me."

"Sore. No. Different. I don't know!"

I suck her relentlessly, plumping up her breast in my fist and pinching the hard tip with my lips. "Be clearer."

"Good! Ah, God. It hurts...good."

She pants and squirms. It's good to have her in the moment with me. I need her to feel, because I get off on her pleasure. I kiss her breasts and fondle her nipples until she's close to hyperventilating, throwing incoherent words and phrases at me.

"I'm going to make you come," I say, "and you can't stop it."

She tenses again, her face a mask of agonized pleasure.

"Say it," I urge, pinching her nipple hard.

She yelps. "Can't...stop it."

"That's it." I suck on her nipple. "Let it go."

She wiggles. "I–I can't."

"I won't stop, Valentina. We'll go all night if we have to, but you're going to give it to me."

She grips my shoulders, her nails digging into my skin, and gives a frustrated sob. "I don't understand what you want from me."

"Just lie back and I'll show you."

Her grip on me tightens, and her neck strains up, fear dampening the arousal in her eyes.

"My cock will stay in my pants. Lie back."

Slowly, the muscles in her neck relax as she lays her head back on the pillow. Once more, her body goes soft beneath me, but this time she's present. There's no more holding back. Her legs go slack, her thighs parting an inch. The slow, raspy lick of my tongue over her nipple is another reward, strengthening her good behavior. When she lifts her shoulders off the mattress, I almost lose control. I suck her nipple to the back of my mouth, eating her breast like a piece of cake, and she throws the reward right back at me by pushing deeper, forcing me to take more and giving me what I've been waiting for. The sweetest whimpers fall on my ears.

So damn hot. My fingers tighten involuntarily around her neck, applying more pressure, showing us both who she belongs to. There's no intent to harm, and her subconscious mind knows this. I lave her other breast with the wet strokes of my tongue, giving the plump curve the same meticulous attention as its twin until she squirms in my hold. Loosening my grip on her neck, I let my palm slide down her throat, between her breasts, and over her stomach. Her skin is slick from my kisses, and the wet trail makes her tummy quiver. Keeping my hand on her stomach, I kiss a path to her pubic bone, nuzzling her skin with my nose. The smell of her desire drives me crazy. She's wet, and the possessive side of me revels in the knowledge that I'm the cause. I'm the master of her desire. I brought her this far. I'll take her over the edge.

She seems barely coherent as I hook my fingers in the elastic of her underwear and pull it over her hips and down her legs. I free her ankles and discard the piece of clothing on the floor. She's turned on enough to take it a level rougher. I push her legs wide open, giving all of my senses access to her deepest core.

It's no secret that I love fucking. This is the part of women I love with reverence. I love their delicate folds, their taste, their smell, and the sounds they make when I invade their bodies. Valentina's cunt is beautiful. Her pussy lips are pink and plump, glistening with arousal. Her clit peeks from between her swollen labia like a pearl. The pucker of her asshole is a rosebud, and the tightness tells me no man has claimed her there. I don't mind her dark, silky pubic hair, but it has to go. I want to see her bare skin when I part her with my cock. I want to see her peachy lips stretch as wide as they can go when I take her deep, but thinking ahead only fucks with my head and torments my aching dick. I close my eyes and focus on her taste, instead. My tongue sweeps over her slit to the tip of her clit. She jerks violently, a sweet cry bouncing off the walls. Her hands dig into my shoulders, shoving and pulling simultaneously. She stopped talking. The only sounds coming from her lips are the moans I was chasing after.

"Just feel," I whisper over her skin. "You have no control, no choice."

She relaxes and opens wider, giving me better access. I spear my tongue into her pussy, and groan as her thighs hug my face in a soft vice. Her honey coats my tongue, the taste a powerful aphrodisiac. I could stay with my head buried between her legs forever, but even my patience, the resolve and control I'm so proud of, has limits. I eat her like a starving man, my teeth grazing and nibbling while my lips pinch and suck. Her nails dig into my skin and her heels kick into the mattress. When I lift my eyes, I'm shocked to see she's staring at me, her brown pools drowsed in desire. Soft, feminine pants and moans lash at me as I suck her harder, feeding my addiction for this, for everything she's giving me.

A little surprised cry fills the air, and her hips lock. I know what this means. I push down with my palm on her stomach to measure her body's reaction, but it's not necessary. I know exactly at which point she comes. She utters a high note and contracts around my tongue with a tangy explosion of moisture. I want to use her orgasm to drench my cock, to make it slick so I can sink it deep into her body, as deep as she can take me, but for now I only kiss and lick her clit, prolonging the shockwaves and reveling in her release. Despite my earlier resolution, I'm more than ready to fuck her, but something is holding me back. For some reason, I feel like it's her first time coming. A hot wave of satisfaction and immense anticipation washes over me as I consider the impossible.

Valentina is a virgin.

And it fucking crushes me.

I can't break something that is whole *and* pure.

Valentina

I'M INEXPERIENCED, not stupid. I know I had an orgasm, but it was my first and I'm devastatingly sad. Ashamed. I gave in to the man who was going to kill my brother, but those hands on my body… I expected force and roughness. Instead, he gave me gentle. It confused the hell out of me. The way his fingers explored my skin soothed me, and when I gave up on my fear, he set me on fire. He knew exactly what to do. There's no doubt he's a skilled and intuitive lover. He touched me like no man ever has, in a way that made my skin come alive. He twisted and primed my body, playing it like an instrument until it gave him the tune he wanted. I thought he was going to rape me. In a way, he did. In a way, this is worse. He raped my senses, took my defenses, and left me vulnerable, but not yet cold. His arms fold around me, pulling my naked back to his clothed chest. Hot, unwanted tears drip on the pillow.

I gave in.

I lost.

My body betrayed me.

Big, hard hands, hands that tortured my nipples into aching points of need, brush over my hip. One arm curls under me, strong fingers locking on my breast, while the other strokes my thigh gently as I battle to get my sobbing under control.

"Shh," he whispers against my ear. Repeating the same mantra from earlier, he gives me absolution. "You didn't have a choice."

There are many things I can take, but not his gentleness. I need to hate him. Prying his fingers open, I roll to the edge of the bed and jump to my feet.

"Get away from me." I jerk my nightgown down my body.

His eyes harden, but he doesn't reach for me. With his dark expression on top of the scars, he looks scarier than any man I've seen.

Lifting up on one elbow, he says, "You should've told me it was your first time."

Why can't I feel indifferent? Indifference won't hurt or cut so deep. The ache and betrayal won't let me go. Using that pain, I mold it into a shield of hatred.

Loathing infuses my tone. "What difference would it have made?"

There's a warning in his voice. "Valentina, I took nothing you didn't promise to give."

"Exactly," I snap. "I promised to give, not to take."

His lips lift in one corner, giving him the same amused expression from this morning when he threatened Charlie's life. "Give and take, now that's a debatable subject. The way I look at it, this was all give on your part. I did all the taking."

I'm fuming. I expected him to use me, but to do it like Tiny. Instead, he somehow managed to make me a partner in whatever he executed.

"Are you angry that I made you come or that you enjoyed it?" he asks, hitting the hammer on the nail.

Shivering with fury, mostly at myself, I wrap my arms around my body. "Is there something else you want? Any other *service* you require?"

He smirks. "All in good time." A wince replaces his cocky smile as he gets to his feet. "I'll have my breakfast at five. Grapefruit, orange juice, coffee, and omelette with chili. Make sure it's ready."

Adjusting his pants over a hard-on impossible to miss, he limps from the room. I wait a good five minutes after the clack of his heels on the kitchen tiles has disappeared before I shut the door, leaning against it with wobbly legs. My shoulders shake with more unwelcome sobs, but I can't stop them. It takes me a few minutes to find my control. I want to have another shower to wash away the remnants of Gabriel's touch, but a glimpse at my phone tells me it's past midnight. I have to wake in four hours, so I slip into bed and give myself over to the escape of a shallow and fitful sleep.

IT'S torture when my alarm goes off at four. Oscar is stretched out on the foot of the bed, purring like an engine. He must've jumped through the window during the night. I can only spare him a quick cuddle, or I'll be late. I put last night out of my mind, making a conscious decision to not dwell on the shameful memory. Torturing myself with the details won't change anything. I'll only make it harder on myself.

After a shower, I dress in the morbid, black dress and tie my hair into a ponytail. Knowing I'll be on my feet all day, I slip on my trainers. Half an hour later, I'm in the kitchen, chopping chili for Gabriel's omelette while the coffee percolates. Cooking comes easy for me. I've fed Charlie and myself since I was fourteen. I miss my brother so much. We've never been apart. It feels as if my anchor has been dislodged, and I'm floating aimlessly in a dark and treacherous sea.

My back is turned to the door, but I know the minute Gabriel walks into the kitchen. I first feel and then smell him. Heat creeps up my spine, making me break out in a cold sweat. The air becomes thick like smoke hard to breathe. My body registers his scent from where I've categorized it in my brain, connecting the dots to the sensual experience from last night, an experience I'd rather forget, but I can't help the powerful association. The clean, spicy fragrance of his skin triggers an unwanted reaction in my belly, contracting my womb with a fluttering echo of my first orgasm. My cheeks flame at the thought. I hope he'll think it's from the hot stove plate.

"Good morning, Valentina."

That voice again. Now that I'm less frightened, it leaves a complex mixture of sensory impressions on me--dark, smooth, bittersweet, and deep. Like burnt sugar. I glance over my shoulder. He's dressed in a dark suit with a white shirt and red tie. His hair is damp and his beard trimmed.

I fold his omelette, doing my best not to let my nerves show. "Good morning."

He comes to stand next to me, so close that our hips almost touch, and reaches for two mugs in the cupboard above. As he pours the coffee with a steady hand, mine holding the spatula starts shaking.

"Sleep well?" He pushes one of the mugs toward me, angling the scarred side of his face away.

Of course not. "Yes, thank you."

"Have you eaten?"

"Later."

"We can share the omelette."

"I can't eat this early."

I'd rather die of hunger than share his omelette. It's an illogical thought, since he gives me the allowance that pays for my food, but I have to hold on to whatever pride I can salvage.

"The doctor emailed your blood test results. You're clean."

Our eyes lock when I involuntarily jerk my head in his direction. We both know what this means. As soon as the birth control takes, he'll fuck me. Unless he uses a condom to do it sooner. Before he can say anything else, I serve his omelette on the plate I heated in the warmer drawer and carry it to the dining room. Then I disappear to start my duties for the day, trying not to think about what he said in the kitchen or that I'd become a maid with benefits. A whore.

I QUICKLY GET a handle on the house routine. Carly gets up at six and leaves the house at seven without breakfast. Marie comes in at eight, places the grocery orders for the day, and starts preparing lunch. I give her my habitual shopping list. My staple diet consists of instant noodles and apples. Apples are cheap, filling, and nutritious. The noodles give me a boost of energy when my blood sugar levels drop too low. I need the bulk of the money I save for Charlie and my studies.

As I make the bed in Gabriel's room, I try not to gawk at his private space, but my curiosity outweighs my manners. Like him, the room is overly masculine. Heavy, silver-gray curtains drape the windows, and his furniture is bulky, modern, and square. The bed is bigger and longer than a king size. The monogramed initials on the sheets indicate they're custom made. The fabric is soft between my fingers. A glance at the label tells me it's a high-thread Egyptian cotton. There are many black and white photos of landscapes and buildings on the wall. The pictures are of foreign places and cities, maybe places he's visited.

A walk-in closet connects his bedroom to his private bathroom. The closet is bigger than my room with suits organized by color and shelves for shoes and ties. Gabriel is painstakingly neat. There are no dirty clothes or towels on the floor. Whatever toiletries he uses are stored in the cupboards. Nothing stands on the shelves, not even a toothbrush. His bathroom tiles are black and white with a gray border running above the twin basins. The taps and fittings are brass, and it's a bitch to polish them to a shine. I scrub until my nails are chipped, but that's the easy part. The not-so-easy part is trying not to feel the shame of my reaction to him as, even in his physical absence, his lingering presence taunts and torments me, forcing me to remember.

Oscar follows me around, keeping me company. By the time the morning deliveries arrive, I'm shaky with hunger. After wolfing down a bowl of noodles and an apple for breakfast, I feel better. Walking into my room for a quick bathroom break, my gaze falls on a box on the edge of the basin. I pick it up to read the label. Birth control pills. My face is ablaze with heat, even as my stomach turns to ice. I've never used birth control. Never needed it. With a shaky hand, I take out the leaflet and read the instructions. It feels like I'm crossing the last line by accepting the pills, but falling pregnant will be a disaster, and as crazy as it sounds to appreciate any gesture from my captor, I'm thankful to Gabriel for his consideration in this regard.

I'M HANGING out the laundry when a whistle catches my attention. The driver from yesterday enters through the courtyard door.

"Morning." He offers me an uncertain smile, eyeing my uniform. "How are you?"

I don't know what to make of his greeting, so I simply say, "Fine, thank you."

"I'm Quincy."

I tug a stray strand of hair behind my ear. "Hi."

When I resume hanging the washing, he cuts the small talk. "I came to warn you not to come outside before clearing it with the guard house."

"The guard house?"

"We live in a staff house at the back of the estate. There's a phone in the kitchen. If you dial the button marked guard house, one of us will pick up."

"Oh."

"Next time, if the door is open," he motions at the garden access, "call before you come outside."

"Why?"

"Gabriel keeps a guard dog. He patrols the garden, and we've had an accident before."

"Okay."

"Well then, have a nice day." He must realize what a stupid thing that is to say, because his cheekbones turn a shade darker. "See you later." With an awkward salute, he hurries away.

Picking up the empty basket, I notice Marie in front of the kitchen window, watching me.

SOMETIME DURING THE DAY, Gabriel and Magda must've left, because they're gone when Carly comes home at five. Judging by her casual clothes and the late hour of her return, she attends a private school. Public schools require uniforms and are out before lunchtime. Marie has already left when Carly finds me ironing in the scullery.

"Valentina, right?" She leans on the wall and bites into a peach.

"That's right."

"My dad didn't say he was hiring a maid." She regards me from under her lashes. "Can you bake?"

"Yes."

"Will you bake me a cake for dessert? Marie made flan. I hate flan."

I crane my neck to check the time on the wall clock in the kitchen. I need to finish earlier tonight so I can do my homework, but I can fit something in if it's not too complicated.

"What do you like?"

She swings the fruit by the stalk. "Anything with coconut."

I know a simple recipe for honey and coconut cake that doesn't take long. The ingredients are common enough. The chances are good I'll find everything I need in the pantry. I switch off the iron. "All right."

When the base cake comes out of the oven, I pour the melted butter, honey, and shredded coconut over the top, and caramelize it to a crispy brown under the grill. Carly leans on the kitchen counter as I remove the cake, her blonde hair hanging in a braid down her back. She's a stunning girl. She doesn't take after her father. Her mom must be gorgeous.

Carly sniffs appreciatively. "That smells good. I'll have a slice now."

She's not a child, but I say what I'd say to Charlie. "You'll spoil your appetite for dinner."

"Come on, Valentina." She pouts. "My mom never lets me have sweets. It's bad for my figure." She motions at her body on which there isn't an ounce of fat. "Daddy will be home any minute now, and I don't want him to know I'm snacking before meals. I'll never hear the end of it."

"You're a big girl." I push the cake toward her. "Don't say it's my fault if you're not hungry for proper food later."

"Oh," she winks, "I won't." She cuts a generous slice and bites into the warm cake, humming her approval. "Oh, my God, this is so good."

"I'm glad you like it." I return to my work, happy that I pleased her. Instinct tells me getting on with Carly won't be smooth sailing.

Twenty minutes later, I'm folding the last of the ironed shirts when Gabriel's thunderous voice bursts through the house.

"Valentina!"

Oscar scoots off the top of the tumble dryer where he's been sleeping and escapes to my room. I jump, burning my arm on the still-hot iron. A second later, Gabriel storms into the kitchen, almost knocking me off my feet as I exit through the scullery door.

He grabs my arm, his fingers digging into my flesh. His face is pale, making the red scars stand out more. "There's a first aid kit in the pantry. Top shelf on the left. Get it and bring it to the television room."

4

Valentina

I jump to execute the command, running through every lounge on the ground floor with a big screen in it until I find Gabriel on his knees in front of the couch in what must be the television room. Carly is lying on the couch, panting through an open mouth. Her skin is blotchy and puffy, and the glands in her neck are swollen. The sight shocks me to a standstill, but Gabriel's calm, strong voice commands me.

"Give me the epinephrine auto-injector. It's a yellow and white box." He loosens his tie and pushes a cushion under Carly's head.

I find the box and hand it to him with shaky fingers. Contrary to my trembling hands, his are steady as he opens the box and retrieves the injector. He removes the gray cap and pushes the red tip against Carly's thigh, then counts out loud to ten. When he's done, he checks that the needle has extended and caps it with the protective cover. I'm a vet student, not a doctor, but I know what epinephrine is for, and I know a severe allergic reaction when I see one.

There's underlying panic in Gabriel's steady voice. "The ambulance is on its way, honey."

"Allergy?" I force from a tight throat.

The only answer I get is his cold, frightening glare. I want to ask what she's allergic to, but the ringtone of a phone cuts me short. A mobile vibrates on the coffee table. Gabriel holds out his palm in silent instruction, his eyes back on his daughter.

When I place the phone in his hand, he glances at the screen, and answers in a flat tone. "The ambulance is on its way." His expression turns hard as he listens to a reply. "Yes, I take full responsibility if anything happens to her, and no, now's not the time to threaten me with sole custody. Come over if you want to see for yourself how she is or wait for us at the hospital, but stop calling every two minutes. It's not going to change a damn thing." He cuts the call and dumps the phone on the couch.

Before I can get my bearings, the doorbell rings. I run to get it, but the door opens to reveal one of the men from yesterday, the one who shot Puff. He leads two paramedics pushing a stretcher inside. A private ambulance is parked in the circular driveway.

"Where?" one of the men asks tersely.

"Follow me."

I lead them to the television room. The medics go inside and shut the door on me. Puff's killer gives me a hard look before he exits the house. While I'm pacing the corridor, a model-pretty woman rounds the corner and stalks my way. Her blonde hair is twisted into a French roll. A white two-piece suit clings to her body, defining her curves. There's a striking resemblance between her and Carly.

"Where are they?" she asks with regal calmness.

I indicate the door. "Through here."

She opens and slams the door, causing it to shake in the frame. Through the door, I hear the heated tones of an argument, but I can't make out the words. Carly's mom must live close by to be able to get here so fast.

Not sure if I should wait or leave, I decide to stick around in case they need me. Why didn't Carly call for me? Maybe she did, and I didn't hear. It can't be the cake. Carly would've told me if she's allergic to eggs or honey. It can be a bee sting. The sliding doors to the pool deck are open.

Seconds later, the paramedics exit, pushing Carly on the stretcher. Gabriel and the blonde woman walk next to the stretcher, Gabriel's face tense.

At the front door, the paramedics stop.

"Only one of you can accompany us in the ambulance," the older man says.

"You go." Gabriel drags a hand through his hair. "I'll meet you at the hospital."

When Gabriel's guard helps the men to lift the stretcher down the stairs, the woman I presume to be Carly's mom turns to Gabriel. "I expect you to deal with this."

"I will," he says tightly.

She looks down her nose at me before clacking a path down the stairs to the waiting ambulance. At the bottom, she throws her keys to Puff's killer. "Rhett, bring my car to the hospital."

Rhett glances at Gabriel, who gives a small nod. Carly's mom gets into the back of the ambulance, and the door is pulled closed from the inside. As the vehicle pulls off with blaring sirens, Rhett gets into a Mercedes sports model and follows.

We are alone in the entrance now, Gabriel and I, and fury replaces the coldness in his eyes.

"You have a lot to explain."

Panic speeds up my breathing. "What?"

"The cake."

To say I'm shivering in my shoes is an understatement. "Oh, no, Gabriel." This can't be happening. "I'm so sorry."

His eyes drill into mine. "Why did you do it?"

"I just wanted to make something nice for dessert."

"*Nice* could've gotten her killed. Or did you know all along? How did you find out?"

"I swear I didn't know. I still don't know! Was it the honey? The eggs?"

"Carly is allergic to coconut."

"What?" My mind is reeling. "She specifically asked for it."

He looks at me with an expression that stops my heart before sending it into overdrive, the beat pounding in my ears.

"If you're lying, you'll pay dearly." He grabs my arm with such a strong grip it hurts to the bone. "You don't want to know what I do with people who threaten my family, let alone try to kill them." He shakes me hard. "Next time, stick to what's expected of you and leave the menu planning to Marie." He shoves me away and takes his phone from his pocket.

I'm hugging myself while he barks out a command into the phone.

There's a dark threat in his words. "Stay with Valentina until I return." After putting away his phone, he hisses, "Be very glad she's not dead and be even gladder Magda is at a dinner party tonight."

A guard comes jogging up the path, an automatic rifle in his hands.

When he reaches the porch, Gabriel says, "Don't let her out, and if Magda returns, don't let her near Valentina."

The guard nods, taking up a position by the door.

I try to calm my breathing as I meet Gabriel's livid stare. He has all the reason in the world to be angry, and the fact that he doesn't hit me makes me fear him more. It means he has control, and men with control are the most dangerous.

"Go inside." The words sound like an ice lake cracking. "Don't even think about running. The windows and doors are protected with an alarm."

I bite my cheek to still my chattering teeth and do as I've been told. I'm scarcely inside when I hear the tires of a car shooting up gravel. Through the lounge window, I see a Jaguar convertible clear the gates.

I'm shaking all over when I get to my room. Oscar is my consolation, offering me affection as I sink down on the bed and sit in the dark until my breathing is more normal. As the minutes roll into hours, I try to calm my mind by studying, but I can't concentrate on what I read. One hour becomes two, then three, four, and five. I don't have the courage to shower or change. All I can do is wait for Gabriel and Carly's return. Not able to stand the tension any longer, I take up a post in front of the window in the dining room that overlooks the street-side of the property.

It's almost eleven before the headlights of a car illuminates the gates. It can be Magda, returning from her dinner party. Relief washes over me when the Jaguar pulls up to the door. A haggard-looking Gabriel gets out and limps around the car to help Carly from the passenger side. With his arm around her shoulders, he leads her up the steps.

I rush to meet them in the entrance. "Carly! Are you all right?"

"She will be," Gabriel says, moving past me.

"I kept the dinner warm."

"I'm not hungry," Carly says.

"You need your strength, honey. Bring it up to Carly's room."

He doesn't spare me a glance as they make their way upstairs. I prepare a tray and knock on Carly's door before I enter.

Gabriel sits in a chair next to the bed, Carly's hand clasped in his. He turns his scars away from me. "Leave it on the table. We'll serve ourselves."

I obey and escape to the false safety of my room. I'm petrified Gabriel won't believe me, but even more terrified that my mistake will cost Charlie's life. 'One wrong move,' Magda said. I don't get why Carly would do something like this.

For another hour, nothing happens. Eventually, my tiredness wins over my anxiety. I have a quick shower and get into bed.

Gabriel

In the solitude of my study, I sit down at my desk to contemplate my options. It's a difficult decision. I watched a playback of the security feed from the cameras in the kitchen. Carly's voice was clear when she asked for a cake with coconut. Valentina told the truth. With a sigh I feel all the way to my bones, I pour a shot of whisky and down it in one go.

I don't understand my daughter. I failed her. There's a gorge so wide between us I'm afraid I'll never bridge it. When the crack started, I can't say. Was it during Carly's toddler years, when I was always absent from home, the family business taking up my days and nights? Is it because Sylvia and I couldn't make things work? If I can pinpoint when it started, maybe I'll find the reason. Carly and I both know there's a problem. We don't acknowledge it, because it's easier to skip the drama. If I believed Carly has a better relationship with her mother, I'd encourage her to stay with Sylvia, but she's old enough to choose, and the fact that she lives here tells me enough.

Despite being scum, I try to be fair. It's the only shred of humanity that stands between the man and the monster, but in my business, fair only applies to family. Putting any staff member above family, right or wrong, won't be tolerated. Such an act could get said staff member killed. Innocent or not, actions have consequences, and Valentina can't escape taking responsibility for hers. Sylvia expects me to inflict suitable retribution. She's not going to forget or let it go. If I don't do it before Magda comes home, Valentina will die for what happened tonight. I don't feel like punishing Valentina for something Carly should pay for, but I don't have a choice.

I refill my glass and shoot back another shot before I pick up my phone and dial Rhett. "Come to my study," I say when he answers.

The fact that something ignites in me, making me hard, when I think about what I'm about to do is proof of how far gone I am. It could be that the alcohol is fuel on my rusty inhibitions. Maybe it's heredity, and it's in my genes. I'm not a made monster. I was born one.

The door opens, and Rhett enters. "You called for me, boss?"

"Take Valentina to the gym."

The twitch that wrings his lips into a smile makes me want to break his nose. I add it to the mistake he made of shooting the dog. Deep down, I know it's not Rhett's fault. He never expected me to let the Haynes' live. He did what he believed was right, but he caused Valentina suffering, and he'll have to pay. Lucky for him, he leaves without question. I could do with another drink, but I won't risk it. I have to be sober. I'll need utter control.

The house is dark and quiet as I make my way downstairs to the basement. It's a windowless room where my guards and I work out, but it also serves as interrogation room when the need arises. For this reason, it's soundproof. Carly can never know what happens in the depths of the house when she's fast asleep upstairs.

5

Gabriel

I flick on the lights and walk around the room, trying to still the upsurge of regret that's not powerful enough to wash out my excitement. The exercise mat absorbs my steps, not giving sound to the unequal harshness of my soles.

Regret makes me weak. Excitement makes me cruel. Anger makes me dangerous. I assess my state carefully. Anger is not part of my repertoire tonight. That's a good thing, or I wouldn't be able to do this. It would be much too hazardous.

Rhett enters the room with Valentina, his hand folded around her upper arm. She's wearing her nightgown, which exposes her toned legs. Rhett's fingers leave white indents on her skin. It shakes up all kinds of sentiments in me, but they're like shredded pieces of paper. I can't make sense of anything, except that I want to chop off his hand and poke out his eyes.

With a flick of my head, I direct him to the back wall. He knows what to do. Her eyes hold mine as he drags her past. The quiet kind of anger I often recognize in myself makes the brown of her irises sizzle with sparks. Within seconds, Valentina is strung up by her arms on a rope knotted to her tied wrists, facing the wall.

"Go," I say to Rhett.

He gives me a questioning look. The surprise and disappointment on his face threaten to unleash my rage. I've never dismissed him when punishment or interrogations are executed, but this isn't a goddamn show for his entertainment. Rhett knows me well enough to read the signs. With a last, confused glance in Valentina's direction, he walks from the room, shutting the door behind him.

When there are just the two of us, I breathe easier. The violence dissipates. It becomes something different, something that turns my already erect cock into a raging hard steel rod. I adjust the rope, stretching it gently through the eye in the ceiling until she's barely touching the mat with her toes, and secure the cord to the hook on the wall. I don't want her to struggle or move. It's safer this way.

She peeks at me from over her shoulder, her eyes big and her cheeks pale. "What are you doing?"

It's not an easy question. There are many layers to it. I unbutton first one, then the other shirt cuff, rolling the sleeves back as I contemplate the answer. I don't lie if I can prevent it. I decide to give her the simple truth.

"Punishment, Valentina." I let her name roll over my tongue, loving the sound of it. Such a pretty name. *Valens*. Strong. It suits her.

She twists in her constraints. "I didn't do it on purpose."

I reach up from behind, grabbing her arms to still her. "I know."

She stops struggling, and her body freezes. "Then why are you doing it?"

I sweep her silky hair over her shoulder and brush my lips down the curve of her neck. "Because I get off on this." Another layer of truth.

A sob tears from her throat. "Please."

My cock twitches. There's begging in that word, but also acceptance. She knows there's no turning back. Even if there weren't Sylvia's expectations or my mother's threat, I can't stop myself. Not anymore.

I kiss the shell of her ear.

"Gabriel…"

She should call me sir or Mr. Louw, but the sound of my name on her lips is a treat I'm not going to deny myself. Already battling to carry her weight, she tips back. I catch her around her waist. My hands dip under the hem of her nightgown, gliding up her soft thighs. Hooking my thumbs into the elastic of her underwear, I pull it down over her hips and calves, leaving it around her ankles.

She shivers under my palms, but wisely doesn't speak. There's nothing she can say to stop this. When I step away, her body sways backward. Like a ballerina, she dances on her toes to regain her balance. A cry leaves her lips when I grip the collar of the nightgown and rip it down the middle. The fabric hangs loosely down her body, giving me a glimpse of her smooth back and the curve of her ass, but I'm greedy. To save time, I use one of the combat knives from the weapon counter, cutting open the arms to free her from the constraining clothing.

I step back to admire the view. Fucking hell. Restrained, with only her panties around her ankles, she's an erotic image that will haunt my dreams. Her frame is a flowing portrait of S-lines, from the slender curve of her neck to the sides of her plump breasts and the narrow diameter of her waist to the swell of her hips and the rise of her firm ass. My eyes follow the trail of her legs from her quivering thighs to the dip of her knees and from the gentle expand of her calves to where they taper to her delicate ankles. My fingers ache to bury themselves in the cheeks of her buttocks and in the warm, wet depth of her cunt. I expel those thoughts almost violently, knowing I can't enter her there. For now, I'm content to have her naked and bound, and if I'm honest, I'll admit this isn't about retribution or proving to my mother I'm not weak. This isn't even about saving Valentina's life. This is all for me.

I cup her breasts from behind and search the soft sweetness of her skin, dragging my lips down the elegant curve of her neck. "If I don't do this, Magda will kill you."

She turns her head to the side, away from my caress and voice.

So be it. She won't defy me much longer. I can never have my fill of looking at her like this, but her arms can only hold her weight so much longer before I risk tearing them from their sockets. I shake my fingers to loosen them and breathe in and out a couple of times to find my control. It'll be easy to go over the edge with her. Too easy. There's something about her that shatters every ounce of willpower I possess, a new experience I'm not sure I like.

I loosen my buckle and pull the belt from the loops of my waistband. Only then does she look at me again. Finally, she understands my intention. Her eyes grow large, and her lips part.

"Eyes in front." I don't mind seeing her tears or hate, but I don't want her to see the lust in mine, the darkness that makes me the monster.

Stepping so close I can smell the raspberry fragrance of her skin, I smooth my hand over her ass. When she clenches her muscles, my cock pushes painfully against my zipper. I knead her ass cheeks, playing with the firm softness of her flesh. Parting them, I can glimpse the pretty pucker of her ass. I draw a finger down her crack, teasing the dark entrance before running the tip down to test her pussy. She's dry. Good. I love the challenge.

I take a step away, widen my feet and find my stance. Drawing my arm back, I practice careful control with my strength, letting the leather collide with her ass hard enough to sting, but not forceful enough to bruise.

Whack.

The red line that welts over her golden skin makes my cock twitch. A drop of pre-cum heats the tip of my shaft.

Whack.

She cries out softly and jerks in her restraints. She's holding back.

Whack.

"Let me hear you, Valentina."

Fire simmers with tears in her brown eyes as she glances back at me. "Fuck you."

"Very well."

The next lash falls over her thighs, just under the curve of her ass.

She squirms and whimpers, grinding her teeth so hard I can hear it. The next smack is gentler, aimed higher to heat her pussy.

Her cry comes involuntarily. She tenses up as the sound escapes. I let the lashes go higher, leaving a crisscross pattern over her back and shoulders. Allowing the tip of the leather to fold around the sides of her breasts, I keep well away from her nipples. My lashes are not hard enough to draw blood or break skin, but before long she's grappling for air, moving as far away as the position allows, which isn't much. I let the belt curl around her waist, letting her feel the bite on her stomach, and move back down to her ass and thighs.

I give her a break to catch her breath, using the time to free her underwear, spread her legs, and tie each ankle to a cuff on a chain extending from the wall. She can move her legs forward or backward, but she can't close them.

I walk around to face her. Grabbing her jaw, I kiss her hard. She's crying into my mouth, her lips defenseless as I sweep my tongue over hers, devouring her like a starving man. Forcing myself to pull away, I steal a last, chaste kiss before taking my place behind her again.

"Ready?"

I test my strength by swinging the leather under the curve of her ass. When her golden skin is left unmarred, I twist the belt one more time around my hand, leaving a shorter bit at the end, and let a succession of soft but fast swats rain between her legs, aiming the leather to heat both her labia and clit. She fights it at first, flinging her head back, and pushing her breasts forward.

"Let me hear you."

I don't stop until she finally breaks for me with a scream. The breath she's been holding escapes, allowing her shoulders to rise and fall with violent sobs. At her surrender, I cast the belt aside and grab her to my body.

I want her. I want her so fucking bad I can't think. For all of my intentions to be gentle, I can't help the rough way my fingers feel between her legs. A groan is trapped in my chest when I find her wet. I need to be inside her. Now.

My hands shake as I undo my pants and let them fall to my ankles to free my cock. My shaft aches with need, the root pulsing as I grab it in my fist and guide it to Valentina's wet pussy. Bending my knees, I spear through her thighs and drag the head of my cock through her folds. I shiver in anticipation as her moisture slickens me, and the heat emanating from her core invites me deeper. Driven by primal hunger, I place the sensitive head against her opening. My only instinct is to impale her, to take her as deep as I can, but it's her frightened whimper that pulls me back from my dark lust.

Barely holding onto reason, I coat my dick in more of her arousal before slipping free from between her legs. I'm too far gone to back off completely, and as much for my sanity as her chastity, I carefully open her ass cheeks, and wedge my slick cock between them.

"Please," she begs, arching her back away from me.

My voice is guttural. I don't recognize the sound. "Relax. I won't fuck you."

She stills at that, but only until I start gliding up and down, folding her ass cheeks around my cock with my palms. I have to push her body against the wall in front for leverage. When I move faster, she starts squirming in all earnest, twisting to the left and right.

"Keep still," I hiss, "or I'll accidently penetrate your asshole."

Again, she goes slack, allowing me to find my release by grinding my cock up and down the crack of her welted ass. I find her breasts and hold her to me as I come, shooting my seed up her spine, the hotness of my release dripping down between our bodies. When there's nothing left to give, I let go, stumbling back a step to look at her. She's marked with the imprint of my belt, and my sperm running between her ass cheeks over her pussy and down her thighs. Intense satisfaction surges inside of me, overriding even the physical high of ejaculating on her skin. It's the most beautiful thing I've seen, and that fucking scares me.

Coming to my senses, I pull up my pants and unlock the cuffs around her ankles. I loosen the rope from the hook on the wall, releasing her arms. Valentina falls backward, but before she hits the floor, I catch her around the waist and use the same knife I used to cut off her clothes to cut through the rope around her wrists. She's crying and shaking, her body limp in my arms. I use her nightgown to wipe her back and between her legs, getting rid of most of the semen, and then I pick her up in my arms and carry her to her room.

Placing her inside the bath, I run a cool shower and sponge her down. She doesn't object to anything. Her pretty eyes are closed, but tears are leaking from under her long lashes, and I have to look away. I find them way too appealing. She's like a ragdoll in my arms when I towel her dry, taking care not to press on the marks of my belt. They'll be gone in a day, but she'll hate me much longer. No marks will be left on her body, but not everyone carries their scars on the outside.

I put her to bed on her stomach, naked, and don't pull the sheet over her. She'll want nothing to touch her skin for a while. Going down on my knees between her legs, I make her come with my mouth until she begs me to stop. Through her begging, I wring one more orgasm from her before I'm satisfied. Then I get onto the bed next to her and pull her onto my chest so that she's stretched out on top of me. I kiss her head and stroke her hair, holding her until her breathing takes on the even rhythm of sleep.

It's after midnight. Magda will be home any minute. Valentina doesn't wake up when I ease out from under her. Looking down at her slender back marred with red welts, I'm filled with the devastating affirmation that I can't play with a perfect, new toy without breaking it.

I WAIT in my study for Magda to return. I prefer to relay tonight's events to her myself, before she hears the news from Sylvia or Carly. I can still taste Valentina on my lips. Her arousal is a powerful aphrodisiac that twists my balls into rock hard knots and feeds my lust. There's peace in knowing I own her pleasure and discord in not being able to take her. Until she's no longer a virgin, I can't bury my cock in her soft body, and I want nothing more than to train her to come with my dick until she gets wet from the mere sight of me. It takes everything I have not to go back to her room and fuck her raw. I drag my tongue over my bottom lip. Savoring Valentina's womanly scent one last time, I pour a drink and down the liquor, drowning the perfume of her skin in alcohol.

Magda is pissed as hell when I give her a brief summary of how the night turned out. It's when I assure her Valentina's been punished, and she watches the video feed of Carly asking for a coconut cake that she calms.

"You have work with Carly," she says. "That girl has issues."

"I know." I rub my eyes.

"Do something about it, before it becomes a disaster we can't fix." She walks from my study without saying goodnight.

I touch the photo of Carly on my desk, having plenty of questions and no answers.

Valentina

IT FEELS like Gabriel took something from me. I knew he was dangerous, but I had no idea how dark he is. What Tiny did to me was almost more bearable, because it never turned me on. What Gabriel did to me last night made me wet, and that makes me sick. I, of all people, should be disgusted by the violence. It wasn't the lashes on my back. It was the intense rhythm of the leather between my legs. I both resented and appreciated that he took care of me--both emotionally and sexually--afterward. It was something I needed desperately, and I hate myself for it.

Wanting to hear a kind, safe voice, I call Kris before she's due at the practice, and speak to Charlie, who sounds as happy as only Charlie can be. It soothes me enough to get me through my Friday morning chores. My body is sensitive from Gabriel's lashing, and each brush of the rough linen of my dress is abrasive on my skin. Carly is at home today, skipping school to recover, and I do my best not to run into her. I only clean her room when she's outside by the pool.

Marie avoids my eyes. If she knows about last night, she doesn't say so. She comes looking for me in the entrance where I'm mopping and fixes her gaze on a spot behind me. "Mr. Louw says the towels in the gym needs washing."

"Okay." I mop past her feet.

"You must take clean ones. Now."

She leaves stiffly, hiding her discomfort behind her brusque manner.

I fetch a clean pile of towels from the linen closet and make my way down the hallway. As I descend the stairs to the gym, my stomach clenches, and my throat closes up. Forcing my feet to move forward, I stop abruptly when the door opens, and Rhett exits, blood all over his naked chest. He's pressing his palm to his nose, his head turned up, and almost bumps into me before I have time to jump out of the way. The reason for the blood seems to be a broken nose. The bridge is swollen and the cartilage askew. His right eye sports a shiner, and the skin on his cheekbone is split. When he notices me, he glares and pushes past, making for the stairs. I'm still staring after him when Gabriel walks through the door dressed only in sweatpants and clutching the ends of a towel draped around his neck. His face and chest glistens with perspiration.

My face flushes at the memory of last night, and my mouth goes dry. Where I come from, I've seen a lot of gangsters who pump iron in the gym all day, but no one as hard or perfectly cut as Gabriel. His upper arms are the size of my waist. Deep lines define his pecs and abs. A trail of dark hair starts beneath his navel and disappears under the pants, the V of his hips cutting sharply down to his groin. It's not the beauty of his body that renders me speechless, but the power of it. Even with his disability, he stuffed Rhett up badly, and Rhett is a hulk. As he advances, I stand there like an idiot with the towels in my arms, not having words.

A smile flirts with his lips. "Training," he says with a shrug, grabbing one of the clean towels off the pile to wipe his face. He gives me his intense stare, searching my face. "How are you?"

"Fine."

"Good." Dumping the towel in the basket by the door, he limps away.

It's the first time I see him in anything but a dress shirt and suit pants. The broadness of his shoulders and the tightness of his ass don't surprise me as much as the way the sight of him, half naked, makes my womb flutter. I can't feel desire for a man who tortured me. It will make me as twisted as him. It will drag me down to a place I won't be able to come back from.

Angry at my unwelcome reaction, I enter the gym and pack the clean towels on the shelf before picking the dirty ones off the floor. I take my time to do what I haven't done last night--take stock of the room. There's a section with free weights in the corner and a small bathroom off to one side. Judging by the metal rings bolted to the ceiling and the hooks fitted on the walls, this is where Gabriel tortures his enemies. A chill fills my veins, and I'm not able to look any longer.

I rush back upstairs, banishing my memories of last night to the depths of the gym. In the lounge, I run into Carly.

She props a hand on her hip. "Hey, Valentina."

I can't ignore her without being rude. "How are you feeling?"

She cocks a shoulder. "I'll be fine."

"Why did you do it?"

"To get you fired."

I don't know if she knows what her dad does for a living, but if she doesn't, it's not my place to disillusion her. I can't tell her I'm here against my will, especially not after Magda's threat to kill Charlie and me for one wrong word. All I can ask is, "Why?"

"I saw the way my father looked at you at dinner."

"What way?"

"A way he never looked at my mom. It's the money, isn't it?" She gives me a wry smile. "It's always the money. Well, plenty of others before you tried, and it always ends the same way. He won't marry you, and you won't get a cent, so save us all the trouble and pack your bags now."

"Yes, it's the money, but not how you think. I can't give up this job, even if I want to."

"You don't belong here. I want you gone."

"So badly that you'll endanger your life?" I ask with a note of anger.

"Oh, come on. Why are you so upset? It didn't work, did it? You're still here."

"I have every reason to be upset. What you did was foolish and irresponsible."

"What's your problem? You're acting like you're the one who almost died."

"My problem is that if you *had* died, I would've carried your death on my conscience for the rest of my life. Have you considered that?"

"Who do you think you are to speak to me like this?"

"Is it the attention? Is that the only way you can get your parents to show you they care?"

She draws back her arm and lashes out. Her palm connects with my cheek, leaving a burning sting. "You know nothing about me."

In that moment, her guard is down, and a vulnerable part peeks out from under her bitchy veneer.

I cup my cheek, pressing a cool palm on my heated skin. The fight goes out of me as I only feel pity for the poor, rich girl who, underneath it all, is just a girl.

I sigh. "Listen to me, Carly. You're young, beautiful, privileged, and healthy. You have your whole future ahead of you. You can have anything you want. It's more than most people get. Don't waste it. Even if you don't see it now, your parents would've been devastated if anything happened to you, and I would never have forgiven myself."

"Yeah?" Tears glisten in her eyes. "Like you know me or my family. Don't you dare preach to me. Maybe you would've liked to be a psychologist, but you're not. You're a *maid,* so stick to your trade." Her eyes turn hard. "I'll be outside. Bring me a turkey sandwich and lemonade. Plenty of ice. When you're done, you can clean my bathroom again. You missed a spot. Then you can iron my new blue dress. I want to wear it to school tomorrow."

I want to say I don't answer to her, but that's not true. By the rules of our kind, I'm lower on the hierarchy than the cat.

THAT AFTERNOON, Carly doesn't touch her lunch. It's a delicious looking lasagna, but she's not to be persuaded to take a bite. Magda and Gabriel treat her with kid gloves. Gabriel goes out of his way to drag a conversation out of her but gives up after a while.

After clearing the table, I salvage the portion from Carly's plate and set it aside to eat later. The rest I scrape into a plastic container I store in the staff fridge for the street dogs. I hate wasting, and I'm famished, hungry for something other than apples and noodles. I'm sure no one will mind if I eat a leftover portion destined for the trashcan.

During my lunch break, I put a cushion from a patio chair on the deck steps and make myself as comfortable as I can on my bruised butt. Then I dig in. The lasagna is rich with white sauce and cheese, the meat dripping with fresh tomato and oregano. I close my eyes as I chew, savoring every bite. Marie knows how to cook.

I'm almost finished when barking draws my attention. Quincy stands at the edge of the pool with a vicious looking Boerboel. The beast is straining on the leash, baring his teeth.

Quincy jerks on the chain. "Quiet!"

The barking stops, but the dog still growls at me, his lips pulled back over his teeth.

"What the hell are you doing outside? I told you to call. You shouldn't be in the garden when the dog is out." Quincy takes a few steps toward me, but stops a safe distance away. "I told Marie I was taking him for a walk."

"I guess she forgot to tell me."

"I'll have a word with her." With a tight nod, he continues on his way, the dog hopping along on three legs.

"What's wrong with his paw?" I call after them.

He pauses. "Don't know. I'm taking him to the vet tomorrow."

It looks painful. I leave the plate on the step and get to my feet.

Quincy looks mildly surprised when I approach, but when I'm almost within reach of the leash, he holds up a palm. "Don't come closer."

The dog goes ballistic, barking and straining toward me.

"Down, boy," I say in a stern voice.

The dog reacts immediately. He stops barking and sits down.

"That's better."

As I reach for the dog, Quincy looks like he's going to have a heart attack. "Valentina! Stay--"

His words are cut short when the beast flops down on his side and turns on his back, all four legs in the air.

I go down on my haunches to stroke his belly. "That's a good boy. It's not polite to make so much noise for nothing."

Quincy stares at me, his mouth agape. "How did you do that? No one is able to touch him but me, and I've trained with him for a year."

"I have a thing with animals."

"You don't say."

Smiling at the surprise in his tone, I look up at him. "What's his name?"

"Bruno."

"Of course it is. Can I have a look at his paw?"

He squints at me. "If he'll let you."

Taking the injured paw in my hand, I study the pad. A broken thorn is lodged in the flesh. The poor baby must be suffering.

"It's a thorn." I point it out to Quincy. "Do you have a pair of tweezers?"

"No." He thinks for a bit. "Wait. Maybe this'll do." He pulls a Swiss Army knife from his pocket and unfolds a small pair of tweezers.

"Perfect." Taking the knife, I scratch Bruno's ear. "I'm going to make it better."

It takes a second to extract the thorn. The area around the wound is inflamed. Handing the knife back to Quincy, I ask, "How long has he been like this?"

"He's been limping all week. I couldn't get an appointment at the vet sooner."

"You'll still have to take him." I straighten. "He needs an antibacterial and anti-inflammatory cream."

He tilts his head. "How come you know all this stuff?"

"An interest."

Bruno rolls back onto his paws and licks my toes.

"No shit." Quincy shoots me a smile. "Thanks for your help. He wouldn't let me touch that paw."

"Don't mention it."

"I'm not sure Gabriel is going to be happy when he learns you turned his guard dog into a drooling puppy."

"It'll be our secret. As far as the rest of the world is concerned, Bruno is a vicious guardian."

He whistles through his teeth. "Come on, Bruno. Time to finish your walk." He salutes, and walks off with Bruno in the direction of the orchard.

MY HOMEWORK IS FALLING BEHIND. I have an essay to finish before Friday next week, but I'm too exhausted to read further than one page. With what happened last night, I didn't get much sleep. I *have* to meet my study deadlines. I won't give up. I can't. It's not only my dream that keeps me motivated, it's knowing that I'll have something to fall back onto when I'm free. Charlie and I will need an income. We're not going back to Berea. I have to build a better future for us, and Gabriel Louw isn't taking that away.

I take a cool shower, still feeling the sting of the water on my back and butt. Since the only nightgown I owned is destroyed, I pull on a T-shirt and a pair of panties before slipping into bed.

Like the first night, Gabriel comes to me when I'm sleeping. I'm not sure if it's the way he softly cups my breasts or the sound of my moan that wakes me, but I'm too tired to fight it. I simply let him hear what his touch does to me. I'm rewarded with a kiss on the mouth, startling me to a fully awake state. It's nothing more than a brush of his lips over mine, but the intensity burns like a fire, and I find it...

pleasurable. His mouth is cool and dry, and his breath smells of mint and alcohol, like whiskey.

Warm air blows over my ear as his lips graze the shell. "Turn over for me, Valentina."

He lifts the sheet for me to make it easier, but my feet get tangled in the duvet at the foot. Carefully, he frees each foot, stopping to caress the bridge before planting a kiss on the sole. The tender act confuses me. I expected him to hurt me like last night, not to trail his hands gently up my body and twist my hair into a ponytail before arranging it on the pillow next to me. Maybe he will. My body tenses. Gabriel is anything but predictable. He lifts my arms and, bending them by the elbows, puts my hands above my head. A tap on my inner thigh makes me lift my head to look at him, but he cups my neck and, with the slightest pressure, pushes my face back into the pillow. He taps on my thigh again. Understanding the cue, I open my legs. The mattress dips as he gets onto the bed behind me. He doesn't undress me, but pushes the T-shirt up to my shoulders and pulls the panties down to the under-curve of my butt.

Heat drenches my skin as he stretches out on top of me without touching our bodies together. Keeping his weight on his arms, he flicks his tongue over a welt on my shoulder, making my nerve endings pop with electricity. Goose bumps break out on my skin when he blows air over the wet trail of his tongue. He continues down my body, treating each lash with the same care, until he reaches the dimples of my ass. As he licks and blows over my ass cheeks, moisture gathers between my legs. This goes on for a long time, until my clit is swollen and pulsing in need.

The first time he lays his hands on me after kissing my bruises is to remove my underwear. Gripping my hips, he lifts my ass. He takes his time to position me like he wants, kneeling with my legs spread and my forehead resting on the pillow. With my ass and sex exposed to him, he sits back and watches. I can't see, but I feel his eyes on my body, burning on my naked parts. His palms glide over my buttocks before he takes a cheek in each hand, parting me like fruit while running his nose from my coccyx to my opening. A shiver runs through my organs. My depraved body knows what's coming and wants it. His tongue flattens on my clit, warm and wet. I cry out as the raspy, hot surface draws over my slit, all the way to my asshole. Somewhere in the back of my mind there's a cry of embarrassment, but it's no use giving rein to the sentiment. Gabriel will do what he wants.

He continues to lap me like this until I'm desperate to come. Unable to stand the slow torture any longer, I moan loudly into the pillow. He hums his approval and finally gives me what I want. Catching my clit gently between his teeth, he flicks his tongue over the nub--fast, but too light.

My hands fist into the sheets. "Ah, God. Please."

"Please what?"

"Please make me come."

As soon as I verbally express my need, he opens me wider with his hands and nips at my folds, alternating the gentle bites with sucking on my clit. It takes me seconds to come with a violent spasm of my womb. Pins and needles prick my genitals. My toes curl. I can't take more.

"Stop. Please."

Begging doesn't help. He milks me dry until I'm a quivering mess, and only then does he push on my back to lower my pelvis to the bed. I'm shaking and boneless. I never thought it could be like this. He lowers over me, at last pressing our bodies together, until my trembling stops. With a kiss on my neck, he lifts from the bed. I turn on my side to look at him, some part of me needing to see his expression, but he turns his face away.

He taps his fingers on my lower back. "Go back to sleep."

Then he's gone.

For a long time, I lie in the dark, trying to understand Gabriel. I don't get it. What is he doing to me?

Gabriel

IT DOESN'T HELP that Valentina is around every hour of every day. I'm a walking hard-on, suffering from constant blue balls. No amount of wanking is enough to relieve my ache. I want inside her. Deep. Deep enough to hurt. The only niggle is her virginity. It's a barrier to me, literally and psychologically. I don't want to be the one to break her that way. Her first time needs to be special, not monstrous. Even I am not that cruel. She deserves a pretty face and gentle kisses, not a scarface who loves to fuck rough.

In this lies the problem. I can't take her virginity, and I can't stomach the thought of someone else taking it, either. I won't last much longer without relief. I consider calling Helga, but when I think of another woman, I can't get it up. The image of Valentina's strung-up body with her underwear around her ankles haunts my nights. I wish I'd taken a photo so I'd have something concrete to jackoff to.

The emergency with Carly is further fuel on my nerves. I'm not sure if I should punish her or call in professional help. I'm not a great moral example. I have no ground to judge or discipline her. If there's one thing I'm sure of, it's that Carly won't live the life I lead. My mother never gave me the choice. She put a gun in my hand when I was twelve and told me to pull the trigger. When I couldn't, she shot me in the foot.

There's no point in talking to Sylvia. Sylvia is way too much like Magda. God knows why I ever thought we had a chance. I loved her. I truly did. I believed she'd learn to love me with time, but the only thing that became clear with time was her ambition. What she wanted was my money and protection, not my love. She married me on her father's orders and got out as fast as she could, as soon as she produced the heir expected of her. Her sacrifice got her what she wanted. As the mother of my child, she'll always have my money and protection. After Carly, she insisted on a hysterectomy, ensuring she wouldn't bear me any more children. Sylvia hated every minute of being pregnant. She was devastated when the doctor confirmed the results of the pregnancy test. Carly stretched and scarred her body. Sylvia never forgave me for that. The minute Carly was born, Sylvia went on a diet and a binge of plastic surgery, letting the nanny take care of our child. Maybe Carly subconsciously felt the rejection. She was a colicky baby. She's never been an easy child, but she's my daughter, and the only human being I love in this world. I wish I knew how to fix this.

Magda's high-pitched voice and fast-slapping heels on the marble floor in the foyer pulls me from my troubles. An itch works its way down my shoulder blades.

"That's it! I've had it."

I pull the door open to see Magda charge down the hallway with Oscar. She's got him by the skin of his neck.

"What's going on?" I barely hide the irritation in my voice.

She doesn't stop in her stride, but calls over her shoulder, "He peed on my Louis Vuitton sofa. Quincy! Get your ass over here."

Quincy rounds the corner, a question on his face.

"Here." Magda pushes the clawing cat into his arms. "Take him to the vet and have him euthanized."

I'm about to tell my mother she's overreacting when Valentina flies from the lounge, a cloth and spray bottle in her hands.

"Oh, no, please, Mrs. Louw, you don't have to do that. It's not his fault. It may be a urinary infection. I'm sure antibiotics will fix the problem in no time."

Magda turns on Valentina. "What makes you the goddamn expert?"

"She's got a point," Quincy says.

The fact that he puts himself between Valentina and my mother isn't lost on me. I don't like it. Not one fucking bit.

"I'm heading out to the vet with Bruno, anyway," Quincy continues. "I can take Oscar."

"I'm not spending another cent on this fur pollution. He's just signed his death warrant."

That figures. My mother never harbored any love for my late grandmother's overweight cat. If it was up to her, she would've abandoned him at my grandmother's house after the funeral, but Carly insisted we bring him here.

"I'll take him," Valentina says quickly. "I mean to the vet. You don't have to pay anything, I promise."

I lean in the doorframe, enjoying Magda's irritation. "It was Grandma's cat, after all," I drawl.

My mother shoots me a dirty look. "Fine," she says to Valentina. "If you've got money to waste, do as you please, but if he pees in the house one more time, he's dead."

"I can take him on Sunday when it's my day off."

"Today or never," Magda says, marching to her study and slamming the door.

Valentina looks at me. There's a plea on her face. I haven't missed how Oscar follows her around or that he sleeps in her bed. She's fond of the shedding fluff ball.

"You can take an hour this afternoon," I say.

Her face lights up, and a smile transforms her features into something angelic, something too good for me. I take it anyway, enjoying the knowledge that I put that expression on her face, giving her something more than physical pleasure.

"I'll drive you," Quincy says.

Immediately, my good mood evaporates. Dark, suffocating jealousy smothers my reason. My bodyguard may mean the gesture in the most platonic way possible, but I want to break every single one of his ribs. The only thing that prevents me from kicking the life out of him is that Valentina doesn't see the way his eyes soften as he drags them over her, because she's looking at me. She's looking at me for permission. The submissive act somewhat calms me. I don't manage more than a nod.

"Thank you," she says, her gaze wary, as if she's reading the change in my temper.

I'll be watching Quincy from now on.

Valentina

THE VET BILL eats a hole into my allowance, money I was going to use for my studies, but the tests are done, and Oscar has medicine. It's a urinary infection as I thought. The vet assures me he'll be back to normal in a couple of days. It was my plan to take him to Kris on the weekend. She would've treated him for free, but I couldn't risk his life, and I don't doubt for a second Magda would've had him put down. To play it safe, I lock him in my room with his litter tray and food, waiting for the frequent urination to stop.

When I get to my room that night, there's a bundle of colorful silk tied with a ribbon on my bed, and a note tucked underneath. Curious, I pick up the piece of paper. The handwriting is neat and square.

Shave your pussy.

Gabriel is the most warped man I know. Flinging the note aside, I pull the ribbon off to reveal seven nightgowns in red, navy, white, pink, baby blue, black, and cherry plum, all with lace and ribbon trimmings. Did he get me new nightgowns because he destroyed mine, or are the sinfully sexy sleepwear something that turns him on?

I should be studying, but I can't stop thinking about the note. There will be repercussions if I disobey. In the shower, I trim and shave my pubic hair. It's a surprisingly lengthy task. After moisturizing my body, I pull on the navy nightgown, which is the least revealing, and sit down on the bed to wait.

It doesn't take long before I hear footsteps in the kitchen. Oscar, who sleeps on my bed, twitches his ears, but he doesn't move. Gabriel's tall frame appears in the doorway. With the backlight from the scullery, his face is in the dark. I can't make out his expression. He flicks on the light and enters the room with slow but purposeful steps. He's a man who always knows what he's doing and who always has a reason for his actions. His gaze slides over me from top to bottom, but there's nothing of Tiny's lustful need for a quick fix in his eyes. They're filled with questions as he runs his fingertips down my arm from my shoulder to my hand. There's a crazy moment when I almost trust him with my body, that I almost surrender my mind. It's like being in a car with a good driver, knowing you'll end up safely at your destination. I must be going nuts. It's the endorphins my body releases when he touches me. Purely hormonal. Biological. Gabriel is a sadist, and he made me a whore. I can never trust him.

He slides a finger under the strap of the nightgown. "It looks good on you."

"Thank you," I say awkwardly. "You didn't have to."

"Yes, I did." He lifts Oscar from the covers and puts him in his cat bed in the corner. "He doesn't need to see this."

I'm not sure if he's joking or serious, but the insinuation behind his words makes my underwear damp. I don't want this reaction, but I'm helpless to stop my body from wanting what he gives.

He drums his fingers on my wrist. Whatever is going through his mind, he's giving it deep thought. Finally, he breaks the silence with a single command.

"Undress."

I can fight and argue, cry and plead, but it won't make a difference. It never does to men like him. Sitting up, I take the hem of the nightgown and pull it over my head. My underwear follows next. I don't want to drag it out. The quicker we get this over with, the quicker I can go back to pretending I don't want him to touch me like this.

Gabriel doesn't hide his arousal from me. He's comfortable with it, like he is with his body and clothes. His erection strains under the fabric of his pants, but he doesn't touch it or go for his zipper. He tucks my hair over my shoulders with a gentle brush and continues with his orders.

"On your knees and open your legs."

Heat creeps up my neck as I take the posture that opens me up for his gaze, but I lift my chin and face him squarely. I won't surrender to my shame, not with him in the room. For a long moment, his eyes fix between my thighs, seemingly pleased that I obeyed his order to shave.

He tests the weight of my breasts, sending an uncontainable shiver over my skin. I can't prevent my nipples from hardening.

"Shoulders back, tits forward."

I give him what he wants and wait.

A rare smile tugs at his lips. "You're so brave, Valentina." Without warning, his hand slips between my legs. He cups a broad palm over my sex. "I love your cunt bare. Do you know what I want to do to you?"

He doesn't wait for my answer, but flicks the forefinger of his free hand left and right over the tip of my breast. The movement is firm and fast, and it makes my already heavy breast turn even more swollen. While he's toying with my nipple, he pushes his middle finger against the opening of my vagina. He doesn't penetrate me, but runs the tip of his finger up and down my slit. The rasp of the rough skin of his pad feels more intense on my shaved skin. Strangely, his touch on my breast echoes in my clit. The nub between my folds swells and throbs with aching need. Wetness coats his finger. I can feel the moisture as he slickens the outer walls of my opening with my arousal. Determined not to give him a sound, I gasp nevertheless when he grips my nipple between his thumb and forefinger with a pinch.

Satisfaction bleeds into his expression. For some reason, he's happy with my reaction. He's happy that he has this effect on me. Another cry leaves my lips as he rolls my nipple.

"Valentina," he says with a moan, "you're everything I want."

Alternating between pinching and rolling my nipple, he works my body into a state of desperate need. The bite of pain followed by the softer caress is too much to bear. No man has ever touched me like this. There's so much wetness, his hand is covered. It takes everything I have not to grind into his palm. I don't have to. He presses the pad of his thumb down on my clit, massaging in circular movements. His deft fingers abandon my tormented breast to start working on the other one. When he gives the curve a soft smack on the side, making it bounce, a gush of liquid heat spills from my body and coats his fingers.

His eyes widen, and his pupils dilate. "You like that."

My lips part, and sounds I don't want to make tumble from my mouth. Nerve endings in my lower body spark with electricity, and an invisible band of fire draws tight around my womb. It implodes, drawing all my feminine parts tight in my core before it snaps and explodes from my clit outward. All the while, I watch his face. I hold his eyes as much as he holds mine. For the briefest of moments, he's exposed, and I understand why he's enjoying this. My pleasure gives him power.

With a hand on my back, he presses my upper body to his chest while he holds my sex in hand, applying gentle but unyielding pressure to my clit while aftershocks from my orgasm wrack my body. I shake in his hold, my energy spent, and my pleasure his. Only when my body turns quiet does he stop his assault on my clit. He keeps his hand between my legs still while he brushes a broad palm over my hair and down my back. His lips are warm and dry as he plants kisses from the arch of my neck down to my shoulder. His breath is a mist of heat on my skin. His erection is a steel rod that presses against my stomach from the difference in height with him standing and me on my knees, but he doesn't pay it any attention. Slowly, he pushes me back on the mattress and straightens my legs. Kneeling on the floor between my legs, he kisses first my clit and then my folds, running his tongue over the wetness and lapping it up until I'm only wet from his tongue, but no longer slick.

When he finally gets back on his feet, he wipes his mouth on the back of his hand. A flush burns on my cheeks.

He smirks and bends over me to plant a firm kiss on the corner of my mouth. My scent is musky on him. He continues to plant kisses down my body, turning rougher. I'm still soaring from my orgasm when he starts nipping my nipples and pinching my clit. It takes him a long time to bring my body to a quick, but intense, second orgasm. His roughness, in contrast to the first orgasm, feels like punishment, but I can't think of a single reason why. His house is spotless, and I stay away from the kitchen. By the time he's done with me, he's panting as hard as I am. He doesn't angle his face away from me like I'm used to, but pulls me into a sitting position on the edge of the bed while his hands go for his pants.

The air squeezes out of my lungs.

He's going to fuck my mouth.

6

Valentina

Visions of me on my knees in the middle of the road for anyone to see make my throat tight. I close my eyes, trying to visualize a black hole in space, anything so I can escape into a dark corner of my mind.

"Open your eyes," Gabriel commands.

I obey. I don't have a choice.

"Unzip me."

He has undone the button of his pants. A trail of hair peaks out from under the open flaps. My hands shake as I pull down the zipper. I'm on eye level with his crotch, and he's towering over me. The difference in strength between us chokes me. He can easily make me swallow him, and there will be nothing I can do.

"Take me out." His voice is quiet and calm. There's nothing threatening about it.

Slowly, I push the elastic of his briefs down his hips to free his erection. He's impossibly big. Free from its constraints, his cock twitches and hardens more. The crest is broad and smooth. Manly veins run over the thick shaft to where the root is cushioned by heavy balls.

He doesn't grab my hair and force himself into my mouth, but simply stands there, watching me as I study his cock. I've never seen one from close-up. I've had Tiny's down my throat, but I deliberately never looked at it. Gabriel's is beautiful, a work of art.

He doesn't object when I slide a finger over his length from the bottom to the top, so I carry on with my exploration, caressing the velvety head. I'm rewarded with a drop of moisture that spills from the slit. In response, liquid heat gathers between my legs, even if I've just had two orgasms. When I wrap my fingers around him, he groans. Loudly. He's not afraid to let me see the power I have. The deep lines that cut from his hips to his groin fascinate me. I abandon his cock to trace them with my fingers, surprised at how hard the muscle is underneath. A white scar runs across his hip, covering bone and flesh. He grits his teeth when I trace it, but doesn't say anything. His cock jerks when I run my hands down to his inner thighs and cup his balls. They're soft and heavy, contracting in my palm.

"Valentina," he moans, "suck me already or zip me up."

He's giving me a choice? Emotion clogs up my chest. I swallow and look up to catch his expression. He's looking down at me with something like hope and acceptance. He'll take whatever I'm prepared to give.

He strokes my hair, his big hand cupping the back of my head. "Take only what you want."

At the verbal confirmation, my fear vanishes. He'll let me stop. He won't hold it against me. I lick my lips to moisten them, uncertain how to proceed. I've never done this without force.

"However you want," he whispers. "There's no right or wrong way."

I inch to the edge of the bed, taking his cock in both hands. Holding him close to my mouth, I flick out my tongue to taste him. A strangled grunt escapes when I lick over the crest. He tastes of earth and sea, a mixture of fertile soil and salty air, and I love it. I lick down to the base to see if it's the same, and when I suck a testicle into my mouth the heady taste intensifies.

"Fuck. Goddammit."

He threads his fingers through my hair, but he doesn't pull. He's holding onto me for support as I take his control. The knowledge gives me more power, and it makes me brave. I slicken the whole shaft with my tongue, using my saliva as a lubricant for my hands. I grip his girth firmly, one hand above the other, and move my fists down while pushing my lips over him.

"Ah, fuck." Air wheezes through his teeth. "Yes."

I suck him into my mouth, hollowing my cheeks, and running my tongue over the head.

He buries his fingers deeper in my hair. "Yes, beautiful, just like that."

When I glide my hands up and down his length where my mouth doesn't reach, he grows even thicker in my mouth. His hold on my hair tightens, and his ass clenches. "Pull out if you don't want to swallow."

I don't want to give my power away, yet. He's letting me do what I want with him, and his cock is jerking in my mouth. He's close. I want to take him all the way. There's agony in his eyes. I recognize the look, know the depth of that kind of pleasure. I felt it at his hands, lips, tongue, and teeth. I open my throat and take him deep, breathing through my nose.

His jaw clenches as he grunts out his pleasure while warm jets coat my tongue. He holds my head in the gentle vice of his palms as he empties himself. Keeping his hips still, he lets me suck him dry rather than moving between my lips. I take every drop like I earned it, drinking down the dizzying cocktail of male ecstasy and feminine power.

Looking spent, he bends over and leans our foreheads together while he catches his breath. I'm still floating on a cloud of warm satisfaction knowing I pleased a man like him, when he tilts my head and crushes our lips together. He kisses me fiercely, tangling our tongues, and sucking my bottom lip into his mouth. When he finally lets go, I'm breathless.

His eyes crinkle in the corners. "You taste good with my cum on your tongue."

A wave of heat creeps up my neck and spreads to my cheeks.

He chuckles and kisses my forehead. "Zip me up."

I bend to pull up his underpants and pants. There are more scars on his leg, but I don't linger there. For now, I'm concentrating on adjusting the clothes over his cock. He's still semi-hard. The velvet feel of his warm skin is pleasantly erotic. He catches my hand and moves it away, finishing the task of zipping his pants up himself. He plants a warm, wet kiss on my mouth and pushes me down to the mattress with a hand wrapped around my neck. For a second he stays like that, watching me, and then he lets go.

"Not yet," he says, as if to himself. "Good night, Valentina."

Then, like last night, he's gone.

It's ten when I go up to Gabriel's room to make his bed. By now, he'd have finished his morning workout and shower. He'd be working in his study. As I'm pulling the sheets over the mattress, the bathroom door opens, and he steps out with a towel tied around his waist, his hair wet and droplets running down his chest.

I gulp and almost choke on my saliva. Heat gathers in my underwear as my imagination completes the picture hidden under the towel. A slow smile spreads over his face. He twists his head, hiding the scars from me, and walks to the dressing room.

"Shall I make the bed?" I ask in a small voice.

He turns to watch me, letting his eyes slide over my dress, making me feel naked. "Unless you have other ideas?"

His smile broadens as a flush heats my cheeks.

I clear my throat. "I meant I could come back later."

He drops the towel, flashing me with a full frontal of his glorious, naked body.

"There's nothing you haven't seen," he says, "so don't let me keep you from your work."

He's wrong. The white, embossed line running diagonally across his knee is new to me. So is the circular mark surrounded by finer lines, like a spider's web, on his foot. He looks like a perfect Frankenstein specimen, angrily stitched together and magnificently hard. There's not an inch of him that's not one hundred percent man, in every right and every wrong way possible.

For an utterly embarrassing moment, I'm frozen to the spot, staring at him like an idiot. It's Gabriel who breaks the spell by walking to a rack of shirts. His ass looks like it's chiseled from marble.

My breath flutters as I force my eyes away and continue the task of making his bed. All the while, I'm aware of him. He pulls on a white shirt and buttons it up. Next follow briefs, black slacks, and silver tie. He sits down on a stool to pull on socks and expensive looking shoes. He opens a drawer and selects a pair of cufflinks, which he fits without difficulty.

I've never watched a man's grooming. There's something intimate about it. It's like a privilege he's given me, allowing me to watch. All dressed up, he leaves the room, trailing his palm over my backside on his way out. The caress is so light, maybe I imagined it. Alone, with no one to see, I fluff out his pillow and push my face into it. I inhale his scent, remembering the taste of him in my mouth. What is it like to be a woman from his world, treasured and respected, and not a maid or sex toy? We're worlds apart, and our worlds don't mix.

For the remainder of the day, I keep a watchful eye on Oscar. His frequent urination stops in the late afternoon. It's safe to let him out of my room. Besides, he can't stay here all weekend when I leave.

Gabriel is out when my weekly shift comes to an end. I'm nervous to leave the grounds even if Magda was clear on the rules, but I'm also anxious to see Charlie and Kris. I shove a change of clothes and the container of food remains into a grocery bag and check that Oscar has enough food before I go. Outside, I find Rhett on the porch.

"Hi." I clutch the bag in my hands. "I'm off until Monday."

"I know."

"I'll need the new key to my flat."

"You're going back there?"

"I need to tie up loose ends."

"Wait here." He disappears inside and exits a short while later with a set of keys he places in my hand. "The big one's for the main lock, and the two small ones for the top and bottom deadlocks."

"Thank you."

"Are you going there now?"

"Probably tomorrow. I'm first going to see my brother." I also want to visit Puff's grave. "Where did you bury Puff?"

"You don't want to know."

"I want to put flowers on his grave."

"You don't want to put shit out there. In fact, I'm not sure you should go anywhere near that neighborhood."

From the look he gives me, I'm scared he's going to prevent me from leaving, so I say quickly, "See you Monday."

He doesn't reply, but doesn't stop me either. When he presses a code on his phone that opens the gate, I rush through with relief. There are no public busses in this area, but if I walk far enough, I'll eventually hit the off-ramp to the highway where I can catch a minivan taxi. I flag one down after a fifty-minute walk. I'm the only white girl in the van and receive nasty remarks about the color of my skin from the other passengers, but the driver is kind and lets me sit up front until he drops me off in Orange Grove.

A Jewish community mostly populates the area because of the synagogue. In Rocky Street, I pause to feed the food remains to the street dogs before hurrying the last two blocks to Kris' house. I enter through the adjoining clinic. A few clients are waiting in the reception area. Kris runs an honest to God good practice for the love of it. She charges way less than what she should, and I know she treats a lot of animals for free when the clients can't afford the medicine or consultations. She barely makes ends meet, and I feel bad for saddling her with my problems, but I have no one else.

There's no assistant. She hasn't replaced me yet. I knock on the consultation room door and push it open.

Kris lifts her gaze from a Yorkshire Terrier and shoots me a smile. "Get me a vaccine shot while you're here, will you?"

I scrub my hands in the basin and enter the small backroom where she keeps the vaccines. She's in over her head, so I stick around and help out where I can.

After seven, she pats my shoulder and jerks her head toward the door. "Go on. Charlie's in the house. I know you're anxious to see him."

"Thank you." I offer her a grateful smile and hurry through the back to the house.

Charlie sits in front of the television in the lounge, wearing a Superman T-shirt and shorts, his fringe falling into his eyes.

When he sees me, his eyes light up. "Va–Val!"

He jumps up and grabs me into a hug, almost crushing my ribs. Sometimes, he forgets his strength.

"Hey." I brush the hair from his face. "How are you? Is Kris taking good care of you?"

"Loo–look." He points at a stack of comic books on the coffee table. "Kri–Kris gave me money to ex–exchange th–them."

"That's great," I say, even if I worry. The comic store is across the road. Charlie has to cross a very busy street to get there. "Have you eaten?"

"Kris is a good coo–cook. She's making ma–macaroni and chee–cheese to–tonight."

"Sounds good." I tie an apron around my waist, and set to work cooking dinner and cleaning the kitchen. Dirty dishes are stacked on every surface. The trashcan needs a good scrub and the floors a wash. Kris has never been tidy, but she spends every free second in the practice. An hour later, the kitchen is spotless, and the lounge and bedrooms vacuumed. I'm busy putting clean linen on the beds when Kris enters, looking shattered.

"Dinner's ready." I pull out a chair by the small table in the kitchen where Charlie is already seated.

She looks around and shakes her head. "You didn't have to."

"Are you kidding? After what you're doing for Charlie?"

"Yeah." Her eyes are probing. "We need to talk about that."

I glance at my brother and give her a pointed stare. "After dinner."

"Okay."

Later, when I've tucked Charlie into bed, I take the clean laundry from the dryer and start folding it. Kris takes two beers from the fridge, cracks the cans, and hands me one.

She leans on the counter and props a foot on the cupboard door. "So, care to tell me about this new job of yours?"

I take a long swig from the beer before I face her. "There's nothing more to tell."

Her eyes narrow on me. "How long?"

"Nine."

"Nine months?"

"Years," I say from behind the beer can.

She sprays the swallow of beer she's just taken over the clean floor. "Jesus, Val." She shoves a hand into the pocket of her jeans and stares at me with an open mouth.

"I know. It's not like I have a choice." I don't go into the gritty details.

"Hold on. Are you telling me you're his live-in maid for the next nine years?"

"Yes." I dab up the spilled beer with a paper towel.

She starts pacing the floor. "What about your studies?"

"I'll still carry on."

She stops. "Will you manage?"

"I'll have to."

"It's a lot of studying. A fucking lot of studying."

"I know."

"Did you sign a contract?"

"I don't need a contract. Paper is worthless to men like him. His word is enough."

"How does this agreement work?"

"The salary he would've paid me goes to settling the debt."

"How could he approve a loan for Charlie? I mean, Charlie. Of all people. There must be a law that prevents institutions from granting loans to disabled people."

"I never declared Charlie incompetent. A big oversight on my part. In any event, fighting him with the legal system won't work. You know every judge in this country is corrupt. The man with the most money always wins."

"Fuck, Val, there must be something we can do."

"Look, I can't change it. I have to make the best of it."

"If you're working for him for nothing, how will you afford your studies?"

"He's giving me an allowance. It'll be enough to pay the portion the bursary doesn't cover, and I was kind of hoping you'll keep me on for Sundays."

"You're going to burn yourself out."

"That's rich coming from you, Miss Workaholic."

She smiles. "You know I'll do whatever to help."

"I'll pay for Charlie's food and expenses. I don't expect you to put him up for nothing."

"Forget about it."

"It's not up for negotiation." I hesitate. "Nine years is a long time."

"Don't worry about Charlie. He's welcome here for however long it takes."

"Thank you, Kris." A heavy weight lifts off my shoulders. "I don't know what I would've done without you."

"What about your flat?"

"I'm selling it. There's no point in keeping it if it's going to stand empty."

"Good luck. You'll battle to give it away for free."

I sigh. "I know. Listen, about Charlie." I twist the tip of my trainer on the floor. "He told me about the comic store. It's a busy road, Kris."

"I taught him to wait for the green light. We did a few practice rounds together. You've got to let go a little, give him some freedom. I know you feel protective, and it's understandable, but you have to push him to be as autonomous as possible."

"I just..." I swallow. "I just don't know. I feel responsible."

She leaves her beer on the table and takes my shoulders. "It's not your fault. It was an accident. You have to let it go."

I wipe at the unwelcome tears in my eyes and look away. "I know."

"Hey." She wipes my face with her palms. "Everything's going to be all right. It'll work out. You'll see."

"Sure." I only say it to placate Kris, because once she's on a roll, she won't stop until she believes she has me convinced. Kris is the queen of positive thinking, and for that I'm as grateful as I am for her giving me a job and taking Charlie in.

"Come on." She hooks her arm around mine and drags me to the lounge. "Let's watch a stupid sitcom and laugh ourselves silly."

"I don't know." I pull back. "I have to get to the flat."

"What, *now*?" She points at the window. "It's pitch black dark outside. How will you get there? I'm not letting you out of this house tonight. You can bum on the couch. By the way, I cleaned up your place and emptied out the fridge."

Tears of gratitude stream over my face. I really need to put a cork in it, but it's as if the dam wall has broken.

"Now, now." She hugs me tightly. "Tomorrow is another day."

I WORK all Sunday in the practice, and after buying a few groceries to stock up Kris' cupboards, I head out to Berea in a minivan taxi before it gets dark. The agent I called that morning is waiting for me in front of the building when I arrive. I wonder about Jerry, but I already see from the street his windows are dark. When we exit the stairs on my floor, my heart lurches. The door stands ajar.

"Wait," the elderly gentleman says, pushing me aside.

He takes a pistol from the waistband of his pants and nudges the door open with his shoe.

Chaos greets us. Every single cupboard is open. Broken crockery is scattered over the floor. The mattress is shredded, foam peeling from cuts in the fabric. The cushions have been destroyed, too.

He lowers the gun. "Is anything valuable gone?"

I shake my head. There was nothing, except for our kitchen utensils. "Why would anyone do this?"

"Destruction. They don't need any other reason."

We study the door together. It's not broken.

"The bastards picked the locks," he says, confirming my deduction.

As I start sweeping up broken glass and porcelain, the agent inspects the ruined space. He ums and ahs, testing the taps and the button to flush the toilet.

"Everything looks clean," he finally says, "but it's tough selling in Berea these days."

My heart sinks, even if I know no one in their right mind will buy a place in the heart of drug valley, and those who'll risk it here don't pay rent. They simply take or vandalize.

"Can you try? I really need the money."

"Don't we all? What about the furniture?"

"I'm having it picked up by a pawn shop." Kris gave me the contact. They offered me a few bucks for our belongings.

"I'll keep in touch."

After he's gone, I ensure the fridge is empty and have a shower before I switch off the geyser. Tomorrow, I'll have the electricity and water cut. It's additional bills I don't have to worry about. The money will go to Kris to help pay for Charlie's part of the living expenses. Tonight is the last night I plan on spending here. I never want to come back. When I'm done paying Charlie's debt, I'll join Kris in her practice and get Charlie and me a place of our own. Kris promised me a full partnership when I graduate from vet school.

It takes a good couple of hours to clean up the flat, after which my grumbling tummy reminds me I haven't eaten since lunch. I drink a glass of water, but the hunger pains won't go away. There's nothing in the cupboards. The thieves took all the tinned and dry food that was left. There's ten bucks in my bag from the allowance Gabriel paid me, but I'll need it for taxi fare. I turn the broken side of the mattress onto the bedframe and make the bed, trying not to think about food. I double-check that the door is locked. The new door is sturdy and comes with a deadbolt on the inside, which I slide into place. It gives me a small amount of added security.

Sometime during the night, there's a thunderstorm. I lie awake, watching the lightning run across the sky and listening to the drops falling on the roof. I long for Charlie and Puff. A selfish part of me wishes they were here so I could hold them in my arms, while the logical part of me is happy that they're free from this hell. It's a miracle that I'm here, unbound, that despite my debt, I have a measure of freedom. It gives me hope. Maybe Magda has some fairness inside of her. My thoughts drift to Gabriel as I fall asleep, and my dreams are filled with disturbingly erotic images of his scarred body.

When the alarm on my phone goes off at five, I haven't slept much, but I can't risk being late for work. The gangs and criminals are mostly active at night. At this time, most of them will be passed out from alcohol or drug abuse. There's little chance I'll run into any unfavorable elements on the street. After brushing my teeth and washing my face, I pull on my clean dress. I lock the door, drag the trash bags with our broken crockery downstairs, and hit the streets.

My trainers fall quietly on the pavement as I dodge the potholes filled with water. The air is fresh after the rain with steam coming off the tar. There's a quiet after the storm, leaving me peaceful and calm, but my tranquility doesn't last long.

A little way down the street, a tall, slender figure emerges from between two buildings.

7

Valentina

My heart lurches in my chest. Maybe he hasn't seen me. I clutch the bag to my body, searching for a side road to slip into, but it's too late. The man heads straight for me. I know that step. There's a slight bend to his knees, and his arms are spread wide. My breathing quickens, and my body breaks out in a sweat, but I lift my chin and give him a defiant stare when he stops in front of me.

"Well, now," Tiny says, "if it ain't Little Red Riding Hood."

"I don't have time for your games."

I try to move past him, but he grabs my arm.

"No time for Tiny? My, my, are you an uppity-ass, now?"

"Unlike you, I work. Let me go or I'll be late."

"High and mighty, huh? Tiny heard you left. Tiny was watching your flat, waiting for you."

His words shake me. I didn't run into him by chance. He *waited* for me.

"Tiny…" I want it to sound like a warning, but there's a wheeze in my voice.

"You still owe Tiny. You'll always owe Tiny. Tiny has waited long enough."

He starts dragging me by my arm toward an alley. I kick in my heels and try to pry his fingers open, but his grip is like steel. Panic gets the better of me. This time is different. If he was going to fuck my mouth he would've done it in the street, as always.

"Tiny, no!"

"You can scream all you like. Nobody gives a fuck."

He shoves me down the foul-smelling alley all the way to the end where the exit is blocked by overflowing trashcans and rips the plastic bag from my hands. Peering inside, he takes out my purse, drops it on the ground by his feet, and throws the rest onto the heap of garbage.

"Come here, white bitch." He takes a wide stance and feels his way up under my dress, dragging his sweaty palms over my hip and stomach.

Oh, God, I'm going to be sick. "Don't."

"Or what?"

My defenselessness infuriates me. The anger boils over. I pull back and punch him on the jaw as hard as I can. For all of one second he's off balance, but before I'm one step away, he grabs my arm and throws me against the wall. My back hits the bricks with a thud. He slaps me so hard my ears ring.

"Fucking bitch."

I scream and scratch, my fingers going for his eyes while my knee aims for his crotch, but he catches my wrists above my head and presses my body to the wall with his weight.

"Wanna fight?" he hisses, the repugnant air from his mouth fanning my face.

"Let me go!"

He laughs and shifts, holding me secure with one hand to stick the other down the front of my panties. "What have you been doing with this cunt, huh?" His fingers drag over my clit, parting my folds.

I press my knees together, but it's no use. He wiggles his fist until it's lodged between my legs, forcing my thighs open.

He licks my neck, inviting a shiver of repulse.

"Tiny's gonna fuck you so hard, you're gonna forget your name."

His upper body crushes me. I almost sigh in relief when he pulls his hand from my underwear, only to cry out in despair when he shoves his pants down over his hips.

Please, no. Not this.

He knocks my knuckles into the wall, but I hardly feel the pain. I need to fight. I struggle like mad person, which only makes him laugh. By the time he has his dick out of his underwear and my dress hitched up to my waist, I'm already panting from the exertion of fighting him while he hasn't even broken into a sweat.

"Tiny." The plea falls from my lips while tears stream down my cheeks.

"Yeah, say my name, bitch."

When he rubs up against me, I bite my lip so hard I taste blood. The fear I've fought against my whole life finally gets to me, making my throat constrict and my heart pump with furious beats. It's difficult to breathe. It happens all over again, the man who raped me. I fight the images that play over in my mind, but I'm back in the bar where the men dragged me, on my back on the pool table while the one with the deep voice unzips his fly, and the rest watch. I'm in a zone where I don't want to be, but I can't come back. Tiny's hand is around his flaccid cock, pumping it to life, but I already feel the tear in my body and the dribble of blood running down my legs.

"Get your hands off her."

The voice that spoke isn't part of the memory. The men cheered him on. They didn't tell him to remove his hands. They were filming it, laughing as I cried.

"Now."

The deadly calm in the baritone voice is dangerous. It's like this morning's quiet before the storm. Tiny freezes, bringing my attention back to him, to the present. He drops his penis and lifts his hands, glancing over his shoulder as he takes a step back.

"Easy, man," he says in a thin voice. "You're interrupting our fun."

"Fun?" The tall, broad figure in the dark steps forward, a gun aimed at Tiny.

His face is in the shadows, but I know it's him. I know his voice, his shape, his smell, his very presence.

"Doesn't look like she's having fun," Gabriel says.

"Whoa." Tiny laughs nervously. "You've got it all wrong, here. Tiny ain't doing nothing wrong. She's Tiny's bitch. Ain't you, honey? Come on, love." He jerks his head in Gabriel's direction. "Tell the man."

Gabriel moves so fast, I don't see it coming. The one minute he's standing at the entrance of the alley and the next he's in front of Tiny, hitting him in the stomach with a punch that sends him flying through the air and falling in the gutter water. Gabriel steps over him, pointing the gun at his head.

"Oh, fuck." Tiny lifts his hands. "I'm sorry, bro. I didn't recognize you."

Gabriel cocks his neck, cracking a bone. "Apologize."

"I'm sorry, Mr. Louw, really I am."

"To her, not to me, you prick."

Tiny licks his lips and glances at me briefly before returning his gaze to the gun. "Sorry. Tiny didn't know you and Mr. Louw are friends."

"Friends?" Gabriel utters a cold laugh that vanishes as quickly as it started. "She's property."

Tiny gulps and starts crying. "Fuck, man."

I'm shivering in my dress, feeling like I'm stuck in a very bad dream.

"Valentina." The firm way in which Gabriel says my name commands my attention. "Walk to the street and wait on the corner."

"No," Tiny says, shaking his dreadlocks, snot running from his nose. "Please, fuck. No."

Gabriel is going to shoot him.

"Gabriel, please..." I take a step toward him. I need to find a connection with him, to reason with him. "Please, look at me."

He doesn't look away from Tiny. "I won't tell you again. Leave the alley and wait at the corner."

I start crying myself, touching Gabriel's arm. "He's not worth it. Don't."

I can't live with myself knowing I'm the reason for another man's death. My father is enough.

Gabriel cups my nape, and drags me closer, pressing me hard against his body without moving his aim from Tiny. He kisses my temple with his gaze fixed on the man on the ground and speaks softly against my ear.

"Go. Now."

In Gabriel's world, there's vengeance and violence. Violence can be dissuaded, but never vengeance. I know how it works. If he doesn't shoot Tiny, Tiny will have to kill him or look over his shoulder forever. I don't want this for Gabriel. I don't want him to carry another life on his conscience, especially not because of me.

"Gabriel--"

Quincy comes running down the alley. He brakes in his tracks when he takes in the scene.

Roughly, Gabriel shoves me toward Quincy. "Take her to the car."

Quincy doesn't hesitate. He drags me kicking and screaming down the alley, all the way to the car where Rhett waits. He bundles me into the back and wipes a hand over his face. Rhett gives me a grim look in the rearview mirror. I huddle in the corner, unable to control my shaking. I wait for a shot to go off, but hear nothing. Gabriel would use a silencer. A few seconds later, he exists the alley, adjusting his cuffs and walking with brisk strides to the car, my purse in his hands.

Once he's in, Rhett pulls off. No one says a word on the way home. Gabriel puts his arm around me, holding me tight, and I close my eyes and cry quietly for the terrible act he committed for me.

Gabriel

AT THAT HOUR, everyone at home is asleep. We park at the back so I can carry Valentina to her room without having to traverse the whole house. She objects when I lift her into my arms, but I don't heed her. Rhett and Quincy will go back to deal with the body. They know the drill. Since that scumbag fucker son of a bitch Tiny wasn't connected to any gang, there are no logistics or payoff to iron out. My priority is Valentina.

Oscar jumps from the tumble drier and runs ahead of me into Valentina's room to keep guard in the windowsill. I lay her down on the bed and remove her trainers before stripping the dress. It's going to the trashcan. I don't want anything that filthy Zambian touched on her skin. Anyway, the dress is threadbare.

Going through the shelves of her closet, I find one T-shirt, a tank top, a pair of jeans that has seen better days, and a pair of shorts. These are all the clothes she owns? I make a mental note to go through her belongings later and grab the T-shirt.

Helping her to sit up, I dress her. After what happened, I don't want her to feel vulnerable, and nakedness will do that.

"What time is it?" she asks.

"Almost six."

"I need to get ready for work."

She tries to get up, but I push her down.

"Stay."

"I'm fine." She looks up at me through her wet lashes, her lips quivering.

Yeah. She looks anything but fine, but she's obstinate and worried that she'll fail in her job and therefore get shot.

"Don't move," I say with enough authority to make her obey as I leave the room.

In the kitchen, I pour a stiff shot of whiskey and take a mild sedative from the medicine kit. The remedy is natural and won't have adverse effects with the alcohol.

Sitting down on the edge of Valentina's bed, I lift her head, slip the pill into her mouth, and hold the glass to her lips. "Drink up."

She doesn't argue. Her blind obedience heats my insides. It's a huge step, and I don't think she realizes how much trust she's showing me.

Depositing the empty glass on the floor, I take her hand in mine. Her bones are delicate and thin in my palm--breakable. There are scratches on her knuckles, but they're not deep. We can worry about that later. The sight of those marks unleashes the monster in me, though, and it takes some effort to calm myself enough to ask, "Do you want to talk about it?" I do, but I'm not going to push. Not now, at least.

She puts a hand on her forehead. "I–I don't feel so good."

My body tenses, every muscle going taught. "What's wrong?"

"I don't know. I just feel weird."

"Tell me what you feel."

"Dizzy. The world is turning."

The effect of the alcohol is kicking in, but instead of relaxing her, it's making her drunk.

"When was the last time you ate?" I ask with caution.

She lifts her eyes to the ceiling while she thinks. "Lunch."

I try to keep my voice normal. "Yesterday?"

She clutches my hand like a riptide is about to pull us apart. "Gabriel?"

"It's just the whiskey I gave you to relax. You need food. I'll get you something to eat."

"You don't have to. I can." There's a slight thickness to her speech.

"I know you can, beautiful."

I pry her fingers open gently and go back to the kitchen to rummage through the fridge. Going for as much carbs, fat, and protein as I can find, I pile a plate high with leftover Bacon Carbonara and add lots of cheese. While the food is heating in the microwave, I grab a fork and paper napkin. Back in her room, I prop her back up against the pillows and twist the pasta around the fork. When I bring it to her mouth, she utters a weak protest.

"Open," I say.

Again, she obeys.

I feed her until the plate is empty before I pull her into my lap. "You should sleep now."

She shakes her head, brushing her cheek over my chest. "Can't. Have work to do."

"It's an order, not a request."

Her eyelids are already heavy. “Thank you for saving me.”

“You’re welcome.”

“Why were you there?”

I run my gaze over her face, drinking in her pretty features as the truth registers in her expression.

“You followed me?” she asks with disbelief, a tinge of hurt thrown into the mix.

“Your phone,” I replied flatly. “I planted a tracker in it before I gave it back to you.”

“Why? Don’t you trust me? Do you think I’ll run?”

If she knows the intensity of my obsession, it’ll expose the one weakness I can’t afford. I’ll lose my power over her, and that’s not something I’m willing to let go, ever, so I give her a warped version.

“You’re worth a lot of money to me, Valentina. I’m protecting my interests.”

Hurt shimmers in her eyes and creeps into the tremulous smile she gives me. “Of course. How could I forget? Four hundred thousand rand.”

I let a note of warning infuse my tone. “You chose. I never forced you.”

“You’re right.” A single tear slips free and runs over her cheek. “I’m sorry.”

Her apology catches me off-guard. “About what?”

“That this morning happened.”

I catch the drop on my thumb and stick it in my mouth, tasting her sorrow. “It wasn’t your fault.” I hesitate, choosing my words carefully. I don’t want to contradict what I just said by making her feel responsible for what happened. “What were you doing back at your flat?”

“Trying to sell it.”

There can only be one reason she would risk it out there to make a sale. The state of her almost bare closet gives me a hint. “You need the money that bad?”

She looks away. “It doesn’t make sense hanging onto the place if neither me nor Charlie is going to live there.”

That's not the point. The point is that no one is going to buy a bachelor flat in Berea. Homeless people and thugs may move in, but they're not going to pay a cent. I get it, though. She's proud. She doesn't want to tell me why she wants the measly money that shithole is worth. I give her more than enough money to feed and clothe her, with plenty left to take care of her brother. It's not that she owes anyone. I checked with the money lords. There's something else.

"How much are you hoping to get?" I ask.

"Ten, twenty thousand, maybe?"

If this is part of a scheme to pay me back quicker, I'll play along for now. In time, she'll understand I'm not letting her go. Anyway, she won't get a lousy buck for the place. If she wants twenty grand, I'll give it to her.

"I'll handle the sale for you." She doesn't have to know I'll be the one to buy it. "You're never going back to that area. Do you understand?"

"Oh, no." Her eyes grow large. "I'm not making my problem yours. I can do it."

"I know you can do it, but I said I'll deal with the agent. End of discussion. There are too many others like Tiny out there."

She goes quiet at the mention of the fucker's name. *Way to go, Louw. Why don't you rub her face in it?*

"You shot him, didn't you?" she asks in a small voice.

I hug her tighter. "He'll never bother you again." I'm afraid to ask, but I need to know if I should call out a doctor. "Did he hurt you?"

"Some."

I go cold, the fury from earlier reviving in my veins. "How?"

"When he slapped me. My hands."

That explains the bruises on her knuckles. "Anything else?"

"Not like *that*."

Relief has me close my eyes briefly. "It wasn't the first time he bothered you." I of all people know when a man is proprietorial, and Tiny acted like she was territory.

"He collected levies for our building. It doesn't matter now."

It does. I can only imagine how he made her pay. The thought has a nerve twitch in the back of my eye, making my eyeball jump in the socket.

"What did he do to you?"

"Nothing."

"It didn't look like nothing."

"It wasn't always like this. Today was different."

The light bulb goes on in my head. "He made you give him head," I state matter-of-factly, keeping the agonizing rage from my voice, because I need to know.

"I gave nothing," she bits out. "He used my mouth, but I didn't give him a single damn thing."

That lowlife fucking son of a bitch. I wish I had more control back in that alley, enough to hold back from shooting him straight away. I should've tortured him to death, starting by cutting off his dick. The irony of the situation isn't lost on me. I'm condemning an already dead man to a slow, painful death for something I'm guilty of myself. I took her and decided to keep her. I eat her pussy every night and get off on her climaxes. I stuck my dick in her mouth and shot my load down her throat. Yes, I'm no goddamn better than the man I killed for her today, but she's *mine*. Tiny had no right to lay his hands on her.

Turning my scars toward the shadows, I bring my head down and brush our lips together. I want to wipe the imprint of every other man's dick on her lips away. I press my lips on the mouth that cocksucker Tiny abused God knows how many times.

"There." Despite my dark mood, I try to keep things light. "All kissed better."

A smile curves her lips. She looks so damn innocent looking at me like this. After what happened to her, the enormity of the oral sex weighs heavy on my shoulders. She's mine like no other person has been, not even my ex-wife. When I took possession of her body, I also committed myself to take care of her feelings. I'm training her body to want me, because God knows I'm too ugly to inspire spontaneous desire in a woman, let alone love, but she needs to understand sucking my cock isn't mandatory.

I smooth my hand over her hair. "You never have to do that again. Not for anyone. Not even me."

She lifts her head to look at me, her brown eyes soft and wide. "It wasn't the same. With you, I wanted to."

The alcohol loosens her tongue, but it also makes her speak the truth. A foreign feeling crushes my chest. Gratitude. It's the first time in my life I feel gratitude toward anyone.

Not knowing what to do with the emotion, I rock her in my arms until she drifts off. For a long time I hold her, until Marie is about to arrive. Easing her limp body down on the mattress, I cover her with the duvet and put Oscar on the bed to keep her company. I go straight to my study to call my PI. I prefer to conduct sensitive calls in a room swept for bugs every day.

Anton answers on the first ring. "Gabriel," he says jovially, "what can I do for you?"

"I need a detailed report on the financial activity of Valentina Haynes and anything you can get on her history."

"Marvin Haynes' daughter?"

"The one and only."

"I'm on it. By when do you need it?"

"Yesterday."

"I don't know why I still ask."

I'm about to head for a shower when Rhett returns.

"The flat was broken into," he says. "I spoke to the agent Valentina met there. Apparently, the place was turned upside down."

Why the fuck would someone burglar her place when it's under our protection? It's a stupid act only an idiot on a suicide mission would risk.

"Any leads?" I ask tightly.

"No. Must be a random break-in, maybe a thief who's new to the neighborhood and doesn't know shit about the hierarchy."

True. There are thousands of murderers and thieves out there. Not everyone is familiar with the families or how we operate. Still, I smell a rat, and I don't like it.

I give him a pat on the shoulder. "Get some rest."

He's been up with me all night. If the business meeting on Saturday hadn't run overtime, I would've been home before Valentina left for the weekend. I was irritated for not being able to see her before she was off for two nights and a day. I tracked her via her phone to Orange Grove, and when she went back to Berea, we spent the night outside her flat, parked in a nearby street. I was lucky I checked the tracker when I did, or I wouldn't have noticed she was on the move, being attacked in a dirty alley by that filthy Zambian. I didn't expect her to leave that early. My bodyguards must think I'm crazy, but they're wiser than to comment. I could've broken down her new door again and dragged her home to safety, but I want Valentina to have an illusion of freedom. Magda wants her to have hope, but I want her to be happy. Suddenly and inexplicably, it's important to me.

Valentina

It's after noon when I wake with a start. Ice fills my veins when the memory of this morning floods my mind. Gabriel shot a man because of me. I know it's not the first man he's killed, and it won't be the last, but I didn't want to be responsible. If I'm to function today, I can't think about it. Pushing the dark memory from my mind, I pull on a uniform and braid my hair.

Marie looks up when I enter the kitchen, her face pulled into a scowl. "Mr. Louw said you're sick. Apparently, so is Carly. Must be a bug going through the house. I made the beds, but you better see to the laundry."

I grab the washing basket and brush past her to fetch the dirty clothes from the bedrooms. Before I reach Carly's room, heated voices coming through the open door stop me in my tracks.

"Dad, come on, I'm old enough to go on a date."

"Not with a boy I don't know from Adam."

"You want to *know* every boy who asks me out on a date? Jesus,

Dad, they're too scared of you to come to our house. I may as well become a nun now and get it over with."

"Watch your tongue, young lady."

"All the girls in my class are going with dates. It's only a movie."

"I said no."

"I'll look like an idiot if I go alone. Everyone will think I couldn't get a date."

"If that's your only motivation for wanting to go with him, you're not doing it for the right reason."

"Dad!"

"If it's really such a big deal, I'll get the Hills' boy to go with you."

"You're mean and cruel! I don't like Anthony Hill. I like Sebastian."

"I don't give a damn. I don't trust a man I don't know, and I don't know Sebastian."

"You're ruining my life!" Carly storms from the room, her eyes brimming with tears. "I hate you!"

She runs down the stairs, her sobs audible until the front door slams behind her. When I look around the door, Gabriel stands in the middle of the room, his eyes closed and his head turned up to the ceiling.

"What are you doing?" Magda says behind me, making me jump. "Eavesdropping?"

"Laundry." I lift the basket.

"Get on with it then."

I get out of her way and load the washing machine, but I can't stop thinking about Carly. In some regards she's a brat, but I feel for her. I remember what is was like when my father told me who I'd marry and that I'd never be allowed to go out with other boys. At the time, it felt like my world had come to an end.

Later, when I wash the windows, I see Carly sitting outside by the pool, her cheeks streaked with tears. I pour a glass of lemonade and carry it outside.

Leaving it on the table next to her, I say, "I'm sorry you're upset."

She crosses her arms. "I'm sure you are."

"He's just being protective."

"He's a pain in the ass."

My mom always paved the way for me with my dad. "Why don't you ask your mom to speak to him?"

She snorts. "Like *that* will help. She's ten times worse."

"When is this big night?"

"Friday."

"Maybe he'll come around."

"If that's what you think, you don't know my father."

I stare down into her unhappy face, seeing myself at a younger age when I already knew I'd never have love, not the kind people marry for, anyway. Maybe it's the futility of my life, of my own unhappy existence that makes me blurt out, "Do you want me to speak to him?"

She jerks her head up, her lips parted. "Will you?"

"I can't guarantee he'll listen, but I can try."

She turns her face toward the pool, staring at the blue water with empty eyes. "I guess you're my only shot. No one else will try."

"All right. Now cheer up. Sulking gives you wrinkles."

A smile almost curves her lips.

Gabriel

I'M PORING over the information Anton sent about Valentina--the general stuff that's easy to come by--when the object of my research walks into my study.

"Excuse me, do you have a minute?"

Lowering the report, I scrutinize her. She looks pale. "Feeling better?"

"Yes." She fixes her gaze on the carpet and shuffles her feet. "Thank you."

She's nervous. "What is it, Valentina?"

"Earlier on, back there," she throws a thumb in a general direction, "I couldn't help but overhear the argument."

I lean back in my chair and narrow my gaze. "With Carly?"

"It's none of my business, but--"

"Damn right, it's not." Carly is *my* daughter, and whatever issues I have as a father are private.

At my tone, her eyes grow large. I can practically see the fear bleeding into them. Making a conscious effort to soften my tone, I say, "Whatever you want to say, I'm sure you mean well, but your opinion is unwanted." I turn my face to the computer screen, not dismissing her, but showing her she no longer has my undivided attention.

For a moment, she says nothing. I believe she's going to bolt, but then she lifts her chin and looks down at me from her meager height.

"Gabriel."

All I want is to throw her over the desk and fuck her, but in this, I have to show her her place.

"It's sir when I'm not going down on you."

Her cheeks turn pink, but she stands her ground, her gorgeous courage making me hot around my collar and hard in my pants.

"*Sir*, I promised Carly I'd speak to you. You can do to me whatever you want, listen or not listen, but I won't break my promise."

The chair scrapes over the floor as I push it back and get to my feet. "I won't tell you again, keep your nose out of my business."

The hem of her dress trembles--her knees must be shaking--but she doesn't back down. "You're making a mistake."

I round the desk and stop in front of her. "Am I, now?"

"You should let Carly decide who she wants to go out with."

"You would know."

"Yes."

"You're not a parent. Until you are, keep your opinion to yourself."

She cranes her neck to look me in the eyes. "No, I'm not a parent, but I've been there. I know what it feels like."

The angry part of me stills as I picture her as a young woman asking her father's permission to go out on a date. From the report I just read, I know she was only thirteen when he died, way too young to date, but I'm curious.

"My father already decided who I was going to marry when I

turned ten. It didn't matter what I wanted or how I felt. My mother was already gathering a trousseau for the day I'd turn eighteen. My father passed away early, saving me from that fate, but if he'd still been alive, I would've been far, far away from here."

There's nowhere far enough she could've run. Marvin would've found her. He was a small fish in a big pond, but he was part of the mob. Every single man in the business would've been looking for her. My curiosity piqued further, I ask, "Who were you supposed to marry?"

"Lambert Roos."

It makes sense. It would've strengthened Marvin's connections, but hearing her say it doesn't sit right with me. Lambert is an old fart. I feel like killing him now just because he once upon a time considered marrying her. Which raises the questions I've been mulling over for the last hour. Why didn't anyone in the family take the Haynes orphans in? Now I want to know, why didn't the Roos family take Valentina and Charles when their mother died? Lambert's family should've claimed them and raised Valentina until she turned a marriageable age. Too many things about Valentina don't add up.

She watches me with her big eyes. "Don't push her away. Give her reason to confide in you, not to do things behind your back. Carly is her own person. She deserves to make her own choices, even if they're mistakes."

Everything she says is true, but the protective side of me is too fierce.

"It's just a date," she continues. "You can't lock her in a glass cage forever. She has to find her way in life."

"I'm not sure I can."

"Of course you can. At least meet the kid before you cast judgment. Invite him over. That way you can decide if she's safe with him."

I consider her words. I'm not the world's greatest father, but I want what's best for Carly.

"You can always kill him if he misbehaves," she says with a hint of a smile.

It's her way of telling me she accepted what happened this morning, not that I need her acceptance. I'm not worried about her ratting on me, either, because I know how desperately she wants to keep her brother alive. Anyway, it won't do her any good. Magda practically owns the police force.

I sigh and wipe a hand over my face. "I have to discuss it with her mother."

Hope lights up the somber depths of her eyes. "Can I tell her you'll think about it?"

"Fine." I shove my hands into my pockets. "I'll think about it, and I'll tell her myself."

"Thank you," she says, as if I just granted *her* freedom to date, which brings another nagging issue to my mind--Valentina's virginity.

I won't be able to hold off much longer. At some point, my control is going to snap. It tears me apart to even think about it, but soon I'll have to face the decision I've been putting off for far too long.

WHEN VALENTINA IS CLEANING UPSTAIRS, I send Marie out on a shopping errand with Quincy, and go through Valentina's room. Except for a few pieces of clothing, a pair of flip-flops, and a change of plain, white underwear, there are raspberry-scented shampoo, body lotion, deodorant, and tampons in her closet. There are no cosmetics, jewelry, or shoes, not even a hairclip.

On the bottom shelf, I find a stack of text and notebooks. From the titles, I deduce they're on veterinary science. Could it be that Valentina is a university student? It should've occurred to me earlier. She's clever, driven, and ambitious. It makes sense that she'd want to further her education. As I'm staring at her neat handwriting, I'm struck by another foreign emotion.

Pride.

The pride I feel for Carly is her birthright, but this is different. This pride is *earned*. A piece of the ever-present coldness in me makes way for a pleasant rush of heat. Valentina wants to be a vet. She'll make a brilliant, gorgeous animal doctor. This is why she needs the money. I finished an MBA after high school, and I know how much hard work it is. She won't keep up this job and her studies. Not for long. The part of me that wants her to be happy wants her to have this, but I'll have to find a way around Magda.

I'm enjoying the sensation of warmth in my chest too much to let it go, but when my gaze sweeps over her belongings, a new feeling dampens my pride. It takes me a while to place it.

Fuck me. I feel compassion. Big, empathic compassion. I always knew Valentina was going to play havoc with my body, but what the hell is she doing to my heart?

Valentina

"Which one?" Carly holds up a pink strapless dress and a blue one with a tight-fitting bodice.

I stop ironing to consider the options. "The pink one." Gabriel will definitely object if she shows off too much of her figure.

She puts the pink one on the ironing pile and lifts her hair on top of her head. "Up or down?"

"You have a pretty neck. I'd say up."

She all but skips from the scullery, leaving me with a smile. I'm glad Gabriel finally agreed to let her go out after meeting Sebastian and his parents. It didn't take a brain surgeon to see Carly was smitten with the boy. He has all the qualities to make a schoolgirl's knees weak, including playing for the school rugby team.

I finish pressing the tablecloth, hiding a yawn behind my hand. I'm exhausted. It's a battle to keep my eyes open past eleven. Every night, Gabriel comes to me. My body has learned not only to respond to him, but also to need the pleasure he gives me like I need food and water. When my body hits the mattress, it starts craving him. I'm wet and aching before he even walks through my door. By the time he fondles and kisses me, I'm begging for release. Sometimes, he lets me return the favor. It's always the same routine. When it's me making him come, he leaves everything up to me. I find comfort and power in this, and I also find I need more. I'm ashamed to admit I want more from Gabriel than oral sex. I'm fantasizing about having him inside my body, feeling him rock a rhythm into me with his cock. I shouldn't want this, not from him of all people. I crave what he does to my body, but I hate him for having this effect on me. I never wanted a man before or had erotic dreams, but now I wake up soaked and needy every morning, my senses super aware of him as he moves around the house. Last night, I was on the verge of asking him to fuck me, but my pride won't let me. Maybe controlling me with powerful orgasms is enough for him, but it's not enough for me. Not only did he make me a whore, he made me a greedy one.

"Meeting in the kitchen," Marie says, breaking my train of thought.

I let my hair fall around my face to hide my flustered cheeks. "Coming."

Magda is waiting for us with a clipboard in her hand. As usual, she jumps straight into business. "It's my son's birthday in four months, and we're hosting a party at the house. I'm hiring caterers and servers, but everyone's help is needed. Make sure you're available on Saturday and Sunday the tenth and eleventh of March. It'll finish late, so, Marie, you'll have to sleep over. You can share Valentina's room. Any questions?"

Both Marie and I shake our heads.

"Good. I'll give you more details closer to the time."

When she's gone, trying to sound casual, I ask, "How old is he?"

"Thirty-six."

"He had Carly young."

"He married Mrs. Louw when they were both only nineteen. They had Carly the following year."

"Was it an arranged marriage?"

Marie pulls her back straight. "You shouldn't ask questions about affairs that don't concern you."

She's right, but I have an insatiable curiosity about my keeper. I'm devastated to admit I want to know everything there is to know about him.

"The table needs to be cleared," she says harshly.

I tidy the dining room and smuggle the untouched food to my room. On my break, I carry the Shepard's Pie outside and make myself comfortable on the low wall separating the garden from the pool.

Gabriel

BEFORE VALENTINA'S ARRIVAL, I never spent time in the kitchen. I never had reason to. Now, I gravitate to that part of the house with increasing frequency. An urge to see Valentina drives me there, but she's nowhere to be seen. Marie can't hide her shock at my presence, more so when I switch on the kettle and take a mug from the cupboard.

"Anything I can do, Mr. Louw?"

"I've got this."

She eyes me warily as I drop a teabag into the mug.

"I can prepare you a tray," she says, "or get Valentina to bring it to your study."

"Where *is* Valentina?"

"Lunch break." The way she wrinkles her nose tells me our maid isn't one of her favorites. Any resentment she has should be directed at me. The little maid came voluntarily, but only because I made sure there was no other choice.

"Shall I call her?" Marie asks, watching me with hawk eyes.

"No." Valentina needs her rest. Her back is breaking under the burdens Magda piles on her.

"As you wish." Her dismay is laughable. If she weren't a loyal employee, I would've kicked her ass out on the spot.

As if sensing my discord, she moves away quickly, busying herself with chopping vegetables. I don't really want the damn tea, but if I abandon the task, Marie will know my ulterior motive for gatecrashing in the kitchen.

I walk to the window while I wait for the water the boil and jolt to a standstill. Valentina sits on the wall with a plate in her hands.

I go colder than the morgue.

Bruno is out. Quincy told me ten minutes earlier he's letting him run free for exercise.

"Valentina!" My voice carries through the window, because she lifts her head with a frown.

Jumping to action, I sprint as fast as my limp allows to the backdoor, my body in fight mode. I clear the house in record speed, but my voice didn't only attract Valentina's attention. The Boerboel rounds the corner, his ears drawn back in alert. My heart stops. My lungs collapse, making it impossible to draw in a breath.

"Quincy!" Where the fuck is he? "Valentina!"

I don't have time to elaborate on my warning. The dog spots her and charges.

8

Gabriel

The chances are in Bruno's favor of making it to Valentina before I do, and I don't have my gun on me. I throw my weight behind my effort, but my disability makes me too slow.

One more second and Bruno is next to the wall. Horrible visions play off in my mind. I reach for Valentina with an outstretched arm, trying to throw myself between her and the dog, but Bruno is at her feet, his enormous jaw going straight for her delicate ankle. I'm about to tackle and strangle the animal when the fact that he's licking her leg instead of tearing her apart registers in my frantic mind. I barely stop myself from crashing head-on into both of them. My hands are shaking, and my skin is clammy. The powerful rush of adrenalin drops as quickly as it has flared, making me feel physically ill. I swallow several times to suppress the urge to puke. While I'm battling to settle my guts, Bruno slobbers all over her.

Valentina gives me a confused look, uncertainty creeping into her eyes. She puts a plate with a half-eaten serving of Shepard's Pie on the wall and pushes it away from her, as if the food is the cause of my reaction. Bruno puts his forepaws on the wall and stretches. When she scratches behind his ear, he closes his eyes, and tilts his head to her touch.

"Is everything all right?" she asks in a small voice.

I must look like I feel--a fucking madman.

Quincy comes running from the back, jogging up when he spots me. He stops with his hands on his hips, looking between Valentina and me. "What's going on?"

I can't look at him right now. The chances are too big that I'll rip his head from his body. Instead, I lock gazes with Valentina.

"What the fuck are you doing outside when the dog is loose?"

She stops petting Bruno and drops her hand. "He doesn't mind me."

"He's a guard dog, not a lapdog."

The vixen dares to challenge me. "He seems friendly enough to me."

"She's right," Quincy adds quickly. "Bruno likes her. He won't attack."

"You," I turn to him with ice in my tone, "are supposed to check that nobody is out before you let him loose."

"It's not Quincy's fault," she says. "I didn't tell him I was coming outside."

She's covering for Quincy? With the aftermath of the adrenalin still burning in my veins and my leg aching like a bitch from the overexertion, this is as much as I can take.

I grab her arm and pull her from the wall, catching her around the waist before she falls. "Inside."

Her face pales at my tone, even if the command was no louder than a whisper.

Quincy lifts his palms. "Gabriel, take it easy."

"Are you giving me an order?"

He backs down. "Of course not."

"Next time, follow instructions," I snarl.

I don't care that Marie stops to look at us as I drag Valentina behind me through the kitchen. I don't stop until I get to the gym. Shoving her inside, I lock the door and turn to face her. She wraps her arms around herself, regarding me calmly, but there's wariness in her eyes.

For a moment, I just look at her. The thought of anything happening to her leaves an acidic, bitter, fucking horrible taste in my mouth. The intensity of the notion shocks me to my core. I hate her for it. I hate her for the crippling anguish I suffered on her behalf. It's a goddamn sick feeling, and it makes me fucking weak. I like my sex wild, and I love a woman's tears, which is why I sleep with women who crave my money enough to take what comes with having sex with me. But Valentina? I never wanted to hurt her up to this moment. When I belted her, it was to prevent Magda from killing her. Yes, it turned me on, but I regretted it. Now, I want to paddle her ass until she screams. I want to punish her for what I feel.

I undo the buttons of my shirt cuffs and fold them back twice. Her eyes follow the movement, but she says nothing. It's only when I walk to the weight bench and sit down that she finds her voice.

"Gabriel, please."

"Come here."

She doesn't move.

"If I have to come get you, you're going to suffer double as much as what I've got planned for you."

Slowly, she moves to me, her eyes flittering between my face and lap.

I point at my knees. "Bend over."

"Gabriel…" Her lip starts to tremble.

"You endangered your life, and your life is mine, which means you put my property at risk."

"Nothing happened."

"Don't make me tell you again."

She shuffles closer until her knees brush my thighs.

"Bend over my lap and press your palms and feet flat on the floor. Keep your legs spread."

She lowers herself across my lap so that her head hangs down one side of my thighs and her legs down the other. The bench is low enough for her hands and feet to touch the ground.

I pull her dress up to her waist and move her panties down to her thighs. "If you move, your punishment will be tripled."

Her smooth, golden ass and plump, pink pussy are exposed to me. I take my time to admire her perfect body, her unmarred beauty and unsoiled innocence. My cock stirs and grows impossibly hard. I lift my hand and take aim.

Smack.

My palm lands on the tight curve of her left ass cheek. She jerks in my lap, driving her belly into my hard cock.

Smack.

The second marks her other cheek. She sucks in a breath, but she doesn't give in to me. Her silence is her defiance. Not giving her time to draw another breath, I land a succession of firm blows over her ass until I find my rhythm. I keep it light enough not to bruise, but hard enough to turn her skin pink. She squirms and whimpers, but she doesn't break her stance. Her ass clenches with each slap. I keep going until not a patch of her skin is left unmarked. When I start to repeat the pattern on her inflamed skin, she finally breaks. A loud cry escapes her throat. I keep at it mercilessly, not giving her reprieve until her body goes slack.

As she relaxes under my touch, her cries become different. The whimpers turn to moans. She mumbles my name and grinds her body down on my cock. I reward her by stopping the blows and reaching between her legs to cup her sex. She's soaked. My cock rises against the constraint of my zipper in satisfaction. I didn't plan on taking it here, but I can't help myself. The fight has gone completely out of me. All that's left is the gnawing lust. I pet her folds for a while, reveling in how they swell to my touch, before I rub my middle finger in circular movements over her clit. I like the vantage point I have on the view. When I bend my head, her pussy is so close I can smell her arousal. It drives me insane. Her beautiful female parts clench, and her lower body shakes. Her thighs and arms quiver as she screams out her orgasm. I let her have it and more. I carry on rubbing and pinching her clit until she begs me to stop, but I don't let up until I'm certain she can't take any more. Only then do I adjust her clothes, help her up, and pull her into my arms with her head cradled against my chest. While she's sobbing it out, I caress her cheek, wiping the tears away as they fall. Every molecule in my body is aware of her. I'm intoxicated with the woman I hold in my arms, the woman I'll eventually have to kill. It's then that I acknowledge the truth. I'm not going to kill her. I was never going to. She's meant to be mine.

When she stops crying, I dry her tears with my palms. "Don't ever do that to me again."

She blinks. She's confused. Hell, so am I. Spanking her makes me hot. Holding her makes me forget why I spanked her in the first place. With her arms wrapped around my neck and her ass cushioning my dick, I can't think straight. All I know, is that I can't lose her.

"From now on, I want Quincy to train you with Bruno."

She lifts her head to look at me.

"You're not allowed outside if he's loose, unless you give me a demonstration that proves you can handle him."

"He won't attack me."

"He's bitten a trespasser before. Fuck, Valentina." I drag a hand through my hair. "Not even Magda risks it out unless he's closed in the back."

"Why do you keep a dog if he's so dangerous, even to your own family?"

"Protection. People who want to break in badly enough will eventually find a way."

"Bad people will also poison a dog."

"He's trained not to take food from anyone but Quincy." I study her tear-streaked eyes. "What did you do to him? How did you get him to heel?"

"I removed a thorn from his paw."

"That's it?"

"It's not hard at all. You just have to show him who has the authority. You can't be frightened. Animals sense fear."

It sounds a lot like me. No surprises there. I'm an animal, at best. I brush my lips over her hair, inhaling her sweet, raspberry scent. "Was my lesson clear enough for you, or will you need a repeat?"

"No," she says quickly. "I get it."

"Do you fear *me*?"

"Why? Do you sense it?"

"Yes," I say gravely. I do, and I'll encourage it, even if it's only to use her fear like a leash, holding her close to me.

I lift her to her feet. "I'll tell Quincy to set aside some time later today."

She brushes her hair behind her ear.

"Do you need a moment?'

She gives a grateful nod. "Please."

I give her the privacy she needs to gather herself. After arranging for dog training with Quincy, I distract myself by catching up on business, and then I access the financial records Anton emailed me. Valentina earned a salary from Rocky Street Veterinary Clinic. When she said she was an assistant, I assumed it was the secretarial type. That explains the white tunic the first night in Napoli's. Debit orders went off from her account for water and electricity, which she stopped yesterday. Her credit card statements show the usual expenses for food and essentials. Other than that, Valentina isn't a spender. Not that she had the means. There are no luxuries, nothing of the things women like, not even a tube of lipstick. Every month, she withdraws a substantial amount of cash, and it's always the same amount, to the last cent.

I call my private banker and arrange for twenty grand to be transferred to her account. Next, I get the agent on the line and offer him a five grand commission to transfer the Berea property to my name. He's happy to oblige. Firstly, he knows who I am. Secondly, he knows he'll otherwise not get a cent for the flat. I arrange for the necessary transfer of ownership documents to be delivered. For Valentina's sake, the sale must look authentic.

With the finances in place, I call the club manager at Napoli's. I'd like to have a word with Valentina's ex-neighbor about the burglary, and Jerry hasn't been home since we took her and her brother. The manager assures me Jerry hasn't been back, so I put word out that I'm looking for him. Whoever wrecked Valentina's flat will pay. I leave the most unpleasant task for last, dialing Lambert Roos. The phone rings for a long time without going onto voicemail. Looks like I'll have to pay Lambert a visit.

It's only when I grow more settled again and reflect on this afternoon's episode that I recall the lunch Valentina never finished. On strict order from Magda, Marie won't serve the food she prepares to the staff. Is Valentina eating our leftovers? Goddamn. An uncomfortable emotion lances into my heart. The pinch in my chest won't let up. I pull our grocery order records. Valentina is living on Granny Smith apples and cheap Chinese noodles. I feel too many things to distinguish one from the other. There are pity, concern, and anger at myself for not discovering the truth earlier. She's starving right under my nose.

This won't do. I need her healthy. I adjust the order and send Marie a note. From now on, Valentina will eat what *I* decide.

Valentina

THERE'S a box with my name on it in the kitchen when I come in from washing the patio.

"That's for you," Marie says, drying her hands on a dishcloth.

"For me?" I lift the flaps to peer inside.

There are meat, cheese, eggs, veggies, fruit, bottled water, and juice. In a smaller box, I find a variety of delicatessens, including olives, nuts, cold pressed cooking oil, and dark chocolate. There must be a mistake.

"I didn't order these."

"It's from Mr. Louw." She scrutinizes me. "Whatever you did, it made him very happy."

I shouldn't feel guilty, but a flush warms my cheeks. I'm ashamed of my poverty. Always have been. Gabriel's gesture only reminds me of the gap between us. The kindness makes me irrationally sad and inexplicably angry. I'm nobody's charity case. I'll return everything, but for now I unpack it in the fridge to prevent the expensive food from spoiling.

When Gabriel comes to my room, I fight the orgasm he forces on me, doing everything in my power not to come, but it's a losing battle. Eventually, the pleasure takes over. My body gives in and delivers what he wants. His power over the physical part of me is complete. He stripped me of my defenses. I can't allow him to strip me of my pride.

Afterward, he pulls me into his arms. His voice is gentle, but stern. "What's wrong?"

"Nothing."

"The harder you fight me, the harder I'll push."

I lower my eyes. "The food… I don't appreciate the gesture."

"Ah." He says it as if he suddenly understands everything that's going on in my head. "Look at me."

I oblige. Grudgingly.

"What are you to me, Valentina?"

"An investment," I bite out.

"What do I do with my investments?"

"Take care of them."

He brushes a thumb over my cheek. "I *like* to take care of you. Is that so bad?"

Yes, dammit. I want to be more than someone's investment. "You can't force food on me."

"Yes, I can. You can eat what I tell you or be force-fed. It's your choice, but it'll please me if you accept it without arguing."

It shocks me how badly I want to please him. What the hell is wrong with me?

"Whatever you need," he continues, "I want you to tell me."

I can only stare at him, not sure what is changing between us, but the balance is shifting.

He runs a forefinger over my lips. "Is there anything you'd like to tell me now?" The air of anticipation that hangs around him makes him seem vulnerable, as if he has more to lose than me in this strange game playing off between us.

"No," I croak, not sure what he wants from me.

As I expected, my answer disappoints him, but he doesn't pursue the matter. He simply kisses me until my desire spikes again before he gets to his feet and unbuckles his belt.

Gabriel

WHAT DID I expect from Valentina? To open up to me? Why is it important to me that she tells me about her studies out of her own, free will? I don't have an answer. I only know I want to hear it from her. Until she admits it, I won't tell her I discovered the truth.

Besides keeping an eye on Valentina's eating habits, worry about Carly's date dominates the rest of my week. On Friday night, I have men placed around the movie theatre. Discreetly, of course. Still, I don't relax until my daughter is home safe and sound, bubblier than ever. If Sebastian put as much as a finger on her, my men would've acted, and I'm glad it didn't come to that. Carly comes to my study to say goodnight. She surprises me with an uncharacteristic kiss on my cheek and a hug.

When the house is quiet, I make my way to Valentina's room. It's a routine I look forward to, a fix to which I'm already addicted. My steps fall unevenly on the kitchen floor. My limp is heavier, tonight. There's rain in the air. The humidity makes my joints ache.

My breath catches when I open her door. She's spread out on the bed, naked. Her golden skin is flawless, except for the tiny beauty spot under her left breast. The small mark of imperfection only adds to her allure. In her sleep, she looks more vulnerable and innocent than when she watches me with her big, frightened eyes. Her folds already glisten with the arousal I conditioned her to have. Walking to the bed, I stare down at her. Usually, my presence is enough to wake her, but she's been tired, lately. Too tired. It doesn't help that I steal an hour of her sleep time, but I have very little control where Valentina is concerned. I take another moment to study her body. I like looking at her when she's sleeping. The voyeuristic act is invasive, but it turns me on and feeds a dark part of me.

After a few seconds, she starts to stir. Her eyelids flutter, and her lashes lift. I read her expression as she rises from her sleep. First, there's recognition and then desire. There's no more fear or resistance. She's ready for the next step.

Keeping my clothes on, I stretch out next to her on the bed, lifting myself up on my elbow. Immediately, she spreads her legs. The submissive act makes me dizzy with desire. If I'd remained standing, she would've sat up on her knees for me, legs wide, just like I taught her. I reward her with a soft kiss, my tongue spearing through her lips and stroking hers while I'm playing with her breasts. I can get drunk on her moans. I want to drown in her arousal, but I have other plans for her pussy tonight.

I run my hand down her stomach to her sex. I stroke the pad of my middle finger up and down her slit, working moisture to her clit. When she's drenched in her own wetness, I clamp my mouth over hers and drive the first digit of my finger into her soaked channel. She's soft like velvet and so fucking wet. So hot. Her eyes fly open, and she gasps into my mouth. I eat the sound like an addict, greedily swallowing the whimpers that follow when I twist my finger a few times. When Engelbrecht examined her he told me there's no membrane--not an uncommon occurrence with virgins--so there shouldn't be any bleeding, but goddammit she's tight. Sucking her lips into my mouth, I drive home, burying my finger all the way inside, and then hold still while I stretch her. This time, she moans loudly into my mouth. I don't mind if she screams. Her room is too far for anyone in the house to hear, but I want to eat her sounds of pleasure like I eat her orgasms. I want to swallow her essence in every sensory way possible to carry it inside of me. I want her to be a part of me in the most literal sense.

She's panting in my mouth, sucking the oxygen from my lungs, and fueling me with rapid breaths of ecstasy. I take as much as I give, drinking her air like a vampire. It becomes a battle of breaths, a sucking and exhaling, a give and take. Putting my free hand on her forehead, I smooth back her hair in a soothing caress, preparing her for what's to come. As she starts breathing more easily from my mouth, accepting only the air I choose to give her, I pull out my finger and push back in. Her internal walls quiver around me. I drive in and out, finding a rhythm that matches the rise and fall of her chest. My thumb finds her clit, pressing down while I curl the finger inside to caress the soft spot under her pubic bone. Her hips lift toward me, chasing my touch, so I give her more, a bit harder, a bit faster.

Her lower body trembles. I want to make her fly so fucking high. The thought has my balls climb up into my body. When the first flutter of a spasm strokes my finger, I glide my palm from her forehead over her eyes to pinch her nose shut with my thumb and forefinger. Before she has time to register my intention, I start fucking her with my finger in all earnest, slapping her pussy hard enough with the heel of my palm to turn her clit pink.

I suck the life from her body with my mouth while I give back with my hand. Her legs scissor. Her ass lifts off the bed, and her toes curl inward. Then she begins to fight. She tries to twist her head in my hold while shoving at my shoulders. Realizing she's no match for my strength, she scratches. My skin burns deliciously hot where her nails leave long gashes in my neck. She bites my tongue. The metallic taste of blood coats my lips and drives me wild. One more second and her body jerks as if she's taken a thousand volts. I can own her life for several more seconds before she'll pass out, but I don't want it to go that far. I only want her to have the pleasure. Two more seconds and she falls limp, taking the relentless fucking of my finger in and on her pussy without fighting it any longer. She does nothing but ride the pleasure I force out of her, allowing me to control her breathing.

Total surrender.

I ease my hold on her nose and mouth, keeping our lips a hairbreadth apart. She sucks in the cool night air with a hoarse gasp, her neck arching from the intensity of the action. Shockwaves ripple through her abdomen, dissipating in her pussy. I keep her pussy in the vice of my middle finger, which is still inside her, and my thumb, which is pressing on her clit, until the tremors pass. Her vagina feels plump and ripe from my workout. I kiss her lips one last time, tracing my tongue over a spot where she bit herself during the struggling, and move down her body until my tongue finds her folds.

She shivers when I push inside to taste her climax. It's uniquely Valentina. She tastes raw and well loved, and I have a shocking desire to taste her with my cum in her body. I'm beyond myself with need. She protests with a meek whimper when I shove her thighs wide and push my hands under her ass, digging my fingers into the fleshy globes to pull her open. I stare at her cunt. She's more than a treat. She's the food I need to survive. I bury my head between her legs and devour her flesh. I eat her like I need her, with no excuses and no mercy.

"Gabriel, no more. Please."

I ignore her begging. The business about finding her a man, a pretty man, to take her virginity has me on edge. I'll give her a handsome man only this once, even if it feels like carving my heart out with a blunt knife, but fuck it, I own her. I need to show us both after all that will happen, she'll still be mine. Her pleasure is mine. Getting her off is my addiction.

I make her come once more with my mouth and twice with my hand. When I'm done, she's boneless. I'm not even sure she's conscious. I settle down beside her and drag her against my body. Folding my arms around her, I hold her until I drift into a haunted sleep.

Valentina

I WAKE up with a weight on my stomach and chest. Gabriel is draped around me, fully dressed, except for his shoes. It's the first time he stayed after making me come. A full-body flush heats my skin when I remember what he did last night. My breasts grow heavy, and my clit starts to throb. It was carnal. Deadly. Somewhere between the last orgasm and Gabriel petting me, I passed out, too tired to lift an eye.

Careful not to move, I revel in the comfort of being in his warm arms. The sun is barely up, tainting the curtains with a golden glow. I don't have to face the reality yet, that he's the man who holds the power over my life. Charlie's life. I bite my lip as I acknowledged the painful truth. I liked what he did. Very much. Once I got over my initial panic, I gave over to him, trusting him to keep me safe, and he did.

Gabriel moves, his hold on me tightening. His breathing doesn't change, but he drags his chin over my jaw and kisses my ear. His beard grates my skin, making me aware of his masculinity in a rough, pleasant way.

"Morning, beautiful." He nibbles on my earlobe and sweeps his palm over the goose bumps that break out on my skin. "Coffee?"

Gabriel is offering me coffee? I turn to face him, trying to read his expression, but his face is blank.

Without waiting for a reply, he swings his legs off the bed and gets to his feet. I don't miss the flinch he tries to hide as he puts his weight on his damaged leg. His white shirt is crumpled, and his black hair sleep-messy. He looks gorgeous. I want to tell him how grateful I am that he didn't leave me last night, how much I needed his arms around me after the intense way he treated my body, but he limps to the door and disappears before I can formulate the words.

I have another ten minutes before my alarm goes. Cuddling under the covers, I feel replete and strangely happy. A short while later, Gabriel returns with a cup of steaming coffee, the welcome aroma filling my room.

I prop myself up on the pillows to take it from him. "Thank you." I'm not sure what else to say. It's such an unexpected act.

"Milk, two sugars," he says.

He knows how I drink my coffee? I blink at him, not sure if I should ask, but he doesn't give me a chance. He wipes a thumb over my bottom lip, over the mark where I bit myself, and drags his heated eyes up to mine. From the way his cock hardens, he's thinking about last night.

He checks his watch and angles his head away from me. "I'll be out tonight. Don't leave tomorrow without saying goodbye."

The minute he walks out of my room, the air changes. A cold emptiness expands in my chest. Needing some warmth, I cradle the cup between my hands. I allow his act of kindness to warm my heart and fill my empty spaces. He's a contradiction of sensations, a very bad kind of good.

Gabriel

WHEN I WALK into my study after lunch, Helga sits in my chair. How the hell did she get past security?

I click the door shut. "How did you get in?"

"Hi to you, too." She leans back in my chair and crosses her ankles on my desk. Her dress rides up to her thighs, exposing black garter stockings. "Chill. Your mother let me in."

I'll have to have a word with Magda. For Carly's sake, I don't invite my bed partners home. Seeing her reminds me that I haven't fucked a woman in a very long time, not since I took Valentina.

"Why did you come?" I approach the desk, irritated with her presence. "You know the rules."

She pouts. "I miss you."

"Carly's home, for fuck's sake."

"You haven't called. It's not like you."

I cross my arms and stare at her. I don't owe her explanations. We fuck when we're both in the mood, and that's that.

"I need you, lover boy."

"I've told you before, don't call me that."

She uncrosses her legs and plants a heel on each side of my desk. No panties. Her fanny is bare, shaved like I prefer. The wide posture gives me a prime view of the goods on offer.

"Tell me what to call you, ugly boy."

Normally, Helga would have my balls in a knot with the act. By now, I would've had her bent over my desk. I would've spanked her pink before fucking her smart mouth, but not today. My cock doesn't stir. Not even a twitch.

"I'm busy."

"It'll only take five minutes."

I smirk. "You know me better than that."

"Okay," she gives me a sly grin, "thirty if you make it a quickie."

"You have to leave."

"Throwing me out?"

"Don't make me. It won't be pleasant for either of us."

She narrows her eyes. "Who are you fucking?"

"No one."

"Come on. I know you. You can't go a day without sex, let alone weeks."

I don't have time for this shit. I round the desk and stop next to the chair, intimidating her with my size and height. "I'll ask you nicely one last time."

She grabs my tie and pulls me down to her level. "You don't scare me. Whatever you want to give, I can take it."

A knock on the door interrupts us, but she doesn't let go or break the stare. I'm going to be a first-class jerk. I give her a calculated smile.

"You won't."

"Watch me," I whisper.

"It can be your daughter."

Carly never knocks. It's probably Quincy or Rhett. "Come in," I call in a loud voice.

Helga's eyes grow large. By now, she should know I never bluff. She brings her knees together and pulls down her dress, but not before the visitor who opens the door gets a full glimpse of her pussy.

Triumphantly, I turn my head to see who the lucky spectator is and freeze. Valentina stands in the doorframe, a stack of white envelopes in her hand and shock in her eyes.

9

Gabriel

"I'm sorry," Valentina says. "I didn't know you were busy."

I free my tie from Helga's grip and straighten, not missing Helga's curious expression. I have to be careful. Helga is perceptive. Raising a brow at Valentina, I encourage her to continue.

She swallows and holds up the envelopes. "Your mother sent me to bring you these."

"Leave it on my desk."

She approaches with averted eyes and puts the stack on the corner. With a small nod, she hurries out of the room.

"New staff?" Helga asks. "You never told me you have a maid. I thought you used a cleaning service."

I grip her arm and drag her to her feet.

"What are you doing?"

"Tell me why you're really here."

She licks her lips. The facade finally drops. "I need money."

I always leave money after fucking Helga, and she'd feel two weeks without a bonus. Letting go of her arm, I take out my wallet and press a couple of thousand in her hand. She bats her eyelashes when I take her wrist and pull her around the desk.

"Does this mean we're fucking?"

"It means I'm walking you out." I all but drag her to the front door where Rhett stands guard. "See to it that she leaves the grounds."

"Gabriel!"

The last thing I see before shutting the door in her face is her disgruntled expression. It's over. I never want to see her again.

Valentina

GABRIEL LOUW HAS A REPUTATION. He's dangerous, and the women who have first-hand experience say he fucks like a horse. Why seeing it with my own eyes hurt so much I can't fathom. It's not like I found out today. What did I expect? Exclusivity? Last night was sweet. The dull ache between my legs reminds me of how Gabriel fucked me with his finger. It's the kind of hurt that feels good, until a few moments ago, before I walked in on a pretty blonde with her naked parts splayed on his desk. It's a game to him. I'm his toy. When he tires of me, he'll cast me aside. The only thing he values is the debt I owe. When I walk free, I don't want to leave a piece of my heart here. That will be too ironic. It's a good thing I walked in on them. No, it's a good thing he *allowed* me to walk in on them. I guess he wanted me to see that, to remind me I'm not special. I'm one of many, and for the moment, I'm convenient.

I get through the day by working myself to a standstill. Even my brain is too tired to think. That night, for the first time, he doesn't come to me. I'm a heap of shivering and aching need when morning comes, cursing him and my body. Visions of him in the blonde woman's bed drive me to maddened tears. He's ruined me for other men. He's ruined me for even myself.

I'm busy with the vacuuming the following morning when he stumbles through the door, Rhett and Quincy in tow. His hair is disheveled, and there's blood on his shirt. His knuckles are bleeding. My heart squeezes, and my pulse quickens. He glances at me, but limps down the hallway without a greeting. I contemplate the reason for his state the whole day, refusing to acknowledge the worry that gnaws on my gut. Worrying means caring, and I don't care.

At five, I have a shower and change into my shorts and T-shirt. I throw my tank top into my bag together with the food for the homeless dogs. I'm not in the mood to face Gabriel, but I'm not so stupid as to ignore his order to say goodbye before I leave.

Like yesterday, he calls me in when I knock on his study door. I don't enter, but only pop my head around the frame.

"Have a good weekend. I'm off." I retract my head, hoping to get away with a quick greeting, but I'm not that lucky.

"Valentina."

I close my eyes and take a deep breath before facing him again.

He gets up from behind his desk. He's wearing a blue shirt with navy pants and a striped tie, looking as hot as ever. "I'll take you."

All I can do is stare at him in confusion. "What?"

"I'll drop you off."

Gabriel is offering me a lift? I'm not sure how I feel about that. I don't want him to be kind to me. "That's not necessary. I can find my own way."

"Like you did last week?"

"Um, yes."

"In a minivan?"

"Yes."

He crosses the floor with menacing steps. "If you ever get into a minivan again, I'll tan your ass so hard, you won't sit for a week."

I blink up at him.

"Do you have *any* idea how dangerous that is?" he asks.

For a white girl, he means. Other people have cars. Nobody dares walking in the street alone. The chances are too good of getting raped, tortured, and murdered. Life carries no value in this city, but in my world, if you don't have a choice, you just have to take your chances.

"You're worth a lot to me, Valentina. I own you, and I protect what's mine."

He returns to the chair and lifts his jacket off the back. Picking up his keys from the desk, he takes my hand and leads me to the garage.

I feel small next to him in the luxurious interior of his car. He says nothing as he steers the sleek Jaguar down the driveway and into the traffic. Instead of heading east, he goes north. He doesn't ask where I'm going, so I keep my mouth shut until he pulls up in front of an exclusive store in Sandton. I get out when he comes around to open the door for me, clutching my bag to my chest as he guides me inside the luxurious shop. It's not like any department store I know. There are no items on display. There's only a leather sofa and a glass desk stacked with clothes, purses, and shoes. A pretty, young lady greets us by the door and waves an arm to the desk.

"Everything's ready for you, Mr. Louw."

He acknowledges her with a curt nod and ushers me forward. "Go ahead. Choose whatever you like."

Dumbfounded, I gape at him.

"What's your color, darling?" the woman asks. "Red will look good with your complexion. White, too. Silver for the evening." She starts pulling dresses from the heap and drapes them over the sofa.

"Um, excuse me." I clear my throat. "May I please have a moment with…" What do I call him in front of her? "…Mr. Louw."

"Gabriel," he corrects.

The woman looks from me to Gabriel. There's judgment in her eyes, even if she tries to hide it. "I'll fetch refreshments. Take your time."

When she disappears into a backroom, I turn to Gabriel. "What are you doing?"

"I'm getting you clothes."

"Why?"

"I threw your blue dress in the trash."

"I don't expect you to replace it."

"I told you I like to take care of you."

Wringing my hands together, I close the distance between us. "I can't take your money."

His eyes darken, the chipped blue turning stormy. "It's legal money."

"It's not that. It just doesn't feel right."

"Feels pretty damn good to me. Are you saying making me feel good isn't right?"

"Don't twist my words."

He grabs me to him so suddenly my breath catches. Holding me around the waist with one arm, he cups my breast and gives my nipple a soft pinch. "Don't test my patience."

Immediately, heat floods my body. It bubbles in my veins and sends blood to my clit. My nipples are as hard as pebbles. I want to hate the feelings coursing through me, but I can't. As my body puts my arousal on display, the same heat I feel reflects in his eyes.

The shopkeeper returns with a pitcher of ice tea and glasses, but Gabriel doesn't let go of me.

She measures our stance. Depositing the tray on the table, she says in a professional tone, "Have you chosen anything yet?"

An hour later, I walk out with a new dress, designer jeans, two T-shirts, a casual trench coat, a pair of ballerina flats, five sets of pretty underwear, and a cute off-shoulder sweater. Gabriel pushed me to take more, but this is already more than I need.

He loads my parcels in the back of his car, and when we're seated, he turns to me. "Where to, beautiful?"

I'm sure he already knows, but I give him Kris' address. On the way there, I try to figure out what just happened. By the time we pull up in front of the practice, I'm still nowhere near understanding Gabriel.

He switches off the engine. "Your flat has been sold."

"Wow, that quickly?"

"I arranged for the money to be paid into your bank account. I hope that's in order."

"Gabriel..." I'm at a loss for words. "Thank you." The words don't express my gratitude, but they're all I can muster.

"No need to thank me. I said I'd handle it."

He reaches over me and opens my door, his arm brushing against my breasts. Before I can object, he gets my parcels and carries them to Kris' house. Charlie meets us by the door, taking me into a bear hug.

"Va–Val!"

"Hey, big brother."

Gabriel holds out his hand for Charlie to shake. "Hi, remember me?"

"You're the ba–bad ma–man."

Gabriel chuckles. "I guess you can say that, but I prefer Gabriel."

Charlie takes a step back and looks at me with big eyes.

"It's okay, Charlie. Gabriel isn't going to hurt us. I work for him, remember?"

After contemplating my response, Charlie's good manners finally win. "Want a jui–juice?"

"Sure." Gabriel flashes me a smile and makes himself right at home in Kris' kitchen.

I'm wary of having him around my brother. I watch him like a hawk while he makes small talk with Charlie, but Charlie quickly warms up to Gabriel. When he leaves an hour later, you'd swear they're best buddies. What game is Gabriel playing? He can toy with me if that's the price I have to pay for Charlie's freedom, but I won't let him disrupt my brother's life.

Gabriel

SINCE CARLY IS at her mother's this weekend, I have the evening and tomorrow to myself. Magda is out with friends. I ensured that no business meetings were scheduled and gave Rhett and Quincy the weekend off. I pour a whiskey and settle into an armchair in the reading room with Valentina's file in my lap. There's not much in her history I don't already know. Her father, Marvin, was involved in a car cloning syndicate. Her mother, Julietta, was a housewife. Valentina grew up in Rosettenville, in the south. When she was thirteen, their

Chevrolet went off a bridge. Marvin was killed on impact. Valentina survived, and Charlie incurred serious injuries resulting in brain damage. One year later, her mother was killed during an armed bank robbery. An aunt took care of Valentina and Charles, moving into the flat her parents owned in Berea when their house was auctioned to cover the outstanding accounts and funeral costs. The aunt died after Valentina's nineteenth birthday, leaving her to take care of Charlie alone.

My earlier question remains. Why did no one take care of Julietta and her kids? In our business, family is everything. We take care of our own. Marvin wasn't at the top of the hierarchy, but he wasn't a petty thief, either. He had enough influence and support to guarantee his widow and children protection, a roof over their heads, and food. Instead, they lived from hand to mouth after his death.

I put the file aside and wipe a hand over my face. The second folder contains Valentina's bank activity of the day. Half of the money I paid her for her flat was transferred to Kris' account. The other half, she paid into an account registered to UNISA. Following up the lead on the University of South Africa, I confirm my assumption. Valentina is enrolled in a correspondence degree in veterinary science. Using my contacts, I have a number for Valentina's mentor at the university within minutes. Even if it's late, I dial the number. It doesn't take me long to convince Mrs. Cavendish to have breakfast with me tomorrow.

I SIT at a table tucked away in a private corner on the Rosebank Hotel rooftop when Aletta Cavendish arrives. She's not the old prude her voice made me imagine. The only reason I know it's her is because she walks onto the rooftop at the exact time we agreed. The tall platinum blonde is in her late thirties. Wedding ring. Big diamond. The husband must have a cozy job, because university professors don't earn that much. Her hair is loose around her shoulders, and there's not a trace of makeup on her face. Even without the help of cosmetics, she's attractive. She wears a white T-shirt and flowing, Indian-print skirt with leather sandals. There must be twenty bangles on her arm. The flower-child type. From her straight back and square shoulders, I gather she has confidence. Her walk is easy and light. Clearly the type who sleeps well at night.

She gives her name to the waiter, and when he motions in my direction, she meets my eyes with a level and friendly stare. For a moment, there's shock on her face when she takes in my features, but her smile doesn't unravel. Her earrings dangle as she approaches my corner. I'm on my feet before she reaches the table.

She greets me with a firm handshake. "Mr. Louw."

"Gabriel, please." I pull out her chair and seat her. "Thank you for meeting me."

Dropping an oversized bag next to her chair, she gives me a scrutinizing look. "I have to admit, if the student concerned wasn't Valentina, I wouldn't be here."

"I appreciate your time." I nod at the waiter. "Shall we order?"

As she studies the menu, I observe her. Aletta is intelligent and doesn't beat around the bush. I like her. She's passionate and dedicated. Must make a good teacher.

We both order coffee and eggs benedict. When the waiter's gone, she says, "You said on the phone you're Valentina's new employer. I didn't know she'd changed jobs."

"It's very recent."

"What does she do for you, exactly?"

"House management."

She tilts her head. "Like a maid?"

I smile, keeping my expression even.

"I'm surprised," Aletta continues. "She loved the job at the vet practice, and it was good experience."

"I made her an offer she couldn't refuse." No lies there.

The waiter returns to serve our coffee. Aletta stirs in one sugar and milk. "In that case, it must be for better money. God knows, she can do with every extra cent."

"I'm concerned about her financial welfare, which is why I wanted to meet. Valentina doesn't know about it, of course. She's proud. I'd appreciate it if we can keep this discussion between us."

She blows on the coffee, watching me from over the rim. "What are you asking me?"

"How much does she owe?"

"Isn't that a question you should ask her?"

"All right. I'll rephrase that. How much does a veterinary degree cost these days?"

"You're looking at roughly fifty thousand a year, excluding books and material."

"I know how much she earned before she started working for me. How did she manage?"

"She has a partial bursary, but it's not enough to cover everything."

"Is she a good student?"

"Honestly? She's hands-down the best I've ever had. Her grades are top, but that girl has a natural vet in her. I've never seen animals react to anyone like they behave toward her."

You bet. "Then how come she secured only a partial bursary?"

"With the financial collapse and political unrest there's very little left in the university coffers. There are no full-time bursaries for vet students. I'm donating her books, but as you said, she's proud. Luckily, Valentina is also strong. Becoming a vet is her dream. She'll find a way."

The food arrives. The waiter arranges the salt and juice, shifting it around several times before he can fit the plates.

I've never had to worry about money. If I want something, I go out and buy it. I can't imagine what it's like to work your fingers to the bone and worry about covering your bills, which is ironic coming from a man who makes money from other people's financial troubles.

I lean back in my chair. "If I'm to create a bursary, can I choose to who it'll go?"

The knife stills in her hand. "Yes." She looks at me with mild surprise. "You can name the beneficiary."

"The beneficiary doesn't need to know who the sponsor is?"

A smile warms her eyes. "You can call the bursary whatever you want. It doesn't have to carry your name, and it can certainly be anonymous."

I lean my elbows on the table and tip my fingers together. "In that case, I'd like to offer a full bursary, all expenses paid."

Her smile turns ten degrees warmer. "I'll put you in touch with the right person in finance."

"Monday." I want to pave this road for Valentina as soon as possible.

"Gotcha." She takes a bite, chews slowly, and swallows. "You know, I had my doubts about you."

"Yes?"

"I thought you were going to tell me Valentina's studies are interfering with her job."

"Oh, no. Nothing like that."

"I'm glad I was wrong."

She has no idea.

AFTER BREAKFAST, I text my private banker and give instruction for the bursary to be set up. Then I head to Rosettenville. I drive past the address in my file, the house in which Valentina grew up. It's a humble miner's house, the cheap, cookie-cutter type the gold mines constructed for their workers and later sold to private owners. In this street, everything looks the same. It's hard to imagine someone like Valentina walking the streets of this average and dull neighborhood. She belongs someplace exotic, someplace beautiful. The main street that houses most of the commercial businesses is quiet. The shops are closed on the weekend. At the mechanic workshop, I park my car and tuck the gun into the back of my waistband. Lambert Roos lives in a house adjoining the workshop. The simple dwelling has a low wall in front, an easy target for thieves. With the fall of Hillbrow and downtown, Rosettenville became a dangerous neighborhood. The fact that he hasn't raised the wall and fitted it with electrified barbwire tells me one of two things. Either he's too poor or he's powerful enough for criminals not to fuck with him. Judging from the peeled paint on the walls and the missing roof tiles, I'm putting my money on the first option.

I jump over the wall and bang on the door. Footsteps shuffle inside.

"Who is it?" a male voice calls.

"Gabriel Louw."

There's a moment's hesitation before the door swings open on a crack. A short, bald man dressed in a vest and a pair of boxer shorts regards me with skepticism. He shoots a look over my shoulder, his gaze traveling up and down the street.

"I'm alone," I say with a cold smile.

"Well, well, if it ain't Owen's ugly duckling. Howzit?"

I should kill him for that remark, but I need information. Shoving past him, I make my way into his house. The place smells like old socks and stale cabbage. The carpets are worn, and the furniture has seen better days. Business must be slow. Or maybe not. On the table, there are several bags filled with white powder. Coke or maybe cat.

His eyes follow mine. A thin layer of perspiration shines on his forehead. "What can I do you for?" he asks with humorless slang. "Want a beer?" He shifts his weight.

He's hospitable enough, but he wants me gone.

"Remember Marvin Haynes?"

Cocking his neck, he blinks twice. "Yeah. Who doesn't?"

"You must've known him well, seeing that you were supposed to marry his daughter."

His puffy eyes narrow, and he utters a forced chuckle. "He lived down the road, but we weren't thick with each other. Saw his missus from time to time in the pharmacy. Why do you ask?"

"If Valentina Haynes was promised to you, why didn't your family take her and her brother in after her mother died?"

He scratches the back of his neck. "With her daddy gone, the deal was off."

"You didn't want to honor the agreement?"

"She's not my type."

Bull fucking shit. "She's a very pretty woman, isn't she?"

"Yeah."

"You don't like pretty? Or you don't like women?"

"Look, she didn't do it for me."

"You backed out because she didn't do it for you?"

"Yeah."

He's lying through his crooked, yellow teeth.

"Why do you want know?" he asks, trying to look nonchalant, but his voice breaks on the last word.

I shrug. "Curiosity."

With a nod, I go back to my car. Before I'm inside, the idiot has his cellphone in his hand, looking at me through the tattered lace curtains as he makes a call. I should've tapped his phone before my visit. It doesn't matter. I'll find out. I text Anton with Lambert's name and address, as well as the date and time, instructing him to get a recording of the conversation and send it as an encrypted message to my private email account.

Valentina

When I step outside Kris' house on late Sunday afternoon, Rhett is waiting across the road next to the Mercedes. He opens the backdoor in silent instruction for me to get in. Not a word passes between us during the drive to Parktown. My heart is sad to leave Charlie. I feel guilty for not being able to take care of him, but more than that, I miss his presence. His joy is innocent and genuine. He's the only piece of uncomplicated truthfulness in the twisted emotions of my life.

Despite my sadness, my body starts humming when we get nearer to the house. Like a conditioned animal, my body becomes aroused at the knowledge that it will soon be with my captor, while my brain condemns the reaction. I hate this division between my thoughts and physical reactions. I'm at constant war with myself.

Gabriel himself waits on the porch. My heart gives an unwelcome lurch at the sight of his muscular shape. He gets the door and my parcels, the new clothes still unpacked and the price tags intact. Rhett disappears to wherever. The minute he's gone, Gabriel brushes his lips over the shell of my ear.

"Welcome home."

The words grate on me. This isn't my home. My home is with Charlie. What Gabriel is doing to us as a family is wrong. I hurry inside and make my way to my room. A minute later, Gabriel steps inside, standing like a menacing, dark energy at the foot of the bed.

"What's wrong?"

"Nothing."

"Aren't you happy you got to spend time with your brother?"

I give him a hard look. "Of course I am."

I start unpacking the clothes, taking my time to fold each item meticulously.

He lets me carry on like this for a while before taking the pile from my hands and leaving it on the bed. "Let's go for a swim."

My jaw drops. He's inviting a house servant for a dip in his pool?

"What do you say, Valentina?"

"I don't have a bathing suit."

"You don't need one."

Without waiting for a response, he takes my wrist, pulls me through the kitchen and out the backdoor. On the deck, he starts stripping his clothes.

I glance around to make sure we're alone. "What are you doing?"

"Swimming naked with you."

"Are you crazy?"

"We're alone. Magda's out, and Carly won't be back before tomorrow."

Gabriel stands stark naked and hard in front of me. His scarred body is terrifying in its brutal beauty. The marks on his foot and knee don't diminish his physical perfection. To me, they add to his appeal, making him breathtakingly perfect in a broken kind of way. Is it the warped attractiveness of imperfection, or is a part of me is just attracted to everything that's dark and destructive?

Flashing me his rock-hard ass, he walks to the deep end and dives. Water splashes onto the side, the sound reminding me of holidays and stress-free times long gone.

"Come on," he calls. "The water's good."

It's tempting. It's been a hot as hell day, and my body feels sticky. I can't remember the last time I swam.

My gaze travels in the direction of the staff quarters. "Rhett--"

"Rhett won't come near the house unless I give him an order. Now I'm giving you one. Get in."

"All right."

Pulling off my trainers and clothes, I walk to the edge of the pool. The minute our gazes lock, there's a shift in his. The ice in his eyes makes way for a molten look of heat. Unashamedly, he ogles my breasts and lower. His cock grows enormous under the water. I wish I wasn't tingling between my legs or that my nipples hadn't hardened, but I'm as helpless to my reaction as I am to his wordless command when he curls a finger at me. Stepping into the cool water at the shallow end, I leave my guilt and judgment behind. No matter how hard I protest, Gabriel will do whatever he wants. The crazy, unequal power play gives me a measure of absolution.

When I'm up to my waist in the water, he swims to me and grabs a fistful of hair. Pulling my head back to arch my upper body, he latches onto a nipple, and sucks my breast deep into his mouth. I cry out as pain assaults the sensitive tip. Immediately, he pulls back to look at me.

"You usually like that."

I cup the sore curve. "It's almost that time of the month. They get overly sensitive."

He studies my breasts with new interest, taking both into his hands. "They're bigger." He jiggles them, making me groan with the discomfort. "And heavier." His hands move down my sides to my hips, and over my swollen stomach. "When's your period due?"

"Tomorrow." I shake a little when I say it. After that, the birth control will be effective, and nothing will prevent him from taking the final step.

He eases up then, setting my body free. "Maybe the water will do you good."

It does. We swim a few laps and just drift around without talking. By the time we get out, my skin is wrinkled. Gabriel fetches towels from the pool house and covers me with one on a deckchair. For a few blissful moments, I forget my circumstances and simply enjoy the rays of the setting sun on my face. I've never been alone with him in the house. There's less tension when no one else is around.

When it starts to get cool, he carries me inside and lies me down on my bed. Like every night he came to my room, he makes me come. He's gentle, avoiding my sore breasts and swollen abdomen. Afterward, he lets me take him in my mouth and stays with me for another hour.

Does he hold other women like this? Does he go out to fuck someone after he's been with me? I've never seen another female in the house except for the woman in his study, but that doesn't mean he's celibate. Maybe he entertains his women elsewhere to protect Carly. For all I know, he has a girlfriend. Maybe it's the woman I saw. Maybe he's fucking her brains out every night after he leaves my room. Our silence is no longer amiable.

I can't help myself from asking, "Are you sleeping with someone?"

His chest vibrates against my back with a chuckle. "Does it matter?"

If the ache in my ribs is anything to go by, yes, it does, but I'd die before admitting it. "Just wondering." Hell, I don't even sound convincing to myself.

"Her name is Helga."

Humph. It's like he punches the wind out of me with a fist in the stomach. I wanted to know, and now I regret asking. I especially don't want to know her name. Pain lances at me from all directions, rendering me vulnerable. Jealousy mounts in my chest.

"She's the woman you saw in my study. That's what you're really asking, isn't it?"

Now that it's out, I may as well go the full nine yards and let myself hurt thoroughly. Maybe the ache will dampen my need for Gabriel. "Did you sleep with her?"

"Yes." After a moment, he continues, "But I haven't fucked her since you arrived."

Something gives in my torso, like an elastic band that snaps. Stupidly, I feel like crying. Correction, I feel like bawling. Damn PMS. "It doesn't matter."

His laugh is knowing. "Of course not."

"Why haven't you slept with her?" I hold my breath for something I can't name.

"I don't want to."

But he may. Gabriel is the kind of man who takes what he wants, not by force, but by making your own body betray you, by stealing your will and breaking every one of your good intentions, leaving you with a hole only he can fill. Where I'm aching now, only his cock can fill the empty feeling. It's twisted. He made me want him--need him--like I need water, while he can walk away on a whim, whenever he doesn't want me. There'll come a day I'll be the next Helga, a day he won't come to my room to make me come, just because he doesn't *want to* any longer. He's an asshole, and I hate myself for being affected.

"You're quiet," he muses. "If you're tired, I'll let you sleep."

Longing for solitude so I can curl into a ball, I let the lie spill from my lips. "That'll be kind."

My heart drops when his weight lifts from the mattress. With a chaste kiss on my forehead, he walks from my room. Finally, I have the solitude I demanded, but I'm utterly and miserably lonely.

ON MONDAY MORNING, Magda awaits me in the kitchen with shocking news. Marie had a stroke.

"You'll take over the menu planning," she says, "and the cooking. Run it past me to approve." She points at the computer in the corner. "You'll find the budget and supermarkets that deliver on the system."

"Will she be all right?"

"I don't know. Her daughter will let me know. It's mighty inconvenient, though, seeing we have a formal business dinner at the house on Friday. Oh, you'll have to see to the catering and serving. I'll email the menu to the kitchen computer. I'm only expecting two or three guests." She writes a code on the message pad. "Here's the password."

She's halfway to the door before I find the courage to speak. "I'm not sure I can manage."

She twirls around to narrow her eyes at me. "Do you have a problem?"

"The cleaning and cooking…it's a lot for one person. It's not that I'm not willing, but it's a big house. I don't want to neglect one or the other."

"Then make sure you don't." Her lips thin into a smile. "Your life depends on it."

I stare at her back as she leaves the kitchen. I hate the haughty clack of her heels as much as I detest the traffic cone color of her lipstick. She may look down on me because I'm poor and treat me like a slave because she owns nine years of my life, but when those nine years are over, I'll never take an order from her again. I'll take Charlie and move to another town, a city where the Louws don't rule. Allowing the intention to strengthen my resolve, I switch on the computer and wait for it to boot up so I can place the grocery order for the day.

MONDAY AND TUESDAY pass in a blur. I wangle some sort of schedule, vacuuming only every second day and ironing later at night. By Tuesday evening, we get an update from Marie's daughter, stating that she won't be back at work for at least six months. Since I don't know Marie's recipes, I don't have a choice but to change the menu. What I know is more my late mother's Mediterranean style. I find a small, local producer of fresh produce, which turns out not only to be organic, but also cheaper. The fruit and vegetables aren't pretty, but they're tasty. I also order less cleaning products. I can wash a floor just as well with a bit of vinegar in water than with an expensive product that smells like a summer orchard, but has been tested on animals. The result is a thirty-percent saving on the weekly grocery bill.

The new work pace is strenuous. On top of that, my period arrived right on time. I've always suffered from a heavy flow that leaves me feeling weak. I order an iron supplement with my personal deliveries to boost me for the big night on Friday. The last thing I want is to fail my first dinner party test when my life depends on it.

Despite my period, Gabriel still comes to me at night, but instead of bringing me to the earthshattering climaxes I got used to, he fondles my body with backrubs and massages. It's strange and out of character for him, not that he's predictable. The more Magda pushes me, the kinder Gabriel acts toward me, which infuriates Magda. It's a vicious circle between the two of them, and I'm caught in the middle.

Carly is cool but not completely unfriendly since she got to go out on her date. Sebastian is allowed to visit her at home with her grandmother or father's supervision, but as Gabriel is always out during the day, it's mostly Magda who keeps an eye on the lovebirds.

On Wednesday, Carly is alone by the pool. When I pick up her towel to put it in the wash, I notice she left her iPad outside again, something she does often. I take it with the intention to put it away in the house, but as I reach the sliding doors, Quincy's voice stops me.

"Hey, Val. Look, Bruno's all better."

Bruno runs on a leash with Quincy, the limp gone. The dog barks and wags his tail furiously when I approach. Leaving the iPad on the wall, I go down on my haunches and get a sloppy dog kiss.

I laugh, wiping my face with the back of my hand. "Glad to see you're back in shape, boy."

"Thanks, again."

"I'm glad I could help." I straighten and glance over my shoulder at the house. "I better get back. Lots to do."

"Yeah." He looks uncomfortable. "Are you coping?"

"Sure."

"Valentina," Magda says from the door, her condescending stare resting on Quincy and me as if she caught us making out or something, "if you've finished socializing, we need to talk about Friday's menu."

"Bye, Bruno." I stroke his back and smile at Quincy in greeting.

His eyes are hard as he directs them to the door where Magda waits with her hands on her hips, but I don't give it further thought as I hurry inside.

IT'S NOT until the following morning when Carly makes a ruckus at breakfast about her missing iPad that I remember leaving it outside.

Magda summons me to the dining room. At first, I'm in the dark when Carly points a finger at me and exclaims, "She took it. It was there last night, and now it's gone."

"Did you take Carly's iPad?" Magda asks. "Don't bother lying, because I'll be going through your room myself."

My insides freeze, remembering where I left it. They go even colder when I look at Gabriel. He's regarding me with a frown. He believes I stole it? Hurt lances into my heart. Why does it matter what he thinks?

"Well?" Magda asks with a flick of her penciled eyebrow.

"I meant to bring it in last night, but I got distracted and forgot it on the wall."

"Distracted with Quincy," Magda says snidely.

A thunderous expression darkens Gabriel's face. Of the three people in the room, right now, I'm most scared of him.

"I'll go get it," I offer quickly, but Carly's already on her feet, heading for the door.

Magda folds her hands on the table and gives me a single instruction. "Stay."

I stand quietly in the uncomfortable silence until Carly's screaming filters through the backdoor. Everything inside of me tightens further.

"It's ruined!" Carly shouts, running into the room with the iPad. It's dripping with water.

Gabriel's tone is flat. "On which wall did you leave it, Valentina?"

"The one by the pool!" Carly shoots daggers at me with her eyes.

"The sprinklers reach there at night," Gabriel says almost distantly.

"This is your fault," Carly continues in hysterics. "Do you realize how many photos I had on here? Not to mention my homework!"

"Carly." Gabriel's quiet but hard voice instantly shuts her up. "Let that be a lesson well learned for leaving your iPad outside. It's not the first time. It was bound to happen."

"Dad!"

He holds up a hand, giving her a dark look. "Let me finish. You can recover your homework and photos from iCloud."

"I didn't activate it!"

Gabriel's tone is uncompromising. Not a flicker of sympathy warms his eyes. "Lesson number two, well learned. From now on, you'll make a backup like I told you." He turns to me, suddenly looking tired. "I'll deal with you after breakfast."

"You'll replace Carly's iPad," Magda says. "It'll teach you to be less forgetful in future." She shakes her napkin out on her lap. "Now, I want to eat in peace. Quiet all of you."

Carly flops down in her seat, her face red.

I'm shaky as I return to the kitchen, cursing myself for my negligence. I can't afford to replace the iPad, not without making more debt.

It doesn't take long for Gabriel to come find me. The words I dreaded most leave his lips. "Go to the gym after you've cleared the table."

Going down to the basement is like a walk to the gallows. He's already waiting inside, his tie removed and his shirtsleeves rolled back.

"Close the door," he says quietly.

I push until I hear the click, but I don't have the courage to turn and face him.

"Come here."

I bite my nail as I gather enough strength to obey, one step at a time.

When I stop in front of him, he pulls my hand from my mouth. "Undress."

My eyes lift to his. I don't mean to beg, but it slips out anyway. "Please."

He doesn't bat an eye. There's no compassion, no mercy. "Undress."

As I pull off my shoes, dress, and underwear, he watches me like a hawk. By now, I'm used to his scrutinizing stare, and it's less embarrassing than during those first few times, but not less frightening. Once I'm naked, he taps a finger on his lips, studying my face. Finally, he drops his arm, as if he's made his decision, and points at the floor. "On your back."

I swallow as I lie down on my back, watching him fetch a bar with a set of handcuffs secured on each end.

"What are you doing?" I ask as he locks my wrists on either end.

He gathers my panties and bundles them into my mouth. "Sorry, beautiful, but I'm not in the mood for dialogue right now."

I mumble a protest when he locks my ankles to my wrists, spreading me open on the bar. He pushes the bar back until it touches the mat, raising my arms above my head and my legs with them. Flat on my back, my ass and pussy are exposed in the most vulnerable way. My hamstrings are on fire. I shift in an effort to relieve the uncomfortable stretch when he fetches an object from the torture shelf.

He returns with a wooden paddle. I shake my head, pleading with my eyes, but he grips the bar and lifts a few times, giving me brief reprieve from the position before he pushes down flat and starts paddling my ass. The first whack on my ass cheek comes as a shock. I scream behind the bundle of fabric in my mouth, even if the sting heats my skin without hurting. The second lash makes me jerk, but when I realize he's caressing my skin rather than inflicting pain, I almost relax. He works his way from left to right on the fleshy part of my ass until my nerve endings are on fire and my clit is a pulsing nub of ache. My vagina feels swollen. The need for release is severe. When I'm no longer begging with my eyes for him to stop, I'm begging him to let me feel the paddle where I crave it most. Only after every inch of my skin is humming with electric sparks does he finally bring the paddle down right in the middle of my pussy, covering my opening and clit. With the tampon inside me, it feels full. And good. I grind up, desperate for more, but he changes to a slower and gentler rhythm, teasing me mercilessly with a few too-soft taps on my swollen parts.

Just when I think I can't take more, he pulls the underwear from my mouth and says, "Beg."

I don't hesitate. "Please, Gabriel."

"Please what?"

"Please, please fuck me."

He goes still. There's a mixture of shock and disbelief on his face, which is slowly replaced with satisfaction. Heat darkens his eyes. His jaw tightens as he looks down at my sex.

"Please."

His chest is rising and falling rapidly, his breathing as harsh as mine. There's only the sound of our pants in the room. Then he exhales with a long, shaky breath. He pushes the paddle down on my clit and starts massaging with circular movements. Everything clenches as I come violent with a spasm that shatters my respiration. I'm out of air by the time he frees the constraints and drags me to my knees. In his haste to undo his pants, his fingers fumble with the button. I grab the waistband and pull it down his hips to help, not bothering with the zip. His cock juts at me, the tip close to my lips. I devour him like a crazy, starving woman, sucking and licking until he grabs my hair for leverage. He clenches his ass with a primal roar and a curse as he empties himself in my mouth. I swallow as best as I can, trying to breathe through my nose. I don't want him to pull out. I want him in me forever.

After a moment, he grips my face in the vice of his giant hands and eases out of my mouth. He uses my hair to wipe himself clean, an act I find strangely and savagely satisfying. Pulling me to my feet, he shoves his tongue between my lips, tasting himself on my mouth. He nips and sucks, bites and laves. I'm aware of nothing but the heated skin of my ass and the wetness of his mouth as he steals my reason. His taste is addictive. I don't know for how long he kisses me before he pushes me away with a gentle shove.

"Get dressed," he says in a hoarse voice. "And leave."

Confused by the change in his behavior, I obey wordlessly, empty and dissatisfied despite the orgasm I just had. At the door, his words make me pause.

He grits out every syllable like he has to push it from his throat. "Put on a pretty dress, tonight. You're going on a date."

Gabriel

WHEN I ASKED her to beg, I expected her to beg for release. Instead, she begged me to fuck her.

She's ready.

I both rejoice and shiver in dread, because the first time won't be with me. No matter how much I want to take her virginity, I made a promise to myself, and I never break my promises. This time I may be pushed to my limits to keep this promise, but I already have a plan.

Magda waits in my study when I get back from the gym. I grit my teeth as I stroll past her.

"Did you do it?"

I know what she means, but I ask anyway, "Do what?"

"Punish her."

"Yes." I sit down and open my laptop.

"How?"

"Appropriately."

Carly learned a valuable lesson. There was nothing to punish Valentina for. I'm a sick bastard for using the situation to feed my own lust.

Magda doesn't budge. "How?"

I shoot her an incredulous look. "You want the juicy details?"

"What is it about her that's got you thinking with your dick instead of your head?"

"Don't insult me, and your reference to my dick is highly inappropriate."

Her eyes, the same watery blue as mine, turn dark with anger. She slaps her palms on my desk, bringing us at eye level. "You're just like your goddamn father."

Keeping my voice calm and my gaze indifferent, I say, "If you can't speak without repeating yourself, and you have nothing new to say, please get out of my office so I can focus on the business of running your business."

Her nostrils flare. The thick layer of foundation around her nose cracks with thin lines. The pores are big with white hairs standing erect in each follicle. Every minute detail of her age catches my attention.

"You won't live forever, Magda."

She straightens and adjusts her jacket. "Neither will you." A superior smile curves her lips. "Who knows? You may die before me." She turns, making it clear she's leaving my office on *her* terms.

There's no love lost between my mother and I, and no amount of introspection to figure out where it went wrong will change that. We are who we are.

I pick up the phone and set out to do what I've been meaning to when I walked through the door.

Quincy answers with a bright, "Yes, boss?"

"Come to my study."

I take a deep breath, and steel myself. A short while later, he enters. I want to break his face, but it's not his fault he's fallen for Valentina. As little as it's hers. She's a gorgeous woman with a courageous heart and a soft spot for animals. How could he not be under her spell?

"Sit." I point at the chair facing my desk.

He takes the seat, his posture at ease.

"I have a mission for you tonight."

He waits quietly for me to continue.

"You're going to fuck Valentina."

10

Gabriel

I may as well have drenched Quincy with a bucket of ice water.

He coughs. "Excuse me?"

"Take her out on a date. Someplace nice. Romantic. Dinner by candlelight, that kind of thing." I flip my credit card at him. "All expenses paid. Take two guards to make sure you're safe."

His eyes grow larger by the second.

The next part is hard for me to get out. I swallow the bitter taste in my mouth. "Then get a room at the Westcliff Hotel and fuck her."

His skin is as pale as the whites of his eyes. "I don't understand."

"There's nothing to understand. Wear a condom and be gentle. It's her first time. Oh, and she's having her period. That kind of thing doesn't put you off, does it?"

"Of course not, but--"

Not able to stomach the conversation any longer, I say gruffly, "You're dismissed."

He jumps to his feet, obviously eager to escape my presence.

"One more thing," I say as he gets to the door, "I don't want to see you until tomorrow morning. Make sure you stay the hell away from me until sunrise, and then I expect a full report."

He all but jumps through the door, leaving me alone with a kind of agony no human being can understand.

IN THE AFTERNOON, a visit from Sylvia puts me further on edge. I meet her in my study. It keeps things professional. She declines my offer for a drink and sits down on the corner of my desk, the slit of her skirt riding up her thigh. At some point in time, I would've kneeled at her feet and kissed my way down that leg, all the way to her toes. Now, there's no desire for the woman who married me in a pretty white dress with a fake smile on her face.

"What's with Carly's new diet?" she asks. "We already discussed this. You're not supposed to change her meal plan without consulting me."

I fight to control my irritability. "I'm not aware of any diet."

"She's wheat intolerant, for God's sake. She's not supposed to eat pasta. What's wrong with Marie? Is she going senile?"

"Marie had a stroke. Valentina's taking care of the cooking."

"The maid who tried to kill our daughter?" she shrieks.

"She didn't do it on purpose. It was another one of Carly's attention-seeking, self-destructive actions."

"Don't you dare take that maid's side over our daughter's."

I sigh deeply. "Relax. Valentina has been punished. It won't happen again."

"I won't relax where Carly is concerned. She has a modeling audition in a month. She can't afford to pick up weight with carbs and creamy pasta sauces."

"She's *not* doing a modeling audition."

"It's not up for discussion."

"Have you called the therapist?"

She stiffens. "Carly doesn't need a therapist. It's hormones. Normal teenager issues."

"Sylvia." I say her name warningly. "Carly never got over our divorce. It's time to face the fact that she may have issues we're not equipped to deal with."

She snickers. "That's rich coming from *The Breaker*."

"Keep the business out of this."

"How can I? It's all that matters in your life."

"Yet, that's why you married me. Security and money, don't you remember?"

"Don't be so dramatic. Why do you always have to bring up the same old accusations? It's boring." She gets to her feet. "Shall I speak to your maid?"

"You lost the right to address my staff when you walked out."

She rolls her shoulders. "Dear God, Gabriel, get over me and move on."

"I am, Sylvia. You have no idea."

"Good. It'll make you easier to get on with." She walks to the door with a straight back. "Tell Carly I dropped in."

"Why don't you call her tonight and tell her yourself?"

She narrows her eyes. "Fuck you, Gabriel. I love my daughter, and she knows it."

"Does she?"

She yanks the door open and slams it hard enough to shake the frame. Dragging a hand over my face, I take a moment to calm myself before I go out for the business of the day that requires the end of another scumbag's life.

WHEN I GET HOME, I shower and spend time with Carly, helping her with her math homework. I don't go down for dinner. I can't bear to look at Valentina. I'm too terrified I'll change my mind. After a whiskey too many, I call Rhett and tell him to meet me in the gym.

He enters cautiously, probably thinking of the last time we wrestled because he shot Valentina's dog.

Dragging a bench from the free weights section to the metal chains attached to the wall, I sit down. "Cuff me."

It takes him a moment to find his voice. "What?"

"You heard me."

Not stupid enough to defy me, he approaches slowly. I hold out my wrists. He secures first the one, then the other in the metal cuffs.

"Take the key with you," I say, "and don't give it to anyone, no matter what."

"The key for the cuffs or for the door?"

"Both."

His head bobs up and down, like a toy dog on a car dashboard. "When must I come back?"

"At six tomorrow morning and not a second before. Got that?"

He gulps. "Yes."

"Go."

His eyes say I've finally lost it, but he doesn't argue. The key scrapes in the lock after he has closed the door, making me a prisoner of free will.

Valentina

WEARING the new dress Gabriel bought, I bite my nails while I wait in the kitchen. I've never been on a date. I should be studying, but I'm curious about what Gabriel has planned. The door opens just after eight, but it's not Gabriel who steps inside. It's Quincy.

"Hi," I say with an easy smile, half-relieved and half-stressed, because now I'll have to go through the waiting anxiety again.

There's a flush on his cheeks as he takes in the red dress. "You look nice."

This is so uncomfortable. "Thanks."

"Ready?"

I blink. Maybe he's driving me somewhere to meet Gabriel. "Um, yes."

"Let's go." He looks me over. "Take a jacket. It'll get fresh later."

I grab my black trench coat and follow Quincy to the car. He drives. Another car follows at a distance. I peer at the headlights in the side mirror.

"Are they going to follow us all night?"

"Protection," he mumbles, his forehead pleated in a frown.

"Where are we going?"

"I was thinking the Thai Hut. It's got five-star reviews for its curry dishes, and it's fancy without being uptight. What do you think?"

I have no idea where or what the Thai Hut is, but my brain is stuck on something else. "Wait, you mean you and I decide? Gabriel's not coming?"

He shoots me a quick look. "Ah, fuck. He didn't tell you."

"Tell me what?"

He clenches the wheel and faces straight ahead. "This is—How do I put it? He set us up on a date."

"Me and *you?*"

"Hey." He utters a wry chuckle. "I know I'm not the world's greatest hunk, but there's no need to say it like you won't go out with me if I'm the last man on earth, which you probably wouldn't, even if it was true."

I'm so gob smacked I have to remind myself to shut my mouth. "I don't understand."

"Neither do I." He shifts in his seat. "Look, I'll be honest with you. All I know is Gabriel ordered me to show you a good time tonight."

"He *ordered* you?" Who the hell orders anyone to go on a date? What am I? A piece of meat up for auction? I narrow my eyes. "What else?"

He steals another glance at me. "What do you mean what else?"

"A good time and what else?"

He wipes a hand over his face. "Dinner, candles, and…"

"And what?"

"He wants me to sleep with you."

"Stop the car."

"Valentina--"

"Now!" I'm already jerking on the door handle.

He brings the car to a screeching halt on the side of the road and grabs my arm. "Please, calm down. We've got his guards watching us."

I still at his words. I can't believe Gabriel set me up with Quincy. For sex. I cover my face with my hands. "I'm so embarrassed."

He pulls my hands away. "It's not your fault. You have nothing to be ashamed of. I don't know what Gabriel's idea with the whole thing is, but we may as well go out and have a good time since he's paying." He adds quickly, "I'm not saying you have to sleep with me. We'll just say it didn't work out that way. I know you don't feel for me like that, and I'm not in the habit of forcing women."

"Thanks." I drag in a shaky breath. "I guess you're right. We'll just go on our make-believe date and order the most expensive dishes on the menu."

"Good." He pats my hand. "Now I can relax. Man, this was eating me. You have no idea."

I can't help but laugh. "Sorry. I didn't want you to stress over sex with me. Must be a terrifying thought."

He gives me another wry smile. "Don't put words in my mouth, now."

The tightness in my chest vanishes a bit, but not the hurt that Gabriel would rather send me off to be serviced like a cow or horse than deal with me himself. I need to change the uncomfortable subject.

"How come you got to train with Bruno?" I ask.

"I was the only one more or less not scared of him."

"You should treat him better. I saw what you're feeding him. May as well give him sawdust."

He chortles. "Yeah? What do you recommend?"

"I'll give you the name of a good brand, but you'll have to order it from the vet."

"Is this an order or a request?" he asks mockingly.

"It's not like Gabriel can't afford the best."

"You're right." His smile is bright. "We'll give it a try."

The Thai Hut is a small wooden house on stilts with colorful fairy lights draped over the porch. The interior smells of curry, and the ambience is warm. Despite myself, I relax with Quincy's easy banter. We polish off a bottle of wine, and by the time we ask for the bill, there are no other diners left. Since Quincy is over the limit, one of the guards drives us back. At home, he kisses me on the cheek and saunters off to the staff quarters.

The night guard lets me in. After a second's hesitation, I take the stairs to Gabriel's room. I want some answers, and I want them now. I push the door open, anger making me brave, but the room is dark and empty. Maybe he's out himself, doing what he wanted me to do with Quincy. Banishing the thought from my mind, I go to my room and try not to think about him as I fall asleep.

Gabriel

THE OVERHEAD TUNGSTEN bulbs buzz with a constant noise. Their blue-white light washes out the shadows with an overly bright intensity. It's been an hour since Rhett left me in the gym. I'm going through the week's business in my mind, trying to focus on planning and figures, but my thoughts keep on drifting to Valentina and Quincy. Where are they? What are they doing? What is she wearing? Is her hair hanging loose down her back, or did she take it up in the messy bun she does on a Sunday? Maybe it's tied in the ponytail she wears for work, and my guard is pulling the elastic from the silky strands right now, letting is spill over her full breasts. Is he pressing his lips against the soft, plump curve of her mouth? Is his hand between her legs?

I jerk on the cuffs, rattling the chains like a beast in a cage. A cry of outrage fills the space. It takes me several long breaths to find some resemblance of calm, forcing my brain to function rationally. I made a promise. This is for Valentina. It shreds my heart to bleeding pieces, but I've seen the way they look at each other. Quincy is smitten with my woman, and she likes him more than she'll ever admit. Daily, I'm forced to witness the way her eyes light up when they run into each other in the garden. His gentleness toward her is shoved down my throat. It's a reminder that I'll never have her like another man can have her, a man with a handsome face and an easy smile. A man without darkness and a need to hurt and own her. She'll never be mine like that--freely--but it doesn't matter. I'll never let her go. In exchange for forever, I'm giving her this one night. She deserves it pretty with a gentle man on top, offering her a handsome face to stare up at and an unbroken body to hold onto.

Does he find her wet?

"No!"

I strain against the chains. My roar sounds animalistic, even to my own ears. I can't do it. I can't stand it. Fuck my promise.

"Rhett!" My voice carries through the room, lifting the roof. "Let me the fuck out! Open the door!"

I shout profanities and utter threats even Magda will be ashamed of, jerking on the cuffs until my skin is chaffed raw and I'm running the risk of pulling my arms out of their sockets. I scream until my voice is hoarse, but the sounds are trapped in the room designed for exactly that purpose.

"Valentina!"

I struggle in a rage so dark that reason flees my mind. I grapple with thoughts that slice my heart open and blind me in the red fury of my possessive jealousy. I wrestle with nothing but the air, as if I can strangle those images torturing my mind and lay them to rest. Clawing and kicking, I twist my body until the bench falls from under me. I kick at the wood with my boots, the splintering crunch as it breaks a satisfying sound that feeds my need for violence. Pain shoots up my injured leg, a sharp stab lancing in my knee. I fight until every part of me is hurting as much as my heart, until I have no more energy left.

Sweat-drenched and battered, I sag in my chains, hanging by the threads of sanity. The irony of where I find myself isn't lost on me. I'm chained in my own torture chamber, suffering a self-inflicted torture far worse than anything I've done to any enemy who's ever had the displeasure of crossing this doorstep.

"Valentina."

Her name is a croak. My throat burns. I can no longer scream. I can only sob and give in to the cruelty of my imagination as it leads me on a graphic tour of Valentina's first time.

SOMETIME DURING THE EARLY HOURS, I wake. I found a position on my knees, my arms pulled up and my head hanging between my shoulders. I must've passed out from physical exhaustion. My throat and eyes are dehydrated. Scratchy. Everything inside of me is raw. I did her a favor, but the selfish part of me is too great, the possessive part of me too complete to accept it gracefully. I glance at the wall clock. It's done.

Too late.

The key turns in the lock, and the door opens. Rhett pauses when he takes in the scene.

"Come get me," I grate out.

He hesitates, but finally approaches with quick steps. As he unlocks me, he avoids my eyes. The minute I'm free he retreats to the far end of the room.

"Leave," I growl, frightened that I'll take it out on him.

He doesn't let me tell him twice. Like an arrow from a bow, he shoots through the door, his steps falling in a fast jog down the hallway.

I wipe a hand over my face, the stubble where there's no beard a reminder that I need a shower and a shave. Every ounce of my body is pulled tight. More than anything, I want to hunt Quincy down and kill him. In less than an hour, I'll face him and listen to his account. I want every fucking detail so I can pretend I've been there, part of it all. I'm too damn jealous to even spare myself the pain.

Walking to the wet bar that's always stocked with bottled water and drinks--torturing people is thirsty work--I pour a whiskey and shoot it back neat. Then another. And another. I need the alcohol if I'm not to crush Quincy's windpipe and rip off his dick. For good measure, I have a fourth. The alcohol burns my stomach and relieves the worst of the rawness in my throat from the vile curses I uttered all night. My skin heats, and my brain blurs enough to dull my emotions, enough to get through the hour that awaits without committing a murder in my own house.

Valentina

AT FIVE, I'm up as usual, but Gabriel doesn't come to the kitchen for his coffee. I leave his breakfast on the hot tray and shrug inwardly. If he had a rough night, I hope he wakes up with a hell of a hangover. It will serve him right for the stunt he tried to pull on me. Still seething with annoyance, I take the washing basket and set out to collect the dirty laundry. In the hallway, my step slows as none other than Gabriel turns the corner, heading my way.

He looks like shit. His hair is disheveled, standing in every direction, and stubble blurs the neatly shaved line of his beard. His eyes are bloodshot and his clothes--the same clothes from last night--are creased. Wherever he's been, it looks like he slithered out of some woman's bed a second ago.

His eyes fix on me with the kind of intensity that isolates us in this moment. Everything else fades away as he nails me with his glacier stare, making me shiver inside. He holds me locked in invisible constraints until he's almost on top of me. Even if I want to, I can't move. I'm frozen to the spot.

He leans an arm above his head on the wall and crosses one ankle over the other, his stance both relaxed and intimidating as he stares down at me.

"So," his eyes run over me from top to bottom, "how was last night?"

There's a bite in his words that's contradictory to the flash of hurt in his eyes. The whiskey that laces his breath drifts to me on the air. He's been out drinking?

I want to tell him he's an asshole, but his masculinity folds around me like a cloak, the power he has over me both frightening and exciting.

"Did he kiss you?" he asks on a drawl, cool amusement masking something else I can't place.

"On a first date?" I say sarcastically. "Some men are gentlemen, you know."

First, he looks surprised, then relieved, and then angry. "Are you telling me nothing happened?"

"Like I said, Quincy is a gentleman."

Predator intent fills his eyes. He moves so close to me, I can see his pupils dilate. "Then it seems it's not a gentleman you need."

I pull myself to my full height, my breasts brushing over his chest in the process, but I don't care. "Why, Gabriel, you look disappointed." I bat my eyelashes in mock innocence. "What were you hoping for?"

He reaches out so fast I jump in fright and drop the basket when he grabs my wrist.

"I offered you a chance to have it pretty." His lips thin. "I offered you beautiful. You blew that chance, and now you're left with hard and ugly." He squeezes to the point of pain. "You're left with *me*."

There's so much meaning in those words, I can't stop the shiver that crawls up my spine.

He releases me with a soft shove and says in a quiet, threatening voice, "Remember, you begged for it."

Picking up the basket, he pushes it into my arms and walks around me like I'm nothing but an irritating obstacle in his way. If I was infuriated last night, I'm ten times more so now.

"You can't pass me around like a toy for your men," I say to his back, "and you can't decide who I sleep with."

He stops and takes two steps back to me. His smile is cold and cruel. "That's where you're wrong. You're *property*, Valentina. You agreed to *any duty* I see fit. I can share you however I want, but you don't have to worry about being a toy for my men. I don't like to share my toys. Last night was a big fucking gift. Not for Quincy. For *you*." Heat and possessive intent darken his eyes, making him look more dangerous than ever. "And it'll never happen again."

He stalks away with a heavy limp, leaving me trembling with something other than anger. Understanding blooms in me. Gabriel wanted my first experience to be with someone normal. He wanted me to have a taste of how sweet it can be before he submits me to the dark lust I sense in him. I brace my back against the wall and take a few deep breaths. I'm not sure what's worse, that I find his intention sweet or that I crave the darkness he's withholding from me.

11

Valentina

That afternoon, Gabriel goes out on a job and doesn't return for dinner. I'm already in bed when I hear his uneven gait in the kitchen. Rummaging sounds come from the pantry. If he's hungry, I left his food in the oven. I'm not ready to face him, but I can't put it off indefinitely. Rather now, than later.

Entering the scullery, I forget my apprehension. Gabriel is removing a bloody shirt over the basin, the medicine kit balanced on the edge.

"Gabriel!"

I run to him, my eyes doing a quick evaluation of his state. There's a cut in his shoulder through which blood is oozing and several scrapes on his stomach and ribs.

He presses the shirt to the wound and opens the tap. "Shh. Where's Carly?"

"She went to bed after dinner. What happened?" I take the shirt from him and dump it in the trashcan. It's torn and stained beyond saving.

"Business."

He flinches when I touch the wound to assess how deep the cut is.

"This needs stitches. Where are Rhett and Quincy?"

"I sent them to bed. It's not that serious." He flashes me an amused smile. "But your concern is flattering."

"This is no time for jokes." Taking disinfectant and sterile gauzes from the medicine kit, I start cleaning the wound.

"Good thing blood doesn't make you queasy."

I don't return his smile. I don't even want to think what sinister activity earned him these injuries.

"Give me a needle and thread," he orders.

Only Gabriel will keep sterile needles and surgical thread in his medicine kit. I locate the items and hold them out to him. He takes a vanity mirror from the shelf and balances it on the counter. I watch as he pulls the thread through the eye of the needle, but when he angles himself toward the mirror and pushes the needle through the skin at the top of the cut, I take over. He lets me, studying me as I work to sew him back together. I'm no nurse. I'm not even a vet, but I've watched Kris stitch up cuts plenty of times. He winces, but he doesn't say a word until the cut is closed and dressed.

"Thank you."

"You're welcome."

I dispose of the used materials and scrub the basin and my hands with disinfectant. When I'm done, I give him a painkiller and anti-inflammatory with a glass of water. He drinks the pills without protest. Fine lines of fatigue mark his eyes and the corners of his mouth. His permanent frown lines run deeper than usual. Taking his hand, I lead him to my bathroom.

"What are you doing?" he asks.

"Getting the blood off you. You should be worried about catching AIDS."

He grins. "Next time, I'll wear surgical gloves."

I snort. He lets me undress him while the water runs warm. I have to undress as well so my clothes don't get wet, but the shower in my bath is too small for both of us to stand comfortably. When I'm with him in the shower, he has to drape me over his body or hold me in his arms. I angle the water away from his wound, and wash the rest of his body, trying to be gentle on his abdomen where he's bruised. When he's clean, I wrap a towel around his waist and take another to pat him dry. I have to stand on the toilet to reach his hair. Judging by the teeth he flashes me, he finds my care amusing, but he doesn't interfere or take over. I dry his back, chest, and arms, and then I go down on my knees to rub the towel up his legs. There are so many muscles on these legs. They knit together in rigid lines, defining the man's hard exterior with an accurate mirror image of what lies inside his soul.

As I'm pushing to my feet, he prevents me with his hands on my shoulders. I look up. He's devouring me with his eyes, his cock tenting the towel at my eye level.

"Valentina."

There's a plea in the way he says my name. I can't help but want to please him. My reply to his unspoken question is to tug on the towel and let it fall to the floor. I take him in my mouth, and like always, he lets me do whatever I want. I suck him as deep as I can take, eating him hungrily. He groans and dips his knees, giving himself over to me. I take his pleasure like I own it, like it's his duty to give it up to me. He's breathing hard when I'm done, but so am I. He hooks his hands under my arms to help me to my feet, pressing our lips together, and dipping his tongue into my mouth like he always does when I've swallowed his seed. He growls deep from his chest as he sucks on my tongue. The primal sound makes liquid heat gather between my thighs. I'm impossibly slick, my body preparing itself for his invasion, an invasion that's yet to come.

After drying the water that splashed on me while I washed Gabriel, I take him to my bed, and make him lie down on his back to avoid putting pressure on his shoulder. I curl up against his side with my head on the uninjured side of his chest.

"Why did you do it?" he asks.

"Do what?"

"Take care of me."

"I don't know." Deep inside, I wanted to. It frightened me to see him hurt.

"It doesn't matter." He cups my sex, stroking a thumb over my clit. "It was sweet."

He delves a finger into my wetness, teasing and torturing me until he drags a long and slowly detonating orgasm from my body.

Later, as he holds me in his arms, I say, "Gabriel?"

"Mm?"

"Are you ever afraid of dying?"

He answers without hesitation. "Every day."

The big, strong man next to me suddenly seems too vulnerable for my liking. "The scars, are they from fights like today?"

He gives a low chuckle. "You didn't think I was born *all* ugly, did you?"

I cup his cheek. "That's not what I said. I just tend to think of you as indestructible. Untouchable."

He places his hand over mine and rubs his cheek against my palm. "I'm not untouchable, Valentina. I'm far from it." He moves my hand to his chest. "I do have a heart."

I kiss the flat disk of his nipple and put my ear on his chest, just for good measure. The beat is strong and rhythmic. It sounds sure and secure. I have to believe nothing will happen to him. If he's gone, our nine-year deal is off, and I'm dead. Magda won't honor the agreement. Of that, I'm certain.

I push up on one elbow to trace the embossed lines on his face. "Tell me how it happened."

He catches my hand. "Not tonight."

"Nothing?" I ask with a tinge of disappointment. I want to know his history. I want to understand the man inside the sadist.

"All you need to know is that I regret them." He moves my palm to the bandage strip covering the cut on his shoulder. "For this scar, on the other hand, I'm eternally grateful. I hope it never fades."

"Why?"

"Now it's a reminder of you." He kisses my temple. "Go to sleep. It's late."

The balance that started shifting between us from the day he bought me food tips to the one side of the scale, the side where affection surpasses the physical. There's no denying it, any longer. I'm starting to care for my jailer. Maybe I'm suffering from Stockholm syndrome. Not that it matters how or why it happened. Whatever sparked my feelings, they're real.

When I wake up sometime in the middle of the night, he's gone. I don't even have a scar to run my finger over, no raised tissue on the surface of my skin that can make me feel closer to him. All I have are the marks he's leaving on my heart.

My period is over. My breasts and womb are no longer sensitive, but my body is primed with a powerful arousal that won't grant me relief. The orgasms Gabriel gives me are no longer enough. He made me like this, a pathetic addict who needs, craves, and aches, and still he denies me the remedy, even when I beg. I lie in the dark for a long time, trying to make myself come. It's not my fingers, my touch, I need. It's not even Gabriel's touch. I want him *inside* me. I don't care that he's ruined me or that he still holds my life in his hands. He's conditioned me, and I'm at the end of how far I can go. I'm at the edge of a dark abyss, and even if I fear the plunge, I can't turn back. Getting out of bed, I pad barefoot through the dark house.

He won.

Again.

Gabriel

LEAVING Valentina in her bed is becoming harder. I want her next to me all night. It's an impractical and dangerous notion. If Carly sees us or Magda suspects I'm taking it further than the game I claim, I stand losing both my daughter and the woman who dominates every minute of my waking hours and even my dreams. The alarm beeps, pulling me from my thoughts.

The red dot on the bedside monitor warns me of movement in the house. Our security is top-notch, but even the best systems are breached. I check the doors and windows on the monitor. No entrances have been compromised. It can be Carly or Magda. Still, I'm not taking any chances. Whoever is moving through my house is at my door. The creak of a floorboard confirms the information on the screen.

I reach for the gun on the nightstand. When the door opens with a soundless swing, I take aim. My finger freezes on the trigger. It's Valentina's slender form that fills the doorframe. A bolt of shock runs through me for how easily I could've shot her. I lower the weapon. The fight leaves my body, but my muscles don't relax. They're tense with a different kind of anticipation. Her white negligee glows pearly in the moonlight. She's staring at me, biting her lip. Putting the pistol back on the nightstand, I flick on the lamp for a better view.

I know what she wants. We both know why she's here.

I told myself I couldn't do it, and yet, I've never wanted anything more. I've belted and spanked her without breaking a molecule on her skin, but if I take her tonight, I won't only break her virgin body, but also my promise. Call me a weak man, but I already lost the battle the night Rhett locked me in the gym. It was only a matter of time. Tonight is a night for broken promises.

I hold out my hand. "Come here."

She walks to the bed and crawls over me. Every inch of my skin catches fire. By the time her pussy is resting on my crotch, I'm a live wire, ready to explode, but I hold back, giving her control, because she came to me and it's the sweetest moment of my entire fucked up life.

I'm not a man to make small talk or beat around the bush. Especially not when something as serious as this is about to happen. When she doesn't move for several beats, seeming uncertain of where to go from here, I roll us over, pinning her underneath me.

"Get rid of the clothes." I give her just enough space to pull the negligee over her head.

Impatient, I pull the panties down for her, and she kicks them free. She wiggles my pajama bottoms over my hips to my knees. I have to lift first one and then the other leg to get rid of them. Stretched out on top of her, naked, static sparks detonate in every cell of my body. My cock is heavy and painfully hard, cushioned between her soft thighs. My balls ache from too many weeks of celibacy and not enough hand and blowjobs. The need to drive into her is so fierce that I have to grit my teeth.

I slip my hand down our bodies and dip my fingers between her legs. She doesn't need foreplay. She's dripping wet. For *me*. The nights of training her body to want and need me are like one long endless stretch of foreplay, and finally, it's about to explode. I've sucked and tweaked her tits, eaten her pussy, and played with her clit for weeks. What's left is to give her every inch of my cock. Once I'm inside her, there's no turning back. Her body belongs to me, but when I'm done fucking her, her soul will be mine. Once my seed spills in her womb, no other man will touch her again. Not tomorrow. Not when her nine years are up. Never.

Spreading her pussy lips with my fingers, I push the head of my cock against her entrance. My head spins as if I'm on a high. I keep my eyes open. I want to see her face the moment I sink into her. I want to remember her expression. I want to know what she looks like when she comes on my dick, and what she feels when I mark her inside with my cum.

She meets my stare head-on, as bravely as I thought she would, and takes my face between her hands.

"Gabriel…" She inhales deeply.

There's hesitation in her voice. I'm ready. So is she, or she wouldn't be here. The only thing preventing me from tearing into her is the air trapped in her lungs along with her unspoken words.

"Say it," I grit out, my need painful.

Placating my libido, I grind down on her pubic bone. The tip of my shaft edges forward, dipping into the slick heat that waits. Almost violently, I jerk back before I lose all reason and fuck her before she's spoken.

"I know you think I'm a virgin," she says softly, "but I'm not."

For a moment, I'm shocked to a pause. How could I have been so wrong? My judgment concerning a woman's body is always on the mark. All this time, I punished myself, withholding from her, making promises I couldn't keep. To think I almost let Quincy have her. I shake the thought. It's not where I want to take my mind, right now. Whoever her lover was, the asshole didn't know how to get her off. In that regard, I'm definitely her first. Anyway, I don't care who her first was. It doesn't matter, because I'll be her last. It makes no difference to me if she's a holy virgin or a whore.

"I don't care," I say gruffly, grabbing my shaft and directing it to the place that will give me access to her soul. It's when you take a woman, when you make her fall apart in your arms, that you see the nakedness of her heart, and all the truths she hides from the world.

"It doesn't matter to you?" she asks with a tinge of disbelief.

"Of course not." I nip at her ear. "Why would it? I'm no virgin, either."

"I just don't want you to be disappointed."

Disappointed? Is she crazy? "Believe me, nothing about this," I rub my dick over her slick folds, "can be disappointing."

A sob tears from her throat. It catches me so off-guard I almost miss the flash of terror that sparks in her eyes.

"Valentina." I pull back an inch. "If you're not ready, you have to tell me now." I used seduction as my weapon to lure her into my bed with good reason. There's no pleasure in it for me if it's by force.

"Is that why you waited? You thought I'm not ready?"

"You know why I waited. What are you really asking?"

"Do you...?" She bites her lip. "Do you want me? I mean, do you want me like *this*?"

"Goddamn, Valentina. This isn't an act of kindness or a favor. The reason you're here is because I wanted you from the moment I first saw you, and a second from now I'm going to fuck you like I've been wanting to for a very long time, so you better tell me if you're having second thoughts."

"It's not that." She sounds ashamed. "I don't know what to do."

"Wait..." If she's not a virgin, but she doesn't know what to do? A cold feeling of rage unfurls in my gut. Bitterness fills my mouth. The truth lodges like a stake in my heart. "You were raped."

"Yes," she whispers, "but it was a long time ago."

The pace of my breathing quickens, changing direction. I go from turned on to raving mad. Fucking furious. I'll kill the son of a bitch with my bare hands, peel his skin from his body, and cut his muscles from his bones. Forcing back my emotions, I let go of my cock, easing up to cup her cheek.

Calmly, so as not to frighten her with the force of my anger, I ask, "Only once?" while holding my breath for the answer.

"Only once."

"When?"

She turns her head to the side.

I won't let it go. I need to know. "Look at me."

She obeys, her eyes begging me not to push, but the more she holds back, the more uneasy I get.

I brush my thumb over her cheek. "When?"

She purses her lips and stares at me with big eyes, as if I'm going to judge her. "I was thirteen."

When I lay my hands on that motherfucker he's going to suffer. There's only one question left to ask. "Who?"

"I don't know."

She's not lying. She doesn't blink or look away, and her pupils don't dilate. She was a random victim. I'll find and kill him for her. If she wants to, I'll give her the gun and let her shoot him herself. If it's the last thing I do, I'll make the bastard pay.

I kiss her lips. "It wasn't your fault."

"I know."

I'm glad she told me. This will require a different skill and attitude. Technically, she may not be a virgin, but physically, emotionally, and mentally she's the virgin I took her for.

Easing over her body, I cup her jaw and hold her in place for my kiss, bruising our lips together. She gasps into my mouth, but lets me take control. As she can't move her jaw, I'm the one nipping, sucking, and molding my lips around hers, taking and giving and making the moment mine. After a while, she starts fighting me, wrapping her arms around my neck and pulling me down for a deeper kiss, her tongue tangling with mine in an urgency that sets me ablaze. I shift my palm from her jaw to her neck, squeezing with dominant control. She embraces the touch, arching up into my hand. I pin her to the mattress with that commanding hold while I shift to her nipples, starting a slow seduction of tongue and teeth on every erogenous zone of her body. I nip the insides of her elbows and bite into the flesh where her pussy meets her thigh. I drag my tongue over the insides of her legs and dig my fingers into her ass, pulling the curvy flesh apart so I can lick down her crack to her pussy. By the time I've kissed my way from her feet to her mound, her legs are wrapped around me, and she's sliding her wet sex over my cock, seeking the friction that will bring her release.

"I want you," she whispers, breathing beauty into my room. "I want you, Gabriel. Please."

A low groan vibrates in my chest. She's begging *me*. She wants me like no other woman has wanted me before--not for my money or protection, but to ease the need I so carefully planted and nurtured inside of her. Her pleasure is mine, and I'm keeping it forever.

"Oh, God, please." She digs her nails into my back. "Fuck me, already."

We're both out of control. I need to be lucid, or I risk hurting her, but she has me by the balls--literally--dragging her sharp nails from my sac up my ass and sending me way beyond sanity.

I grip my shaft and squeeze the root hard, praying the bite of pain will keep me within reason. Pushing up on one arm, I pull myself from the vice of her thighs and part her legs with my knee. When she's wide and open, I take only a second to enjoy the sight before I lodge the head of my cock in her pussy. Her lips spread wide around my girth, stretching to accommodate all of me. I have precious little control left.

"Look at me," I demand.

She opens her eyes. They're hazy with desire and smoky with need, but they're focused on me. I rest my elbows on the mattress so I can cup her face between my hands, needing to catch her expressions like a prayer between my palms. The movement shoves me another inch into her. She gasps, and her eyes widen. She's tight and hot, her unused channel already pushing to expel the foreign object lodged in her entrance. I push deeper, feeling her like a velvet fist around me. I'm big, and she's fragile, small. Her slickness helps, but it's like pushing into a narrow chamber of hot, melting lava. The deeper I go, the more she squirms. I see it all in her face--the shock, pain, trust, and all-consuming need.

Sweat beads on my brow and torso. My skin is on fire. Her breaths explode from her chest.

"Gabriel..."

It's a plea for mercy. It's moving too slow. I can drag out the discomfort or make it hurt hard and quick before fucking it all better. Pulling back until only the head of my cock is held in place by the stretching muscle in her opening, I hold on to her face tightly and drive home. Tearing through feminine tissue, I bury myself inside her body as far as I can go. It's the moment I've been dreaming of, of hearing her sounds, seeing her surrender, inhaling the scent of our sex, and feeling her body stretch for my cock. She's shaking, her fingers digging into my hips.

"It's almost over, beautiful. It won't hurt for long." I kiss her jaw and move, taking her with long, careful strokes until her body surrenders just like her mind, her tight channel embracing my dick rather than pushing it out.

Her moans turn to panting. It's music to my ears. When she throws her head back, I let go of her face, holding only her eyes. I play with her body, petting her breasts and clit as I stroke deeper and faster, taking everything she can give, everything that makes Valentina a woman. I knead and massage until she's soft and pliant in my arms. She molds like wet, earthy clay under my touch, until her hips start moving to the rhythm of my fingers on her clit.

And then it's over.

She breaks.

Her body sucks me deeper, catching my cock in a trap of painful ecstasy. Her pupils dilate like shooting stars, and her gaze flies away from me like a comet as she comes and leaves a burning trail in my soul. In this moment, she can ask me anything, and I will bust my balls to give it. I'll fetch her the moon and the stars, if that's what she wants, but she only says, "Hold me," and I give her what she desires.

Valentina

GABRIEL'S ARMS are safe around me. He's given me uncountable orgasms, but this one was different. This one was deeper and more intense, stirring the buried emotions I haven't had the courage to look at for so long. After my assault, I shied away from men. The event prevented me from exploring my sexuality. I was afraid to go down that road in the fear of uprooting everything I experienced that awful night, but what I shared with Gabriel was nothing like that. It was a carnal, guilt-free, and necessary need. He took my freedom and made my body a slave to his, but right now, there's nowhere else I'd rather be. This is where I belong. This is where *he* belongs. As much as he took me, I took a part of him, too. I took something of him for myself, and I'll always keep it in my heart. I feel connected to him as I lie in his embrace, enjoying the afterglow of my orgasm. Now that I've had him inside me, I'm hungrier than ever for more. I'm starving for information that goes beyond the sex we share. I want to know why his beautiful physique is broken. I want to know everything about him.

I slide my hand down his body to trace the scar on his knee. Maybe he'll tell me tonight. "How did this happen?"

"Got my kneecap shot away by one of our rivals," he says matter-of-factly.

"And this?" I stroke his hip.

"Baseball bat."

"And this?" As I'm about to cup his cheek, he catches my hand.

"Shrapnel. Explosion. A debtor tried to blow us up with the building where he was laundering the money he stole from us."

"Did he survive?"

He gives me a forced smile. "What do you think?"

"Have you ever considered having it fixed?" I ask as gently as I can.

He replies in a cold voice. "This *is* fixed."

Horror, not because of the ugliness, but because of the sadness, invades me. How did he look before, if this is *after*?

He utters a small sigh. "My bones were crushed. Underneath the skin, there's mostly metal. The risk of the muscles collapsing with more plastic surgery is too high."

I wrap my arms around his waist, holding him tight to me. Saying his mask of pain doesn't bother me will only sound frivolous, even if it's true.

I rest my cheek on his chest. "Your foot?"

All of his muscles go tense. It takes him several seconds before he relaxes under me again. Just when I thought he wasn't going to tell me, he says, "My mother shot me."

I barely manage to swallow my gasp. "Why?"

His tone is flat. "When I turned twelve, she gave me a gun and told me to shoot a man. I couldn't."

A lump in my throat restricts my speaking. I can't imagine the kind of childhood he had. A part of me relates to that and understands. There's quiet accord between us as we hold and comfort each other, two damaged people with different scars.

It's still dark when Gabriel wakes me with a kiss on the mouth. I stretch, feeling the roughness of his loving in the tenderness between my legs, even if he's been as gentle as I guess he can be.

"Good morning." He nips my bottom lip.

His cock is hard against my hip, a reminder of last night and of what I can have again.

"Gabriel." My voice is breathy.

He chuckles. "If I weren't so concerned about not letting you sleep enough, I would've been buried between your thighs an hour ago."

I shiver at the thought, desire making me wet.

A shadow creeps into his eyes. "You have to go. Carly will be up soon."

It's a logical comment, but it hurts, and that's a surprise. Maybe it's because creeping down the dark hallway like I have something to hide, like what I did with Gabriel belongs to the shadows, kills the emotional upsurge of last night.

"You're right." I sit up, clutching the sheet to my breasts.

Groping around under the sheets, I find my nightgown and underwear and pull them on. As I swing my feet off the bed, he grabs my arm. I pause, but I don't look back at him. I'm scared he'll see what I feel in my eyes. That I care.

He kisses my shoulder and brushes his lips up the curve of my neck to my ear. When he releases me, I take it as my cue to leave. I close his bedroom door quietly behind me and glance down the hallway to make sure it's clear before I sneak back to my room. The room looks empty and cold. Out of nowhere, I have an attack of inexplicable loneliness, followed by a bout of guilt because Oscar is sleeping alone on my pillow.

I pick him up and hug him to my chest. "Poor baby. I'm sorry I left you all alone last night."

He purrs and rubs his face against my jaw, not halfway as unsettled as I am.

Gabriel

THERE'S NOT much information in the country Anton can't lay his hands on, so when he tells me Lambert Roos' phone records have been wiped, I know the rat I smelled is real. I order Anton to dig into Lambert's history, present and past, and to flag anything suspicious that comes up, especially pertaining to the Haynes family. Lambert did business with Marvin. I want to know why he stopped brokering the car cloning business after Marvin's accident. I also want to know who Valentina's rapist is, but I'll have to get more information from her, a delicate situation I don't look forward to. I already checked the police records. The family didn't report her rape. My own research produced nothing helpful.

The remainder of my time is dedicated to preparing for tonight's dinner meeting. Despite her protests, I ship Carly off to Sylvia for the weekend. I don't want her around for the dinner party, not with the guests Magda invited. We'll be catering for the Ferreira drug cartel men, Jeremy, the owner, and his son and future heir, Diogo. It's tough enough stomaching the political pawns Magda likes to entertain. I don't like hosting drug thugs in our home, but Magda is wheeling a deal to open a new financing franchise in Westdene, the heart of Jeremy's territory.

From the minute they walk through the door, I dislike them. Jeremy has the close-set eyes of a crocodile who acts asleep to snatch his non-suspecting prey. He grabs my hand in a jovial shake, treating me like his long-lost son, while Diogo, a smooth, handsome man in his late twenties, gives me a measuring look that tells me he finds me too short, not in the literal sense, of course. He may be ten years younger than me and blessed with a whole body, but I have years of experience over him and a darkness he can't begin to understand.

They kiss Magda's hand and accept the cocktails and hors d'oeuvres she offers in the lounge. Their chitchat and pretense at civility irritate me. If it was up to me, I would've cut through the bullshit and gotten to the point. We want exclusivity in their area. They want our money. Simple. We pay a kickback, and no other loan sharks get in. A deal also guarantees that we don't fuck with them, and they don't kill our men.

Magda navigates through a whole family tree of questions about their wives, kids, grandmothers, and whatnot before she finally announces dinner is served. The tux I'm wearing for the occasion, these affairs being sordidly formal, is too hot. I hook a finger between my neck and the collar of my evening shirt and tug. The bowtie gives marginally, but I only breathe easier when Valentina walks into the room in her somber black dress and hair pulled back in a neat bun in the nape of her neck.

I watch her unabashedly as she serves our starters. The curve of her neck is long and elegant. Her fingers are slender, but they serve with efficient and sure movements, not spilling a drop of the gazpacho soup. A smell of raspberry fills my nostrils as she brushes past me, the fabric of her dress touching my chair. She's present in all of my senses, even in my thoughts with a memory of how her body surrendered to mine last night. My cock hardens. It's a good thing we're seated.

It's hard to tear my attention away from her, but I need to concentrate on the negotiation and the subtle nuances of the conversation. I'm good at reading body language. I may not say much, but if our partners try to fuck us over, I'm always the first to get the hunch. With difficulty, I return my attention to the people seated at the opposite side of the table, but as I lift my eyes, I notice the way Diogo stares at Valentina. Anger explodes in my body and courses through my veins. The only thing that prevents me from reaching over the table and drowning him in his bowl of soup is that Valentina leaves the room, cutting his ogling short. I can't wait for this night to be over.

Halfway through the main meal, we come to an agreement. The minute we shake hands on the deal, Magda's tenseness evaporates. She becomes the engaging hostess she's known for, drawing Jeremy into a friendly argument about the opposing rugby teams they support. Diogo asks for directions to the bathroom and excuses himself.

The skin between my shoulder blades pinches. I push back my chair. "Excuse me. I'm going to check on dessert."

Magda shoots me a look, but I'm blind to the annoyance in her eyes. My soles are quiet in the carpeted hallway. In the entrance to the kitchen, I come to an abrupt halt. Valentina has her back pushed against the wall and a kitchen knife aimed at Diogo.

12

Gabriel

The knife in Valentina's hand makes me see images that will haunt me forever. A million scenarios pop into my head. The thought of Valentina hurt or Diogo's hands on her, pulls me from reason into a state of madness. In a flash, I pounce on Diogo, throwing him on the floor. I slam his face into the tiles and pin him down with my knees, my fists pounding into his ribs. The sounds of his strangled grunts and bone cracking aren't enough. I want him to cough up blood until his lungs drown in it.

"Gabriel!"

Valentina's voice pierces the ugly bubble of my rage. The piece of shit under me is struggling for his life. Slowly, I return to the distant part of humanity inside me, the little that's left in my soul. Magda and Jeremy come running into the room, probably alarmed by Valentina's scream.

"What in God's name?" Magda grabs my arm and tries to pull me off the man sprawled out on the floor.

I shake her off, but it's Valentina's round, fearful eyes that beckon me to let the scumbag go.

Getting to my feet, I adjust my jacket. "Get up, you son of a bitch."

"What the hell's going on?" Jeremy takes Diogo by his shoulders to help him to his feet.

Pulling him up is a struggle. It looks like he has trouble breathing. I must've knocked the wind out of him and broken a few ribs. His nose is bleeding from the blow on the tiles.

Magda flutters around him like a hen. "Gabriel! Are you out of your mind?"

I jab a finger at Diogo. "If you put a finger on her, asshole, you're dead."

Magda and Jeremy turn their heads toward Valentina. She's still standing with her back against the wall, her body trembling and her eyes fixed on Diogo.

I take the knife from her hand and leave it on the counter. Lowering my head, I put us on eye level. "Look at me." Once I have her undivided attention, I ask, "Did he touch you?"

"No," she whispers.

Magda starts speaking, but I cut her short. "What did he do?"

"He wanted to–to..."

She doesn't have to say it. I know men like Diogo. I know the things they want to do. I turn to Diogo with cold calculation. "If I didn't walk in here, what were you going to do?"

He spits blood from a split lip on the floor. "Have myself some fun. She's only a maid, for Christ's sake."

My voice is soft, but my anger carries in my tone. "That gives you the right to assault the people living under my roof, the people I protect?"

"Hold on, son." Jeremy steps between us, his palms raised. "You're not going to risk our newly forged relationship over a maid, are you?"

I turn my vengeance on the old man. "She's not just a maid. She's property."

Jeremy knows what that means. In his and my world, property is more untouchable than a man's wife. You may fuck someone else's wife and pray you don't get caught, but you don't lay a finger on another man's property without accepting that you're going to get your hand chopped off.

"Whoa." He utters a nervous laugh. "Honest mistake. Diogo didn't know. We're used to helping ourselves, if you know what I mean."

"Are you insulting me by insinuating my house is a brothel?"

"Jeremy," Magda takes his arm, "your son needs medical attention. I'll cover all the costs, of course. I do apologize for this unfortunate misunderstanding."

It's a subtle way of telling him to leave. Magda knows me too well. I'm a lunatic, and right now, I'm about as stable as an active volcano.

Jeremy frees his arm. "Let's go, Diogo."

Diogo sneers at me as he passes, clutching his side. He should've just carried on walking, but the mistake he makes is to turn back in the doorway.

"You know what your problem is, honey?" he says to Valentina. "You're too damn pretty. It's a shame you're also a prude. I think you would've enjoyed it if I'd jumped you against the wall."

Just like that, my frayed control unravels. Magda grabs for the hem of my jacket as I lurch forward and catch the cocksucker around the neck. Jeremy is cussing and trying to pull my arms away from his son, but not a hundred horses are enough to tear me away. I drag him by his scrawny neck to Valentina and force him down on his knees at her feet. I grab a fistful of his perfectly styled hair and jerk his head back. Reaching for the same knife Valentina used to defend herself, I push the tip against his lilywhite, pretty-boy neck.

"Apologize."

"Diogo," Jeremy says from behind me, a tremor in his voice, "do as he says."

"Gabriel." There's consternation in Magda's tone, but she doesn't touch me. The situation is too volatile. I'm too unpredictable. A flick of my wrist and Diogo's life will bleed out at Valentina's feet. Only, I don't want another man's blood on her conscience. She already feels responsible for Tiny's death. Diogo doesn't deserve the guilt she'll suffer over him.

"I'm sorry," Diogo grits out.

I jerk harder on his hair, making him cry out in pain. "Say it like you mean it."

"I'm really fucking sorry."

I lodge the tip of the knife under his skin. "Beg." A thin trickle of blood runs down his neck under his collar.

"Forgive me," he says. "I beg you."

I look at Valentina. "Do you forgive him?"

She looks at me with owl eyes. "Yes."

"You're more compassionate than me." I yank him up by his hair until he finds his feet. "Get the fuck out of my house. The deal's off, and you better pray I don't run into you on the street. You better stay very far away from me."

When I let go, Diogo stumbles to his father. Magda is paler than the white tiles on the floor, quiet for once. Jeremy gives me a narrowed glare, but he takes Diogo's arm and escorts him from the room. You don't insult a man in his own house. Jeremy knows this. He knows I can cut Diogo's throat for that, and none of his business associates will retaliate.

Magda rubs the back of her neck. "I'll see you out." She turns to Valentina. "You better go to your room and not come out until morning. If I see your face before, I may not be able to suppress the urge to kill you."

When it's just the two of us in the kitchen, I take her in my arms and give her a hug. "You okay?"

She nods. "I didn't want to cause trouble."

"You did the right thing." I kiss her nose. "I'm proud of you."

"You put your life at risk. They're going to kill you."

"They'll try, but so is every other criminal and cop in the country. You're mine, Valentina, and nobody touches you."

The clicking of Magda's heels down the hallway makes me go rigid. "Go to bed."

"The kitchen--"

"Can wait for tomorrow. Go."

She obeys wordlessly. By the time Magda reenters the room, Valentina is out of sight.

"In my study." Magda stalks from the room, not waiting to see if I'm following.

She holds the door for me and slams it when I step over the threshold.

"Are you out of your goddamn mind?"

"You know I am, Magda."

"Do you have any idea how hard I worked to secure that deal?" She pushes her finger in my face. "What gave you the right to blow it away? Over a fucking maid!"

I grab her finger and move it away with force. The act catches her off-guard. She stumbles a step back and gapes at me with a mixture of disbelief and fear.

"If you ever push your finger in my face again, I'll break it."

"Gabriel," she exclaims on a gasp, "I'm your mother."

"You've never been a mother to me. Don't claim the designation now."

"What's gotten into you? You blew a multi-million-rand deal, for God's sake!" She straightens her back, her fear suddenly gone. "Don't think you're above my punishment because you're my son. You're taking this game you're playing with the girl too far. You've had your fun. Let her slip up and kill her so we can all go back to our lives."

"I'll decide when the fun's up."

"Is part of the fun buying her fancy clothes? Playing with a doll isn't enough for you? You have to dress her, too?"

"Are you checking my bank statements?"

"I know the owner of the boutique where you took your slave on a shopping spree."

"That's none of your business."

"You're fucked in the head, you know that? Just like your father."

"How can I forget when you're doing such a great job of reminding me?"

She wipes a hand over her face. "I need a drink." Propping her hands on her hips, she regards me from under her lashes. "Get her out of your system, Gabriel. Do whatever it takes. Eventually, you're going to have to kill her."

"Good night, *Mother.*"

I leave her alone in her study, going to my own for a stiff drink and to mull over the evening. I should've broken Diogo's nose the minute he stepped over my doorstep. That way, I would've saved myself a whole evening of his unpleasant presence. My thoughts don't dwell on the cocksucker for long. As always, my attention is reserved for Valentina. I'm not sure in what emotional state she'll be when I go to her room, but I'll be there for her, regardless. She should feel safe under my roof, knowing I won't let anyone harm her. The kind of hurt I want to give her, that's something entirely different. The kind of pain I like to inflict is as much for her pleasure as mine.

When I walk through her door, I don't find her curled up in bed or huddled in a corner. She's spread out on the bed, naked, waiting for me. My balls draw tight. My cock swells.

I can't look away from her fingers where they rest between her legs. "You played with yourself?"

"Yes."

"Did you come?"

"No, I was saving that for you."

"Good, because otherwise I would've had to punish you. I own your orgasms. Say it."

"You own me, Gabriel. All of my orgasms."

I swallow away the hoarseness in my throat. "Show me. Play with yourself."

"Later." She wiggles her hips. "I want *you* inside me."

Holy fuck. What she does to me. I strip my clothes and climb between her legs. Even if she's offering herself, I want to hunt her. I want to catch her in the wild, wild, darkest woods of our desires and conquer her body. I want to tame her soul. I've got her, but I'm terrified I'll lose her. I need to pin her down and constrain her, keep her in the cage of lust I so carefully constructed to trap her.

I flatten my palm on her pelvis, keeping her lower body in place as I push two fingers inside her pussy. She's wet. The suction of her inner muscles welcomes me. I can't wait. I grip the root of my shaft and place it at her entrance, but she shakes her head. It takes every ounce of willpower I possess not to give in to the urge to tie her up and make her have it my way. It takes strength to lift my hand from her abdomen and allow her to escape, but she doesn't run away from the monster in her bed. She embraces the need that's chasing us both by turning over on her hands and knees. She looks back at me from over her shoulder, putting her beautiful cunt on display.

"Take me like this," she whispers.

The animal in me rises to the occasion. I open her pussy with my thumbs, align my cock with her slick folds, and drive home. Her back arches from the fast and hard intrusion, but she slams back, meeting my force with an urgency of her own. I'm giving her my all, thrusting our groins together with enough force to bruise her skin.

"More," she pants. "You're holding back."

I'm fucking the air from her lungs, and she's begging for more.

"Harder, Gabriel. Please. Please, God. Let it go. Make me forget. Make me forget what happened tonight."

I do. The walls of my constraint break, crumbling around her, and I take her like I've never taken a woman before.

Valentina

GABRIEL IS POUNDING INTO ME, hurting me inside, but I need more. With him, I'll always need more. He steals my breath, takes my pleasure, and owns my desires. I am so filled with him, I can't take more, and, yet I want him in every crevice and corner of my body.

Reaching between my legs, I caress his testicles, feeling their charged sway as he slams his groin against my ass.

"More," I moan. "Please."

"If I fuck you harder, I'll break you."

I want him to bleed into my cells until we are inseparable, until our DNA is entangled and my life is grafted with his. Together, we're invincible. As long as he's with me, no one else can touch me. Like this, there's no ugly. No Diogo. No men like Tiny. Only Gabriel who makes me forget everything, even that he owns me.

"Fill me, Gabriel. Fill me more."

"Goddammit, Valentina. You kill me."

I look back at him from over my shoulder. His face is scrunched up with pent-up desire, his cool eyes dark with lust, and his jaw tense with control. Without breaking his pace, he lets go of my hip to stick his forefinger in his mouth. He opens my ass with his free hand and sticks his wet finger into my dark entrance. I fall forward and catch my weight on my arms. With the intrusion in my ass, the pressure in my pussy increases two-fold.

"Yes," I whimper. "Like that."

I brace myself for the impact. His hands being otherwise occupied, he can no longer support my hips. The force is too much. My body is helpless under his brutal hammering. Every thrust shifts me higher up the mattress. He follows me, pulling out and pushing back in, his cock and finger working in synchrony. One hand moves around to the front of my body, finding my clit. A few fast strokes and I come, yelling his name. I expect him to come with me, but he doesn't. While I'm riding the incredible wave of my release, he stretches me by adding a second finger to the first in my backside. I'm overfull, but I don't care. I'm contracting and sizzling, my body a canvas of receptors for pleasure. I'm floating in a space of euphoric bliss. I don't care what he does with my body.

After a while, he pulls his cock free. Only his fingers are punishing my ass. This, too, stops. His touch disappears.

"Don't move."

Exhausted, I melt into the sheets. I'm not going anywhere. The bed dips, and then he's gone. Cupboards open and close in the kitchen. What is he doing? I have my answer when he returns with a bottle of cooking oil. He places it on the floor and continues right where he left off, working two fingers into my ass. The sensation is wrong and thrilling. A forbidden kind of pleasure runs up my spine. After a moment, he withdraws his fingers and opens my crack. Cold liquid squirts into my ass. After the heat, the cold comes as a shock. I squirm to escape the onslaught, but he grabs me between the legs and holds me still while more of that slippery liquid fills me up. The oil. It feels like when he comes inside of me, only colder. He smears the substance around the tight ring of muscle, and when he pushes his finger back, it slips right in. I arch my back in response, needing more of the friction. The second finger joins the first, and soon a third finger stretches me. It doesn't hurt, but it's too full. I'm about to say so when his hand disappears and a hot, smooth surface pushes against my dark entrance. I look over my shoulder to see him positioning his cock where his fingers have been.

I try to lift my upper body, but he pushes me down with a hand on my lower back, working himself into me an inch. It burns like hell. I moan and squirm and try to push him out, but the harder I clench my backside, the harder he pushes.

"Relax," he says in a tight voice. "I'll take your ass regardless."

I know he will, and I want him to. I take a deep breath and try to let the tension go, but when he moves deeper, I cry out and bite into the pillow to muffle the sound.

"Almost there," he says, rubbing his palms over my ass cheeks.

God, it hurts. I'm not sure I can take it. "Gabriel."

"Hush, beautiful." He bends down and kisses my spine. "Take a deep breath."

He talks me through it, making me breathe in and out until he has buried all of him inside me. The last inch is the worst. I gasp and swallow air. When he moves, I scream, grinding my pelvis to the mattress to escape the touch, but he chases after me, fucking me deeper. With every thrust he pounds the breath out of me until my voice is raw, and then he stills, keeping his cock in my body. I'm barely aware of anything but the invasive hardness. Carefully, he slips two fingers into my pussy. The pad of his thumb rests on my clit, stimulating my need. As my desire starts climbing again and my muscles contract around him, he moves again. He takes me to a place I didn't know existed, where pleasure and pain are one, and the effect of having both sensations simultaneously on my body makes it impossible to discern where the one starts and the other stops. He's kindling the biggest need in me yet. I'm full and fulfilled. I'm aching, but he's soothing me. I'm hovering on the edge. If I tumble over, I may not stop falling, but I'm powerless to prevent it.

My body tightens. As the wave starts rolling, he drags his wet fingers from my pussy. His hands fold around my neck, squeezing just enough to cut my airflow. I need to fight, but I'm too weak. I don't have enough energy left. I can only lie there with electric shivers running through my clit, and Gabriel's cock ramming into my ass while white spots start to dance in my vision, and my pulse hammers in my ears. The minute he gives me back the gift of oxygen, of life, I come with a force that shatters my body and mind. Thousands of volts of pleasure course through me, pulling every muscle, finger, and toe so tight my body is one, great spasm. I must've fallen over that edge, because I'm drifting like a feather, and everything around me turns into a comfortable darkness where the brutal pleasure mercifully stops.

Gabriel

FUCK. Shit. It's the first time I fucked a woman unconscious. I turn Valentina's limp body on her back and slap her cheeks.

"Wake up, baby."

She doesn't move. Not even her eyelashes flutter. The euphoria of my climax evaporates. Fuck, fuck, fuck. I pick her up in my arms and carry her to the shower. I can barely squeeze inside with her draped over me. I adjust the water to a lukewarm setting and, tipping her head back, let it run over her face and hair.

She frowns and stirs.

"That's my girl. Come on, Valentina."

She gasps and coughs. Her eyelids lift to reveal tiger-eye gemstones staring at me. "Gabriel."

Relief washes over me, and the tightness in my chest expands marginally. "I'm here, beautiful."

I hold her to me, letting her find her feet without releasing my grip on her waist. Allowing her to pass out wasn't part of my plan. I'm furious with myself. She deserves better than a sadist who pushes her to the limits of pleasure, all the way into fucking fainting. The only way I know to make it right is to give her comfort. Like she took care of me the night I was stabbed, I take care of her, washing her hair and her body from the top of her head to the tip of her toes as best as I can in the confined space. I'm careful with the tender part between her legs and especially her ass. After drying and dressing her, I put her to bed. It tears me up, but I have to go to my own. I'm too exhausted to risk staying with her. If I fall asleep, I may not wake up before Carly. I don't want to leave her like this, but I must. For how much longer can I keep up the pretense?

AFTER MY MORNING workout with Quincy and Rhett, I meet Sonny and Lance, two of my franchise owners, about a dispute over territory. Lance has been casting his nets in Sonny's reservoir, and as much as I hate playing ombudsman, I prefer to step in before we have a war on our hands. It's a glorious day, and we're having our discussion by the pool. My leg has been bothering me more than usual after last night's sexual marathon, and the exercise in the water does me good. I swim a few laps before stretching out on a deckchair in the sun, listening to the squabble between the grown men. When it gets close to one o'clock, I interrupt their bickering.

"No eyes on the housekeeper."

Sonny and Lance exchange a glance, but comprehension dawns on their faces when Valentina exits from the kitchen, a tray loaded with food in her hands, and walks our way. Sonny looks up at the sky while Lance fixes his gaze on his toes.

Her figure is slender in the dark dress. With tendrils that escaped her ponytail, she looks feminine and vulnerable. I want her next to me, in my arms, not at a distance acceptable for a servant, not with a barrier between us that lets me enjoy the sunshine while she's standing there in her black garb, sweating in the sun.

There's not a stitch of resentment in the brilliant smile she gives me. "Can I get you anything to drink?"

"Lemonade." I turn to Sonny and Lance, who are looking anywhere but at Valentina. "Beer?"

"Please," they say in unison.

"Anything else?"

I'm suddenly bothered that she has to serve men not worthy of kissing her feet. "No."

Her smile is genuine and pure, a ray of beautiful that doesn't fit in the filth of my world. "Just shout if you need me."

As she walks back to the kitchen, I can't help but stare after the frail set of her narrow shoulders with an emotion that, this time, isn't foreign to me.

Longing.

I'm consumed by longing.

Valentina

Nothing is worse than the helplessness I felt at the hands of men who bullied and assaulted me. Tiny lifted the tightly sealed lid on those emotions. What Diogo tried to do made me relive those feelings. Those forbidden sentiments, the ones I banished to the depths of my mind, make me shaky with shame and anger. I hate not being able to defend myself. Then there's Gabriel. The things I feel when I'm with him are too complicated to examine, and I'm too scared of what I'll find. What I need is not to analyze what's happening between me and my keeper--I can't change it, anyway--but to learn to protect myself from people stronger than me. Maybe I could get a weapon and learn how to use it.

I'm sweeping up the leaves on the pavement, fantasizing about my options, when Magda walks up.

"I want all the leather sofas treated with beeswax and polished to a shine today. Carly is complaining her cupboards are full of dust. Unpack everything and wipe down the shelves. Her closet can do with a good reorganization."

"Yes, ma'am."

"I want dinner to be served an hour earlier, tonight. I have an appointment after."

"I'll make sure it's ready."

"Tomorrow you need to start taking down the curtains and wash them. Start with the bedrooms. You can do one room every day."

"Yes, ma'am."

She checks her watch. "Don't wait for the afternoon to sweep the pavement. It has to be done every morning at eight. The neighbors must think we're pigs living in a pigsty."

"I'll do it at eight."

"Are you any good with a sewing machine?"

"I've never used one."

"Better learn. You can adjust the hems of the new curtains I bought for the lounge."

The delivery van pulls up, thankfully saving me from more tasks she can think up, as I have to check and sign for the produce.

For the rest of the day, I race through my chores, skipping lunch and teatime. It's hard not to stress over screwing up a task or failing to execute it when your life's in the balance. I haven't slept enough in weeks, and I haven't studied in days. I missed deadlines for two assignments and only got extensions because of my good grades, but no matter how fast I work, there's always more work and too little time. My mentor warned me if I miss another deadline, I'd get a zero for the assignment. She can't keep on making exceptions for me.

During the next two weeks, Gabriel is hardly home. When he comes to me at night, there are lines of strain on his face. I don't ask about his business, but from the way he takes me, hard and relentless,

I know in his own way, he's as stressed as I am, so I don't complain. When I'm at Kris' house, I cook, clean, help in the clinic, and spend as much time with Charlie as I can. At night, I try to catch up with my outstanding projects, but I'm several weeks behind. I sleep between four and five hours per night, returning to my studies when Gabriel leaves me to go back to his own room. I don't dare confess to him in the fear that he'll take it away from me, and I can't lose my dream. Despite the explosive sex, I'm still property. Nothing but an amusing toy. Gabriel takes care of me like one would maintain an expensive car or look after a cute pet. Copious amounts of coffee keep me awake and jittery during the day. It's only by sheer willpower that I finish the tasks Magda doles out. The harder she pushes me, the harder I try. The more she demands, the more I deliver.

It's a bright December morning when half a kudu carcass is dropped off in the kitchen.

"A gift from business colleagues who went hunting," she says, regarding the piece of meat with her hands on her hips.

It's not hunting season. "Where does it come from?"

"A friend did some culling on a game farm up north."

"What shall I do with it, ma'am?"

"Marie used to process the meat. The leg is good for biltong. You can use the offcuts for sausage."

I've never chopped up half an antelope, but I'm not going to admit it. When she's gone, I do an internet search and come up with page that gives detailed illustrations on how to process a carcass. It's too heavy for me to handle alone, so when Quincy walks past the kitchen with Bruno, I ask him to help. Together, we use the meat axe to chop the meat into smaller, more manageable pieces. He helps me to set up the electric meat saw and grinder on the island counter. While he's cleaning the blades for me, I order the intestines for the sausage from a local butcher.

"All ready," he says. "Need some help with the grinding?"

"I'm good, thank you." I'm proud that I figured it out.

"Just shout." With a wave, he's off.

For the next hour, I cut the bigger pieces into smaller parts, keeping the strips for the biltong aside, while soaking the offcuts in a solution of vinegar and salt for the sausage. It's a long and time-consuming process. I'm stressed about preparing dinner, but I can't cook in the dirty kitchen. I'll have to disinfect the countertops, first.

My phone beeps while I'm pushing the meat through the blades to make sirloin steaks. Normally, I won't interrupt my work to check my messages, but the beep tone tells me it's from my mentor, Aletta. I flick the switch on the saw and gingerly fish the phone from my apron pocket between my thumb and forefinger. The message hits me like a hammer between the eyes.

Come see me. You failed your cell biology test.

My hand trembles as I leave the phone on the counter, reading the text over and over. The repercussions are enormous. The test scores are taken into consideration at the end of the year. If I fail one subject, my partial bursary will be revoked. I'd have to drop out. Devastation crashes over me. I want to remain positive, but the realistic side of me brings my mind to a standstill to evaluate the facts and face the truth.

I'm not going to make it.

There's a terrible finality in the notion. It's as if an anchor has been cut from my life, and now that I'm no longer grounded to a dream, I'm floating meaninglessly in a life which only purpose is to keep Charlie alive. Swatting at the moisture building in my eyes, I try to let my pride keep me strong. I won't cry over this, but my heart is not on par with my mind. Fresh tears blur my vision as I switch the saw back on and start feeding the meat through the blades. I work on autopilot, letting the rhythm of my hands and the noise of the machine dull me to a state of unfeeling, automated movements. It liberates my mind to think. Not making my dream come true will hurt my heart, but failing my brother will destroy me, so I make peace with giving up the dream.

The very moment I make the decision, a hot sensation explodes in my right hand and travels up my arm. I look at the slicer and the meat I clutch in my hands, but I don't make immediate sense of the scene. My brain registers the blood squirting from my thumb long before it does the pain.

13

Valentina

The first digit of my thumb is gone. I cut it just above the metacarpal bone. My mind switches down, and my body goes into automatic functioning mode. I open the cold-water tap and hold my hand under the stream. Water-diluted blood swirls down the drain. The first thing in reach is a clean drying cloth. I turn off the tap and wrap the cloth tightly around my hand to stop the bleeding. I switch off the slicer by the wall and, careful of the blades, go through the reservoir until I find my severed thumb. I feel sick and dizzy, like I'm about to vomit and pass out, but adrenalin keeps me going. After putting the top of my thumb in the mini icebox, I retrieve an icepack from the freezer for my right hand. I grab my purse with my identity card and walk through the house, looking for someone, but only Carly is in her room.

"My dad's out," she says without looking up from her book.

I can't afford an ambulance, and I don't have medical insurance. Private insurance costs a fortune in this country. I'll take my chances with the public hospital, but I need a ride.

I go out the front and find Rhett by the door. "I need a lift to the hospital. Can you please drive me?"

He takes one look at the bloodstained cloth around my hand, and takes the car keys from his pocket. He opens the door for me and helps me into the Mercedes.

"Joburg Gen is the nearest," I say.

He nods and steers the car down the road with a speed that will most likely get us killed before we arrive at the hospital. On the way, he dials Gabriel on voice commands via the hands-free kit and is directed to his voicemail.

"It's Rhett. I'm driving Valentina to the Joburg Gen. She..." He looks at me.

"Cut my finger," I fill in for him.

"I'll keep you posted." He disconnects and dials another number to instruct a guard to take up his post by the Louw residence front door.

When he hangs up, he shoots me a sidelong glance. "You okay?"

"Yes." As if on cue, the pain intensifies. I lean back and purse my lips. My hand is throbbing like a giant heart.

The emergency entrance drive is blocked with vehicles, so we go to the underground parking. The state of the place comes as a shock. Garbage litters the surface up to my ankles. We take the lift to the emergency floor, and when we exit, I'm halted by the rows of people sitting on the floor in the hallway, all looking ten times worse than me. Some of them have gaping wounds, and others have invisible ailments that seem no less fatal judging by the lifeless shine of their eyes. The corridor stinks of vomit and urine. I haven't seen the inside of a hospital since the age of ten when I fell and needed stitches on my head. This makes me never want to come back. We walk past a man with a fracture, the bone sticking through his skin. Another one has a gush in his arm so deep, I can see the tendons. The woman next to him has a broken beer bottle still lodged in her cheek. Violence screams at us as far as we go.

I feel for Rhett's hand with my good one, clutching his fingers as we make our way through misery and despair to a front desk where a bored-looking nurse looks up.

"What's your problem, love?"

When I sway, Rhett catches me. "I cut my finger."

She pushes a clipboard with a form across the counter. "Fill that out." She scratches her head with a pencil and points at an area at the far back. "Waiting area's over there."

We pass an examination room. A naked man lies on a bare mattress. He's handcuffed to the iron bedpost. A nurse is washing blood from his legs. The floors are dirty, and the walls are stained. There are no pillows, sheets, or dividers. Our eyes connect. I avert mine quickly, but feel his follow me until we're out of sight.

All the seats are taken, but I don't want to risk sitting on the germ-infected floor. Rhett takes the pencil from me and calls out the questions while I tell him what to write.

From the way the cloth is soaking up the blood, the bleeding hasn't stopped. I'm starting to feel the effect of the blood loss, or maybe it's delayed shock that's making me feel like fainting.

"Come on," Rhett says gently, taking my arm to lead me back to the reception desk when the questionnaire is completed.

The nurse takes the form, but is in conversation with a colleague and doesn't look up to acknowledge us.

"How long does she have to wait?" Rhett asks tightly.

"What's that, love?"

He jerks his head toward the long line of people. "How long?"

She chuckles. "See that man over there?" She points at the one with the gash in his arm. "He's been waiting for twelve hours."

He opens his mouth to argue, but there's no point. These people are in as much need, if not more, than me.

I touch his arm and say softly, "I think we should do it at home." I won't be able to hold the severed piece in place and stitch. "Can you help me?"

The nurse's attention is already on her colleague again. They're laughing together, sharing a joke.

He nods at my hand. "Show me."

I unwrap the cloth slowly to reveal my thumb. Blood pumps from the digit as if bubbling from an underground fountain.

Rhett blanches. "Jesus Christ." He sweeps me up in his arms and starts walking with long strides back in the direction from where we came.

"Rhett! What are you doing?"

"There's a private clinic in Brixton. It's only seven kilometers from here."

"I don't have medical aid. I can't afford a private clinic."

"I'll pay." He shifts my weight in his arms. "Don't worry about the money, okay? I'm not leaving you in this dump for one second longer."

"We can do it at home," I insist.

He doesn't say anything, but the hard set of his jaw tells me he disagrees.

Twenty minutes later, we're going through the same procedure at the Garden Clinic, but the change is remarkable. The building is clean and sterile. A nurse takes charge of me the minute we enter, and no less than ten minutes after Rhett put down the cash for my treatment —which was required upfront—I'm wearing a hospital robe, lying on a gurney outside the operating room. Rhett is pacing the hallway, his figure passing from left to right and back in front of the door window, his phone stuck to his ear. The doctor who introduces himself as the surgeon tells me the good news is that he can try to save my thumb, thanks to my foresight to recover and bring the missing piece. As they start pushing me toward the operating room, the door slams into the wall, and Gabriel rushes into the corridor, his limp heavy and his short hair messy.

"Excuse me," the doctor exclaims. "You can't barge in here."

He doesn't look at the doctor. He finds my eyes and holds them. "She's with me."

"I don't care if she's with the queen of England."

Gabriel's blue eyes grow hard. His face sets into a frightening mask, and when he turns it on the doctor he says in a cold voice, "I'm staying with her."

Gabriel reaches for my uninjured hand, but the doctor cuts him short.

"Get out or I'll have you removed."

His gaze fixes on my covered wound, and like Rhett, he pales.

"Good thing you're not squeamish, huh?" I smile at him, feeling a little high from whatever they injected me with to kill the pain.

"Call security," the doctor tells the nurse.

Gabriel lifts his palms. "Calm the fuck down. I'm leaving."

"I guess no one is eating meat tonight." The thought sends a sudden rush of hysteria through me. "Oh, my God, Gabriel. The dinner." I trip over my own words, trying to get them out. "It was a stupid accident. I didn't pay attention. I'm so sorry. Please don't let Magda kill me."

"Forget about the goddamn dinner," he says harshly. When the doctor shoots him a warning look, he continues in a softer tone, "I'm taking care of everything."

He holds my gaze as the medical staff rush me toward the swinging doors. As I look back at him, standing there by himself, I have this weird notion that he's alone in the world. Suddenly, I long for him, inexplicably and completely. In this scary moment, it's him I want by my side. I reach for him, recognizing the helpless expression on his face, and then the doors shut out his image. Coldness washes over my body and invades my soul as the doctor pushes a mask on my face and tells me to count to ten. I get to three before the memory of Gabriel's face fades.

THE DOCTOR KEEPS me overnight and discharges me the following day at noon. He tells me the operation went well, and that he gave me a tetanus shot. A tense and tired-looking Gabriel enters my room with a huge bunch of white lilies when the doctor leaves after examining me.

"Hey, beautiful." He kisses my lips. "How do you feel?"

"I'm fine, thanks."

"Come on." He helps me to get dressed, and even if I protest when a nurse pushes a wheelchair into the room, he lowers me into the chair. "It's the chair or my arms." He gives me a smile, but it's weak.

The expression in his eyes is shuttered, making it hard for me to read him.

"I have your prescription from the doctor," he says. "We'll stop at the pharmacy before we go."

We leave armed with antibiotics and painkillers from the hospital pharmacy. On the way home, Gabriel clutches my fingers, and when he shifts gears, he places my bandaged hand on his thigh.

It's only when we take the off-ramp to Parktown that he speaks. "Don't ever do that to me again."

His anger sparks annoyance in me. It's with difficulty that I keep my temper in check. "It was an accident."

"You have no idea what you put me through."

"I can guess. You were worried about your investment."

He swerves and brings the car to such a quick stop on the shoulder of the road that my body is thrown forward, and the seatbelt cuts into my chest. I utter a shocked cry, but it's lost in his mouth when he grabs my shoulders and presses our lips together. His kiss is frantic and brutal. His teeth cut my tongue, and the force of his caress bruises my lips. My jaw aches when he finally lets me go. We're both breathing hard, our chests rising and falling rapidly. I can only stare at him, both turned on and frightened.

"Valentina…" A flash of something tightens his eyes and makes his nostrils flare. "You have no idea…" He drags a hand through his hair, messing it up more.

I swallow away the constriction in my throat that makes it hard to speak. "I said I was sorry."

He cups my cheek and brushes a thumb under my eye. "Not as sorry as I am."

In that moment, he lets me see his anguish. I remember what he said about having a heart the night I asked him about his scars. Compassion replaces my irritation.

I place my hand over his. "It's going to be all right."

A flicker of a smile plucks at his lips. "I'm supposed to say that, dammit."

"Then say it." I dare him with my eyes, urging him to let go of whatever darkness took hold of him.

"It's going to be fine, Valentina."

"That's better." I bring his palm to my mouth and plant a kiss on it.

"I'm supposed to do that, too," he says with a hint of sadness.

I wordlessly offer him my palm, but he doesn't kiss the inside. He draws my hand to his lips and sucks my forefinger into the warm depth of his mouth, biting down gently on the tip. Heat floods my underwear as he swirls his tongue around the digit. Then he pulls my wet finger from his mouth and dries it on his shirt. The kiss he leaves on the top of my hand is the opposite of what he did to my mouth. It's sweet, tender, and careful. After holding my eyes for another second, he puts my hand in the same position as earlier on his thigh and steers the car back into the traffic. When he's not shifting gears, he plays with my fingers, rubbing his thumb over my knuckles.

At home, Rhett opens the door and helps me from the car. "If you need help with anything, you only have to say."

"Thanks for driving me, yesterday."

Gabriel's dark expression stills Rhett. I'm not sure what Gabriel's problem with Rhett is, but the guard immediately excuses himself and leaves.

Inside, Quincy and Carly rush to greet us.

"Show me your hand," Carly exclaims. "You could've told me."

I hold up my bandaged thumb. "It's not so bad."

"Lunch is in the oven," Quincy says. "We had to improvise, but it's edible." He turns to me, looking guilty. "I shouldn't have left, yesterday. I should've stayed and helped."

"It's not your fault."

"Come on, Dad," Carly hooks her arm around Gabriel's. "I'm starving."

He hesitates for a second before he follows her to the dining room, his eyes finding mine over his shoulder.

To be honest, I'm happy for the time alone. I haven't dealt with the shock, yet, and I want solitude to process what happened. Oscar greets me by the entrance to the kitchen, rubbing his soft body against my legs.

"Hey, baby." I take a moment to pet him and check that he has food.

There's no place to put the enormous bouquet of flowers in my room, so I borrow a vase from the crystal cupboard and leave them on the counter in the kitchen. Thankfully, Quincy left the kitchen tidy. I'm prohibited from using my hand or working for a week, but I won't allow that to give Magda a reason to kill me. Or Charlie. She's only biding her time, waiting for the right excuse. Packing the dishwasher and doing a few minor chores, I find that I cope well enough with one hand, but Magda grudgingly tells me to take the rest of the day off. I use that time to rest, catching up on sleep.

Much later, Gabriel comes to my room. He covers every inch of my skin in kisses and makes love to me gently. When he holds me afterward, I allow the warmth of his arms to soothe me. Uninvited tears flow over my cheeks. The grief of giving up my studies and the shock of the accident come tumbling down on me, pushing me under a wave of sorrow that makes it hard to breathe. Sobs wrack my shoulders as I cling to him, holding onto the man who took my freedom. In what feels like my darkest hour, he's all I have. It's so damn screwed up. How much more can I handle before Gabriel completely destroys me?

He pulls me into his lap and kisses the top of my head. "Hush, beautiful."

"Gabriel." I bury my face in his neck, inhaling the spicy fragrance of his skin. "Set me free, I beg you."

He rests his chin on my head and inhales slowly. "You may as well ask me to cut off my arm."

When I fall asleep a long time later, I dream that I'm standing on one end of a hospital corridor and Gabriel on the other. Between us, there are rows of people with horrendous injuries, the number of patients too big to count. I'm pushing my way through the bodies, trying to reach him, but when I get to the other side, he's gone. I wake up in a fit of pain, sweating, and alone in my bed. I take a painkiller and count a hundred sheep ten times before I drift off again.

Gabriel

THE FIRST THING I do the following morning, is have the meat saw driven to the dump. The second is to take out medical insurance for Valentina. As long as I'm alive, I'll cover her bills, but I may not live as long as I'd like, especially not with my kind of business. I almost fired Rhett for his stupidity of taking her to the goddamn Joburg Gen. The only thing that saved his skin is that I couldn't punish him for my negligence. I should've thought about Valentina's health the minute she crossed my doorstep. I should've informed my staff in the case of an emergency, she's to be treated like any member of the family. All sorts of bad things could've happened. She could've bled to death. She could've caught an infection. With all the filth and blood around the Joburg Gen, she could've contracted AIDS. To think she considered sewing back her own thumb. That she didn't panic gives me a new level of respect for her. It's one thing to stitch me back together, but quite another to pick your thumb off the floor and not raise the roof in hysterics.

She's managing with one hand, like she always does, but this isn't what I want for her. She's been in my house for less than a quarter of a year, and my perfect doll is already broken. I threatened her with the whip if she doesn't rest. Magda isn't happy with the turn of events, but she only raises the issue when we're alone in the car on our way to one of the loan offices.

"Why did you do it?"

I glance at her from over the rim of my sunglasses. "Do what?"

"Pay Valentina's hospital bill."

"Jesus, Magda, did you expect me to sit back and let her lose her thumb? Anyway, Rhett paid for it. I only reimbursed him."

"You're investing in dead meat."

"We've been through this enough times already."

"When are you going to let go?"

"When I'm ready."

"When will that be?"

I gave her a hard look. "When I'm damn well ready and not a second before."

"I've been lenient with you, but my patience is wearing thin. Don't make me choose a date."

"I'll choose a date," I say evasively, placating her for now. Maneuvering the car down the steep hill into Braamfontein, I ask the question that, for the last few weeks, has been foremost on my mind. "Why do you want her dead?"

She blinks and looks away. "I told you, to make an example out of her."

"Why her?"

"Why not?"

"If it's just about the money, I'll settle her debt."

She turns in her seat. "You're willing to buy that little slut?"

Anger spurts into my veins, setting my heart off at a dangerous beat. "She's anything but a slut."

She gives a cynical snort. "Maybe you prefer a different term, but she's your fuck toy, and in my opinion that makes her a slut."

"Easy, Magda," I say evenly. "You're pushing me too far."

"Gabriel," her voice takes on a softer tone, "you can never trust her. If you lower your guard, she'll stab a knife in your back or steal you blind."

I can't say for sure about the knife in my back. I'm sure Valentina has wished me dead plenty of times. What I do know is that she's not a thief.

"She's been managing the food budget since Marie's stroke, and she's saving us a lot of money."

"That doesn't say anything."

"It says she's trustworthy where money's concerned. Don't think I'm unaware of the money Marie pocketed for herself with the kickback she got from the suppliers."

"It's small money."

"Doesn't change the principle. Stealing is stealing, which makes Marie a thief. Yet, you never lashed out at her."

"That's different. Marie is practically part of the family. Her mother worked for my mother. Your fuck doll is neither family nor loyal. I don't care how much money she's saving us, her time's running out."

"Let it go."

At the cold deliberation in my tone, she turns her head to look through the window. "Anyway, I'm not interested in selling her. You won't settle her debt."

I let it slide, making an effort to calm myself. "I called our old cleaning service company. They'll stand in until next week."

My mother scoots up straighter. "You did what?"

"Valentina is booked off. You know that."

"This is the perfect opportunity to let her fail."

I clench my jaw. "Don't make me repeat myself."

"Fine." She waves a hand in the air. "Treat her like a princess and wrap her in cotton wool. It'll make her fall so much harder."

My fingers tighten on the wheel. I feel like leaning over my mother, opening her door, and shoving her out of my car and my life. We keep on clashing heads over this, and if she can't accept that Valentina is a part of our lives for good, it's going to get ugly.

THE WEEK DRAGS on with Valentina being withdrawn and quiet, keeping to her room. At least she has time to rest and maybe study. She still hasn't told me about her studies. I'm not sure if she's hiding something else from me, or if it's the after-effect of the anesthesia that's giving her the blues, but she's not herself. I suppose it's normal, given what she's been through. All I can do is give her my support and care until she's back in the kitchen in her black dress. I'm not happy about it, but I haven't found a solution to the dilemma, yet, and Magda won't budge.

On top of my worry about Valentina, I need to raise a difficult issue with Carly. Carly doesn't normally eat in the morning, but since Magda isn't present today, I ask my daughter to have breakfast with me so we can speak in private.

I wait until Valentina has left us after serving bran muffins before I say, "I know you love your mother and our divorce was tough on you. We didn't discuss it much when the breakup happened. I think it's important that you have someone neutral to talk to."

She stares at me with wide eyes. "It's a bit late for that."

"It's never too late."

"It won't help." She hides her face behind her hair.

"You can't say unless you've tried."

She pushes the fruit around on her plate.

"Stop hiding behind your hair and look at me."

She lifts her head, her eyes throwing daggers at me. "There's only one thing that'll help, and that's if you and mom get back together."

I sigh deeply. "It's not going to happen. You have to accept it."

She bangs her fork down on her plate. "Why not? Why can't you live together like a normal couple?"

"Your mother and I, we don't love each other any more. That doesn't mean we don't love you."

"Bullshit." She pushes her chair back and jumps to her feet. "You don't know the meaning of the word."

Grabbing her bag, she sprints for the door.

"Carly!"

I want to order her to come back and finish her breakfast, but my common sense tells me to give her space until she has cooled down. Dwelling on my parental problems, I finish my breakfast alone, even if I no longer have an appetite.

Valentina's voice pulls me to the present. "Can I clear the plates?"

The new melancholy that has invaded her makes her big, sad eyes more haunting than ever. I gather my plate and glass to carry it to the kitchen, and return with the tray while Valentina takes the rest. Knowing how proud she is, I try to make things easier for her without making it obvious. While I'm loading my plate in the dishwasher, I notice that she scoops Carly's untouched muffin from the plate, carefully wrapping it in a paper napkin. The rest of my half-eaten muffin she packs into an ice cream container half-full with bones, bits of meat, and cooked vegetables, which she keeps in the staff fridge. I've never seen her clear the table before, but it's obvious she's in the habit of collecting the left overs. What does she do with the food that's meant for the compost bin? My morning conference call is due, so I don't give it further thought, but leave the kitchen with a feeling I can't place. It's as if my time with both Carly and Valentina is running out. I don't like it. The last time I felt like this was right before I tripped a wire and was left for dead with half of my face blown to pieces.

I TIME my meetings so that I'm free during Valentina's lunch breaks to check on her. Before going outside, I spend a few undisturbed minutes observing her through the kitchen window. I love looking at her like this, when her guard is down. The perverseness in me likes to invade her privacy, stealing a part of her I'll otherwise never have. I came to accept that Valentina will never be one hundred percent open with me. Our forced relationship isn't the kind that nurtures an unconditional sharing of the soul.

As always, she's sitting on the low wall by the pool. Bruno is lying next to her on the grass, his head on his paws, staring up at her with doting eyes. Her hands are cupped around an object, like the petals that protect the stigma of a flower. She opens them to reveal something round and white. What is she holding? It looks like a paper napkin. Folding the napkin open carefully, she breaks the muffin that's inside in two, and feeds one half to Bruno while she eats the other. The dog gobbles it up in one gulp, and wags his tail optimistically, watching to see if more is coming. She eats slowly, like a person who tastes every bite.

Everything inside of me slams to a standstill. What I'm witnessing is an ordinary scene of a woman nourishing her body, but it shatters me. I've seen many atrocious deeds and tortures that will make most grown men crumble, but *this*--Valentina eating our leftover food--this does something to me not even a killing does. I'll double her allowance and buy her more food. I'll put her brother in a fancy institute. I'll do anything it takes for her to never have to eat the crumbs from someone else's table again. That bursary better come through soon. I go back to my study and call my CFO, who ensures me it's a matter of days now. Some red tape at the university is slowing down the process.

When I go to her that night, I decide to broach the subject. I strip her naked and drive my cock into her, keeping us both on a precipice of pleasure. I drag it out until neither of us can tolerate it any longer.

Her nails dig into my shoulders. "Gabriel, please." She rocks her hips against mine, trying to create more friction.

I pull out almost completely and still my movements. "Who do you belong to?"

She shivers when I press my thumb on her clit. "You."

"Who takes care of you?"

"You."

"How do I take care of you?"

"However you like."

"Damn right. How the hell ever I like." Her back arches when I pinch her nipple. "Who makes you come?" I shove back into her.

"You," she cries on a gasp.

"Who dresses you?"

"You."

I move again in all earnest. "Who feeds you?"

"Ah, God, Gabriel! You."

"That's right, beautiful." I kiss her lips. "Me."

I slam our bodies together so hard I have to cup her head to prevent it from hitting the wall. She cries my name as she comes with a violent spasm, her pussy sucking me deeper and milking me dry. There's nothing more satisfying than coming inside her. I empty my body in hers, making her take every drop, but I don't pull out. Her cheeks are flushed, and her hair sticks to her damp forehead.

I frame her face between my hands. "Anything you need, you've got it. You only have to say the word. Understand?"

She closes her eyes.

"Look at me, Valentina."

When she opens them again, they're moist with tears. "Why are you doing this? It's not part of our deal."

I kiss each eyelid and then her nose. "Because I'm everything you need."

The sadness in her gaze intensifies, fueling my fear, which in terms spurs my anger. "Say it."

She licks her lips, but doesn't reply.

I wrap my fingers around her neck and squeeze. "Say it, damn you."

Her body tenses, but she doesn't fight my hold. Instead, her shoulders sag as she slowly lets out a breath. "Yes, Gabriel. You are my everything."

Heated satisfaction warms my balls, spreading all the way up my spine. My cock grows hard inside her again. I have her in every way I want, but I still need her in so many ways. Rising on my knees, I hook her legs over my shoulders and use my cum to lubricate her ass. She screams when I enter her there, but with my fingers in her pussy and on her clit, she quickly gives me the moans of ecstasy I'm after. Long after she had her second orgasm, I'm still punishing myself with new pleasure. It takes a long time before my second release. With her, I can go all night, but she needs her rest, so I gather her body against mine and hold her until she falls asleep.

Valentina

My mother used to say if something bad happens, celebrate something positive. That way, you'll never become depressed. Maybe that's how she survived when my dad died and we lost everything. She never left the house without red Estee Lauder lipstick.

"If you're sad, Valentina," she used to say, "put on your red lipstick."

I fish the tube I ordered with my supplies from my bag and apply the lipstick in the mirror. The red stands out on my tanned skin. I scrunch my curls around my face, letting their natural glossiness stand out. I'm wearing the pink T-shirt, jeans, and flats from the Sandton boutique. On the outside, I look pretty. No one will know how broken I am on the inside. Maybe, one day, I'll be able to just look at the pretty and forget that I've been a whore to the most dangerous killer in the city.

When I say goodbye to Gabriel for the weekend, he looks at me like he may object to me leaving the house with the makeup on my face, but I'm not his daughter, and this is *my* time.

He swallows as he studies me, jiggling the keys in his pocket. "I'll drive you."

I don't argue anymore. It's pointless. On the way, I ask him to stop at the corner bakery to pick up a Black Forest Cake. I could've baked it for half the price, but that's not the point. I've never purchased a cake in my life. I hold the fancy shop cake in its plastic container on my lap, the black cherries shiny with sugary syrup on top of the whipped cream.

Gabriel glances at the cake and then at me. "Whose birthday is it? I know it's not yours."

"No one." I look from the window at the passing cars.

"What's the occasion?"

"Nothing."

He purses his lips, but doesn't continue the interrogation. Near Rocky Street, I ask him to stop again so I can feed the hungry dogs. The minute they see me, they come running. Gabriel leans against the car with his ankles crossed, watching me as I distribute the food between them. I wipe the plastic container out with a paper towel, and wrap it in a plastic bag to wash later. A shadow of a smile plays on his lips as I get back to the car.

"What?"

He tucks a strand of hair behind my ear. "You're every kind of good."

"No, I'm not."

"To me, you are."

He doesn't give me a chance to reply. He opens the door and helps me inside.

When he drops me off across the road from Kris' place, I wait until his car turns the corner before I head over to the house. Charlie nearly knocks me off my feet as I enter through the kitchen door.

"Hey." I laugh and deposit the cake on the counter. "How are you?" I take him into a big hug. There's more meat on his bones and a tube around his middle.

"Ca–cake!"

"It's for after dinner." I squeeze his shoulders and sit down next to him on the couch, switching off the television.

We play Chinese Checkers until Kris locks up the practice. As habitual, I cook, and she gets to take a much-needed break after she spends the first ten minutes freaking out about my thumb. When Charlie is seated with a big slice of cake in front of his favorite cartoon, she takes the chair opposite me at the kitchen table.

"What's with the cake?" she asks through the motion of chewing.

"We're celebrating."

"We are?"

"Yep." I lick the chocolate filling off my spoon.

"Can you be a little less secretive?"

I shrug. "We're celebrating that I have more free time and money. I can now pay you proper board for Charlie."

She makes big eyes at me. "Did he give you a pay rise? More off-time?"

I take a big bite. My mouth is too full to answer.

"Well?"

I wipe the cream from the corner of my mouth with my good thumb and lick it clean. "Not exactly."

"Val." Kris pushes her plate away and folds her arms on the table. "What's going on?"

"I dropped out of uni."

I'm saying it like I just told her it's hot today, hoping she'll let it go, but I already know better.

"Like in, quit your studies?" she exclaims.

Charlie looks up from the television.

"Shh." I give her my best angry frown. "You'll make him think something's wrong."

"Something *is* wrong."

"Kris."

"Why?"

"Look at it this way, I don't have the burden of paying a huge school bill any longer, or worries about exams, and spending late nights studying anatomy."

She dips her head, searching for my eyes. "Why?"

I sigh. "The cook had a stroke. I took over her duties."

"They're going to hire another cook, right? You can't give up. Val, you've completed more than half of the course!"

"I can't keep up the job and the studies. It's too much."

Her lips thin. "You're letting them win."

"I don't have a choice," I say through gritted teeth. "I work until dinner is served and the kitchen is clean, which means I'm lucky if I get off at ten. God, I'm lucky if I go to bed by midnight, and I'm up at four every morning." I don't say that Gabriel occupies another hour or more of my day, fucking me senseless and giving me orgasms until I pass out.

Emotions play on her face. Thank God she doesn't say something meaningless like she's sorry.

"It's for Charlie." I lower my voice. "Nothing will matter anyway if he's dead. He's all I've got."

She covers my hand with hers. It is a big, strong hand with cat scratches and dog bite marks, and a calloused skin that tells its own story. "You've got me, babes."

Warmth spreads through my chest, making tears build at the back of my eyes. "Thank you."

"You can still work here. I mean, after…"

"I know." After nine years, I'm not sure I'll still have the stomach for this city. "Eat your cake. I paid a lot of money for it."

"You better hide the rest or Charlie will devour it in the night."

Worry nags at me. "He's picking up weight."

"Sorry. I'm not here much, I'm afraid, or I would've taken him out for exercise."

"I have an idea."

"Uh-uh. When you get that light bulb moment look, I get worried."

I prop my foot on the seat of my chair, hugging my knee. "He can walk the dogs."

"You mean *them*?" She throws her thumb at the door adjoining to the clinic.

"Yes! He crosses the road by himself, right? We can try with one dog first and see how it goes. I can go with him tomorrow."

"I suppose it can't do harm."

"It'll be good for him to get out more, breathe in some fresh air."

She snorts. "What fresh air? In case you haven't noticed, this is Joburg."

I'm not having my spirits dampened, not tonight. "Charlie and I'll do the first doggie walk together."

"You're a good sister, Val. Charlie's lucky to have you."

"No, I'm lucky to have him."

I'm still raw about my studies, but there's a reason I'm doing this. The reason is a beautiful, innocent boy trapped in the body of a man who sits on Kris' couch with a huge smile on his face. All it takes to make Charlie happy is a piece of cake. I should learn from him.

Gabriel

The therapist knocks on my door at ten sharp, as agreed. Dorothy Botha is a short, attractive woman in her late forties. She's wearing tight jeans and a stretch shirt, not the attire I imagined for a psychiatrist. At the rate I'm paying for the house call, I expected her to show up in Dior or Gucci.

She shakes my hand, and offers a smile. "Mr. Louw."

"Call me Gabriel. Thank you for meeting Carly at home. It's more comfortable for her in her own environment." And there's less chance for one of our enemies to discover my daughter has instability issues. They'll use anything they can against me.

I show her to the reading room where Carly sits on the couch, her legs pulled up under her. My daughter gives me a cutting look when we enter and doesn't offer Dorothy a greeting. Every part of her body languages says she's not happy about spending her Sunday morning with a shrink.

"Carly, this is Mrs. Botha. Say hi."

"Say hi," Carly parrots.

I'm about to lose my cool and give her a lecture about proper manners, but Dorothy lays her hand on my arm.

"You can call me Dorothy." She takes the chair opposite Carly and looks up at me expectantly.

I get it. She wants me to leave. "Coffee, tea?"

"No, thank you." She's pleasant, but firm.

"All right, then." I close the door, hoping to God Dorothy will accomplish what neither me nor Sylvia is able to do--get Carly to open up.

While the women are talking, or *hopefully* talking, I clear the table from our late breakfast, and feed Oscar. He's got a new brand of food, the same as Bruno. With the price on the tag, they must put gold flakes in the kibbles. The brand's worth its weight in gold, though, because Bruno's allergies have disappeared, and Oscar's coat is thick and glossy. Bruno's food is delivered to our door from our local vet. I pay the bill. No cat food is included. The specialty food isn't available at supermarkets. If Valentina doesn't order it with our daily groceries, where does it come from?

Magda walks into the kitchen, dressed up in her black and white Chanel suit. "Where's Carly? I want to invite her for lunch."

I cross my arms, and lean on the counter. "Where?"

"The McKenzies."

My back immediately turns rigid. "Not interested."

"Come on, Gabriel." She props her clutch bag on her hip. "Carly's never going to take your place. She hasn't got it in her. Our only chance is finding her the right husband."

"I said no."

She advances two steps, stopping short of me. "Do you have a cleverer idea? What if something happens to you? Or me? Who's going to take over our business? Not that gold-digging, ex-wife of yours. Word's going around she's got her sights set on Francois. If she marries him and we can't provide a successor, that slimy rat will take over as Carly's stepdad. Is that what you want?"

Acid burns my mouth. Francois is a pretty boy five years Sylvia's junior, but that's not what's bothering me. It's the idea of him playing stepdad to Carly that I can't digest.

"Answer me. Is that what you want?"

"Is that all you care about, finding a successor for the business? What about Carly's happiness?"

"Happiness?" She laughs. "Carly is my granddaughter, but by God, she's a spoiled child. You got her used to this." She waves her arms around the room. "You give her everything her heart desires. You think she's going to ever settle for less? I don't think so."

"Don't project your sentiments on Carly."

"Oh, money is as important to her as it is to me. Let's face it, even if she's not a leader, she's a Louw. She'll do her duty for our name."

"Don't you dare treat her like a pawn in your business. Carly's not going to lead the life I live."

"The life *you* live? You want to live the life of one of our debtors? Want to see what it's like on the poor side of the fence? Do you know what happens to you and your daughter at night when you don't have enough money for an alarm system that criminals can't break through?"

"I know what happens. I've seen it."

"You haven't *felt* it. Believe me, you don't want to live any other life than this life." She scrutinizes me. "You're getting soft, Gabriel. It's that girl, isn't it?"

My hackles rise. "She's got nothing to do with this. Valentina or no

Valentina, I'll never marry Carly off to Benjamin McKenzie."

"I hope for your sake you're growing tired of fucking your toy."

Every muscle in my body tenses. My injured leg protests against the strain. "What's that supposed to mean?"

"A cat only plays with a mouse for so long before he goes for the kill. Why isn't she dead, yet?"

My heart drops like an ax splitting wood. "I'm not ready."

"I've been patient with you. I gave you the toy you so badly wanted. We made a deal. Now I'm giving you a direct order. Kill her, or I'll do it for you."

I almost jump on her. I'm a hairbreadth away from her face before I stop myself. "You'll do nothing for me, do you hear me?"

"You have one last chance. Make it sooner than later." She smiles sweetly. "You're not twelve any more. Don't make me shoot you in the foot."

My vision goes blurry. I'm about to strangle my own mother in our kitchen. The only thing that stops me from reaching for her scrawny, white, wrinkled neck, is Carly's figure that appears in the doorframe.

There's a chill in her voice. "We're done."

"I'm going out for lunch, Carly dear. Why don't you join me?"

"Magda is having lunch at the McKenzies," I say, knowing how much Carly hates Benjamin.

"No thanks, Gran. I've got homework." She trots down the hallway, pretending I don't exist.

When Carly is out of earshot, I narrow my eyes. "Let me handle my own affairs and leave Carly out of the business." Giving my mother my back, I walk from the room, feeling the tension in my leg.

"Softness will get you killed, Gabriel," she calls after me.

Dorothy waits in the reading room.

I close the door and take a seat. "How did it go?"

She wipes her fingers over her brow. "She's tough to talk to. Of course, I need to win her trust first." She looks at me from under her lashes. "I pick up a need for approval and acceptance. Are you spending enough time with her?"

"Not as much as I'd like."

"Busy job?"

"It's not that. Carly would rather spend time with her friends than her father."

"It's normal. Try to strengthen her self-esteem by complimenting her for homework well done or good deeds, anything positive, but be authentic. Make sure she knows you're noticing her and taking an interest in her life."

"I assure you, I am."

"I don't doubt that, or I wouldn't be here. Just make sure you show her as well as tell her. It will help, of course, if I can have a joint session with you and your ex-wife to agree on a consistent strategy that will reinforce your daughter's self-image."

"I'm afraid you won't find much cooperation from my ex-wife."

"Ah, well." She wipes her hands on her thighs and straightens. "Let's see how it goes after a couple of sessions. Try to maintain the status quo at home. Don't introduce any new or stressful situations if you can avoid it, at least not for a while."

"Such as?"

"A stepmom."

"Carly's worried about that?"

"She mentioned it. I know this is a personal question, but are you seeing anyone, maybe a lady friend your daughter doesn't get on with?"

"No." Not that Carly knows of, at least.

"Then Carly's fear is unfounded. It's not uncommon for children to feel lost after a divorce. Carly's frightened of losing you or her mother to someone else. Reassure her of your affection whenever you can."

"Of course."

"I'll see you next week, same time."

"I'll walk you to the door."

Even as I speak, my mind is drifting to a reoccurring thought. How will Carly react if she ever finds out about Valentina?

Valentina

REGRET IS NOT A CONDUCIVE SENTIMENT. Still, I can't help from feeling it when I read the letter addressed to me that Gabriel brings to the kitchen on Monday morning. Reading it with my back to him, I curl my fingers in a fist until my nails cut into my skin. I want to cry, but he's hovering at the coffee machine.

"Good news?"

I glance at him from over my shoulder. He's dressed in a dark suit with a blue shirt and yellow tie. He makes the ensemble look perfect. The tailored pants stretch over his narrow hips, which emphasizes the broadness of his chest. His unique fragrance beckons me, but I need to be alone to deal with the news.

I shrug.

"All right." He says it like a threat, making me understand he'll let me get away with my disobedience of not giving him a reply for now, but maybe not later.

I hold my breath until he has left the room. Only when I'm alone do I allow the emotions to explode inside of me. I grab the edges of the counter so hard my arms shake from the strain. The letter crumples in my fist. I scrunch it up until it's a tiny ball. Of all the sick jokes in the world, this one must have the best timing. I bang my fists on the counter, setting the bowls and knives and spoons clanging. For all of three seconds, I allow myself every single destructive emotion that lances into my heart, and then I lift the lid of the trashcan and dump the letter informing me of my all-inclusive scholarship inside. When the lid falls back with a clang, something inside of me ceases to exist. What's left is the hollow echo of a dream and nothing more than the will to survive.

Gabriel

THE LETTER that arrived from the university this morning should've made Valentina ecstatic. There's a change in her I don't understand. After doing my morning rounds at our franchises in town, I head to her friend's place where Charlie lives. The woman waiting in reception with a Miniature Doberman shrinks back when she looks up at my face. Walking past her with practiced ignorance, I venture to the food section and lift my sunglasses to read the labels. I pull a bag of the urinary diet brand Valentina bought for Oscar from the shelf and carry it to the till. A few minutes pass before a peroxide blonde in a white overcoat exits. Hard lines mar her weathered face, and her fingernails are broken. Her eyes give away nothing as she assesses me. They flitter from me to the bag of food standing on the counter.

"Can I help you?"

"Is this the best brand you've got?"

"By far."

I lean an elbow on the counter and check out the board with the rates for neutering and vaccinations. "My housekeeper buys it for my cat. I don't know the brand, but I thought I'd get the same."

Her eyes flare for the briefest of seconds before she narrows them. "Your housekeeper is a clever girl."

"She sure is, but she should've told me she's paying for the food out of her own pocket."

"Maybe she couldn't, because she knows you don't care much for your cat."

The lady with the Doberman is watching us, her head bobbing between the vet and me.

"It's true. I don't care for the hair that he sheds in my house or the fact that he tears my curtains to pieces, but my housekeeper seems to like him, so here's the deal. I'll open an account and send a driver once a month to collect the food." I point at the large breed dog food of the same brand. "You can throw in a couple of bags of that, as well."

It almost looks as if she's going to refuse me, but the state of her waiting room tells me she needs the business. After a moment of measuring me, she says, "I'll take down your details."

She writes my address and phone number down in a book. In this day and age, nobody uses a book, not even my most unsophisticated loan sharks. She has a patient waiting, and me taking a chunk of her consultation time. What she needs is a computer and an assistant. No wonder she's operating in a run-down building, charging fees lower than the going rate.

I tap my fingers on the countertop as she scribbles down my order. "You should go electronic."

She lifts her head to give me a cutting look. "I'll upgrade when I can afford it."

I don't blame her for hating me. What makes her different than the rest of the world? In any event, I'm not out to win anyone's love. I can forget about getting information on Valentina's emotional state of late from this woman. She won't give me a glass of water if I'm dying.

She slams the book closed. "Are we done?"

I let the sunglasses fall back over my eyes. "For now."

Saluting her, I take the food and walk to the door. The Doberman whines as I pass her owner who leans as far away from me as she can without falling out of her chair.

Valentina

This lasagna can't flop. I'm so engrossed in letting the white sauce thicken without forming lumps that I don't notice Rhett until he's right next to me. Startled, I drop the whisk. It bounces on the stovetop, rolls off the edge, and hits the ground. It's the first time he's set foot in the kitchen since I arrived. He bends down to retrieve the whisk and rinses it under the tap before handing it back to me.

"Thank you." I use my left hand to stir the sauce.

He motions at the bandage on my thumb. "How's the hand?"

"Good, thank you."

He gives a wry smile. "I didn't get a chance to apologize for driving you to the Joburg Gen. If I had any idea the place was that bad, I would've gone directly to the clinic."

"You did what I asked."

"I wasn't thinking straight. I saw the blood and kind of blanked out."

I can't help but smile. "You? Seriously?"

He lifts his palms in a gesture of surrender. "It wasn't the blood as much as it was *you*. I thought Gabriel was going to kill me."

"For what?"

"It happened on my shift."

"It wasn't your fault."

"Wouldn't have mattered. I was the messenger."

I stop stirring to look at him. "I'm sorry if I got you into trouble."

He grins. "Not as much trouble as you got yourself into. No more kitchen accidents, okay?"

"I'll do my best." I return my attention to the sauce.

He leans on the counter and crosses his ankles. "I was thinking of getting you a puppy."

"A puppy?"

"I already cleared it with Gabriel." He shifts his weight around. "I can get you one of those fluffy dogs women like. A Maltese Poodle or something."

"I don't want a dog."

He looks disappointed. "Why not?"

"I've lost enough. I don't want to care about another dog."

He uncrosses his ankles and crosses his arms, not meeting my eyes.

When he doesn't speak, but doesn't leave either, I remove the sauce from the heat, and turn to face him squarely. "Why did you shoot Puff, Rhett?"

His chest expands, as if he's taking a breath, and when he lifts his gaze again, he regards me with a level stare. "I didn't want to leave the dog to fend for himself on the streets."

"What?"

"I've seen enough of dogs to know that mongrel wasn't going to make it on his own. Leaving him would've meant a drawn-out, cruel death of starvation."

"Leaving him?"

His voice takes on a quiet tone. "When we broke into your flat that morning, it was with explicit orders."

The blood drains from my head, leaving me with a fuzzy feeling. Rhett was certain we weren't going to get out alive, neither Charlie nor me. Oh, my God. Gabriel wasn't there just for Charlie. He was going to kill us both. I put the information away in the back of my mind to deal with later. Alone.

"I don't know why Gabriel changed his mind, but I can assure you, it's never happened before."

My laugh is forced. "My mother used to say I have a guardian angel. Maybe she was right."

"If it'll make you feel better, Gabriel fucked me up good for killing your dog."

"That day you came out of the gym with a broken nose."

"Yep. Look, I'll sleep a whole lot better if you'll let me get you that dog."

The look he gives me is so remorseful that my compassion wins over my vengeance over Puff. Logically, I understand why he did it. It doesn't make it right or better, but I'm not in a position to deny anyone redemption. I'm still chasing after absolution for what happened to Charlie. Wiping my hands on my apron, I consider his proposal. Another living being will only make me more vulnerable than what I already am, because that's what caring for someone or something does.

"I don't want a dog. I want you to train me."

He looks at me like I lost my mind. "What?"

"Teach me self-defense. We can practice in the gym."

"Gabriel will kill me."

"Not if he doesn't know. We can do it when he's out."

"It's a crazy idea, Valentina."

"Is it? Have you ever stood helpless while men took the money you busted your ass for? Have you ever been held down and violated, unable to do a goddamn thing about it?"

He averts his eyes, unable to hold mine.

"Please, Rhett. I'm not going to use it against anyone in this house. I'm not stupid. I just don't want to feel helpless any longer."

He swallows. "Ask me anything else. If Gabriel finds out--"

"He won't, not unless you tell him."

He looks at me again, a war waging in his eyes. Finally, it's his guilt that wins out. "Fine, but not a word to anyone, not even Quincy."

"All right."

He straightens from the counter, but his shoulders sag. "I'll let you know when the coast is clear."

"Thank you."

"Consider us even." There's a hint of apprehension and even fear in his expression as he walks from the room.

Gabriel

THE REPORT from Anton only confirms what I already know. No one knows anything about Valentina's rape. I drop the pen on my desk and rub my tired eyes. I'm not surprised Marvin didn't go to the police. His family was shamed. The way he would've dealt with the crime was to avenge his daughter's stolen innocence by killing the man responsible. Since he died in the same year she was assaulted, I'm not sure he got around to it. Is that why Lambert abandoned his promised fiancée? Because she was spoiled goods? Find the bastard who raped her I will, but for now I have a bigger priority--Magda's threat.

Never underestimate Magda. I know what she's capable of better than anyone. If I don't kill Valentina, she *will* do it, and as punishment for my disobedience she'll do it in a way that will hurt me. I'm not shy about my habits. My mother knows I fuck like some people take up a hobby. She knows I'm territorial and the most possessive bastard on the face of the earth. She knows me well enough to understand that the thought of another man's hands on Valentina will drive me to my knees, especially after what I did to Diogo. Valentina's death is a place

I can't even go. If Magda has to finish the job for me, Valentina will most likely suffer gang rape followed by a horrendous and slow death of torture. I have to find a way to keep her, but there's nowhere I can hide her where Magda's network of business associates won't find her. And then there's Charlie. What do I do with him? Where do I keep him safe? I made a deal with Valentina and, knowing how much Charlie means to her, this is one I intend to honor. Every problem has a solution. I just have to look hard enough.

Seeing that I have precious little time, I should be searching for a way to keep my beautiful toy, not slamming my study door, and stalking the hallway like a crazed man, my steps taking me where they always do, Valentina's room. It's late. Magda and Carly have long since gone to bed, but I still keep a watchful eye.

Just a few minutes. I need a break to clear my mind. Chasing improbable solutions to escape Magda's promise has sent me in circles like a dog chasing his own tail. I need to hold her, see her, taste her, breathe her, to calm the clawing fear of losing her.

When I walk into her bedroom, she steps from the bathroom, her hair wet and her body damp. She stops in the doorframe. The bandage is dry. Good. The last thing I want is more worry. I need her too much.

For a few seconds, we have a stare-down, each one of us waiting for the other to make a move. There are a million things I can do with her. I should punish her for this morning's obstinance when she gave me the cold shoulder, but I won't touch her like that when she's injured. I haven't yet made up my mind when she closes the distance between us, placing her delicate body in front of mine like a vulnerable white pawn in the path of the black stallion's hooves. The position is a physical reminder of the difference in power between us. I can throw her on the bed and eat her pussy from the inside out, I can fuck every hole in her body, or kiss her until she can't breathe. She's mine to do with as I please. I overcompensated for my looks by becoming a master of physical pleasure. I can't give her a pretty face, but I can make her scream with orgasms until there's not a breath of air left in her lungs.

Her hands reach for my shirt. I'm curious. Is she going to undress me? She grips the edges of the fabric above the first button and yanks them apart. Fuck dammit. There's a tearing sound and buttons flying everywhere. She goes up on her toes to push the shirt over my shoulders, but the sleeves get stuck on my upper arms. Abandoning her efforts with the shirt, she focuses on my belt instead, her fingers fumbling with the buckle.

My heart is beating like the hooves of that dark horse she unleashed, and I'm frightened that the beast will crush her when he lets his passion rein free, but I'm too weak to stop her. Finally managing to pull the leather from the loops of my waistband, she folds it double and pushes it into my hand. It's there in her eyes, what she wants me to do. The brown of her irises is mud-stained and murky, like a dam after a landslide.

Under normal circumstances, I'd tie her up and give her what she wants, spank her while I fuck her, but it hasn't been a normal week. When I don't move, she cups my balls and squeezes them through my pants. Her tongue is hot and wet on my stomach, licking a line of molten lava up my chest. Her small teeth latch onto my nipple. I jerk when she bites. Bloody hell. She lets go to bite into the muscle of my pec, then pulls back to study the marks she left on my skin. Her hands snake around my neck, pulling me down to her lips. The nip she gives my bottom lip draws blood. Her nails dig into my scalp. She kisses me like a mad woman, moaning and rubbing her body against mine.

As suddenly as she grabbed me, she lets go, falling back onto the bed with open thighs. Her pussy is ripe for me, wet and swollen. I follow as if she's got me on a tight leash, but before I can straddle her she rolls over and gets up on her knees, offering her ass and pussy. It is a sight so alluring I almost lose my reason. I don't move my eyes from the clean-shaved triangle between her legs as I kick off my shoes and almost tear the zipper to get out of my pants. I take no more than a second to pull off my socks. Gripping her hips hard, I drag her to the edge of the bed, placing her where I need her.

"Take me, Gabriel. Take me hard." I'm about to do exactly that when she says, "Make it hurt. Make it hurt really bad."

My lust jerks to a halt. I get off on hurting her, but her pain ultimately brings us both pleasure. I'm using pain to train to her body to need me, but I won't allow her to use physical pain to escape her feelings. That's reserved for monsters like me, and I have no intention of turning her into a monster. I need her sweet and innocent. I need her for who she is.

She looks at me from over her shoulder. "Gabriel."

Her cry is a plea while her eyes are filled with fear--fear that I won't oblige. There aren't many things I'll deny her, but this I won't give.

"Gabriel!"

Her tiny hand folds around my shaft. I'm so hard I scarcely feel the pressure of her fingers as she guides me to her asshole. I know how an ass fuck without proper preparation feels for a woman. I made my lovers describe every sensation to me in detail. The fact that she wants this shows me how badly she's hurting inside.

"Fuck me already if you're a man."

I know what she's trying to do. "Provocation isn't going to work with me, beautiful."

Grabbing her around the waist with one arm, I shift her up the mattress. When I go down on my side, I bring her body with me, pressing her back to my chest.

"Fuck you, Gabriel!"

She struggles in all earnest, trying to break free, but I trap her in the constraint of my arms.

"Let me go!"

I hold her in place and plant the gentlest of kisses in her neck.

"No! Don't you dare."

I kiss her ear, her hair, and her temple with a soft brush of my lips. "You're so beautiful, Valentina. Have I ever told you that?"

Her voice breaks. "Please, don't."

I throw my leg over hers, confining her kicking legs while I push her upper body into the mattress to kiss her spine. Sobs shake her body, but I kiss every vertebra, working my way to the curve of her ass and back up.

"Not like this," she cries. "Not gently. Not like you care."

I give her all the tenderness I'm capable of, stroking my fingers over her firm ass and between her legs, testing her folds. She's wet. Always ready for me, just like I trained her. When I direct my cock to her entrance, she starts fighting me again, wiggling her upper body, and kicking with her legs. All I can do is hold her shoulders down with my arms and keep her legs trapped between mine while I enter her slick body, inch by slow inch until she's taken all of me. She's so hot and tight she makes me dizzy. With her thighs pressed together the friction is too much. With every stroke, I risk coming like an inexperienced adolescent.

"I hate you." Her words are muffled by the pillow, but her body is already rocking with mine. "Why can't you do it? Why don't you hurt me?"

I won't cut her air, I won't bury my cock in her ass, and I won't take my belt to her. It's my business to understand her needs, and what she needs right now is to be loved.

"Why didn't you kill me, Gabriel?"

I still. "What are you talking about?"

She turns her face to the side. "Rhett told me."

That fucker.

"That's why he shot my dog," she whispers. "We weren't supposed to make it out alive."

I start moving again, trying to still her with our pleasure, but she won't let it go.

There are tears in her voice. "Why Gabriel? Tell me, damn you."

"Because I wanted you," I grit out.

She pushes her ass up against my groin. "Is it this? You needed a fuck?"

I thrust deeper, making her moan. "You know why."

"You spared my life to make me your whore."

"Not my whore." I kiss the soft, golden skin of her shoulder. "My property."

"What's the difference?" she asks bitterly.

The difference is that property belongs. I find her lips, kissing her like she's mine, trying to show her that however much I trained her to need me, I need her in equal quantity. This time, she doesn't resist the gentleness of my touch. She kisses me back, our rhythm slow and revering. I glide my body over hers, the slickness of my sweat-damp skin making the friction smooth. The movement drives my shaft deeper. I feel her on every inch of me. A deep groan tears from my chest.

Goddammit, this is heaven. My balls pull up into my groin, and sharp needles pierce into the base of my spine. Fuck, not yet. I want to last. I still for a moment to bite back the pleasure. I drag my hands over her hair and down her shoulders, over the soft curves where her breasts are pressed flat against the mattress. She's soft and resilient and so much woman. I revel in invading her body, making her secrets and feelings mine. I push as deep as I can go, until my cock hits a barrier. A small gasp escapes her lips. I must be pushing against her cervix. Carefully, I ease back and push again. She throws her head back and whimpers, her moans changing from cries of defiance to need. Just a bit deeper and I'd touch the place in her body where miracles happen, where a child can grow from a seed in her womb. The only thing more beautiful than a woman is a pregnant woman. When your seed takes root in her womb and her breasts grow plump with the wonder of new life as her belly expands with your child, you want to love her and fuck her with your child growing between you. Valentina will scare me with the rawness of her beauty as motherhood changes her.

My body tenses with a building ejaculation so powerful it hurts. As my release explodes an idea erupts in my mind. While I empty myself in her body, I find the answer I've been looking for. I know how to irrevocably save her.

It's depraved and immoral.

It's dubious.

It's perfect.

14

Gabriel

It takes a day for my doctor to deliver the placebo birth control pills. While he's there, I make use of the opportunity to explain to him what I need for next week's house call.

From next month, Valentina won't be protected. I'm an asshole, but falling pregnant is her only hope. The one line Magda will never cross is killing the mother of her grandchild. I'm not naïve enough to believe Valentina will ever want a baby with me. She can never know I took the choice from her hands. It'll be easier to accept if she thinks it was an accident.

Being pregnant will be tough on her. I have no illusions about the psyches of 'women in waiting'. Sylvia detested every minute of being pregnant. She hated what the pregnancy did to her body. My mother never lets an opportunity go by to remind me how she suffered to give birth to me. According to Magda, the pain of bringing me into this world was worse than torture. She resented not being as agile or mobile as normal. She got varicose veins and backaches that drove her nuts. The only time that Magda sympathized with Sylvia was when she was pregnant with Carly. Yeah, it won't be an easy road, especially not for a young woman who hasn't completed her studies. I don't even want to think about our age difference. I'm heading down a hell of a bumpy road, dragging a young woman along against her knowledge and will. You don't get more depraved than that.

After my morning gym workout, I have a shower, and close myself in my study to go over the financial reports. I'm not ten minutes into my work when my phone rings. My CFO's name pops up on the screen.

"Harry, what can I do for you?"

"I just had a call from UNISA. Miss Haynes dropped out."

"What?" I heard him loud and clear, but it makes no sense. "I'm not sure I understand."

"Would you like to withdraw the scholarship, or are you willing to consider another student?"

"I'll get back to you." I end the call and get Aletta Cavendish on the line. "I just found out Valentina quit her studies."

"Oh, dear. I thought she told you."

Of course she hasn't. She doesn't know I know about her studies. "Did she say why?"

"Only that her priorities have changed."

"Is it too late to have her cancellation reversed?"

"I can hold onto it for a while, but not long. Her assignments are overdue, and the exams are coming up in less than two weeks. It doesn't help that she already failed a test."

"I know how badly she wants this degree. Give me a chance to speak to her."

"I hope you can sway her."

"I will."

"I'll be waiting for your call then."

I hang up and lean back in my chair. So, this is what's been eating Valentina. Rhett told me she even refused the puppy he offered. If she can hang in there for a few weeks longer, everything will change.

For the rest of the day, I chase leads to Valentina's rape, but doors close in my face as far as I go. It's a futile effort that leaves me agitated and exhausted. By the time I get home in the late afternoon, I'm worked up into a state that leaves Quincy with a bleeding lip after our wrestling exercise in the gym. A thunderstorm is brewing on the horizon when I have my shower, casting the sky in an ominous, purple light with a touch of gold where the sun penetrates the dark masses. Coming downstairs for dinner, Magda announces we have a surprise guest. Sylvia is seated next to Carly, her blonde hair braided in a French plait and a virginal white dress clinging to her body like a glove. She lost weight.

"Gabriel." She acknowledges me with a tight nod and a cold smile.

I kiss my ex-wife's cheek. "You look beautiful, as always."

She touches her diamond necklace, a gift from me for our first wedding anniversary. "Thank you."

I take my seat and start pouring the wine. I'm going to need a few glasses. "To what do we owe the visit?"

"Nothing. I don't need a reason to visit my daughter, do I?"

Across the table our gazes lock in a non-verbal battle. Mine is torn away from hers when Valentina enters with the starters. My maid's demeanor is one of professionalism as she serves us, but I don't miss the way Sylvia glares at her.

"I'm going over to Sebastian after dinner," Carly says, bringing my attention back to her.

I nod as Valentina hovers beside me with the asparagus. "I don't remember you asking."

"I already said yes." Sylvia drapes the napkin over her lap, challenging me to defy her.

The reason for Sylvia's visit suddenly becomes clear.

"I still don't like that boy." Magda gives Carly a hard look. "He's not our type."

"Grandma," Carly groans. "It's none of your business."

I'm too tired to deal with this tonight. "Mind your tongue, young lady. You won't speak to your grandmother like that."

"She started." Carly pouts and crosses her arms.

Magda snorts. "What can you gain from a relationship with him? Who are his parents? No-good average workers with a business in textiles."

"She's not asking to marry him," Sylvia says. "Anyway, she's my daughter. You don't have a say."

"Our daughter," I remind her.

Magda picks up her fork. "We're not going to fight over this at the dinner table."

"We're not," Sylvia says sweetly. "The decision is already made."

"It's not about the boy," I say. "It's about going behind my back without asking."

"As I said," Sylvia adds with force, "she asked me."

For once, I agree with Magda. This is not a fight that needs to play out here. I'll have a word with Sylvia after dinner about her conniving ways with Carly.

"Well," Sylvia's shoulders set in a straight line, "that's handled then." She pats Carly's hand with more affection I've ever seen her deal our daughter.

Something is up with Sylvia. She hates poverty as much as Magda, which puts Sebastian under her radar line of suitable boyfriend material.

The rest of the meal is tense. I'm relieved when the ordeal is over. Sebastian's mom comes over with her son to fetch Carly and politely declines our offer for a drink. From the porch, I watch Sylvia say goodbye to Carly.

"Be back by eleven," I call, giving Sebastian a look that tells him not to fuck with me.

When the car pulls off, Sylvia comes back up the steps and hands me her jacket to drape over her shoulders. "Good evening, Gab. I'll let you get back to fucking your maid."

I grab her wrist. "It's the last time you'll call me that, and the last time you'll make a snide comment about my maid."

Jerking her arm from my grip, she hisses, "We'll see how well your future works out for you," and then she strides to her sports car with a stiff back. She waves through the window before pulling off with screeching tires.

There was a time she called me Gab. It was a time I trusted her and believed she cared. She's a damned good actress.

"That's what you get for marrying that whore," Magda says behind me.

I look over my shoulder to see her watching from the doorstep. "You'll be wise to keep quiet now."

She only chuckles as she turns on her heel and disappears into the house.

In the lounge, I pour a stiff drink and wait an hour. There's no way I can go to bed before Carly is home. I dial the kitchen.

Valentina's voice comes over the intercom. "Yes?"

"Come to the lounge."

She steps into the room five minutes later, regarding me with mistrust where I sit in the armchair.

"Come sit with me." I hold my hand out to her.

Instead of climbing onto my lap as I would've liked, she stops at the edge of my seat, and drapes herself on the carpet by my feet. I push her head down on my thigh, stroking her silky hair. Like she accepted my pain, she's learning to accept my tenderness. I'm enjoying our tranquil moment, but there are two issues of importance I have to bring up. I don't have the luxury of waiting for her to confide in me, any longer. I've given up on hoping for her trust.

"Why did you drop out of school?"

Her body goes rigid. It takes her a moment to answer. "How did you find out?"

"Does it matter?"

"You're right," she whispers. "I don't want to know."

"You're going back."

She jerks her head up to look at me. "Don't. I've dealt with it. I don't want to go down that road again."

I fist my hand in her hair. "You'll go back."

"Gabriel." Her eyes fill with tears. "Please."

"Marie will come back. Things will go back to normal." It's a lie, but I can't tell her how I'm planning on changing her circumstances.

"Things will never be normal for me."

That's true, but she better accept it. She'll take whatever I choose to give her. My hand tightens in her hair. "You'll call tomorrow and withdraw your cancellation."

"Why?" she whispers.

Because despite everything, I still want her to be happy. "You'll obey me, like you promised."

Hurt flickers in her eyes. "Are you threatening me?"

"I'm the biggest damn threat of your life."

Her bottom lip starts to tremble. "Of course. How could I forget?"

My hand is aching to tan her ass. If it weren't for her injury, she'd be draped over my lap right now, her panties around her ankles.

"Don't push me, Valentina. You'll do as I say without question, because I know what you need, and it's my job to give it to you."

That same acceptance with which she submitted to my lashings and fucking filters into her expression. It's not so much a choice as an understanding that there's no choice.

"Good girl."

I bend down to kiss her, tasting the sweetness of her submission as her lips quiver under mine. If I don't pull away, I'll take her right here in the lounge, and I still have plenty to say.

"There's something else you're going to do for me." I watch her face carefully as I choose my next words. "You're going to tell me about the man who raped you."

Panic flares in her eyes. Her cheeks pale, and her lips part. For a moment, she only stares at me. From her reaction, it's clear she's never spoken to anyone about it, not in the healing sense, at least.

"Who have you told?"

She swallows. "It was a long time−−"

I pull gently on her hair. "That's not what I asked. Who did you tell?"

"My−my...no one."

"Let me rephrase that for you. Who knows or knew?"

"My family."

"Who in your family?"

"My mom, dad, and my brother."

"No one else?"

She shakes her head.

"They didn't make you go to a doctor, the police, a therapist?"

"My mom got me the morning-after pill."

I already know why. Her family would've tried to bury the shame. What I need are details so I can track the fucker down.

"Start by telling me where you were when it happened."

A sob escapes her throat. "I don't want to go back there."

I loosen my fingers in her hair and drag them down the long strands. "I'm here for you, baby. You're not going through this alone."

"I can't do it."

She tries to get up, but I push her down. If I could find out the truth without putting her through this, I would, but I'm at a dead end.

"You don't have to go into the details. Think of it as a movie. Look in from the outside. Go back to the scenes and tell me where you were."

"Gabriel, no." She gets onto her knees and clutches my thighs. "Please, I beg you."

I almost falter. Valentina on her knees in front of me, begging, is more than what I can handle, but she needs to heal, or she'll never be free. The man who stole her virginity will always own a piece of her as long as she keeps it bottled inside, and the fucker doesn't deserve her peace of mind or pain. I press her face down in my lap, running my fingers through her hair.

Steeling myself, I say in a stern voice, "Start at the beginning."

She rubs her cheek on my thigh. A big tear rolls from under her long lashes, the wetness penetrating the fabric of my pants. She licks her lips and opens and closes them twice before she gets a word out.

"Mom sent me to take Dad's dinner. He was working late."

"Where?"

"At the workshop."

"Was it dark?"

She thinks for a while. "It was still light. I think it was before six, because it was right after the afternoon sitcom."

"Good. Carry on."

She swallows again. "A car pulled up."

"What kind of car?"

Her whole body goes rigid. "I don't remember."

"Don't feel, baby. Just tell me who drove the car."

"I–I don't know. I only know they were old."

They? She said only one man raped her. "How many?"

"Five. Six. I think six. I was scared. I didn't want to look at them. I kept my eyes on the ground."

"Don't feel." I brush my thumb over the tears that spill down her cheek. "What did they say?"

"I can't remember. I don't think they said much. One grabbed my arm. Daddy's lunchbox fell on the ground. His sandwiches dropped out. I remember thinking how angry he was going to be if there was sand on them."

"Go on," I say when she falls quiet, rubbing my hand up and down her back.

"They laughed. They laughed a lot."

Anger boils up in me. I feel like breaking something.

"They took me."

"Where?"

She blinks. "I don't know."

"Did they take you by car? Did they make you get inside?"

"No. They dragged me into the building. A bar."

"Can you remember the name?"

"I didn't see."

If she walked, it was not far from where she lived. "Maybe you saw when you went past there later."

"I never walked that road again."

"What did the inside look like?"

"It was dark. Smoke. It smelled of cigarette smoke. There was a counter and bar stools, and a neon sign above the mirror, I think. There was a room at the back with a pool table."

"Were there other people inside?"

"A man behind the bar. I remember him because I screamed for help, but he turned away."

"What did he look like?"

"Fat. Bald. That–that's all I remember."

"You're doing well, sweetheart. Where did they take you?"

She starts shaking, her frail body trembling between my knees. "The back."

"It's a movie. It's not happening to you. Can you see it?"

"They ripped off my clothes and held me down."

Enough. I can't stand it, but I can't let it go, either. "What did he look like?"

"I kept my eyes closed. I couldn't look."

"Only the one?"

"Yes," she says meekly.

I bite back my fury. "What happened after?"

"They left me."

"How did you get home?"

"I woke up in an alley. It was dark."

"You woke up?"

"They beat me. I must've passed out."

God help me, I will tear their limbs from their bodies and make them swallow their dicks before I skin them alive.

"I tried to walk, but I was hurting and bleeding. I didn't get far. That's where my brother found me. When I didn't get home, my mom got worried. She called my father. They started looking."

"He took you home?"

She nods, exhaling a shaky breath. "Mom treated my wounds. I stayed home until the bruises were gone. My father said he'd find the men responsible."

"Did he?"

"I don't know. I didn't want to remember. I didn't want to ask."

"Can you remember the date, Valentina?"

"Thirteenth of February."

Two months later, her father died in the car crash, and her brother suffered brain damage. The mafia who was supposed to be their family rejected them, and here she is, on her knees in front of me. I hook my hands under her arms and lift her onto my lap, cradling her head against my chest.

"They're going to pay."

The tenseness eases somewhat from her small frame as she sits in my arms, allowing me to soothe her and keep her safe.

I kiss the top of her head. "I won't let anyone ever hurt you, again."

For the first time in my life, I have no desire to take cuddling further than holding a woman in my arms. There's satisfaction greater than the high I get from sex in providing her with strength and protection. Even better is that she allows me take care of her, to be the man for her I couldn't yet be for any woman.

We sit together like this for a long time. My only desire is to carry her upstairs and lay her down on my bed, to hold her until the day breaks, but it's close to eleven, and Carly will be home soon.

My thought is scarcely cold when the front door bursts open, and Carly flies through it, sobs and tears following in her wake as she runs through the entrance and up the stairs. Valentina jerks in my arms. She scurries off my lap as fast as I'm trying to get to my feet with my useless leg. She looks at me with wide eyes, concern etched on her face.

"She hasn't seen us," I say.

I have to leave Valentina to go after my daughter. If that dickhead of a pretty college boy touched her, he'll get what he deserves. On the landing, I hear her door slam. My hip aches as I rush to her bedroom.

"Carly?" I call, knocking on the door.

"Go away."

I try the knob. It's locked. Her sobs reach me through the wood.

"Open the door, Carly."

"I said go away!"

"If you don't open this door right now I'm going to break it down."

"I don't care. I don't give a damn."

"Carly!" I'm more worried than angry, but it's the anger that sounds in my voice. "You have three seconds."

"Go to hell."

That's it. I take a few steps back and get ready to charge. I'm about to throw my weight against the door when Valentina comes running up the stairs.

"Gabriel!" She grabs my arm. "What are you doing?"

"Stay out of this."

"You'll scare her."

It's the plea in her eyes that makes me pause. I don't want to frighten Carly, but my fatherly instincts are in overdrive.

I drag my hands though my hair. "Something's wrong."

My concern is mirrored on Valentina's face. Maybe it's the subject we discussed just before Carly's turbulent entry, but we're thinking the same thing.

Valentina walks to the door and taps gently on it. "Carly? Are you all right? Your dad's really worried about you. Please come out and talk to him before he does something stupid."

A hiccup and a snort-laugh comes from inside.

Laughing is good. Whatever happened can't be that bad.

"I don't feel like cleaning up the mess he's about to make," Valentina continues, "not to mention facing your grandmother when he wakes her up with the noise."

The mention of Magda does it. Footsteps approach the door. The key turns. The door opens on a crack, and Carly's tear-streaked face appears around the frame, black mascara smeared under her eyes and her hair a mess. I have to clench teeth, hands, and muscles not to shove the door open, and march into her room.

Carly sniffs and looks between Valentina and me. "I don't want to talk about it, Dad. Go to bed."

"Not until you tell me what's wrong."

"Nothing."

I motion at her face. "This doesn't look like nothing."

"You won't understand!"

It's times like these that I hate Sylvia with an unfair fierceness for walking out on us. "I'll try my best."

"No, thanks." She adds sarcastically, "Can I go to sleep, now?"

"Fine. I'll have to drive over to Sebastian's."

"Dad!" Fresh tears build in her eyes.

I can't stand to see her tears. Moving forward, I hold my arms open for a hug, but she takes a step back into the room and starts closing the door. Only when I stop in my tracks does she let go of the door.

"Can I speak to you, Valentina?"

Valentina shoots me a look. I motion for her to go ahead. I'm desperate. I'll use any measures to get Carly to open up.

"Sure." Valentina clears her throat. "Do you want to talk in your room?"

Carly takes her by the arm and drags her inside, the door shutting behind them.

Why am I surrounded by females who are set on making my life difficult? I go to my study and activate the security system. For my family's safety, every room in the house is equipped with hidden microphones. You never know. It's less than honorable to eavesdrop on my daughter's conversation with Valentina, but only a father will understand how I feel. I pour a whiskey and take a seat behind my desk.

Carly's voice comes over the speaker. "We had a fight."

"Oh, Carly. I'm sorry, honey. Fights happen, you know."

"Not these kinds of fights."

"Was he mean to you?"

"Not exactly. Actually, he was quite polite. I just don't understand. I don't get guys."

"What did he do to upset you?"

"He broke up with me."

"Oh. I didn't know you were going steady."

"He asked me on our first date."

"Then he breaks up a few weeks later?"

"He met someone else. He cheated on me. He lied to me."

"That must hurt an awful lot."

"He says I'm too girlie for him. I'm so humiliated. I hate him."

"You shouldn't look at it like that. Someone not liking you for who you are is nothing to be humiliated about."

"He's a first-class jerk. He's dating Tammy Marais."

"I don't know Tammy, but I know you're beautiful and clever. You're also still very young. There's lots of time for you to meet the right man."

"How do you know I'll meet someone? What if there's no one out there for me?"

"There are plenty of good men out there."

"How can I make sure they'll like me?"

"By being yourself."

"Did you have a lot of boyfriends? Do you have one, now?"

"I didn't date."

"Why not? Don't you like men?"

"I was busy. I had my studies and a job."

"Are you sorry now that you're old?"

Valentina laughs softly. "I'm not that old."

"Are you? Sorry?"

"Sometimes, but it's no use crying over things we can't change."

"I want him back, Valentina. Tell me what to do."

"You want my opinion? He doesn't deserve to have you back."

"If you don't have experience with men, how do I know I can trust your advice?"

"You don't have to trust me. Trust yourself. I'm sure you know you're worth more than lies and deceit."

"You're right. I'm worth more than Tammy Mousy Hair."

"And elegant young ladies aren't nasty."

Carly giggles. "You're no fun. I can't gossip with you."

"See? You're feeling better, already."

"I guess. Thanks for…uh…putting things in perspective."

"No worries. How about hot chocolate with marshmallows?"

"My mom won't approve."

"Hot chocolate *without* marshmallows?"

"I suppose, as long as it won't make me gain weight."

"You're a skinny thing. You don't have to worry about one hot chocolate."

"Okay. Will you bring it to my room?"

"Only if you go say goodnight to your dad. He's worried because he loves you."

"I know. It's just…I can't talk to him about boyfriends. He'll get upset."

"Tell him how you feel. If he understands, he'll be more patient."

"Will you talk to him for me, like you did for going out with Sebastian?"

"I think you can handle him all on your own."

"Thank you, Val."

"You're welcome. Go see your dad. I'll leave your chocolate on your nightstand."

I cut the security link and tip my hands together. Valentina was right all along. It wasn't necessary to make a fuss about Carly going out with Sebastian. The problem took care of itself. Valentina was good with Carly tonight. I'd trust my only daughter with her any day.

15

Valentina

After I opened up to Gabriel about my rape he became more possessive than ever, but he also lifted a weight off my shoulders. My parents' advice was to pretend that day never took place, and until Gabriel, no one knew exactly what happened. My mom didn't want to hear the details. She wanted to spare me the pain of reliving them. I would've confided in Charlie, but I didn't have a chance. After my attack, my parents did everything in their power to please me. When I said I felt like chocolate cake, my father loaded Charlie and me in the car, and then the accident that changed our lives forever happened.

Gabriel calls me to his study every night after dinner. I sit at his feet with my head on his thigh as he reads and comments on my assignments or watches the news while stroking my hair. Afterward, he takes me depending on how he interprets my needs and mood. Sometimes it's tender and sometimes hard. I revel in whatever he gives me, needing his body with an intensity that doesn't diminish, no matter how many times per night he makes me come.

Things are looking up in my life. Since Carly reached out to me about her breakup with Sebastian, our relationship is friendlier. Aletta said if I hand in my assignments, she'll hold onto my study cancellation, giving me a second chance at my dream. I can still be something other than a maid after nine years. With the bursary, I have more money to spend on Charlie and Kris. I can even afford to take them out to lunch on Sunday. I choose a restaurant in Rosebank, close to El Toro, a delicatessen shop where Marie used to buy Spanish chorizo. Magda told me to make paella on Monday, and she only eats this particular brand of sausage in the dish. Since El Toro doesn't deliver, I profit from picking up my order while spoiling Kris and Charlie.

We get a table on the terrace at Roma's and order spaghetti with scallops in basil-flavored cream. Charlie is working his way through his second Coke float. His eyes shine, and his cheeks have a healthy color. He's even lost a bit of the flabbiness around his waist.

"The change in him is remarkable, Kris."

She takes a sip of her wine. "He's a good dog walker. Plus, it saves me a pack of time."

"It makes me happy to see him like this. I wish I could do more."

"So, what's with the lunch?" she asks after we've eaten, direct as always.

"I have good news. The university granted me a full bursary."

"I thought you dropped out."

"I did, but Gabriel said Marie should be back at work soon. I'll have time to study again, and with the full bursary I won't need to worry about the shortfall."

Leaning back, she crosses her arms. "What's going on with him, Val?"

"Nothing." I pick at my napkin, tearing off small pieces. "Why?"

I can't tell anyone what happens behind the closed doors of Gabriel's house. Especially not Kris. She won't understand. Hell, sometimes *I* don't understand.

"He's been to the practice."

I still. "Why?"

"To buy cat and dog food, apparently. He's got a standing order."

"He didn't tell me."

"You're sleeping with him, aren't you?"

I jerk my head up and glance at Charlie, but he's engrossed in his drink. I can't lie to her in her face, so I say nothing.

"He's a loan shark, and you're indebted to him for nine years. You want to know what I think? I think you're his sex toy. His favorite toy. For the moment, he dresses you up--yes, I saw the parcels he carried to my house--and he covers your bills. Hey, I'm not complaining. I need the business. All I'm saying is don't fall in love with him."

I look away to where a mom and dad are having lunch with a cute little girl. "It's not like that."

"How is it? Are you parading around for him in a French maid's costume? Is that his fantasy?"

I give her a chastising look. "Stop it."

"Every boy eventually grows tired of his toys, even his favorite toy."

"I don't have a choice," I say in a lowered voice. "He's not all bad, Kris. I think he tries really hard to treat me well."

She leans forward. "He's a goddamn killer. A criminal. *The Breaker*, Val. Do you need me to remind you *how* he kills people?"

"No."

"Don't sugarcoat him because he's nice to you. Never forget who he is. More importantly, never forget who *you* are and what you are to him."

"What am I?"

"Debt repayment. You're a slave."

"Call it whatever you want, but I made a deal to save Charlie's life. I'll slave, whore, bust my ass, and work my fingers to the bone to keep him safe."

"What about *your* life?"

Kris doesn't know my history. She doesn't know how Charlie picked me up in the gutter, battered and left for dead, and carried me home for more than two miles. She doesn't know he sat next to my bed and held my hand every night after my assault when I was too afraid to close my eyes to sleep.

"I made a choice, Kris. I made a promise to Gabriel Louw. You don't break your promises to Gabriel. Give it a rest, will you? I'm doing the best I can."

"Jesus, Val. If this is your best, you're heading for a cluster fuck. You cut off your finger for Christ's sake." She wipes a hand over her brow. "How is this going to play out?"

"After nine years, I walk away, get a job, a nice house for Charlie and me, and get out of your hair."

"You're not in my hair, kiddo, but I worry about you."

"I know." I push my chair back, desperately needing air. "I'm taking Charlie for a walk."

"I'll order dessert. Tiramisu?"

"Sounds good. Come on, Charlie." I take my brother's arm and cross the Rosebank Square to stroll down the walkway past the shop fronts. Charlie stops to stare at every window. It's not as much the objects he likes as the colors.

"Charlie?"

He points at a red bicycle in the sports shop. "Loo–look."

"What?" I want him to say it. I want to know what's going on in his head.

"Pre–pretty."

"What's pretty?"

"Lo–look." He points again, getting frustrated.

"The bicycle?"

He's already moved on, stuck in front of a shelf of colorful cycling helmets.

"Li–like."

"Which one?"

He rolls his shoulders like he does when he gets annoyed and carries on down the path with a brisk pace.

I run to catch up, taking his hand. "Do you remember how you used to walk me home from school?"

He hurries on toward the street. Once Charlie is on a mission, it's difficult to distract him. He throws his whole weight into a task and won't stop until he's accomplished what he's set out to do. I'm longing for the connection we once had. I'm aching to have my brother back, to give him back to himself, but he's in his own world, and I sometimes wonder if I'm even part of it.

We stop in front of a red Ferrari parked on the curb. This is what attracted his attention. When he puts out his hand to touch the shiny bodywork, I snatch it back.

"Don't touch the car. What did I say about touching things that aren't ours?"

"That's all right," a male voice says.

I twirl around to where the voice comes from. The man facing us has blond hair and a tanned face with friendly, green eyes.

"You can touch it if you like," he says to Charlie. "It's mine."

The man is as beautiful as his car. It's the kind of sinful beauty that will make a woman forget her male companion at a party.

I tug on Charlie's hand. "We should go."

"I can take him for a spin, if you like."

"Spi–spin."

"Uh, thanks," I push my hair behind my ear, "but my friend's waiting for us."

"Pity." He holds out his hand. "I'm Michael."

I reach out tentatively, but before I can make up my mind, he folds his broad palm around mine and squeezes. When I don't say anything, he gives me an amused smile.

"Your name?"

"Valentina."

"That's pretty." He lets me go and shakes hands with Charlie. "You have good taste, eh..." He lifts a brow and waits.

"Charlie," I say.

"Pleased to meet you both. Maybe we can talk about that spin. If you give me your number, I can call when it's convenient."

"Our dessert is ready." The word 'dessert' will catch Charlie's attention. "Thank you, anyway."

Charlie lets me lead him back across the square to our table.

"Who's that?" Kris asks.

"I don't know. Charlie liked his car."

"Ditto." She waves her spoon at the plate in front of me. "Dig in. It's delicious."

It's hard to say goodbye to Charlie. At least he seems happy. I let that thought soothe me as I cross the street to where Gabriel's Jaguar waits. It's Rhett who exits.

"Hi," I say, surprised. Gabriel said he'd fetch me.

"Gabriel's busy," he says with a wink, holding the door for me.

I wait until we pull off into traffic to ask, "Where is he?"

"Business."

A shiver runs over me. Is he breaking someone's bones? Killing someone?

Rhett gives me a sidelong look. "It's better not to ask."

"I wasn't going to." I glance through the window to escape his piercing eyes.

"On the upside," he continues brightly, "we can train."

I turn back to him quickly. "Really?"

"He'll be busy until late."

My mood picks up. I have to learn how to handle myself. Gabriel won't be there to protect me forever. Like Kris said, he may grow tired of his new toy sooner than later.

Rhett changes gears and speeds up when we hit the highway. "Why the sad face? Is your brother all right?"

"Sunday blues." I try to smile, but it's a weak effort.

We don't talk for the rest of the way. At home, I change into my shorts and T-shirt and join Rhett in the gym. It's weird to be here out of my own, free will. The gym represents a place of erotic pain and deep-seated pleasure for me. My body reacts at the thought, sending moisture to my folds. I shake my head and jiggle my fingers, physically expelling the unwelcome arousal at the memory of what Gabriel does to me here.

"Ready?" Rhett walks around me like a boxer measuring his opponent.

"Give me your worst."

He laughs. "You're a funny one."

I fling around and punch him in the stomach. "Like this funny?"

My knuckles hurt, and he doesn't even flinch. Before I know what's happening, he kicks my feet out from under me with a swift swing of his leg, making me land on my ass with a humph.

"This move is child's play, perky tits. You've got a far way to go before you can handle my worst."

"Okay, short dick." I hold out my hand for him to help me up.

He only laughs at the diminutive name. When he's halfway in the motion of pulling me up, I yank hard, using the momentum to bring him down to the floor. He does a graceful shoulder roll and flips his leg over me, pinning me face down on the mat.

He chuckles. "You've got spirit, I'll give you that, perky tits."

"Fuck you, short dick."

"Wanna see? You'll take back your words."

"No thanks. Kicking you in the balls when your pants are around your ankles won't be fair play."

He laughs again. "Yep, you're funny." He gets to his feet and pulls me up by my arm. "We'll start with some basic defense moves, and when you've gotten the hang of them, I'll teach you how to use an attacker's strength to beat him."

The minute I'm up, I kick at his feet like he did with me, but he catches my leg, holding me captive.

"You're a quick learner, and you've got more courage than brains, but let me do the teaching. I don't want to hurt you."

I hop around on one foot to keep my balance. "It'll take a bit more than that."

"As I said, more courage than brains. You're small. You've got to learn to fight clever."

"Okay."

He releases me. "Ready?"

For the next hour, he drills me. By the time he calls it a day, I'm sweating.

"You better have a shower. Gabriel will be home soon."

"I want to learn to use a gun, too."

He props his hands on his hips and regards me from under his eyebrows. "Valentina."

"It's a big, bad world out there. I won't live here forever."

After a moment, he sighs and shakes his head. "In for a penny, in for a pound."

I'm happy with my progress. Finally, I'm getting out of my vulnerable bubble. There's just enough time to shower before Gabriel enters my room.

He walks up and stops flush against my back. "How was your weekend?"

"Good."

He pushes my hair aside and kisses my neck. "We're having a dinner party at home on Tuesday. It'll be a late night."

"Okay. Do you have a menu in mind?"

"Magda will brief you. It's important to her." He doesn't need to say more. He wants me on my best behavior. "Don't forget your checkup tomorrow."

I dress the wound religiously, but it's still red and puffy.

He puts his arms around my waist and pulls my back against his chest. "Bend over and put your hands on the wall."

His tone is clipped, like when he's desperate and can't wait. My body grows deliciously warm and wet. I bend my back and brace myself on the wall. He lifts my skirt up over my waist and jerks my panties down. The metal clang of his belt sounds in the room, followed by the scratchy pull of his zipper. His cock pushes against my folds. Without warning he plunges forward, impaling me in one, hard thrust. My back arches from the friction.

"Fuck, Valentina." He holds still, either to give my body time to stretch around his too large penis or to get a hold on his control.

"Take me as you want," I pant, unable to keep still for much longer.

"Oh, I will."

Gripping my hips between his palms, he pulls out almost all the way and slams back in. Pleasure ripples through my womb. He wastes no time in working me up to a climax, fucking me hard. When I come, it's explosive, but so is his release. He grunts and keeps going until his cock is too soft to stay inside me. Only when his shaft slips out does he go on his knees and suck my clit into his mouth. It's impossible to come again so soon, but he's relentless. He has his teeth on my clit and his fingers in my pussy and ass. Our sounds mingle until there's only the unique blend of our moans in the room. He makes me come again in his mouth, driving me to the edge of pleasure. My legs can't carry my weight. When I collapse, he catches me around the waist and carries me to bed. He holds me until it's dark outside, and then he fucks me on my back and on my hands and knees until my throat is hoarse from screaming. My body is depleted. I can't give him any more, but I want more from him. I'm insatiable, and he's to blame.

My heart aches with something I can't name when he leaves me. I lie in the dark until I can't suffer it any longer. There's only one thing to do. I sneak through the dark house to his room. He's standing in the doorframe, waiting, as if he expected me. Jumping into his arms, I cling to him. I'm a stranger to myself, not understanding this woman who can't breathe without her captor. He wraps his arms around my ass to hold me up and kisses me long and sweet. Gently, he lies me down on the bed, pulling me to his chest. Only then, safe and happy, do I fall into an exhausted sleep.

THE DOCTOR'S appointment is at four the following day. As I get ready, Gabriel calls me on the internal intercom and summons me to his room. If we don't leave soon we'll be late. Why does he want to see me now? Before I can knock, he opens the door. I freeze with my hand midway in the air. A disposable sheet is laid out on the daybed, and a gurney with monitors and scanners stands next to it. The same doctor from before, Samuel Engelbrecht, waits in the room. I look at Gabriel for answers, but he says nothing. He only pulls me inside and closes the door.

"Undress and lie down," the doctor says.

I assumed I was going to see the doctor who operated on me at the clinic, and what Gabriel's doctor demands doesn't make sense. "You need me to undress to examine my finger?"

Gabriel takes my hand. "After what you told me, I want to make sure you're all right. You could've suffered internal injuries you're not aware of."

A blush works its way up my neck, warming my cheeks. "Why didn't you tell me?"

"I didn't want to stress you."

I pull my hand from his. "This isn't necessary."

His eyes turn hard. "Get your clothes off, or I'll take them off for you."

I'm so humiliated I don't know where to look. I don't doubt for a minute Gabriel will execute his threat. Angry tears burn in my eyes as I turn my back on them and pull off my trainers, uniform, and underwear. Draping my clothes over the armrest of the chair, I lie down on the daybed.

The doctor approaches with a probe. "Bend your legs."

I do so grudgingly, avoiding Gabriel's eyes. The doctor pulls a condom over the probe, lubricates it with gel, and inserts it gently in my vagina. The scanner beeps to life. He says nothing as he examines me. He only gives Gabriel a nod when he pulls the probe free. My abdomen is next. I am not sure what he's looking for, and I can't imagine why Gabriel wants to know if the rape damaged my body. After the ultrasound, the doctor takes my blood pressure and weighs me. It's when he brings a needle to my arm that I start protesting again.

"What's that?"

Gabriel takes my wrist, brushing his thumb over my pulse. "It's a vitamin boost."

"I don't need it."

"I told you already, your health is my responsibility."

There's a note of steel in his voice. He'll hold me down if he has to. I don't have a choice but to accept the injection and whatever is in it.

With the injection done, the doctor lets me get dressed and makes me sit on the bed to examine my finger. His face is blank, but he stares at the wound for a long time.

"I'm going to prescribe a stronger antibiotic. I want to see you every day."

"What's wrong?"

"A small infection," he says, as if talking to a child. "You've got to keep it still. Don't use the hand."

I bandaged it tightly when I wrestled with Rhett, and we were careful. I'm also cautious with the housework.

The doctor looks at Gabriel. "Any chance you can keep her still for a couple of weeks?"

The set of Gabriel's jaw is enough to give us the answer. Magda will never let him.

"Well, then." The doctor starts gathering his equipment. "Tomorrow same time?"

"Yes," Gabriel says.

When he's gone, I gather the courage to confront Gabriel. "Why?"

"Don't make me repeat answers I already gave you."

"Isn't he going to take his apparatus?" I motion at the gurney with the monitors.

"It'll stay here for a while."

"What are you doing, Gabriel?"

He cups my cheek. "Looking after you."

When he pulls my head to his chest, I can't resist. I can only melt against him, letting his erratic heartbeat seduce me into thinking he actually cares about more than my body.

From the careful menu planning it's obvious that Tuesday night's dinner is important to Magda. She chooses a caviar mousse starter followed by salmon and spinach crumble with sweet pastries for dessert. I pay special attention to the cooking, ensuring I do nothing to jeopardize our deal. I twist my hair into a neat bun in the nape of my neck and scrub my nails, which are stained orange from the curry I often cook with. The mousse has just set when Magda rings the bell for me to serve. Balancing a tray on one hand, I push the swing door to the dining room open with my shoulder. Looking up, I freeze on the spot. The man sitting opposite Gabriel is the one from Rosebank, the one with the Ferrari. Next to him sits a pretty redhead with freckles on her nose.

"Valentina!" Michael jumps to his feet and holds the door for me to pass.

Gabriel goes rigid. Magda's mouth turns down, her Pit Bull eyes drooping in the corners.

"You know each other?" Gabriel asks, his ice blue eyes narrowed on me.

"We met on Sunday." Michael takes his seat again. "She wouldn't give me her number." He takes the redhead's hand and smiles. "Seems the fairy godmother of fate is still doing her job."

"Valentina isn't available," Gabriel replies coldly. He turns to me. "Where exactly did you meet?"

I clear my throat. "In Rosebank."

"What were you doing there?"

What I do with my free time is none of his business, and his jealous attitude is unwarranted and unreasonable, but Magda can still put a bullet in my head for back chatting or dropping a spoon, so I answer obediently. "I went to El Torro to buy the chorizo."

"I went to El Torro to pick up a bottle of Magda's favorite wine," Michael says. "You see? Divine intervention."

"She's below your class," Magda says. "We picked her up in Berea."

I walk around the table, serving the people who talk about me as if I'm not in the room. I want to dump the mousse on their laps. *Charlie. Think about Charlie.*

"I don't care where she's from," the woman says. "We're not snobbish that way."

She has a rock of a diamond on her ring finger. She must be Michael's wife. Are they into threesomes? I can't get out of the room fast enough. In the kitchen, I inhale and exhale to control my anger. I'm sick of being looked at as a piece of meat.

For the rest of the dinner, the stress mounts every time I step into the dining room. Michael gawks openly while his wife pays me compliments on my physical appearance. Magda is red in the face with annoyance. The one who scares me most is Gabriel. He's quiet. Quiet is never good.

By the time I serve the pastries in the lounge, my stomach aches with tension. My hope of escaping is squashed when Gabriel calls me back as I'm about to exit.

"Valentina." There's authority in his voice. "Come here."

Four sets of eyes are watching me. Magda sits on a single chair at the short side of the coffee table. Her stare is both scornful and hopeful. She hopes I'll disobey. The consequences should be fun to watch. Michael looks on with open curiosity while his wife has a glimmer of excitement in her eyes. My gaze locks with Gabriel's. In silent instruction, he takes a cushion from the armchair and throws it on the floor next to his feet. I don't have a choice. I walk over to him, the tightness in my stomach growing with every step. As I've done so many times before, I sit down next to him. A smile of approval warms his face. He looks at me as if he sees no one else. He cups my cheek and tilts my head to rest on his thigh. Then our brief, private moment is over. Gabriel continues his conversation in a businesslike manner while playing absently with my hair.

Magda looks like a puffed-up dragon about to spit fire. Michael and his wife are obviously used to this kind of behavior. My posture on the floor while Gabriel pets me doesn't take up more of their attention, except for the occasional envious glance Michael shoots Gabriel.

While they're discussing a lease contract for new business premises, Gabriel feeds me sips of champagne. When the tray with sweet pastries is passed around, he takes his time to study the selection and chooses a mille-feuille that he pops into my mouth. His thumb lingers on my tongue. After I've chewed and swallowed, he wipes the icing from the corner of my mouth before licking his finger clean, giving the action his full attention. There's a smile in his eyes as he looks down at me. Again, we're sharing a moment the other three people in the room aren't part of.

After the dessert, he swaps the champagne for whiskey. I'm not a big drinker. Already buzzing from the champagne, I shake my head when he presses the glass to my lips, but his fingers tighten in my hair, pulling back to arch my neck. He takes a drink from the glass and brings his mouth down to mine. I only understand his intention when he spears my lips with his tongue, forcing them open, and feeds me the whiskey straight from his mouth. I gulp and swallow in shocked surprise. He keeps my head in place to drag his tongue over my bottom lip, licking it clean. Only then does he let go of my hair. My face is ablaze with embarrassment. If Mr. and Mrs. Michael find it shocking, they don't show it. Only Magda shifts around on her seat. When Gabriel brings the glass to my lips the second time, I open without argument. Being force-fed in front of his mother and friends isn't an experience I'd like to repeat. It's as if Gabriel is making a point by demonstrating his ownership of me.

At the end of the evening, and three glasses of champagne and a whiskey later, I've gone from a buzz to feeling tipsy. I'm aware of what's happening around me, but I'm seeing double, and my nose is numb. I'm also extremely lethargic. I'm grateful when Michael gets to his feet and announces their departure.

He saunters over to us. "May I kiss the lady, Gabriel?"

Gabriel puts a broad hand on my shoulder. "You may not."

He makes a face of mock disappointment. "I understand. I would act the same if she was mine. You make me long for a sub again."

"She's not a sub," Magda bites out. "She's property."

Michael sighs, barely sparing Magda a glance. His eyes find mine. "Even better."

His wife crosses the floor to lean her head on Michael's shoulder. "If you ever grow tired of her, Gabriel, let us know. I'll be happy to offer her a position."

"That won't happen," Gabriel says through thin lips. "She's too valuable to me."

"You mean her debt is too high," Magda corrects, her glare communicating something with Gabriel I don't understand.

Michael pats Gabriel's shoulder. "Well, goodnight my good man. Next time dinner is at our place." He looks at me. "You should bring your…"

Property. Toy. Four hundred thousand rand-asset.

"Maid," Magda says.

Gabriel gets to his feet. "I'll walk you out." He addresses me with a single command. "Stay."

While Gabriel and Magda see their guests off, I remain as Gabriel ordered. My head is spinning, and I'm not in the mood for punishment tonight. When they return, Gabriel's shoulders are tense, and Magda's mouth is pulled into a hard line.

"Goodnight, Magda," he says pointedly.

Magda isn't that easily dismissed. "You embarrassed me. I won't tolerate this kind of behavior in front of our guests."

Gabriel smirks. "They didn't seem embarrassed to me."

"I'll remind you this is *my* house."

"You insisted we live here."

"For security reasons. There are a hundred or more people who'd have your head on a plate."

"Agreed. It's easier protecting us all under one roof. That doesn't mean you can tell me what to do. As you said yourself, I'm not twelve any longer."

Her nostrils flare. "Are you dealing with what we talked about?"

"I am."

"How long?"

"Soon."

She regards him for a moment in silence. I'm half relieved when she stalks from the room. The other half of me tenses now that I'm alone with Gabriel. His mood is dark. Is he going to punish me? He offers me a hand and pulls me to my feet. My legs are stiff from sitting in the same position for hours, and I stumble, crushing into his chest.

"Sorry," I mumble. Oh, God. My tongue is slurring.

He sets me on my feet with his hands on my hips, testing my

balance before he lets go. When I manage to stand without falling over, he steps aside and points at the door. Interpreting it as my cue to leave, I take a few steps, but I have to hold onto the furniture to walk straight. I don't make it to the sofa before his hands stop me. With one arm around my shoulders and the other under my knees, he scoops me up and carries me to the stairs.

"The kitchen," I protest, pointing in the opposite direction.

His chest rumbles with his deep voice. "The kitchen can wait."

In front of his bedroom, he fumbles with his doorknob. When the door swings open, he carries me inside and kicks it shut. The medical equipment is still there. I vaguely wonder when the doctor is going to send for it.

Lying me down on the bed, he undresses me and then himself. His body is hard and rough, the broken lines and deep scars adding to his masculine, forbidden beauty. He climbs over me, pinning my arms above my head. The alcohol loosens my inhibitions. This is not a good idea. I may do and say things I'll regret in the morning.

"Gabriel." His name comes out as a needy gasp. "I think I'm drunk."

"Good. A drunk woman never lies."

He moves down and takes my nipple in his mouth. I arch up, crying out as pleasure ripples through my body.

He licks over the pebbled tip. "Do you find him attractive?"

His raspy tongue sends goose bumps over my skin. I strain my neck to look at him. "W–what?"

He licks the other nipple before sucking it deep into his mouth.

"Ah, God! Gabriel." I fall back, panting.

"Michael. Do you find him attractive?"

He grips my wrists in one hand and moves the other between my legs, parting my folds and stroking my clit. My hips lift to him, but he removes his touch.

"Answer me, Valentina."

I gasp as he presses the pad of his thumb on my clit. "Yes. Yes, he's very pretty."

His face contorts in a mixture of hurt and acceptance, as if he knew the answer but wanted to punish himself by hearing it. It's an unusual display of emotion. He's an open book as he stares down at me, maybe because he believes I'm incoherent, but the alcohol sharpens my awareness and senses. Strangely, my fear retreats to the far corners of my mind, leaving me perceptive to everything else, to the feelings flowing between us and especially to his fingers as he parts me and slips one digit into my wetness, taking me slowly with his finger.

"Would you like him to fuck you?"

I frown, trying to imagine Michael in Gabriel's position. The idea of any other man touching me fills me with distaste. "No."

"You can be honest. I won't punish you for the truth."

I clench my inner muscles, trying to take his finger deeper, and grind my sex against his palm. "Don't you understand what you've done to me? I want *you*, Gabriel."

The pain in his eyes doesn't ease. There's relief, but grief still sets his face into hard angles that emphasize his harsh features. The shadows of the room hide the scar tissue on his cheek, but not the somber light of his ice blue eyes as he stares at me. To me, he's perfect. I love the stark lines that define his unusual masculine beauty and even the sorrow that's permanently etched on his face. Needing to touch him, I pull on his grip, but he tightens his hold.

"Please, Gabriel." I beg him with my eyes, my voice, and my hips.

He groans as I rotate my lower body, trapping his hand between us. Slowly, the squeeze of his fingers on my wrists relaxes, allowing me to lift my hand to his face. I cup his cheek and brush my thumb over the devastating map of scars. It's frightening to look at him, but when you find the courage to look, to really look, the power of the beauty that lies underneath the physical destruction is blinding. I've seen the beauty inside of him, too. He's a good father to Carly, and he gives me much more than he takes, even if I'm nothing but property to him.

"I only want you," I whisper.

For a moment, he leans into my touch, brushing his scarred cheek over my palm, but then he turns his head away, angling his face to the darkness.

"Gabriel." I moan in protest.

He pushes my legs open wider, positioning his cock at my entrance.

"Gabriel."

I say his name, trying to bring him back to me, to catch the moment we've lost, but he braces himself on his arms, putting more distance between us. The only connection between us is his cock that slams violently into my body. An ache spreads inside of me. He pulls back and does it again, stretching and burning me with that dull pain that tells me he's too rough. He fucks me so hard my body shifts up to the headboard. Over and over he pounds into me, and all I can do is wrap my legs and arms around him, holding on while I give him everything I've got. With every thrust he growls, keeping his face turned away from me. He's never taken me this brutally before, and even as it hurts, my soul revels in his possession. For now, I don't care that I'm property. I don't care that I'm a price tag and an empty body. I just want to be his.

"Only you," I say.

He lances into me harder, his grunts louder, punishing me for something I don't understand. The rougher he treats me, the softer I mold my body around him.

"Only yours."

He snarls, driving into me with such force I'm scared he'll break me.

"Damn you, Valentina. Don't you dare lie. Not about this."

"I want to be yours."

He grabs my face between his palms and jerks his head toward me, putting our noses inches apart without slowing the hard pace of his hips. "Look at this face. Look at me!"

"I *am* looking."

Angers pulls his features into a fearful mask. His nostrils flare, and moisture brims in his eyes. "Stop it."

"Yours."

He utters a raw cry and grinds his groin against mine. Throwing back his head, he clenches his teeth and bites off the sounds as liquid hotness fills my body. He shakes with his release, his body slick with perspiration. I need him. He made a hole in my heart, and only he can mend it. Snaking my arms around his neck, I pull him down for a kiss, but he untangles my wrists and arranges my arms next to my body. He only rests his forehead against mine for the briefest of moments before he lifts up on one elbow to look at me. Our eyes remain locked as he lets his cock slip free to fill the empty space with his fingers. Using his release, he lubricates my clit and brings me to a quick orgasm, all the while watching me.

When the aftershocks subside, he takes me to the shower and washes me. Too weak to stand on my feet, he sits on the bench with me straddling him, my head resting on his chest. The water stings my private parts, and I flinch when he soaps me down there. He towels us dry, carries me back to his bed, and then he disappears into the bathroom again. When he returns, he hands me a glass of water and a tablet.

I look at the white pill. "What's this?"

"Paracetamol. You'll need it if you don't want to wake up with a headache."

He puts the pill on my tongue and makes me drink all the water. The bed dips as he settles behind me, pulling me to his chest.

"I should leave," I say sleepily.

"I set the alarm for five." He kisses my shoulder. "Rest."

I snuggle closer, enjoying the warmth of his embrace. Even if it's only for a few hours, I'll take what I can get. I'm used to living off scraps.

I'm almost drifting off when his voice pulls me back from my sleep.

"There was this cat."

I lie still, waiting for him to continue.

"It was a kitten. Nothing special. Just an alley cat, but to me she was beautiful. She had a soft pelt, black as the night, and eyes like yellow moons. The cat showed up out of the blue at my best friend's house. He called her Blackie. From that day on, Blackie always followed my friend around. She stayed in his room and slept on his bed."

His chest expands with a breath. "I was jealous of him. I wanted the cat to come to *my* house. I wanted her to follow *me*, but she didn't, so I smuggled pieces of fish and steak to his house, luring her through his bedroom window. She ate the food, but still wouldn't follow me home. One day, when my friend was at rugby practice, I went to his house and took the cat. I locked Blackie in my room, hiding her from Magda and our maids. I made a bed for her in my closet, and I fed her treats my friend could never afford to give her. I kept her closed in for two weeks. By that time, I reckoned she would have accepted her new, more luxurious home."

"What happened?"

"The day I let her out, she ran straight back to my friend's house." He strokes my arm for a while, then says quietly, "He thought she'd run away, like strays do."

"Did she continue to live with him?"

"I don't know. I stopped being his friend after that day."

"Why?"

"I couldn't bear to look at that cat."

What is he trying to say? I turn in his arms to look at him.

He kisses my lips softly. "If you set something free, it doesn't come back to you, no matter how well you treat it."

A deep sense of uneasiness settles in my gut. Is he telling me he won't let me go?

"Sleep." He kisses me again, the gentle act conflicting with the soreness inside my body that acts as a reminder of his earlier roughness. "You'll be tired, tomorrow."

I close my eyes to hide my turbulent emotions from him. His story shocks me. It tells me three things. One, he'll take whatever he wants. Two, he believes himself undeserving of love. Three, he'll keep me for as long as my body serves him. What shocks me more is that I yearn to trust him. As long as he holds Charlie and my life in his hands, I can't. For the first time, I consider that he won't honor our deal. He's not going to set me free like the black kitten. A man like Gabriel doesn't repeat the same mistake twice. That's what he was telling me with his story. Tears build up behind my closed eyelids. I turn my back on him again so I can shed them quietly into his pillow. He leaves me with no option. If he doesn't let me go when I've settled Charlie's debt, I'm going to have to run away.

16

Gabriel

Awake long before the alarm goes off, I pull Valentina's soft, warm body closer and mull over last night. Getting Valentina drunk wasn't planned. It's too soon for her to conceive, so I wasn't risking her or a developing fetus' wellbeing. The idea popped into my head while Michael fucked her with his eyes. Sylvia was always brutally honest when she had a drink too many. That was how I found out she never loved me. It shouldn't have come as a surprise. I wouldn't have been so damn gullible if I hadn't been desperate for a woman I could call my own.

Yeah, the truth comes out when a woman is drunk, and unlike men, they don't whisper lies in their moments of passion. When a woman is a second away from coming, that's when you see her true feelings in her eyes. Valentina needs me. That's what I trained her to want. Like the kitten, I lured her with pleasure and orgasms, driving her to her limits and beyond, ensuring that no other man can ever give her what I can, because no other man will have the balls to hurt her to make her come harder. Then why am I gutted? Women want me for my money, for sex, or for the security that comes with being connected to me. Valentina wants me because I designed it so. It's too much, hoping she'll ever want me for me. Girls like her want men like Michael and Quincy. It's nature. There's not a damn thing I can do about nature, except twist, force, and bend it my way. If I need to make her my captive forever, so be it. Soon, she'll be bound to me in blood. Our child will be a connection she can ever break.

At five, I still my bitter thoughts, switch off the alarm, and start the sad task of waking her. If I could, I would've left her sleeping in my bed. I love having her between my sheets. She groans as I wipe her hair over her shoulder to kiss the gracious curve.

"Wake up, beautiful."

"Gabriel." Her voice is sleepy.

With much regret, I throw the sheet off, letting the fresh morning air cool our bodies. Goose bumps break out over her arms. She turns on her back, rubs her eyes, and stretches.

"What time is it?"

I switch on the nightstand lamp. "Five."

She sits up and swings her legs over the bed. Her back is a perfect portrait of frail vertebrae covered with silky skin.

She gives me a shy look from over her shoulder. "May I please use your bathroom? With all I drank last night, I won't make it to mine."

"Go ahead." I want her to touch everything that's mine. The thought of her fingers trailing over the objects that belong to me makes my skin contract with pleasure, as if she touches *me*.

Her slender hand brushes over the mattress as she gets up. She takes my shirt from the chair and pulls it on. Warmth at the sight of her wearing my clothes fills my chest. When she closes the bathroom door behind her, I get up to select my clothes for the day, but stop dead. Blood spots my sheets. It's not much, only a few drops, but enough to tell me I've broken her again.

I jerk a suit from a hanger with a scowl. God knows I don't deserve anything as beautiful and perfect as her, but I can't let her go.

The door opens, and Valentina enters. Her cheeks are pale, and there are dark circles under her eyes. She smiles at me as she crosses the floor with small steps. Before she reaches the door, I cut her off. I pull her to me with my arm around her waist, cupping her sex gently with my free hand.

"Are you all right?"

She winces at my touch. "Just tired."

Fury directed at myself combusts in my chest. "We'll go to bed early tonight."

She gives me a weak nod. "I better go before Carly or Magda wakes up."

Reluctantly, I withdraw my touch. "I hurt you."

"You wanted to."

"Not like this. You should've told me."

Her gaze holds mine. "No, Gabriel. You didn't want to hear what I was trying to tell you." Without another word, she walks gingerly from my room.

I let her go because I don't have a goddamn choice. Abandoning the suit, I pull on my exercise gear, go down to the gym, and slam my fists into the punching bag until they bleed.

IT'S GOING to snow in the middle of summer. Carly is having breakfast with us. She's unusually chatty, to the point that Magda escapes with her coffee to her study.

"Dad," she says after an exceptionally long account of her week at school, "I've got something to tell you."

My gut twists inside out. I'm not going to like what's coming. I brace myself as I wait silently with a stoic face.

"I've decided to move back in with Mom."

The blow hits me right between the eyes. I don't know what I expected, but it wasn't this. I lower my cup and take a long, deep breath to calm myself. Sylvia's unexpected visits and easy agreement to let Carly go out on dates suddenly make sense.

I'm careful to keep my voice even. "What prompted the sudden decision?"

"Mom misses me."

The guilt card is a dirty one for Sylvia to play. "You don't have to make a hasty decision. Why not think it over for a while?"

"I've been thinking about it for a long time, already. It's not like you'll only see me every second weekend. I can come visit whenever I want."

"Of course. Your room will always be here."

"Thanks, Dad."

There's no point in arguing with Carly once her mind's made up. She takes after me in that regard. I don't trust Sylvia as a mother. She's only ever proved to me she's not capable of the job, and I don't like Sylvia's new boyfriend. All I can do is be there for Carly when she needs me.

"You're not mad?" she asks.

"Of course not." Disappointed, sad, but I'm not mad at my daughter.

"I'm packing some of my things today. Mom will fetch me tonight. Will you be here to say goodbye?"

So soon? "Of course." The day, which has started out bad, goes several shades darker. "Let me know if you need a hand."

"Thanks, but I'm cool."

Unable to contain my emotions, I push back my chair. "I'll pick you up after school."

"Uh, Dad?"

I pause, waiting for her to speak.

"Me and some girls from my class are going to Mugg & Bean after school."

"Who's driving?"

"Mom."

"I'll see you before you go, then." I walk to the door before she sees the anguish I'm feeling in my eyes.

"Have a nice day," she calls after me.

Just like that, my daughter, my precious gift from Sylvia, is ripped from my house.

What I need is a fight. I take Rhett with me to drive around Valentina's old neighborhood. The chances of finding the bar she mentioned are slight. Many of the old places don't exist any longer. The neighborhood has, like so many others around, turned into a cesspool of crime. The buildings are dilapidated. Some are broken down to the ground. I requested the city plan for twelve years ago from the municipality, but like the rest of the government, they're a corrupt bunch of uneducated officials. The records have long since been displaced with the collapse of the system. It's a joke this country is still functioning. It's people like me and the rest of the thugs on the street who pull the strings. Politicians are merely the puppets. There are a million ways to go to hell, and I've earned them all.

None of the old crowd who knew the neighborhood is left. My father's cronies from way back who collected money on this beat are gone. Steven died of a heart attack with his pants around his ankles on the can. Dawie kicked the bucket when he fell down his front steps and broke his neck. Barney went out the old-fashioned way, gunned down in his front yard. Mickey passed away from cancer, and Conrad caught AIDS from the whores he pimped. My father's death, going peacefully in his sleep, is the most gentle and uneventful of them all, contrary to the violent lifestyle he led. How will my end come? Will I die for the *business*, with a bullet in my brain, or like my father in my bed?

Rhett pulls up to the curb and nods at the flaky house with the missing roof tiles. "This one?"

"Yeah." I cock my gun and slip it into my waistband. "Let's go."

Lambert has the door open before I'm strolling through the weeds in his front yard.

"Gabriel." He gives a nervous laugh. "You'll give me the wrong idea, calling on me all the time."

I motion for him to enter. Rhett and I follow. The firm click of the door when I shut it makes Lambert go tense. His yellow skin takes on a pasty color.

"What can I do you for?"

I hate his slang, but I swallow my insults. "Tell me about the bar that used to be around here."

"The bar?" His shoulders relax visibly.

"Neon sign, bald bartender, pool table at the back."

He scratches his head and thinks for a while. "Ah," he says after a moment, "that'll be Porto, but the place doesn't exist, anymore." He sneers. "Won't find much other than squatters living there."

"Who's the owner?"

"Bigfoot Jack."

The name rings a bell. My father mentioned him once or twice.

"Where can I find him?"

"Six feet under."

Shit. Another dead-end. "Who protected him?" Everyone in the hood had protection from someone. You couldn't survive otherwise.

"He was with the Jewish guys from Kensington."

"Jewish? In Portuguese territory?"

"His wife is Jewish. The big boss made a deal with the Porras to cut Bigfoot out of the loop. Why do you want to know all this stuff?"

"I'm writing a history book," I say drily.

His nose wrinkles, burying his tiny pig eyes in layers of skin. "You're shitting me."

The guy is really thick.

"Where can I find the wife?"

"Won't do you no good. Sophia's got Alzheimer's. She doesn't recognize an ant from a fly."

This doesn't help. I wipe a hand over my face.

Lambert doesn't seem to know where to put his feet. He shifts from the left to the right. "Want a beer?"

"Come on." I nod at Rhett and make my way back to the car.

Inside, my bodyguard turns to me. "Do you mind telling me what's going on?"

"I need Lambert's phone records."

"I'll call Anton."

"I already did. They've been wiped."

"From how long back?"

I give him the date on which I first visited Valentina's almost-husband.

"I know a hacker at Vodacom who's discreet. I'll call him and see what he can do."

While I'm driving, he calls his contact. Before I pull into our driveway, he has a number for me. I park and punch the numbers he reads out loud into my phone. Already by the fourth digit, I know who the number belongs to. As I type in the last digit, Magda's name pops onto the screen.

I fling the door open and make my way to the house with long strides.

"Gabriel!" Rhett jumps from the car and runs after me.

"Stay out of this," I call back.

I find Magda in her study. "Why did Lambert Roos call you?"

She leans back, regarding me from over the rim of her glasses. "He wanted to know why we're sniffing around in his territory." She folds her arms. "Why are we, Gabriel?"

"Did you know Bigfoot Jack?"

"Not personally, but everyone in the business knows who Jack was."

"What do you know about him?"

"Same as you--not much. Why this sudden interest in Bigfoot?"

"I'm trying to piece together Valentina's history, but it's all dead-end streets."

"Why?"

"I'm interested."

"Don't get attached to her, Gabriel. I've warned you, already."

"So you have."

"Are you?"

"Am I what?"

"Getting attached?"

"I don't think I'm capable of attachment."

"You've always been a soft boy, too soft for what it takes."

"What does it take, Magda?"

"Do your job."

"You mean kill her."

"As agreed."

I don't agree at all, but a text comes in from Rhett, informing me the doctor has arrived. I order him to wait upstairs and go in search of Valentina. She's walking Bruno with Quincy, and seeing them together in friendly banter only escalates my irritability.

"Hey," she says when she sees me.

Her warm smile cools at my explosive state.

"The doctor's waiting," I say.

At my tone, Quincy mumbles a greeting and takes his leave.

"I know. I suggested we get started, but he insisted on waiting for you," she tells me.

"I'm here now, so let's go."

In my room, I tell the doctor to repeat the same tests from yesterday. Yesterday, I wanted to ensure Valentina hasn't sustained internal injuries that could prevent her from having children. Today, I need to know I haven't damaged her.

"Again?" he says, his voice not giving away his thoughts.

I raise my brow in challenge. I pay him enough not to ask questions.

He turns to Valentina. "You know what to do, my dear."

"I don't understand."

"Do it, Valentina," I say more harshly than what I intended.

She flinches at my tone but obeys. Only when the doctor tells me that she's fine do I relax. I'd instructed him to inject her with a fertility treatment yesterday to increase her chances of conceiving. She'll be ovulating a week from today, and my seed will be in her morning, afternoon, and night, until it takes.

I hold out her dress for her to step into and button up the front before guiding her back to the daybed. The doctor unrolls the bandage on her thumb, exposing an angry, red wound. I don't need his confirmation to know the antibiotics aren't helping. Neither does Valentina.

She looks at me with big eyes. "I hoped it would be better today."

The doctor gives me a grim look. "She'll have to go to the clinic. Now."

My world comes to a standstill for a third time that day. I take

Valentina's hand in mine. Her palm is cold and clammy. "Is there a risk of her losing her thumb?"

"I don't know. I'm not a surgeon." He pulls off the medical gloves and throws them in the trashcan. "Do you need me to call an ambulance?"

"No." I squeeze her fingers. "I'll take her."

I get Quincy to drive us so I can sit in the back with Valentina, my arm around her shoulders. Her frame is tense, but she leans into my touch when I grip her chin to kiss her lips. From spanking her, I know her pain threshold is low. That's why she was so pale this morning. I want to tell her it will be all right, but there are already enough lies between us, and I simply don't know.

On the way to the hospital, I call my personal insurance broker and get her to arrange pre-admittance at the clinic. It's peak hour traffic at five, but Quincy knows the back roads and manages to get us there in little over thirty minutes. With Valentina already admitted, we walk straight to an examination room where a young surgeon waits on us. He takes one look at her finger and orders tests to be done.

"What's the course of action?" I ask tightly.

"One thing at a time. Let's get the results, first."

"How long will it take?"

"An hour, maybe ninety minutes. We have the lab on site, and I requested the tests as a priority. I can get you a private room where you'll be comfortable, or you can wait in the cafeteria."

"Get us a room, please." I can't stand crowds, and I doubt Valentina is in the mood for hospital coffee.

A nurse shows us to a room with bright yellow walls and a single bed with a blue bedspread. Quincy takes up a position by the door while I make Valentina sit on the bed. I check the time on my phone. It's almost six. I'm about to shove it back into my pocket when it rings. Carly's name appears on the screen.

"Excuse me." I press a kiss on Valentina's temple and walk to the corner of the room. "Hello, princess. Where are you?"

"I'm home. Where are you?"

"At the hospital."

"Is something wrong?"

"I had to bring Valentina. Her wound is infected."

"Oh, no. Tell her I hope it's going to be okay. Listen, Mom's here. Rhett is loading my stuff in the car."

"Already?" I glance at Valentina. "When are you leaving?"

"We can't wait long. Mom's got something on. I can stop by next week."

I'm torn in two. I don't want to let Carly go without saying goodbye, but I don't want to leave Valentina, either.

Valentina hops from the bed and lays her hand on my shoulder. "Carly?" she whispers.

I nod.

"Go," she says. "I'll be fine."

"Give me a minute, Carly." I put the call on hold. "I'm not leaving you. Not now."

"Quincy is here. You heard what the doctor said. It may take an hour or more. Go say goodbye to your daughter. I'm a big girl. It's just an infection. I'll get a shot of potent medicine, and then I'll be back."

I stare at her face, her full lips, and her sad, murky eyes. Rationally, what she says makes sense, but I can't get myself to tell Carly I'll be home in thirty minutes.

"Go on," she urges. "Your daughter is moving out of your house. You're not going to let her go like this, without even being there."

I pinch the bridge of my nose and take a second to make my decision before taking back the call. "I'll be home in thirty minutes."

"Okay," Carly says brightly. "I'll wait for you."

I press a hard kiss to Valentina's lips. It's on the tip of my tongue to tell her I love her, but I swallow the words back just in time. A shiver of shock runs down my spine. What the fuck is wrong with me? The thought tumbled into my mind from nowhere. Habit. It must be habit. Whenever I had to leave Sylvia in a difficult situation, I always needed to reassure her of my feelings. I backtrack to the door and say, "I'll be back later."

Her smile is warm and easy. It's a smile meant to soothe. I escape the feelings crashing down on me, leaving them in the confines of the hospital room as I flee outside.

"Stay with her," I say to Quincy, "and call me when there's news. Anything she needs, anything at all, don't hesitate."

"Yes, boss."

"Give me the car keys. I'm going to the house, but I'll be back as soon as I can."

He fishes the keys from his pocket and hands them to me.

"Don't move away from this door. Keep her safe."

He flicks his jacket aside, showing me the gun that's tucked in his waistband.

I leave the hospital with mixed feelings. If Sylvia was reasonable, I would've asked her to wait, but she's not, and she'll be especially difficult where Valentina is concerned.

The traffic is a nightmare. It takes me more than forty-five minutes to get home. Sylvia and Carly are waiting outside next to Sylvia's overloaded convertible.

"Dad!" Carly runs to me when I get out of the car. "I knew you'd come. Told you, Mom."

She lets me hug her, a rare occurrence. I look at the boxes and suitcases piled up on the backseat of the Mercedes. "Wow, when did you accumulate all this stuff?"

She jabs me with an elbow in the ribs. "You should know. You paid for it."

"Can you even wear all of that?"

"It's not only clothes," she says indignantly. "There are books, too."

"What, ten?"

Sylvia walks up to us in a tight-fitting, pink pencil-skirt suit. "We have to go."

"Carly, if you need anything--"

"I'll call."

"No more than an hour on your phone per day and no dates without my permission."

"Gabriel." Sylvia gives me a hard look. "I'm her mother. I'm capable of handling these decisions."

"But we'll make them together."

She moves away, doing her best not to appear abrupt in front of Carly. "She's growing up. Accept it."

I'm not getting into a fight with Sylvia. Not today. I kiss Carly's cheek. "I love you, princess. You know that, right?"

She wipes her palm over her cheek. "Yuk, Dad! Since when are you all mushy?"

"Since my baby girl is growing up." I was going to say leaving, but I don't want her to feel guilty for spending time with her mom.

"Stop it." She swats my arm. "You'll make me cry, and I don't want my mascara to run."

"Carly." Sylvia starts tapping her foot.

The two women make their way to the car and get inside. As the vehicle clears the gates, a feeling of desolation creeps up on me. The house is empty and purposeless. Its framework stands like a big, white elephant behind me. The pool, garden, televisions, everything was for Carly. It's like a piece of me has left with my daughter.

My phone vibrates in my pocket, drawing my attention back to the present. There's a text message from Quincy.

Valentina's in surgery.

17

Valentina

I wake up in a hospital bed without a piece of me. It's not the end of the world to lose a thumb. Worse things can happen, but I'll never hold a needle and thread again. To be a veterinary surgeon, you need all your fingers. It happened too quickly for me to process. Twenty minutes after Gabriel left, the doctor returned with the news. The digit they sewed back didn't take. I had gangrene in my thumb. To stop the infection from spreading, he had to amputate above the knuckle. Fifteen minutes later, I was wheeled into the operating room.

The door opens, and a nurse enters. "You're awake." She looks at the chart by the foot of the bed and adjusts the drip in my arm. "Ready for visitors? Mr. Louw is anxious to see you."

I'm not. I want to be alone to process what happened.

"Push the button if you're in pain." She leaves a call button within reach of my good hand and calls brightly through the door, "You can see her now."

When Gabriel enters, my heart shatters. His hair is messy and his shirt creased, like he slept in it all night. The skin under his eyes is a blue-ish color. He limps to my bedside, his face an unreadable mask. Despite his tall frame and all those muscles, he looks utterly vulnerable. A deep need to soothe him makes me reach out, cupping his cheek.

"What time is it?"

"Just after six." He adds, "In the morning."

"Did you stay the whole night?"

"Of course."

"You didn't have to."

He says nothing, but turmoil suddenly twists his face.

"It's just a thumb," I say.

He grabs my fingers and squeezes so hard it hurts. When I cry out he lets go, seeming uncertain what to do with my hand. Finally, he places it on top of the bedspread.

"You're not the only one who can brag. I've got my own scar, now."

"I've already spoken to the doctor about a prosthesis."

"I don't want an artificial thumb."

"Why not? It'll look natural."

"It won't function."

"No." He avoids my eyes. "It won't."

"I don't care about how I look." When his eyes turn stormy, I try for humor. "Damn, I'll never be able to hitchhike."

A smile breaks through his dark expression. "You don't have to. You've got me."

Not forever.

He traces a finger along my jaw. "There are other things. Veterinary assistant. Nurse."

It's like telling me there are other men than him.

"Yes," I say softly, "there are other things."

TIME FLIES by during the next few weeks. Christmas comes and goes. I shared a quiet lunch with Kris and Charlie. Instead of buying each other gifts, we donated money to a charity for stray animals. Gabriel, Sylvia, Carly, and Magda had a party with their associates and friends. Magda hired caterers, so my help wasn't needed. Gabriel gave me a spa voucher for Christmas that included every imaginable pampering treatment. My gift to him was of a more depraved nature. He asked to tie me up and film spanking and fucking me. He didn't need my permission, but my free will was the gift he wanted. It was another way of twisting more submission from me, of making me fall deeper into the darkness that is us. Afterward, he made me watch it. Like the perverse being I've become, it turned me on, and the reward for my reaction was a tender marathon of slow lovemaking.

The house is quiet without Carly. She comes to visit every second weekend for a couple of hours. I can tell Gabriel misses her. After New Year, the house turns even quieter when Magda leaves for Cape Town. I don't know what kind of work she's doing there, and I don't ask. Gabriel is often out on business, leaving me alone in the mansion. Gabriel, Quincy, and Rhett treat me like an invalid, carrying the washing basket and anything else I can easily enough pick up. For some tasks, I switch to my left hand. Others, I manage with four fingers.

Marie comes back to work, her speech impaired and her disposition brusquer than before. As the traveling between home and work becomes too much for her, she moves into a bedroom in the house. I have a strong suspicion she tattles to Magda. She watches me like a hawk. For that reason, even if Magda and Carly aren't present, I still don't spend whole evenings in Gabriel's bed. Some nights he comes to me, and some nights I go to him. When we're together, I'm his sex object. His pet. When Magda enters the equation, I'm property. Gabriel is careful to tone down the affection he shows me in private when Marie or Magda is around.

Kris is supportive. She said I could still buy into the practice, even if we both know I'll never be able to afford it on a maid or veterinary nurse's salary. Aletta was sad when I told her the news. Shortly after, she informed me they awarded the bursary to another, needy student.

Charlie got very involved with the dog walking. He takes the task to heart, and the responsibility seems to do him good.

It's only me who's not doing well. On a non-physical level. My checkups are good. The doctor says the infection hasn't spread. I'm stuck in Gabriel's house, submitted to his mercy, and I can't say he's mistreating me. I've come to crave the spankings and beltings. He buys my food and clothes. Anything I want, I only have to mention it, and I'll find it in my room the next day. It's as if he's trying to make up for the loss of my dreams and the dark needs he submits me to with material compensation. His gifts range from cosmetics to books and even a new iPhone.

Sex with Gabriel is always explosive, even when it's gentle. Lately, there's a lot of gentle. That's why I can't understand my growing sadness. The kinder he acts toward me, the sadder I feel. I can't bring the man in my bed together with the man who holds Charlie's future over my head. I want to hate both, but I know better. It's been a long time since I felt only desire for Gabriel. I care about him, and I hate that I do.

As always, Gabriel picks up on my mood. That night, he arranges my naked body on the mattress so he can look at me. He cups my breast gently, stroking his thumb over my nipple.

"Ouch." The sensation is almost too much to bear.

Testing the weight of my breast, he gives me a thoughtful look. "You're close to having your period."

He almost looks disappointed. It's not like he hasn't made love to me during my period. I don't understand his silent dejection.

"Yes." I turn on my side, facing the wall, relieved to understand the reason for my depressive feelings. It's just a heavy bout of PMS.

He rubs a palm over my stomach and presses his cock between my legs. "I'll be gentle." Without waiting for my consent, he rolls me onto my stomach and settles between my thighs. "Open for me, beautiful."

I open my legs, giving him the view he wants. He strokes and teases me for a long time, until his fingers are soaked with my wetness. Only then does he push inside, slow and easy. It's then that it hits me. Since I've been back from the hospital, he's only taken me from behind. How could I have missed this before? He's fucked me against the wall, on his desk, in his armchair, in the pool, and in a variety of other, creative places, but my butt was always pressed against his groin, my face looking away from him. Is it me? Does he find me unattractive? I twist under him, starting to squirm.

"Valentina."

"Let me up."

I don't expect him to, but he obliges. He watches me warily as I switch positions, turning him on his back.

"What are you doing?"

"Looking at you."

"Why?" he says with a pained expression.

"Because I like to."

I lower myself over his cock, taking him into the depth of my body. I let the pleasure show on my face, letting him see what he does to me as I start rocking, my nerve endings coming alive for him.

"You don't have to," he says.

"Do you like to look at me?"

"You know I do."

"Then stop talking and fuck me."

It's as if a dam inside of him breaks. He growls and grips my hips, keeping me in place while he pounds into me, taking me to the edge I want to go.

As my body tightens, he cries out his climax. It's the quickest we've come together since the week he started fucking me. I drape my body over his chest, holding him inside of me. I wish I could stay like this, but I'm not naïve enough to let myself belief this will last. It matters nothing to him. He has no emotional obligation to me. He can fuck anyone he wants without explanation.

"Gabriel?"

He strokes my back. "Yes, beautiful?"

"Do you fuck other women?"

His hand stills. "Why?"

I shrug. "Don't I need tests for STD?"

The caressing resumes. "There's only you, Valentina. I told you before."

"It was a long time ago. It could've changed."

"I'll tell you if it does."

My heart feels like it has just gone through a blender. It can change. I was right. I swallow my tears, angry at my irrational feelings. I have no right to expect more from him. It's my own damn, stupid fault I fell for my tormentor.

THREE WEEKS LATER, I resume my secret training with Rhett. My amputated thumb has healed enough to undertake more strenuous exercise. I'm out of shape, even if I tried to stay fit by using the Walker in the gym. He floors me every time, throwing my ass on the mat. It's during our session on Thursday evening when Gabriel is out on business that I burst into frustrated tears.

Rhett looks at me, aghast. "Did I hurt you?"

"No." I wipe at my cheeks. "I'm just emotional."

My damn period hasn't started yet. The sooner it does, the sooner I'll get over this depressed state.

He offers a hand to pull me up. I'm scarcely on my feet when the evening's dinner pushes back up my throat. I rush to the bathroom, making it to the toilet just before I empty my stomach. Rhett runs in after me, coming to a halt next to the toilet.

Dry heaves wrack my body, making my eyes tear up.

"Jesus, Valentina." He takes a stash of paper towels and hands them to me. "Are you all right?"

"I'm fine."

Feeling slightly better, I rinse my face and wash my hands.

He touches my arm. "Are you...?"

"No." I shake my head. "I'm not sick."

"I meant are you pregnant?"

My lips part in shock. The blood drops straight from my head to my feet, leaving me feeling dizzy. "No, of course not."

I've never missed my pill. I am however a little late. Oh, God. What if? Gabriel will kill me.

Impossible.

I've been careful.

I take another towel from the dispenser and wipe my mouth, noticing how much my hands are shaking. "I think I'll call it a night."

"Can I get you anything?"

"No, thank you. I just need an early night to catch up on sleep."

He watches me leave, not saying a word.

I crawl into bed after a shower, but I don't close an eye. It's late when Gabriel returns. He strips naked and climbs into bed beside me. I'm wet for him, but he takes his time to lick and tease my folds. He doesn't stop until I've come twice, and only then does he fuck me. The way he loves my body is incredible, but my mind isn't there. My mind is searching for solutions to problems I haven't even confirmed, yet.

"Where are you?" he finally asks, kissing my breasts.

"I'm sorry. I'm just tired."

He covers my body in kisses, all the way from my stomach to my feet. He's so gentle, I want to cry.

When he's kissed his way back up to my neck, he hugs me tightly and says, "Go to sleep."

AFTER BREAKFAST, I walk to the staff unit. Rhett is sitting on the porch, sipping his coffee. He gets to his feet when he sees me.

"You look like shit."

"Thanks." I give him a wry smile. "I need a favor, please."

"Anything." He leaves the cup on the rail.

"I need you to go to the pharmacy."

His look is pitiful. "All right."

"Gabriel can't know. Do you hear me?"

"Valentina."

He walks down the steps and reaches for me, but I pull away.

"He can't know, Rhett, not until I know for sure."

He swallows and nods. "I'll be back soon."

A SHORT TIME LATER, I sit on the seat of the toilet, staring at the two blue lines on the strip.

Positive.

I'm expecting Gabriel's baby.

A mixture of feelings rushes through me. I'm faint with wonder. I'm also sick with fear. Will he blame me? He'll be furious. Worse, he'll think I did it on purpose to trap him. Gabriel will never want a baby with a woman who's property. I don't mind raising a child on my own. Gabriel doesn't have to give me a cent. I won't expect support from him, but what if he doesn't want me to have this baby? What if he forces me to have an abortion? If he drives me to a clinic, there won't be anything I can do to stop him. He still owns me, and now he owns the baby growing in me, too.

There's only one thing I can do to save the little life inside me. I quickly pack a bag, my hands trembling so much I drop my phone twice. I wrap the pregnancy kit in a plastic bag, and discard it in the trash outside where no one will look. Only Rhett will guess, but by the time Gabriel confronts him, I'll be long gone.

In Gabriel's study, I write a quick note.

I can't honor my promise. I hope you'll forgive me.

Leaving it on his desk, I pull the door close, knowing Marie won't enter his study. Then I call a private taxi. It's going to cost an arm and a leg, but I can't afford to take a minivan. I need to disappear fast. Rhett left with Gabriel a short while ago, and Quincy is walking Bruno. I walk past the guards at the gate with a wave, my bag slung over my shoulder, acting as normal as I can. They've only seen me leaving the property on foot once, but I'm leaving on a regular enough basis for them not to stop me.

A block from the house, I pause to wait. Two minutes later, the taxi pulls up to the street corner I gave the driver. Looking over my shoulder to make sure no one is following, I jump inside.

"Go, please. Quickly."

I don't glance back as the driver speeds away. I cup my hands over my stomach and stare straight ahead.

I have to.

For my baby.

~ TO BE CONTINUED ~

ALSO BY CHARMAINE PAULS

Diamond Magnate Novels

(Dark Romance)

Standalone Novel

(Dark Forced Marriage Romance)

Beauty in the Broken

Diamonds are Forever Trilogy

(Dark Mafia Romance)

Diamonds in the Dust

Diamonds in the Rough

Diamonds are Forever

Box Set

Beauty in the Stolen Trilogy

(Dark Romance)

Stolen Lust

Stolen Life

Stolen Love

Box Set

The White Nights Duet

(Contemporary Romance)

White Nights

Midnight Days

The Loan Shark Duet

(Dark Mafia Romance)

Dubious

Consent

Box Set

The Age Between Us Duet

(Older Woman Younger Man Romance)

Old Enough

Young Enough

Box Set

Standalone Novels

(Enemies-to-Lovers Dark Romance)

Darker Than Love

(Second Chance Romance)

Catch Me Twice

Krinar World Novels

(Futuristic Romance)

The Krinar Experiment

The Krinar's Informant

7 Forbidden Arts Series

(Fated Mates Paranormal Romance)

Pyromancist (Fire)

Aeromancist, The Beginning (Prequel)

Aeromancist (Air)

Hydromancist (Water)

Geomancist (Earth)

Necromancist (Spirit)

ABOUT THE AUTHOR

Charmaine Pauls was born in Bloemfontein, South Africa. She obtained a degree in Communication at the University of Potchefstroom and followed a diverse career path in journalism, public relations, advertising, communication, and brand marketing. Her writing has always been an integral part of her professions.

When she moved to Chile with her French husband, she started writing full-time. She has been publishing novels and short stories since 2011. Charmaine currently lives in Montpellier, France with her family. Their household is a lively mix of Afrikaans, English, French, and Spanish.

Join Charmaine's mailing list
https://charmainepauls.com/subscribe/

Join Charmaine's readers' group on Facebook
http://bit.ly/CPaulsFBGroup

Read more about Charmaine's novels and short stories on
https://charmainepauls.com

Connect with Charmaine

Facebook
http://bit.ly/Charmaine-Pauls-Facebook

Amazon
http://bit.ly/Charmaine-Pauls-Amazon

Goodreads
http://bit.ly/Charmaine-Pauls-Goodreads

Twitter
https://twitter.com/CharmainePauls

Instagram
https://instagram.com/charmainepaulsbooks

BookBub
http://bit.ly/CPaulsBB

TikTok
https://www.tiktok.com/@charmainepauls